THE FINAL CUT

MICHAEL DOBBS

Cover designed by The Book Designers

Published by Sourcebooks Landmark, an imprint of Sourcebooks, Inc.
P.O. Box 4410, Naperville, Illinois 60567-4410
(630) 961-3900
Fax: (630) 961-2168
www.sourcebooks.com

Originally published in 1994 in Great Britain by HarperCollins Publishers.

Library of Congress Cataloging-in-Publication data is on file with the publisher.

Printed and bound in the United States of America.
VP 10 9 8 7 6 5 4 3 2 1

"That we shall die, we know; 'tis but the time
And drawing days out, that men stand upon."
—Brutus, William Shakespeare's *Julius Caesar*

INTRODUCTION

The Final Cut was written in 1994. All these years later the British are still arguing about Europe, the Cypriots have discovered a vast ocean of hydrocarbon wealth beneath the Mediterranean, and the Greeks and Turks are still arguing about the future of that sadly divided island. What I also hope the reader will find timeless is the enduring wickedness of FU.

PROLOGUE

Troodos Mountains, Cyprus—1956

It was late on an afternoon in May, the sweetest of seasons in the Troodos, beyond the time when the mountains are muffled beneath a blanket of snow but before the days when they serve as an anvil for the Levantine sun. The spring air was filled with the heavy tang of resin and the sound of the breeze being shredded on the branches of great pines, like the noise of the sea being broken upon a pebbled shore. But this was many miles from the Mediterranean, almost as far as is possible to get from the sea on the small island of Cyprus.

These were good times, a season of abundance even in the mountains. For a few weeks in spring the dust of crumbling rock chippings that passes for soil becomes a treasury of wildflowers—erupting bushes of purple-flowered sword lily, blood-dipped poppies, alyssum, the leaves and golden heads of which in ancient times were supposed to effect a cure for madness.

Yet nothing would cure the madness that was about to burst forth on the side of the mountain.

George, fifteen and almost three-quarters, prodded the donkey further up the mountain path, oblivious to the beauty.

His mind had turned once again to breasts. It was a topic that seemed to demand most of his time nowadays, depriving him of sleep, causing him not to hear a word his mother said, making him blush whenever he looked at a woman, which he always did straight between her breasts. They had an energy source all their own, which dragged his eyes toward them, like magnets, no matter how hard he tried to be polite. He never seemed to remember what their faces looked like; his eyes rarely strayed that far. He'd marry a toothless old hag one day. So long as she had breasts.

If he were to avoid insanity or, even worse, the monastery, somehow he would have to do it, he decided. Do IT. Before he was fifteen and three-quarters. In two weeks' time.

He was also hungry. On the way up he and his younger brother, Eurypides, thirteen and practically one half, had stopped to plunder honey from the hives owned by the old crone Chlorides, who had mean eyes like a bird and horribly gnarled fingers—she always accused them of robbing her, whether they had or not, so a little larceny used up some of their extensive credit. Local justice. George had subdued the bees with the smoke from a cigarette he had brought along specifically for the purpose. He'd almost gagged—he hadn't taken to cigarettes yet, but would, he promised himself. Soon. As soon as he had had IT. Then, maybe, he could get to sleep at nights.

Not far to go. The terraced ledges where a few wizened olive trees clung to the rock face were now far behind; they were already two kilometers above the village, less than another two to climb. The light had started to soften, it would be dark in a couple of hours and George wanted to be home by then.

He gave the donkey another fierce prod. The animal, beneath its burden of rough-hewn wooden saddle and bulging cloth panniers, was finding difficulty in negotiating the boulder-strewn trail and cared nothing for such encouragement. The beast expressed its objection in the traditional manner.

"Not over my school uniform, dog meat!" Eurypides sprang back in alarm, too late, and cursed. There was a beating if he did not attend school in uniform. Even in a poor mountain village they had standards.

And they had guns.

Like the two Sten guns wrapped in sacking at the bottom of one of the panniers they were delivering, along with the rest of the supplies, to their older brother. George envied his older brother, hiding out with five other EOKA fighters in a mountain lair.

EOKA. Ethniki Organosis Kyprion Agoniston—the National Organization of Cypriot Fighters—who for a year had been trying to blast open the closed colonial minds of their British rulers and force them to grant the island independence. They were terrorists to some, liberation fighters to others. To George, great patriots. With every part of him that was not concerned with sex he wanted to join them, to fight the enemies of his country. But the High Command was emphatic; no one under the age of eighteen could take up arms. He would have lied, but there was no point, not in a village where everyone knew even the night of his conception, just before Christmas 1939. The war against the Germans was only a few months old and his father's brother George had volunteered for the Cyprus Regiment of the British Army. Like many young Cypriots he had wanted to join the fight for freedom in Europe, which, once won, would surely bring their own release. Or so they had thought. His uncle's farewell celebration had been a long night of feasting and loving, and he had been conceived.

Uncle George never came back.

The younger George had much to live up to. He idolized the uncle he had never known, but he was only fifteen and almost three-quarters and instead of marching in heroic footsteps was reduced to delivering messages and supplies.

"Did you really do it with Vasso? Seriously, George."

"Course, stupid. Several times!" George lied.

"What was it like?"

"Like *peponia*, soft melons of flesh," George exclaimed, gyrating his hands in demonstration. He wanted to expand but couldn't; Vasso had taken him no further than the buttons of her blouse where he had found not the soft fruits he had anticipated but small, hard breasts with nipples like plum stones.

Eurypides giggled but didn't believe. "You didn't, did you?" he accused. George felt his carefully constructed edifice wobbling beneath him.

"Did."

"Didn't."

"*Psefti*."

"*Malaka!*"

Eurypides threw a stone and George jumped, stumbling on a loose rock and falling flat on his rump, fragments of his dream scattered around him. Eurypides's squeals of laughter, by turns childishly high pitched and pubescent gruff, filled the valley and cascaded like acid over his brother's pride. George felt humiliated; he needed something to restore his flagging esteem. Suddenly he knew exactly how.

George loosened the string neck of one of the panniers and reached deep inside, beneath the oranges and side of smoked pork, until his fingers grasped a cylindrical parcel of sacking. Carefully he withdrew it, then a second slightly smaller bundle. In the shadow of a large boulder he laid both on the carpet of soft pine needles, gently removed the wrappings, and Eurypides gasped. It was his first trip on the supply run; he hadn't been told what they were carrying. Staring up at him from the sacking was the dull gray metal of a Sten gun, modified with a folding butt to make it more compact for smuggling. Alongside it were three ammunition mags.

George was delighted with the effect. Within a few seconds, as his older brother had taught him the week before, he had prepared the Sten, a lightweight machine gun, swinging and locking into position the skeletal metal butt, engaging one of the magazines. He fed the first bullet into the chamber. It was ready.

"Didn't know I could use one of these, did you?" He felt much better, authority reestablished. He wedged the gun in the crook of his elbow and adopted a fighting pose, raking the valley with a burst of pretend fire, doing to death a thousand different enemies. Then he turned on the donkey, dispatching it with a volley of whistled sound effects. The beast, unaware of its fate, continued to rip at a clump of tough grass.

"Let me, George. My turn," his brother pleaded.

George, the Commander, shook his head.

"Or I'll tell everyone about Vasso," Eurypides bargained.

George spat. He liked his little brother who, although only thirteen and practically one half, could already run faster and belch more loudly than almost anyone in the village. Eurypides was also craftier than most of his age, and more than capable of a little blackmail. George had no idea precisely what Eurypides was planning to tell everyone about him and Vasso, but in his fragile emotional state any morsel was already too much. He handed over the weapon.

As Eurypides's hand closed around the rubberized grip and his finger stretched for the trigger, the gun barked, five times, before the horrified boy let it fall to the floor.

"The safety!" George yelped, too late. He'd forgotten. The donkey gave a violent snort of disgust and cantered twenty yards along the path in search of less disturbed grazing.

The main advantages of the 9 mm Sten gun are that it is light and capable of reasonably rapid fire; it is neither particularly powerful nor considered very accurate. And its blowback action is noisy. In the crystal air of the Troodos, where the folds of the mountains spread away from Mount Chionistra into mist-filled distances, sound carries like a petrel on the wing. It was scarcely surprising that the British army patrol heard the bark of the Sten gun; what was more remarkable was the fact that the patrol had been able to approach so closely without George or Eurypides being aware of their presence.

There were shouts from two sides. George sprang to retrieve the donkey but already it was too late. A hundred yards beneath them, and closing, was a soldier in khaki and a Highland bonnet. He was waving a .303 in their direction.

Eurypides was already running; George delayed only to sweep up the Sten and two remaining magazines. They ran up the mountain to where the trees grew more dense, brambles snatching at their legs, the pumping of their hearts and rasping breath drowning any sound of pursuit until they could run no further. They slumped across a rock, wild eyes telling each other of their fear, their lungs burning.

Eurypides was first to recover. "Mum'll kill us for losing the donkey," he gasped.

They ran a little more until they stumbled into a shallow depression in the ground well hidden by boulders, and there they decided to hide. They lay facedown in the center of the rocky bowl, an arm across each other, listening.

"What'll they do if they catch us, George? Whip us?" Eurypides had heard dream-churning tales of how the British thrashed boys they believed were helping EOKA, a soldier clinging to each limb and a fifth supplying the whipping with a thin, ripping rod of bamboo. It was like no punishment they received at school, one you could get up and walk away from. With the Tommies, you were fortunate to be able to crawl.

"They'll torture us to find out where we're taking the guns, where the men are hiding," George whispered through dried lips. They both knew what that meant. An EOKA hide had been uncovered near a neighboring village just before the winter snows had arrived. Eight men were cut down in the attack. The ninth, and sole survivor, not yet twenty, had been hanged at Nicosia Jail the previous week.

They both thought of their elder brother.

"Can't let ourselves be captured, George. Mustn't tell." Eurypides was calm and to the point. He had always been less excitable than George, the brains of the family, the one with prospects. There was even talk of his staying at school beyond the summer, going off to the Pankyprion Gymnasium in the capital and later becoming a teacher, even a civil servant in the colonial administration. If there was still to be a colonial administration.

They lay as silently as possible, ignoring the ants and flies, trying to melt into the hot stone. It was twelve minutes before they heard the voices.

"They disappeared beyond those rocks over there, Corporal. Havnae seen hide nor hair o' them since."

George struggled to control the fear that had clamped its jaws around his bladder. He felt disgusted, afraid he was going to foul himself. Eurypides was looking at him with questioning eyes.

From the noises beyond the rocks they reckoned that another two, possibly three, had joined the original soldier and corporal, who were standing some thirty yards away.

"Kids you say, MacPherson?"

"Two o' them. One still in school uniform, Corporal, short troosers an' all. Cannae harm us."

"Judging by the supplies we found on the mule they were intending to do someone a considerable amount o' harm. Guns, detonators. They even had grenades made up from bits of piping. We need those kids, MacPherson. Badly."

"Wee bastards'll probably already huv vanished, Corporal." A scuffling of boots. "I'll hae a look."

The boots were approaching now, crunching over the thick mat of pine debris. Eurypides bit deep into the soft tissue of his lip. He reached for George's hand, trying to draw strength, and as their ice-cold fingers entwined so George started to grow, finding courage for them both. He was the older, this was his responsibility. His duty. And, he knew, his fault. He had to do something. He pinched his brother's cheek.

"When we get back, I'll show you how to use my razor," he smiled. "Then we'll go see Vasso, both of us together. Eh?"

He slithered to the top of the rock bowl, kept his head low, pointed the Sten gun over the edge and closed his eyes. Then he fired until the magazine was empty.

George had never been aware of such a silence. It was a silence inside when, for a moment, the heart stops and the blood no longer pulses through the veins. No bird sang, suddenly no breeze, no whispering of the pines, no more sound of approaching footsteps. Nothing, until the corporal, voice a tone deeper, spoke.

"My God. Now we'll need the bloody officer."

The officer in question was Francis Ewan Urquhart. Second Lieutenant. Age twenty-two. Engaged on National Service following his university deferment, he personified the triumph of education over experience and, in the parlance of the officers' mess, he was not having a good war. Indeed, in the few months he'd been stationed in Cyprus he'd barely had any war at all. He craved action, all too aware of his callow youth, desperate for the chance to prove himself, yet he had found only frustration. His commander had proved to be a man of chronic constipation, his caution denying the company any chance to show its colors. The EOKA terrorists had been bombing, butchering, and even burning alive so-called traitors, setting them in flames to run down the streets of their village as a sign to others, yet Urquhart's company had broken more sweat digging latrines than hauling terrorists from their foxholes. But that was last week. This week the company commander was on leave, Urquhart was in charge, the tactics had been changed, and his men had walked four hours up the mountain that afternoon to avoid detection. And the surprise seemed to have worked.

At the first crackle of gunfire a sense of opportunity had filled his veins. He had been waiting two miles down the valley in his Austin Champ and it took him less than fifteen minutes to arrive on the scene, covering the last few hundred yards on foot with a spring in his step.

"Report, Corporal Ross."

The flies were already beginning to gather around the bloodied body of MacPherson.

"Two boys and a donkey? You can't be serious," Urquhart demanded incredulously.

"The bullet didnae seem to unnerstand it was being fired by a bairn, sir."

The two, Urquhart and Ross, were born to collide, one brought into the world in a Clydeside tenement and the other by Highland patriarchs. Ross had been burying comrades from the Normandy beaches while Urquhart was still having his tie adjusted by his nanny.

A year earlier Urquhart had been the officious little subaltern who had busted Ross from sergeant back down to private after a month's liquor allowance had disappeared from the officers' mess at Tel-el-Kebir and Urquhart had been instructed to round up suitable suspects. Ross had only just been given back the second stripe, still making up the lost ground. And lost pay.

Urquhart knew he had to watch his back, but for now he ignored the other's insolence; he had a more important battle to fight.

The children had stumbled into a remarkably effective natural redoubt. Some twenty feet across, the scraping in the mountainside was backed by a picket line of boulders that effectively denied a clear line of either sight or fire from above, while the ground ran gently away on the valley side, making it difficult to attack except by means of a frontal and uphill assault, a tactic that had already been shown to be mortally flawed. Clumps of bushes hugged the perimeter providing still further cover.

"Suggestions, Corporal Ross?" Urquhart slapped the officer's Browning at his belt.

The corporal sucked a little finger as though trying to remove a splinter. "We could surrender straightaway, that'd be quickest. Or blow the wee bastards into eternity, if that's what you want, Lieutenant. One grenade should do the job."

"We need them alive. Find out where they were headed with those arms."

"They're weans. Be famished by breakfast time, come oot wavin' a white flag an' a fork."

"Now, we need them *now*, Corporal. By breakfast time it will be all too late."

They both understood the urgency. EOKA supply drops were made at specified times; any more than six hours overdue and the hide was evacuated. They needed shortcuts; it made early capture essential and interrogation techniques sometimes short on patience.

"In life, Ross, timing is everything."

"In death an' all," the Clydesider responded, indicating MacPherson.

"What the hell's your problem, Corporal?"

"To be honest, Mr. Urquhart, I dinnae hae much stomach for the killing of weans." MacPherson had a son not much younger than the boys hiding in the rocks. "I'll do it, if I huv tae. If ye order me. But I'll tak nae joy fae it. You're welcome tae any medal."

"I'll remember to include your little homily when I write to MacPherson's parents. I'm sure they'll be touched."

The tangerine sun was chasing through the sky, splashing a glow of misleading warmth across the scene. Delay would bring darkness and failure for Urquhart and he was a young man as intolerant of failure in himself as he was in others. He took a Sten from the shoulder of one of his men and, planting his feet firmly in the forest floor, unleashed a fusillade of bullets against the amphitheater of boulders at the back of the bowl. A second magazine followed, dust and sparks spitting from the orange-blond rocks; the noise was awesome.

"You boys," he shouted. "You cannot escape. Come out, I promise no one will get hurt."

There was silence. He directed two other members of the section to empty their magazines against the rocks, and suddenly there was a youthful cry of pain. A spent bullet had ricocheted and caught one of the lads a glancing blow. No damage, but surprise and distress.

"Can you speak English? Come out now, before anyone gets hurt."

Silence.

"Damn them! Do they want to die?" Urquhart beat his palms with frustration. But Ross was on his knees, fiddling with a Mills grenade.

"What on earth…?" Urquhart demanded, but could not avoid taking an involuntary pace backward.

The corporal had bent the pin so that it could not fall out, then with meticulous care and using the stock of a Sten gun for torque he proceeded to unscrew the top of the grenade, lifting it away from the dull metal body complete with its detonator. The powdered explosive poured out easily into a little pile on the rocks beside his boot. He now reassembled the harmless bomb, and handed it to Urquhart.

"If this doesnae scare those rabbits out of their hole, nothing will."

Urquhart nodded in understanding. "This is your last chance," he shouted to the rocks. "Come out or we'll use grenades."

"*Eleftheria i Thánatos!*" came the reply.

"The EOKA battle cry. Freedom or Death," Ross explained.

"They're only children!" Urquhart snapped in exasperation.

"Brave wee buggers."

Angrily Urquhart wrenched the pin from the grenade, letting

the noise of the spring-loaded firing pin drift out across the rocks. Then he threw the grenade into the bowl.

Less than two seconds later it came hurtling out again. The reaction was automatic, the instinct for self-preservation overriding. Urquhart threw himself to the ground, burying his head among the pine needles and cones, trying to count the seconds. There came a muffled pop from the detonator, but nothing more. No blast; no ripping metal or torn flesh. Eventually he looked up to find the figure of Ross towering above him, framed in menacing silhouette against the evening sky.

"Let me help you tae yer feet, sir." Derision filled every syllable.

Urquhart waved away the proffered hand and scrambled up, meticulously thrashing the dust from his khaki uniform to hide his humiliation. He knew that every Jock in the section was mocking and by morning the tale would have filled all four corners of the officers' mess. Ross had exacted his revenge.

A rage grew within Urquhart. Not a blind rage that blurs judgment but a wrath that burned and whose light brought appalling clarity.

"Fetch two jerricans of gas from the Champ," he instructed.

A soldier went scurrying.

"What are you intending to do, Mr. Urquhart?" Ross asked, the triumph evaporated from his voice.

"We need information or examples. Those terrorists can provide either."

Ross noted the change in the boys' status. "Examples? Of what?"

Urquhart met the other man's gaze; he saw fear. He had regained the advantage. Then the jerricans arrived.

"Corporal, I want you to get around behind them. Use the cover of those rocks. Then empty the gas into their hide."

"And then what?"

"That will depend upon them."

"They're nothin' but bairns..."

"Tell that to MacPherson. This is a war, not a tea party. So they can come out in one piece or with their tail feathers scorched. Their choice."

"You wouldna burn them out."

"I'll give them far more chance than EOKA would." They knew the bloody truth of that, had both seen the blackened carcasses, hands stretched out like claws in charred agony, fathers and sons often dragged out of church or from the desperate clutches of their families, burned, butchered. As examples. "And the message will get around, serve as a warning. Make it easier for us next time."

"But, sir..."

Urquhart cut him short, handed him a jerrican. "We'll give you covering fire."

Ross took one step back, shaking his head. "Ah'll no' burn them oot. I dinna fight that way. Against bairns."

There was an audible stirring of support from the section's other members. Ross was able, experienced; some of the men owed their lives to that.

"Corporal, I am giving you a direct order. To disobey is a court-martial offense."

"I hae lads of my own."

"And if you don't follow my orders I'll make sure you're locked up so long they will be grown men by the time you next set eyes on them."

Agony had carved deep furrows across the corporal's expression, but still he refused the jerrican. "Rather that, than never being able to look my boys in the eye again."

"This is not me ordering you, Ross, it's your country."

"You do it then. If you hae the stomach fer it."

The challenge had been struck. Urquhart looked around the others, five men in all, saw they had sided with Ross. He knew he couldn't court-martial the entire section; it would reduce him to a laughingstock. Ross was right; if it were to be done, he would have to do it himself.

"Give me covering fire when I'm around behind them." He eyed the corporal. "No, not you, Ross. You're under arrest."

And he had gone. Ducking low, pacing rapidly through the trees, a can in each hand, until he was well behind the hide. He signaled and one then another of the troops opened up, sending barrages of sound across the scene. Quickly and as quietly as he was able, Urquhart edged up to one of the taller boulders, almost the height of a man, which stood directly behind where the boys were hiding. The cap was off one can; he stretched and spilled all four and a half gallons of stinking fuel down the rock face and into the bowl. The next four and a half gallons followed immediately. Then he retreated.

"You have thirty seconds to come out before we fire the gas!"

Within their rocky hide, George and Eurypides's faces spoke of their dread. As fast as they tried to crawl away from the swamping fuel, they were forced to duck back beneath the blanket of ricocheting bullets. What was worse, the fuel had begun to make the elevations of the rocky bowl slippery, the nails on their boots finding little purchase on the smooth stone. The inevitable result in such a small place was that their clothes became soaked in foul-smelling gas. It made them retch.

"Fifteen seconds!"

"They won't do it, little brother," George tried to convince himself. "But if they do, you jump first."

"We mustn't tell. Whatever happens, we mustn't tell," Eurypides choked.

"Five!"

It was longer than five. Considerably longer. Urquhart's bluff had been called. There was no turning back. He had retained a rag half-soaked in gas; this he tied around a small rock so that the fuel-impregnated ends hung free. He brought out his cigarette lighter, snapped it into life, and touched the rag.

Events moved rapidly from that point. The rag burst into flame, almost engulfing Urquhart's hand, scorching the hair on his arm. He was forced to throw it immediately; it performed a high, smoky arc in the sky above the rocks before plunging down. Ross shouted. There was a crack. Hot vapor danced above the hide like a chimney from hell. Then a scream, a terrified, violent, boyish shriek of protest. Two heads appeared above the bowl, then the tops of two young bodies as they scrambled up the side. But as the soldiers watched the smaller one seemed to lose his footing, to slip, stumble, he disappeared. The older boy froze, looked back down into the ferment, cried his brother's name and sprang back in.

It was impossible to tell exactly what was happening in the bowl, but there were two sets of screams now, joined in a chorus of prolonged suffering, and death.

"You miserable bastard," Ross sobbed. "I'll no' watch them burn." And already a grenade had left his hand and was sailing toward the inferno.

The explosion blew out the life of the fire. And stopped the screaming.

In the silence that followed, Urquhart was conscious that his hands were trembling. For the first time he had killed—in the national interest, with all the authority of the common weal, but he knew that many would not accept that as justification. Nothing was to be gained from this. Ross stood before him, struggling to compose himself, his fists clenched into great balls that might at any moment strike out. The other men were crowded around, sullen, sickened.

"Corporal Ross, this was not what I had wanted," he started slowly, "but they brought it on themselves. War requires its victims, better terrorists than more like MacPherson. Nor do I wish to see you ruined and locked away as a result of a court-martial. You have a long record of military service of which you can be proud." The words were coming more easily now, his hands had stopped trembling and the men were listening. "I think it would be in everyone's interests that this incident be forgotten. We want no more EOKA martyrs. And I don't want your indiscipline to provide unnecessary work for the Military Provosts." He cleared his throat, uncomfortable. "My Situation Report will reflect the fact that we encountered two unidentified and heavily armed terrorists. They were killed in a military engagement following the death of Private MacPherson. We shall bury the bodies in the forest, in secret, leave no trace. Deny the local villagers an excuse for retaliation. Unless, that is, you want a fuller report to be lodged, Corporal Ross?"

Ross, the large, lumbering, caring soldier-father, recognized that such a full report might damage Urquhart but would in all certainty ruin him. That's the way it was in the Army, pain was passed down the ranks. For Urquhart the Army was nothing more than a couple of years of National Service, for Ross it was his whole life. He wanted to scream, to protest that this had been nothing less than savagery; instead his shoulders sagged and his head fell in capitulation.

While the men began to search for a burial site in the thin forest soil, Urquhart went to inspect the scene within the rocky bowl. He was grateful that there was surprisingly little obvious damage to the dark skin of their faces, but the sweet-sour stench of scorching and gas fumes made him desperately want to vomit. There was nothing of military value in their pockets, but around their necks on two thin chains hung crucifixes engraved with their names. He tore them off; no one should ever discover their identities.

It was dusk when they drove back down the mountain with MacPherson's body strapped in the back. Urquhart turned for one last look at the battle scene. Suddenly in the gathering darkness he saw a light. An ember, a fragment of fire, had somehow survived and been fanned by the evening breeze, causing it to burst back into life. The young pine that stood in the middle of the bowl was ablaze, a beacon marking the site that could be seen for miles around.

He never spoke of the incident on the mountain again but thereafter, at times of great personal crisis and decision in his life, whenever he closed his eyes and occasionally when he was asleep, the brilliant image and the memory of that day would return, part nightmare, part inspiration. The making of Francis Urquhart.

ONE

I prefer dogs to humans. Dogs are easier to train.

The door of the stage manager's box opened a fraction for Harry Grime to peer into the auditorium.

"Hasn't arrived, then," he growled.

Harry, a leading dresser at the Royal Shakespeare Company, didn't like Francis Urquhart. Fact was, he loathed the man. Harry was blunt, Yorkshire, a raging queen going to seed who divided the universe into thems that were for him and thems that weren't. And Urquhart, in Harry's uncomplicated and unhumble opinion, weren't.

"Be buggered if that bastard'll get back," Harry had vouchsafed to the entire company last election night. Yet Urquhart had, and Harry was.

Three years on, Harry had changed his hair color from vivid chestnut to a premature orange and shed his wardrobe of tight leather in preference for something that let him breathe and allowed his stomach to fall more naturally, but he had moved none of his political opinions. Now he awaited the arrival of the Prime Minister with the sensibilities of a Russian digging in before Stalingrad. Urquhart was coming, already he felt violated.

"Sod off, Harry, get out from under my feet," the stage manager snapped from his position alongside the cobweb of wires that connected the monitors and microphones with which he was supposed to control the production. "Go check that everyone's got the right size codpiece or something."

Harry bristled, about to retaliate, then thought better of it. The Half had been called, all hands were now at their posts backstage and last-minute warfare over missing props and loose buttons was about to be waged. No one needed unnecessary aggravation, not tonight. He slunk away to recheck the wigs in the quick-change box at the back of the stage.

It was to be a performance of *Julius Caesar* and the auditorium of the Swan Theatre was already beginning to fill, although more slowly than usual. The Swan, a galleried and pine-clad playhouse that stands to the side of the RSC's main theater in Stratford-upon-Avon, is constructed in semicircular homage to the Elizabethan style and has an intimate and informal atmosphere, 432 seats max. Delightful for the performance but a nightmare for Prime Ministerial security. What if some casual theatergoer who loved Shakespeare much yet reviled Francis Urquhart more, more even than did Harry Grime, took the opportunity to...To what? No one could be sure. The Stratford bard's audiences were not renowned for traveling out with assorted weaponry tucked away in pocket or purse—Ibsen fans, maybe, Chekov's too, but surely not for Shakespeare? Yet no one was willing to take responsibility, not in the presence of most of the Cabinet, a handful of lesser Ministers, assorted editors and wives and other selected powers in the realm who had been gathered together to assist with celebrations for the thirty-second wedding anniversary of Francis and Mortima Urquhart.

Geoffrey Booza-Pitt was the gatherer. The youngest member of Francis Urquhart's Cabinet, he was Secretary of State for Transport and a man with an uncanny eye for opportunity. And for distractions, of all forms. And what better distraction from the shortcomings of Ministerial routine than to block-book a hundred seats in honor of the Master's anniversary and invite the most powerful men in the land to pay public homage? Two thousand pounds' worth of tickets returned a hundred-fold of personal publicity and left favors scattered throughout Westminster, including Downing Street. That's precisely what Geoffrey had told Matasuyo, car giant to the world and corporate sponsor to the RSC, who had quietly agreed to pay for the lot. It hadn't cost him a penny. Not that Geoffrey would tell.

They arrived late, their coming almost regal. If nothing else, after the eleven years they had lived in Downing Street, they knew how to make an entrance. Mortima, always carefully presented, appeared transported onto a higher plane in an evening dress of black velvet with a high wing collar and a necklace of pendant diamonds and emeralds that caught the theater's lighting and reflected it back to dazzle all other women around her. The wooden floors and galleries of the playhouse complained as people craned forward to catch a glimpse and a ripple of applause broke out among a small contingent of American tourists, which took hold, the infection making steady if reluctant progress through the auditorium to the evident embarrassment of many.

"Le roi est arrivé."

"Be fair, Bryan," chided one of the speaker's two companions from their vantage point in the First Gallery, above and to the right of where the Urquharts were taking their seats.

"Fair? Can we possibly be talking about the same Francis Urquhart, Tom? The man who took the professional foul and set it to Elgar?"

Thomas Makepeace offered no response other than a smile of reproach. He knew Brynford-Jones, the editor of *The Times*, was right. He was also clear that Brynford-Jones knew he knew. Lobby terms. But there were limits to what a Foreign Secretary could say in a public place about his Prime Minister. Anyway, Urquhart was his friend who had repaid that friendship with steady promotion over the years.

"Still, you have to admire his footwork, a true professional," Brynford-Jones continued before offering a wave and a smile in the direction of the Urquharts who were turning to acknowledge those around them. "There's not a man here without the marks of your Prime Minister's studs somewhere on his anatomy. Good old FU."

"Surely there's more to life than simply providing you with copy, Bryan." On Makepeace's other side a third man joined in. Quentin Digby was a lobbyist, and a good one. He not only had an involvement in professional politics but, in his own quiet way, was also something of an activist, representing many charities and environmental concerns. Makepeace didn't know him well but rather liked him.

"I wondered which of us three was going to play the moralizing toad tonight," Makepeace mocked.

The house lights dimmed as the Managing Director of Matasuyo stepped forward onto the stage to claim his place before the public eye and offer a speech of welcome. The light thrown onto the stage bounced up onto the faces of Makepeace and his companions, giving them a shadowy, conspiratorial look, like witches attending a cauldron.

"Seriously, Tom," Brynford-Jones continued, anxious to take advantage of the Cabinet Minister's presence. "He should have gone on his tenth anniversary. Ten bloody years at the top is enough for anyone, isn't it?"

Makepeace made no comment, pretending to concentrate on the Japanese gentleman's homily, which was attempting to establish some form of spiritual connection between culture and car bits.

"Wants to go for the record. Outscore Thatcher," Digby offered. "I wouldn't mind, but what's the point? What's he trying to achieve? We've got half the country's trash cans crammed full of Harrods wrapping paper, which local councils can't afford to collect while the other half go begging for something to eat."

"You lobbyists always spoil your case with exaggeration," Makepeace rebuked.

"Funny, I thought that was a politician's prerogative," the editor came back.

Makepeace was beginning to feel penned in. He'd felt that way a lot in recent months, sitting beside editors or standing before his constituents with a pretense of enthusiasm when there was only weariness and disillusionment inside. Something had gone stale. Someone had gone stale. Francis Urquhart. Leaving Makepeace with much that he wanted to say, but little he was allowed to.

"He's had a good run, Tom. The country's grateful and all that, but really it's time for some new blood."

"His blood."

"A fresh start for the Government."

"For you, Tom."

"We all know the things you hold dear, the causes you stand for."

"We'd like to help."

"You know the country isn't what it was. Or could be. This country has too big a heart to be beholden for so long to one man."

"Particularly a man such as that."

"Hell, even the illegal immigrants are leaving."

"It should be yours, Tom. Makepeace is ever as good a man as Urquhart."

Respite. The man from Matasuyo had subsided and the play was about to begin; Makepeace was grateful. His head was spinning. He wanted to dispute their claims, play the loyal hound, but couldn't find the words. Perhaps they were right about Urquhart. Without doubt right about himself. They knew he wanted it, enough that at times his mouth ran dry like a man lost in a desert who spots an oasis, only to discover it is a mirage. Power. But not for its own sake, not for a place in the history books like Urquhart, but for now. Today. For all the things that so desperately needed doing and changing.

Both Brynford-Jones and Digby had a strong interest in change, editor and lobbyist, professional revolutionaries by their trade. Having the world standing still was no more an option for them than it was for him, Makepeace thought. Perhaps they would make useful allies, one day, if war ever came. After his friend Francis had left the field. Or perhaps they would all go to hell together among the rogues.

And then there was laughter. Caesar had made his first appearance on stage with a face adorned with heavy makeup that made him look uncannily like Francis Urquhart. The same long profile. Piercing eyes. Receding silver hair. A straight gash across his face for a mouth. A mask that showed neither mirth nor mercy. The arguments backstage had been long and furious when they had learned of Urquhart's imminent presence. Harry had argued vociferously for a boycott and threatened to throw his body into all forms of picket lines and protests but, as the property manager had so successfully argued, "Give it a rest, love. It's been years since your bottom 'alf lived up to the promises of your top 'alf. Bloody years since you last saw your bottom 'alf, I'll bet. Must do it all from memory."

So they had compromised. In true thespian tradition the show would go on, laden with a little ideological baggage. Yet Harry, once more sneaking a look from prompt side to test the mettle of his protest, was to be disappointed. The living mask slipped. From his privileged position beside Booza-Pitt at the front of the stage Urquhart, an experienced trouper in any public arena, had spotted the danger and responded. Not only was he leading the laughter but he also made sure that everyone knew it by taking out a white silk handkerchief and waving it vigorously at his protégé.

As the play progressed, Makepeace agonized. Loyalty meant so much, for him it was a political virtue in its own right. Yet he hadn't been sleeping well, a disturbed mind and troubled heart had robbed him of rest, doubts beginning to crowd in on his dreams. And he knew that if he did nothing, simply chafed beneath those doubts, he would lose his dreams as well.

"The abuse of greatness is when it disjoins remorse from power..."

Loyalty. But to what? Not just to a single man. Great men have their day, only to find that their reputation must fall from the sky like leaves before the autumn storm.

"And therefore think him as a serpent's egg, which, hatch'd, would, as his kind, grow mischievous..."

Every Prime Minister he'd ever known had demanded too much, been dispatched. Sacrificed. Bled. By colleagues.

And finally the deed was done. *"Et tu, Brute?"* An exceptionally pitiless portrayal of the assassination, and at every step Urquhart's handkerchief waved and waved.

"Sodding man!" Grime snapped as he stamped about the quick-change box helping the deceased Caesar into his ghost's garb.

"Your little plot didn't work, luvvie," Julius mocked. "Didn't you see him? Laughing his bloody head off at us, so he was."

"Hold still, Big Julie, or I'll run this pin up your arse," Harry snapped. "Anyway, what would you know about plots? The last miserable screenplay you spawned didn't even make it as far as the typist."

"It had a few developmental problems," Julie acknowledged.

"As much sense of direction as a horse up a hedgehog."

"At least I act. You couldn't even play the skull in *Hamlet* on a good day."

"Bitch," Harry pursed, and subsided.

In the auditorium the house lights had announced the interval and thunderous applause reflected the audience's appreciation of a production remarkable for its freshness. It had been a long time since anyone could remember laughing so much through a tragedy but, up in the First Gallery, Digby appeared distracted. Makepeace probed.

"Sorry. Wondering about the new car," the lobbyist apologized.

"About the mileage? Whether it's environmentally friendly? Recyclable?"

"Hardly. It's four liters of testosterone encased in the silkiest and most explicit Italian styling you can find in this country without getting arrested. Ferrari. Rosso red. My only vice. And parked outside."

"And you're worried whether all the wrapping paper is going to be removed from your trash can by the end of the week," Makepeace taunted.

"More worried that in this brave new world of ours the stereo system will have been ripped off by the end of this performance. What do you think, Secretary of State?"

"Contain yourself, Diggers," Brynford-Jones interjected. "Nothing lasts forever."

The editor and lobbyist enjoyed the banter, but Makepeace's mind had drifted elsewhere. He was gazing down onto the floor of the auditorium where Urquhart, surrounded by enthusing acolytes and attended closely by Geoffrey Booza-Pitt, was replacing his handkerchief.

"Everything pukka, Tom?" Brynford-Jones inquired.

"Yes, of course. Just thinking how right you were. You know. About how nothing lasts forever."

The red leather box lay open on the backseat, papers untouched. The Minister, Frederick Warburton, had fallen asleep as soon as they reached the motorway—it had been a heavy working dinner and the old boy's stamina wasn't what it once was. He was snoring gently, mouth ajar, slumped awkwardly to one side. Should've worn his seat belt. The driver studied him carefully in the rearview mirror for some time before deciding he could risk it. Cautiously, while ensuring that the Jaguar's engine maintained its constant soothing cadence at a steady eighty-three miles an hour, he reached for the volume button of the radio. They were just about to kick off at Upton Park and the next ninety minutes would decide an entire season's effort. He didn't want to miss it.

He paused as through the drizzle ahead emerged the rear lights of an old Escort, trying to prove it was still sparking on all its plugs and not yet ready for the breaker's yard. The Escort's youthful driver cursed; the rotted rubber of his wipers had transformed the motorway into a smear of confusing messages and he was straining to make sense of the scene ahead. He had no eyes for what lay behind. The Minister's driver decided not to risk waking his passenger by braking suddenly, not with the match about to start. He drew over to the middle lane to pass the other vehicle on the inside.

Some events in life—and death—lie beyond reasonable explanation. Afterward men of learning, experience, and great forensic ability may gather to offer their views, yet all too frequently such views serve less as explanation than excuse. Sometimes it is as easy to accept that there are moments when Fate rouses herself from an afternoon nap and, sleep still heavy upon her eyes, points her finger capriciously and with chaotic intent. For it was just as the Minister's driver was leaning toward the radio button once more, less than six feet to the rear and on the inside of the other vehicle, that the Escort's rear offside tire burst. Fate. It swerved violently in front of the Ministerial limousine whose driver, one-handed, snatched at the wheel. The Jaguar hit the central reservation and turned a full, elegant circle on the damp road before crossing the hard shoulder and disappearing down an earth bank.

It came to rest against the trunk of an elm tree. When the driver recovered from his shock he found the Ministerial box battered and torn on the front seat beside him. And so was the Minister.

TWO

I hate outbreaks of unnecessary violence. They strip the violence that is essential of its pleasures.

"Francis Urquhart, peacemaker?"

Brynford-Jones made no attempt to hide the incredulity in his voice and he stared closely at Makepeace to gauge the reaction.

"We live in an exciting new world, Bryan. Anything is possible."

"Agreed. But Francis Urquhart?"

They had stood in line with the other guests on the stairs of Downing Street, waiting to be greeted formally by the Urquharts before being introduced to the Presidents of the divided Cypriot communities. The previous day, on the neutral territory of the ballroom of Lancaster House and under the public eye of the British Prime Minister, Turk and Greek had agreed on the principles of peace and undertaken to settle all outstanding details within three months. The Confederated Republics of Cyprus were about to be born, conflict eschewed, the Right Honorable Francis Urquhart, MP, Acting Midwife, Peacemaker.

Now came celebration. The powers that be within the land had been gathered together in the first-floor reception rooms of Downing Street in order that they might offer thanks to peace and to Francis Urquhart. It was a leveling, for some almost humbling, experience. No matter how wealthy or well-known, they had been treated alike. No cars, no eminence, no exceptions. Stopped at the wrought iron gates barring entrance to Downing Street from Whitehall. Scrutinized by police before being allowed to walk with their wives the full length of the street to the guarded front door. Being made to wait while their coats were exchanged for a wrinkled paper cloakroom ticket. Five minutes spent in line shuffling piously up the stairs, step by single step, past the portraits of former leaders, the Walpoles, Pitts, Palmerstons, Disraelis, Churchills, and the one and only Margaret Thatcher. "To those we have crucified," Brynford-Jones had muttered. Then the formal introduction by some red-coated alien from another galaxy who seemed to recognize no one and had great trouble with pronunciation. "Mr. Bimford-Jones" had not been impressed, but then he rarely was.

"It must have been like this at the Court of Versailles," he offered. "Just before the tumbrels arrived."

"Bryan, your cynicism runs away with you. Great changes require a little ruthlessness. Credit where it is due," Makepeace protested.

"And are you ruthless, Tom? Ruthless enough to snatch old Francis's crown? Because he's not going to hand it over for Christmas. You're going to have to snatch it, like he did. Like they all had to. Do you really have what it takes?"

"You need luck, too, in politics," Makepeace responded, trying to deflect the question but showing no anxiety to finish with either the conversation or the editor.

"Men should be masters of their own fates."

"You know I'd love the job but the question doesn't arise. Yet."

"It never arises when you expect it. You want to achieve great things, you grab Fortune by the balls and hang on for the ride."

"Bryan, at times I think you're trying to tempt me."

"No, not me. I simply present ambition to a man and see if ambition tempts him. I'm strictly a voyeur, the prerogative of the press. The dirty work I leave up to you guys—and girls!" he exclaimed, reaching out to grab the elbow of another guest as she edged through the throng.

Claire Carlsen turned and smiled, her face lighting up in recognition. She was also an MP, at thirty-eight a dozen years younger than Makepeace and the editor.

"And what have you done to earn your place amid this glittering herd?" Brynford-Jones inquired. "I thought nobody below the rank of Earl or Archbishop was allowed at this trough. Certainly not a humble backbencher."

"It's called tokenism, Bryan. Apparently professional middle-aged moralizers like you like to have a bit of skirt around to remind them of lost youth. You know, slobber a bit and go away happy. That's the plan." The smile was warm but the autumn-blue eyes searching. She was tall, almost eye-to-eye with the rotund editor who enjoyed the glint of evening sunlight shining through her blond hair.

Brynford-Jones laughed loudly. "You're too late for confession. I've already owned up to being a voyeur and in your case I'll happily plead guilty. If ever that husband of yours throws you out, you'd be more than welcome to come and stir my evening cocoa."

"If ever I throw that husband of mine out," she corrected, "I'd hope to be stirring more than cocoa in the evenings. Anyway, what have you two been plotting? Strippergrams to the Synod, or something frivolous?"

"I was inquiring whether our friend here has what it takes to succeed in politics, the necessary qualities of energy and ambition to become the next Prime Minister. Would you lay money on him, Claire?"

She arched an eyebrow—she possessed a highly expressive face and, when relaxed, an aura of refreshing mischief. In response to Brynford-Jones's invitation she examined Makepeace as though for the first time, the end of her nose puckered in skepticism, seeming to reach some conclusion before deliberately throwing their attention in an entirely different direction.

"If energy and ambition were all, then our next leader is surely standing over there by the window."

"Not our Geoff? I'd rather emigrate," the editor chuckled, irreverent though not entirely incredulous.

They turned to follow her gaze. In the bay of a grand Georgian window overlooking the garden, the Transport Secretary had pinned the Governor of the Bank of England against the elegant drape.

"Liquid engineering," Claire continued. "He handles it so smoothly the Governor won't even realize when he's been set aside for the next name on the list."

"Our Geoff's got a list?" the editor inquired.

"Surely. Typed on a card in his breast pocket. He has an hour here, so he asks for a copy of the invitation list beforehand, sees how many people he wants to impress or to harangue, then splits his time. Six minutes each. Digital precision."

In silence they watched as Booza-Pitt, without pause for breath or apparent reference to his watch, took the Governor's hand and bade farewell. Then he was moving across the room, shaking hands and offering salutations as he passed, but not stopping.

"Chances are he'll end the program with somebody's bored wife," Claire continued. "It's a regular routine, particularly since he separated from his own wife."

"His second wife," Makepeace corrected.

"Fascinating. The man goes up in my estimation," Brynford-Jones admitted. "Which, I'm forced to admit, still doesn't take him very far. But how do you come by all this delicious and wicked information?"

She pursed her lips. "You know how we girls like to gossip. And you don't think he types his own list, do you?"

The editor knew she was mocking more than Booza-Pitt. He noticed how steady the blue eyes remained throughout her conversation, examining, judging. She didn't miss much. He suspected she used men much more than she was used by them. Her clothes were expensively discreet from some of Knightsbridge's most fashionable couturiers, her sexuality unobtrusive but apparent and all her own. His desire for her was growing by the minute, but he suspected she was not a woman to cross, or to fall for one of his customary "would you like to discuss your profile over supper" ploys. It would be a mistake to miss the woman within by merely tracing over the superficial packaging.

"I believe I should talk to you more often, Claire," he offered.

"I believe you should."

"Aren't you the Booza's parliamentary twin?" he continued. "I seem to remember reading somewhere. You both came into the House together, what—seven years ago? Same age. Both wealthy, darlings of the party conference. Both tipped to go far."

"If only I had his talent."

"Foreign Secretary, d'you think, in a Makepeace Cabinet?" He turned back to his original target.

Makepeace paused, as though to emphasize his words with elaborate consideration. "Not in a million dawns," he replied softly. "The man wouldn't recognize a political principle or an original idea if it were served up en croute with oysters."

"Ah, at last! A breach in your famous collective Ministerial loyalty, Tom. There's hope for you yet," the editor beamed, delighted to have discovered a point of such obvious antipathy. He turned to Claire. "I feel an editorial coming on. Although to tell you the truth, my dear, I'm a little worried by all his talk about principles and original ideas. It's not good for an ambitious man. We're going to have to work on him."

She laughed, a genuine expression full of white teeth and pleasure. "You know, Bryan, I think we are."

THREE

Great men are usually bad men. I intend to be a very great man.

Civilian Area, Dhekelia Army Base, British Sovereign Territory, Cyprus

"Greetings, my Greek friend. Welcome to a humble carpenter's workshop. What part of Allah's bounty may His servant share with you?"

"Sheep. Seven of them. A week on Friday. And not all fat and sinews like your wife."

"Seven?" the Turk mused. "One for every night of your week, Glafko. For you I shall endeavor to find the most beautiful sheep in the whole of Turkish Cyprus."

"It's Easter, you son of Saladin," Glafkos the Plumber spat. "And my daughter's getting married. A big feast."

"A thousand blessings on the daughter of Glafkos."

The Greek, an undersized man with a hunched shoulder and the expression of a cooked vine leaf, remained unimpressed. "Chew on your thousand blessings, Uluç. Why was I five shirts short on last week's delivery?"

The Turk, a carpenter, put aside the plane with which he

was repairing a broken door and brushed his hands on the apron spread across his prominent stomach. The sports shirts, complete with skillfully counterfeited Lacoste and Adidas logos, were manufactured within the Turkish sector by his mother's second cousin, who was obviously "taking the chisel" to them both. But the Greek made a huge markup on the smuggled fakes, which were sold through one of the many sportswear outlets in the village of Pyla, in a shop owned by his nephew. He could afford a minor slicing. Anyway, he didn't want a damned Greek to know he was being cheated by one of his own family.

"Shrinkage," he exclaimed finally, after considerable deliberation.

"You mean you've been pulling the sheet over to your side again."

"But my dear Greek friend, according to our leaders we are soon to be brothers. One family." His huge hand closed around the plane and nonchalantly he began scraping at the door again. "Why, perhaps your daughter might yet lie with a Turk."

"I'll fix the leaking sewers of hell first. With my bare hands."

The Turk laughed, displaying black teeth and gruff humor. Their battle was incessant, conducted on the British base where they both worked and at various illicit crossing points along the militarized buffer zone that separated Greek and Turkish communities. They could smuggle together, survive and even prosper together, but that didn't mean they had to like each other, no matter what those fools of politicians decreed.

"Here, Greek. A present for your wife." He reached into a drawer and removed a small bottle marked Chanel. "May it fill your nights with happiness."

Glafkos removed the top and sniffed the contents, pouring a little into the open palm of his hand. "Smells like camel's piss."

"From a very genuine Chanel camel. And very, very cheap," Uluç responded, rolling his eyes.

The Greek tried to scrape off the odor on his shirt, then examined the bottle carefully. "I'll take six dozen. On trial. And no shrinkage."

The Turk nodded.

"Or evaporation."

Uluç entered upon another hearty chuckle, yet as quickly as it had arrived his pleasure was gone and in place a gray cloud hovered about his brow. He began stroking his mustache methodically with the tip of a heavily callused finger, three times on each side, as though attempting to smooth away an untidiness that had entered his life.

"Wind from your wife's cooking?" Glafkos the Plumber ventured.

Uluç the Carpenter ignored the insult. "No, my friend, but a thought troubles me. If we are all told to love one another, Turk and Greek, embracing each other's heart instead of the windpipe—what in the name of Allah are you and I going to do?"

FOUR

If ignorance is bliss then Parliament must be filled with happy men.

As individuals most were modest, middle class, often dull. And proud of it. Collectively, however, they shared a bloodlust of animalistic intensity that found expression in waves of screamed enthusiasm that were sent crashing across the court.

"Changed, hasn't it?" Sir Henry Ponsonby mused, his thin face masked by the shade of a large Panama. He didn't need to add that in his view this could not have been for the better. As Head of the Civil Service he took a deal of convincing that change was anything other than disruptive.

"You mean, you remember when we English used to win?"

"Sadly that's ancient history of a sort that isn't even part of the core curriculum anymore." He sniffed. "No. I mean that every aspect of life seems to have become a blood sport. Politics. Journalism. Academia. Commerce. Even Wimbledon."

Down on the court the first Englishman to have been seeded at the All England Tennis Championships for more than two decades scrambled home another point in the tiebreak; a further two and he'd survive to fight a deciding set. The crowd, having sulked over the clinical humiliation of its national hero throughout the first horn and a half, had woken to discover he was back in with a chance. On the foot-scuffed lawn before them a legend was in the making. Perhaps. Better still, the potential victim was French.

"I may be an academic, Henry. Even an international jurist. But deep inside there's part of me that would give everything to be out there right now."

Sir Henry started at this unanticipated show of emotion. From unexceptional origins Clive Watling had established a distinguished career as an academic jurist and steady hand, QC, MA, LLB, and multiple honorary distinctions, redbrick reliable, a man whose authority matched his broad Yorkshire girth. Flights of physical enthusiasm were not part of the form book. Still, everyone was allowed a touch of passion, and better tennis balls than little boys.

"Well, that's not exactly what we had in mind for you, old chap," Sir Henry began again. "Wanted to sound you out. You know, you've established a formidable standing through your work on the International Court, widely respected and all that."

Another point was redeemed for national honor and Watling couldn't resist an involuntary clenching of his fists in response. Sir Henry's thin red line of lips closed formation. The mixture of tension and heat on Number One Court stifled any further attempt at conversation as the tennis players squared up once more.

A blow. A flurry of arms and fevered shouts. Movement of a ball so fast that few eyes could follow while all hearts sailed with it. A cloud of English chalk dust, a cry of Gallic despair, and an eruption of noise from the stands. The set was won and from the far end of the court came the sound of hoarse voices joined together in the chorus of "Rule, Britannia." Sir Henry raised his eyes in distaste, failing to notice his companion's broad grin. Sir Henry was a traditionalist, unaccustomed to expressing emotion himself and deprecating its expression by others. As he was to express to others in his club later that week, this was scarcely his *scene*. They were forced to wait until the inevitable wave had washed across them—good grief, was Watling actually flexing his thighs?—before being allowed to resume their thoughts.

"Yes, I've been fortunate, Henry, received a lot of recognition. Mostly abroad, of course. Not so much here at home. Prophet in his own country, you know?" And grammar school achiever in a juridical system still dominated by Oxbridge elitists. Like Ponsonby.

"Not at all, my dear fellow. You're held in the very highest regard. We English are simply a little more reticent about these things."

Sir Henry's words were immediately contradicted by an outburst of feminine hysteria from behind as the players resumed their places for the final set. It was noticeable that the many expressions of patriotic fervor emerging from around the stands were becoming mixed with vivid Francophobia. Such naked passions made Ponsonby feel uncomfortable.

"Let me come straight to the point, Clive. The Cypriots want to settle their domestic squabbles. Shouldn't be beyond reach, both Greeks and Turks appear to be suffering an unaccustomed outbreak of goodwill and common sense. Maybe they've run out of throats to cut, or more likely been tempted by the foreign aid packages on offer. Anyway, most of the problems are being resolved, even the frontiers. They both know they've got to make a gesture, give something up."

"Are their differences of view large?"

"Not unduly. Both sides want the barbed wire removed and most of the proposed line runs through mountains, which are of damn all value to anyone except goatherds and hermits."

"There's offshore through the continental shelf."

"Perceptive man! That's the potential stumbling block. Frankly, neither side has any experience of sea boundaries so they want an international tribunal to do the job for them. You know, give the settlement the stamp of legitimacy, avoid any loss of face on either side. All they need is a little bandage for national pride so they can sell the deal to their respective huddled masses. They're already surveying the waters, and they've agreed an arbitration panel of five international judges with Britain taking the chair."

"Why Britain, for God's sake?"

Ponsonby smiled. "Who knows the island better? The old colonial ruler, the country both Greeks and Turks mistrust equally. They'll choose two of the judges each, with Britain as the impartial fifth. And we want you to be the fifth."

Watling took a deep breath, savoring his recognition.

"But we want it all signed and sealed as soon as possible," Ponsonby continued, "within the next couple of months, if that could be. Before they all change their bloody minds."

"Ah, a problem."

"Yes, I know. You're supposed to spend the summer lecturing in considerable luxury in California. But we want you here. In the service of peace and the public interest. And, old chap, His Majesty's Government would be most appreciative."

"Sounds like a bribe."

A double fault, the crowd groaned. Ponsonby leaned closer.

"You're long overdue for recognition, Clive. There's only one place for a man of your experience." He paused, tantalizing. "You'd make a tremendous contribution in the House of Lords."

Ponsonby offered an impish smile; he enjoyed dispensing privilege. Watling, by contrast, was trying desperately to hide the twitch that had appeared at the corner of his mouth. As a boy he'd dreamed of opening the batting for Yorkshire; this ran a close second.

"Who else will be on the panel of judges?"

"Turks have nominated a Malaysian and some Egyptian professor from Cairo..."

"That would be Osman. A good man."

"Yes. Muslim Mafia."

"He's a good man," Watling insisted.

"Of course, they're all good men. And so are the Greek lot. They've chosen Rospovitch from Serbia—nothing to do with him being Orthodox Christian, I hasten to add. The thought would never have entered a Greek mind."

"And the fourth?"

"Supplied by Greece's strongest ally in Europe, the French. Your old chum from the International Court, Rodin."

"Him!" Watling couldn't hide his disappointment. "I've crossed judgments with that man more often than I care to remember. He's as promiscuous with his opinions as a whore on the Avenue Foch. Can't bear the man." He shook his head. "The thought of being cooped up with him brings me no joy."

"But think, Clive. The panel is split down the middle, two-two, by appointment. You'll have the deciding vote. Doesn't matter a damn about Rodin or any of the others, you can get on and do the job you think is right."

"I'm not sure, Harry. This is already beginning to sound like a political poker game. Would this be a proper job? No arm-twisting? I'll not be part of any grubby backstage deal," the lawyer warned, all Northern stubbornness, drawing in his chins. "If I were to handle this case it would have to be decided on its merits."

"That's why you've got to do it, precisely because you're so irritatingly impartial. Let me be frank. We want you for your reputation. With you involved, everything will be seen to be fair. Smother them in Hague Conventions and peaceful precedent. Frankly, from the political point of view it doesn't matter a dehydrated fig what you decide, in practice it will be little more than a line drawn across the rocks. A half mile here or there on which you couldn't grow a bag of beans. But what it will do is enable the Cypriot politicians to sew up a deal they badly need. So come down on whatever side you like, Clive, there'll be no pressure from us. All we want is a settlement."

They paused. The crowd was rising to the boil once more as the decisive set began to take shape. Watling still hesitated; it was time for the final nudge.

"And I suspect it would be appropriate to speed things along at our end, too. No need to wait in a long line, I think we could ensure your name appeared in the very next Honors List, at New Year's. Wouldn't want any uncertainty clouding your deliberations." Ponsonby was laughing. "Sorry about the hurry. And about California. But there's pressure on. The Cypriots have been at war with each other for a quarter of a century; it's time to draw the curtain on their little tragedy."

"You're assuming I'll say yes? In the interests of a peerage?"

"Dear fellow, in the interests of British fair play."

Further exchanges were rendered impossible, buried beneath the weight of noise. The French player had lunged, tripped, become entangled in the net as in desperation he tried to save a vital rally. Break point. The crowd, as one and on its feet, bellowed its delight.

The captain of the seismic vessel *Happy Valley* flicked the butt of his cigarette high above his head, watching it intently as it hung in the heavy air before dipping and falling reluctantly out of sight beyond the trawler's hull. His lungs were burning; he tried to strangle a cough, failed, shivered violently, spat. He'd promised his wife to give up the bloody things and had tried but, out here, day after day spent under callous skies, crisscrossing the featureless seas of the eastern Mediterranean, he found himself praying for storms, for mutiny, for any form of distraction. But there was none. He'd probably die of boredom long before the weed did for him.

He ached in his bones for the old days, running tank spares into Chile or stolen auto parts into Nigeria, his manifests a patchwork of confusion as he confronted the forces of authority, slipping between their legs with a cargo of contraband as a child evades a decrepit grandparent. Yet now his work was entirely legitimate; he thought the dullness of it all would crush his balls.

So those Byzantine bastards in Cyprus had agreed to exorcize their ghosts and reach a compromise. Peace to all men, whether Greek or Turk and no matter whose daughters they'd raped or goats they'd stolen. Or was it the other way around? Hell, he was French Canadian and loathed the lot, but they wanted their offshore waters surveyed so they could agree to an amicable split. And the sanctions-busting business wasn't what it used to be, not with peace breaking out everywhere. Seismic was at least a job. Until the next war.

From the sea behind him came the explosive thud of compressed air. Once, he remembered, it had been bullets and mines. He'd never thought he'd die of boredom. He squinted into the setting sun at the lines of floats and hydrophones that trailed for three thousand meters beyond the *Happy Valley*, crisscrossing the seas on a precise grid pattern controlled by satellite while bouncing shock waves off the muds and shales below the seabed and down the throats of the computers. The damned computers had the only air conditioning on the vessel while the men fried eggs in their underwear. But, as his bosses at Seismic International never ceased to remind him, this was a thirty-thousand-dollar-a-day operation, the captain and his crew were the cheapest part of it and by far the easiest to replace.

He spat at a seagull that had perched on the rail beside him. The bird rose languidly into the skies behind the vessel, examined the creamy wake for fish and, finding none, gave a cry of contempt before departing in search of a proper trawler. Christ, even the bloody birds couldn't stick the ship. And what was the point? Everyone knew there was nothing but a lot of scrap iron and shards of old pottery down there; not even any fish to talk of, not after they'd blown the once thriving marine world apart with old grenades and other forms of indiscriminate fishing.

He couldn't stick this outburst of peace. He wanted another war. And another cigarette. He coughed and began searching his pockets.

FIVE

A nation's pride was never defended successfully by good men. Good men find it impossible to reach the depths required.

He was standing in his dress shirt, bow tie cast aside, staring out through the shardproof curtains of the bedroom window across St. James's Park when she came in. The room was in darkness, his face cast like a wax mask in the reflection from the lighting beneath the trees in the park. Francis Urquhart, shoulders down, hands thrust deep into his dress trouser pockets, looked miserable.

"They turned old Freddie off," he whispered.

"Darling?"

"Old Freddie Warburton. The car crash? On life support? They decided there was no point, Mortima. So they turned him off."

"But I thought you said he was useless."

Urquhart spun around to face his wife. "Of course he was useless. Utterly and comprehensively useless. I'm surprised they could even tell when his brain had stopped functioning. But that's not the point, is it?"

"Then what is the point, Francis?"

"The point, Mortima, is that he was the only surviving

member of my original Cabinet from all those years ago. They'll say it's the end of an era. My era. Don't you see?"

Mortima had begun taking off her jewelry, methodically preparing herself for bed in the semilight while she considered her husband's fragile mood. "Don't you think you're overreacting a little?" she ventured.

"Of course I am," he replied. "But they'll overreact, too, the wretched media always do. You know how the poison has begun to drip. Should've retired on his tenth anniversary. An aging administration in need of new ideas and new blood. An age that is passing. Now with bloody Freddie away they'll say it's passed. Gone." He sat down on the edge of his bed. "It makes me feel so…alone, somehow. Except for you."

She knelt on his bed and began to work away at the tension in his shoulders. "Francis, you are the most successful Prime Minister this country has ever had. You've won as many elections as anyone, in three months' time you will have passed Margaret Thatcher's record of time in office. Your place in the history books is assured."

He turned. She could see the jaw muscles working away, making his temples throb.

"That's it, Mortima. I feel as if I'm already history. All yesterday, no longer today. No tomorrow."

It was back, his black mood, when he raged at the pointlessness of his life and the ingratitude and incompetence of the world around him. The moods never lasted long, but undeniably they were lasting longer. The challenge had lost its freshness, he needed dragons to slay but instead they seemed to have crawled away and hidden between the subclauses of interminable policy documents and Euro regulations. The cloak of office hung heavily on his shoulders, ceremonial robes where once there had been armor. He had towered like a giant above the parliamentary scene, quite beyond the reach of his foes, but something had changed, perhaps in him and certainly in others. They speculated openly about how long he would last before he stepped down, about who would be the most likely successor. His reputation for slicing through the legs of young pretenders was formidable, but now they seemed to have formed a circle around his campfire, skulking in the shadows, staying just beyond his reach, finding safety in growing numbers while they waited for their moment to step into the light. A few weeks ago he had appeared in the Chamber at Question Time, ready as always to defend himself against their arrows, carrying with pride the shield that bore the dents and scars of so many successful parliamentary battles. Then a young Opposition backbencher whom Urquhart scarcely recognized had risen to his feet.

"Does the Prime Minister know the latest unemployment figure for this country?"

And sat down.

Impudence! Not "Will he comment on" or "How can he excuse" but "Does he know." Of course Urquhart knew, two million or other, but he realized he needed not an approximation but the precise figure and had searched in his briefing notes. He shouldn't have needed to search; he should have known. *But the damned figure changed every month!* And as he had searched, his glasses slipped, and the Opposition benches had erupted as he scrabbled. "He doesn't know, doesn't care!" they shouted. He had found the answer but by then it was too late.

A direct hit.

It was unlike Francis Urquhart. He had bled, shown he was mortal. And the black moods had increased.

"I sometimes wonder what it's all been for, Mortima. What you and I have to look forward to. One day we'll walk out through that door for the last time and...then what? Hot chocolate and woolen underwear?" He shivered as her fingers reached the knot at the back of his neck.

"You're being silly," she scolded. "That's a long way off and, anyway, we've discussed it many times before. There's the Urquhart Library to establish. And the Urquhart Chair of International Studies at Oxford. There's so much we will still have to do. And I met a publisher at the reception this evening. He was enthusing about your memoirs. Said the Thatcher books went for something like three million pounds and yours will be worth far more. Not a bad way to start raising the endowment money we need for the Library."

His chin had fallen onto his chest once more. She realized the talk of memoirs had been misjudged.

"I'm not sure. Not memoirs, I don't think I can, Mortima."

"We shall need the money, Francis. As much as we shall need each other."

He turned sharply to look at her, staring intensely. In the dark she couldn't detect whether the cast in his eye betrayed mirth or yet deeper melancholy.

"No memoirs," he repeated. "Setting down the old falsehoods and inventing new ones. I couldn't write about my colleagues in that way, speaking such ill of the departed. God knows, I uttered lies enough to bury them, I couldn't pursue them beyond the grave. Not at all. Not for a King's ransom." He paused. "Could I, Mortima?"

Hakim was angry. His coffee was cold, his mustache growing white, his talents underappreciated, his bank unsympathetic, and everyone knew him simply as Hakim. Not Air Hakim, not *Yaman* Hakim, not *Old Friend and Colleague* Hakim. There was a small sign on his office door to that effect; they would carve it on his coffin, "*Hakim the Forgotten.*" Then they would forget him, the wife, the kids, the bosses, his bank manager. All of them. Especially his bank manager. He sipped the lukewarm mud in his coffee cup and pursed his lips in disgust. A lifetime's conscientious work and yet all he would have to take with him when the time came to go were his unfulfilled dreams.

He paused to consider. What would he most like to take with him into the afterlife? Young girls? Gold? An air-conditioned Mercedes? The vineyard he had always coveted? Probably young girls, he decided. No, on second thought he would take his bank manager. Then they could both burn.

He smiled to himself, then coughed painfully. The damned pollution was getting to his chest again. It was one of the many problems of building a capital city in the armpit of Anatolia where they burned filthy brown coal and choked the streets with gas fumes. And they were slowly, remorselessly congesting his lungs. A lifetime's service in order that he could choke to death. And be forgotten.

If he just locked the door from the inside and rotted, would anybody notice? His was a miserable office, even by the unexceptional standards of TNOC, the Turkish National Oil Corporation—shelves crammed with old manuals and reports, walls plastered with charts covered in bizarre patterns, a desk dusted with coffee stains and cigarette ash, the dusty accompaniments of his work as a geophysicist. For all he knew the office's previous occupant might still be hiding within the bowels of the small document cupboard in the corner—even though this had been Hakim's office for fourteen years.

He turned back to the computer screen and reexamined the seismic cross sections that had started coming in from the survey. There seemed to be little of interest, everyone knew there was nothing in the seas around Cyprus—TNOC wouldn't have bothered buying in the seismic had Cypriot waters not abutted Turkey's own. All other parts of the Eastern Mediterranean seemed to have oil, not only the Turks but the Libyans, Syrians, Egyptians, even damned Greeks—everyone except little Cyprus, who perhaps needed it more than most.

Dry as dust. God's mystery. A desert amid a sea of black gold. Such is the oil business.

He looked again. They all laughed at him, old Hakim the Forgotten, but he had the patience for the tedious work of analysis, not like these youngsters whose only interest was in football and fu...He stopped. He experienced a strange tingling in his fingers as they hovered over the keyboard, a sensation that he had been here before, or somewhere much like it. A long time ago. Where could it have been? He polished his glasses, giving himself time to remember. These were sedimentary rocks, that was for sure, but sedimentaries bearing oil were like Greeks bearing gifts. Rarely genuine. What type might they be?

Then he understood. He had not only seen it on geological logs, he'd even stuck his hand in the bloody mud. Thirty years ago, as a student at the Petroleum Institute when they had visited an exploratory well being drilled near the sea border with Cyprus. It had pulled up all the right geological formations, the sandwich of spongy sandstones that in theory might have held a billion barrels of oil but had yielded not a single drop. Now he thought he knew why. One of the seismic lines from the recent survey had been shot up to the site of the dry well and went straight through what was obviously a fault plane, a slippage in the earth's crust that played hell with the geology.

He started coughing again, nerves this time. Somewhere he reckoned he still had a copy of his Petroleum Institute report and its detailed findings from the old well. The document cupboard. The thin metal door squealed in protest as with shaking fingers he began ransacking the contents—no skeleton guarding the pirate's doubloons but ancient treasure nonetheless. It was in his hands, a slim ring-bound document that trembled like leaves in an autumn wind as he turned the pages.

It was all there. The right structures. Traces in the drill cuttings of residual oil. But no accumulation, the raw wealth drained by some unknown action.

And the screen yelled at him. "*Fault!*"

Without the seismic revealing the fault plane there had been no way thirty years ago to understand why such suitable sandstones had been bone-dry. And without detailed knowledge of the sandstones revealed by the well, there was no way to understand from the seismic alone what the structures might portend.

But Hakim the Geophysicist knew, and he was the only soul in the world in a position to know.

The fault plane had fouled up everything. Trashing all the logic. Tilting the geological structures. Draining the sandstones dry.

And Hakim thought he knew where a billion barrels of oil had gone.

SIX

I regard being called a hypocrite as something of a compliment. It means I can see both sides of the question.

"I hate memorial services. The cant. The falseness. The empty phrases and hollow praise. I *hate* memorial services."

Urquhart was in one of those humors again. He had stamped impatiently as he had waited at the east door of St. Margaret's Church to be escorted by the rector, and his face had been set in stone while walking to his appointed pew, past the acquiescent, nodding faces with their spaniel smiles and synthetic sympathies worn above black ties and scarves. They had thought his countenance denoted sadness, distress at the loss of such a good friend and colleague as Freddie, Baron Warburton, and indeed his emotions were fractured, but not in pity for others.

The turbid mood had begun the previous night when he had opened his red box to discover that his press officer, thinking it might be appropriate, had enclosed a few of old Freddie's obituaries. The bloody fool. Reading that Warburton's passing marked "the end of an era" and that he had been "the last of FU's dirty dozen" had done little to enhance the Prime Minister's enthusiasm about either the press or his press officer.

"Can't stand it, Mortima. They hound a man into the grave then, soon as he's dead and gone, reach for their sopping tissues and try to prove what a great man he was, how his loss somehow threatens culture, the country, civilization as a whole. The only reason I kept Freddie was because he followed like a lamb. Everybody knew that. But now he's a dead lamb they speak of him as a lion. Not a single mention anywhere that his veins had been swept quite clear of blood by alcohol. Nor of that little tangle in Shepherd Market when two ladies of the night abandoned him without either trousers, wallet, or his Downing Street pass."

"He was loyal, Francis."

"I had his balls in a vise, Mortima, of course he was loyal!" Urquhart brought himself to a sudden halt, closing his eyes. He'd gone too far. He should be used to honoring the dead at Westminster; there had been so many over the years, but such memories only brought out the worst in him. "Forgive me. That was unnecessary."

"Forgiven."

"It's just that...what will they say about me, Mortima? When I've gone?"

"That you were the greatest Prime Minister of the century. That you rewrote the record books as well as the law books. And lived a long and contented retirement."

"I doubt that. How many great leaders have ever truly found contentment in retirement?"

She searched for a name, but none came to her.

"I don't want to grow old and bitter, after all this has gone. I just don't have a vision of myself retiring, being replaced. Ever." He waved a hand at her. "Oh, I know I'm being pathetic but... retirement for me isn't filled with long summer evenings but endless nights dancing with ghosts. The ghosts of what might have been. And of what once was."

"I understand."

"Yes, I know you do. You're the only one who does. I owe you so very much."

She sat beside him now, in the church of St. Margaret's at Westminster, which stood in the lee of the great Abbey, as they listened to the choristers singing a plaintive anthem. Mortima's eyes were fixed on the young treble soloist, a boy of perhaps twelve with fair hair falling across his forehead and the tender voice of an angel that filled the church like the rays of a new sun. What a difference it might have made, he considered, if they had been able to have children; it could have touched their lives with a sense of immortality and brought music to their souls. Yet it was not to be. She had bound the wound until it scarred and toughened, never complaining, though he knew the hurt at times cleaved her in two; instead she had invested all her emotional energy in him and his career. Their career, in truth, for without her he could not have succeeded or sustained. For Mortima it had been a barren crown, a sacrifice in many manners far deeper than death, and all for him. He owed her everything.

The choir had finished and she looked around at him, a fleeting softness in her eye that he knew brimmed with regret. How much easier retirement would be to contemplate, had they had children. Instead all they would leave behind them were a Library and the fickle judgment of history. *Après moi, rien.* Once he had thought that would be enough but, as the years passed and mortality knocked, he was no longer sure.

> *"Rejoice in the Lord always: and again I say, Rejoice. Let your moderation be known unto all men…"*

Clerical hyperbole and half-truth, a momentary suspension of political life in the pews behind him while piously they honored death and, like birds of prey, plotted more.

"Finally, brethren, whatsoever things are true, whatsoever things are honest, whatsoever things are just, whatsoever things are pure."

Men sang such tunes in sleepy ritual then woke to ignore them so blithely. Yet, on the day of reckoning, what would be his own case? He suffered a pang of momentary doubt as ghosts crowded into the shadows of his mind, but then he was clear, as he had always been. That what he had done was not for himself, but for others, for his country. That the affairs of men require sacrifices to be made, and that the sacrifices he had made had always been motivated by public and national interest. Sacrifice of others, to be sure, sometimes in blood, but had not he and Mortima made sacrifices of their own, two lives devoted to one cause in the service of others?

"...that all things may be so ordered and settled by their endeavors, upon the best and surest foundations, that peace and happiness, truth and justice, religion and piety, may be established among us for all generations."

Crap. Life was like setting sail in a sieve upon a wild and disorderly sea. Most people got sick, many drowned.

"In silence, let us remember Frederick Archibald St. John Warburton."

Best damned way to remember the man. In complete bloody silence. But it was not the way Urquhart intended to go.

"Thy will be done on earth..."

And there he drew the line. No, that was not good enough, never had been good enough for Urquhart. Some men used morality as a crutch, an excuse—always the men who failed and achieved nothing. Morality was not the way through the swamp but the swamp itself, waiting to ensnare you, bind your limbs, drag you under. Great empires had not been built or sustained on such poor footings, or the British people protected from the plottings of envious foreigners by prayer. In the end, those who honored weakness were weak themselves. A great man was judged by how high he climbed, not by how long he could remain on his knees.

When the time came, he would not go in silence, he would depart with so much clamor that it would echo through the ages. Francis Urquhart would be master of his own fate.

"Amen."

Geoffrey Booza-Pitt revealed an unusual degree of self-consciousness as he faced his Prime Minister across the desk of the Downing Street study, hands clasped together, knuckles showing white and a smile seeming painted and fixed. It was not unusual for him to seek a private audience, and within limits Urquhart encouraged it; Geoffrey was a notorious gossip and adept at stealing others' ideas, which he could either claim as his own or abandon with ridicule depending on the reception given to them by his master. He was without doubt the finest ankle-tapper in the Cabinet, displaying fastidious team loyalty in public while dexterous at sending his colleagues sprawling in front of goal, usually clipping them from the blind side and always with an expression of pained innocence. A useful source of information and amusement for Urquhart, who relished the sport.

Urquhart had assumed that Booza-Pitt would be laying the ground for a change of responsibility at the next reshuffle. Geoffrey was a young man constantly on the move; ever since he had kicked open the door of the pen with a series of brilliant pyrotechnic displays at party conference he had proved impossible to pin down to any job or, for those who had memories for such things, to any guiding political principle. But in that he was not unique, and his effervescent energy, which is the hallmark of some slightly undersized men, more than made up for any lack of depth in the eyes of most observers. Geoffrey was going places—he left no listener in any doubt of the fact and such enthusiasm to many is infectious. And it was no secret around Westminster that Geoffrey would welcome a new job. As Transport Secretary for the last two years he had long since grown exasperated with the futility of trying to siphon twentieth-century cars through London's nineteenth-century road system and desperately wanted to escape the gridlock for some new challenge—any new challenge, so long as it came in the form of perceptible promotion. Move on before you grow roots and others grow bored was the Booza-Pitt rule, a creed he followed as much in love as in politics. He'd already scraped through two marriages; his ribald and envious colleagues referred to his Westminster house as the In & Out Club. Geoffrey's response had been to make a dubious virtue of necessity and to eschew further matrimonial entanglement, instead choosing his companions on an à la carte basis from the lengthy menu provided by the women of Westminster. Being single, it merely enhanced the dynamic impression.

Yet in the subdued lighting of Urquhart's study, the Transport Secretary belied his image. The neatly trimmed sandy hair had tumbled across his forehead, the eyes cast down, the broad and slightly crooked chin that normally afforded an aura of rugged athleticism tonight looked simply askew. A schoolboy come to confess.

"Geoffrey, dear boy. What news do you bring from the battle front? Are we winning?" He laid aside the gold-ribbed fountain pen with which he had been signing letters, forcing Booza-Pitt to wait, and suffer.

"Polls seem to be...not too bad."

"Could be better."

"Will be."

Urquhart studied the other man. The eyes were rimmed in red; he thought he could detect the bite of whiskey on his breath. Trouble.

"Come to the point, Geoffrey."

There was no resistance; his composure drained and the shoulders drooped. "I've got...a little local difficulty, FU."

"Women."

"Is it that obvious?"

The Minister was known to be a man of modest intellect and immoderate copulation; Urquhart had assumed it was only a matter of time before he stubbed his toe in public. "In this business it's always either women or money—at least in our party." He leaned forward in a gesture of paternal familiarity, encouraging confession. "She wasn't dead, was she? Almost anything can be smoothed over, except for live animals and dead women."

"No, of course not! But it's...more complicated than that."

More than a stubbed toe—a broken leg, perhaps? Amputation might be called for. "Well, so far we have one—one?—live woman. Tell me more."

"The chairman of my local party is going to divorce his wife on the grounds of adultery, citing me."

"It is true, I assume."

Booza-Pitt nodded, his hands still clasped between his knees as though defending his manhood from the enraged husband.

"Embarrassing. Might make it difficult to get yourself reselected for the next election with him in the chair."

Booza-Pitt sighed deeply and rapidly several times, expelling the air forcefully as though attempting to extirpate demons within.

"He says he's not going to be there. He's very bitter. Plans to resign from the party and go to the newspapers with the story."

"A tangled web indeed."

"And make all sorts of ridiculous allegations." This was almost blurted. Control of his breathing had gone.

"That you seduced her..."

"And that I got her to invest money in property on my behalf."

"So?"

"Property that was blighted by proposed road building schemes."

"Let me guess. Schemes that were about to be canceled. Scrapped. So lifting the blight and greatly increasing the value of the property. Inside information known only to a handful of people. Including the Secretary of State for Transport. You."

The lack of response confirmed Urquhart's suspicions.

"Christ, Geoffrey, you realize that would be a matter for not only resignation, but also criminal prosecution."

He wriggled like a worm on a hook. Piranha bait. Urquhart left him dangling as he considered. To convict or to assist, punish or protect? He had just buried one Cabinet member; to bury a second in such rapid succession could look more than unfortunate. He swiveled his pen on the blotter in front of him, like a compass seeking direction.

"You can assure me that these accusations are false?"

"Lies, all lies! You have my word."

"But I assume there are land registry deeds and titles with dates that to the cynical eye will appear to be more than coincidence. How did she know?"

"Pillow talk, perhaps, no more than that. I...I may have left my Ministerial box open in her bedroom on one occasion."

Urquhart marveled at the younger man's inventiveness. "You know as well as I do, Geoffrey, that if this comes out they won't believe you. They'll hound you right up the steps of the Old Bailey."

The fountain pen was now pointed directly at Booza-Pitt, like an officer's sword at a court-martial, in condemnation. Urquhart produced a sheet of writing paper, which he laid alongside it. "I want you to write me a letter, Geoffrey, which I shall dictate."

Awkwardly, with the movements of a man freezing in the Arctic desert, Booza-Pitt began to write.

"'Dear Prime Minister,'" Urquhart began. "'I am sorry to have to inform you that I have been having an affair with a married woman, the wife of the chairman of my local association.'"

Geoffrey raised pleading eyes, but Urquhart nodded him on.

"'Moreover, she has accused me of using confidential information available to me as a Government Minister to trade in blighted property and enrich myself, in breach not only of Ministerial ethics but also of the criminal law.' New paragraph, Geoffrey. 'While I have given you my word of honor that these accusations are utterly without foundation, in light of these allegations…'"

Booza-Pitt paused to raise a quizzical brow.

"'…I have no alternative other than to tender my resignation.'"

The death warrant. A sob of misery bounced across the desk.

"Sign it, Geoffrey." The pen had become an instrument of punishment. "But don't date it."

A dawning of hope, a stay of execution. Booza-Pitt did as he was told, managed a smile. Urquhart retrieved the paper, examined it thoroughly, and slid it into the drawer of his desk. Then his voice sank to a whisper, like a vault expelling the last of its air.

"You contemptible idiot! How dare you endanger my Government with your sordid little vices? You're not fit to participate in a Francis Urquhart Cabinet."

"I'm so dreadfully sorry. And appreciative…"

"I created you. Made a space for you at the trough."

"Always grateful…"

"Never forget."

"Never shall. But…but, Francis. What are we going to do about my chairman?"

"I may, just possibly, be able to save your life. What's his name?"

"Richard Tennent."

"Have I ever met him?"

"Last year, when you came to my constituency. He chewed your ear about grants for tourism."

Slowly, without taking his eyes off Booza-Pitt, Urquhart reached for his phone. "Get me a Mr. Richard Tennent. New Spalden area."

And they waited in silence. It took less than two minutes for the operator to make the connection.

"Mr. Tennent? This is Francis Urquhart at Downing Street. Do you remember we met last year, had that delightful discussion about tourism? Yes, you put the case very well. Look, I wanted to have an entirely confidential word with you, if you're agreeable. Bit unorthodox, but I have a problem. Did you know that you've been put up for an honor, for your political and public service?"

Evidently not.

"No, you shouldn't have known, these things are supposed to be confidential. That's why I wanted an entirely private word. You see, I've just been going through the list and, to be frank, after what you've done for the party I thought you deserved something a little better. A knighthood, in fact. Trouble is, there's a strict quota and a bit of a waiting list. I very much want you to have the 'K,' Mr. Tennent, but it would mean your waiting perhaps another eighteen months. You can have the lesser gong straightaway, though, if you like."

The voice dripped goodwill while his eyes lashed coldly across Booza-Pitt, who showed little sign of being able to breathe.

"You'd prefer to wait. I entirely understand. But you realize that this must remain utterly confidential until then. Won't stop you and Lady Tennent attending a Downing Street reception in the meantime, though? Good."

A tight smile of triumph.

"One last thing. These things get pushed through a Scrutiny Committee, look at each individual case to make sure there are no skeletons in the closet, nothing that might prove a public embarrassment, cause the honor to be handed back or any such nonsense. Forgive my asking, but since your name will be carrying my personal recommendation, there's nothing on the horizon that might…?"

A pause.

"Delighted to hear that. I must just repeat that if anything were to leak out about your upcoming award…But then the party has always known it can rely on you. Sir Richard, I am most grateful."

He chuckled as he threw the phone back into its cradle. "There you are! The old Round Table gambit always works; give 'em a knighthood and a sense of purpose and they always come aboard. With luck that'll keep his mouth shut for at least another eighteen months and possibly for good."

Geoffrey had just begun to imitate the Prime Minister's bonhomie when Urquhart turned on him with unmistakable malevolence. "Now get out. And don't ever expect me to do that again."

Geoffrey rose, a tremble still evident in his knees. "Why did you, Francis, this time?"

The light from the desk lamp threw harsh shadows across Urquhart's face, bleaching from it any trace of vitality. One eye seemed almost to have been plucked out, leaving a hollowed socket that led straight to a darkness within.

"Because Francis Urquhart and *only* Francis Urquhart is going to decide when Ministers come and go from his Cabinet, not some shriveling cuckold from New Spalden."

"I understand." He had been hoping for some acknowledgment of his own irreplaceable worth.

"And because now I own you. Today, tomorrow, and for as long as I wish. You will jump whenever I flick my fingers, whether it be at the throats of our enemies or into your own grave. Without question. Total loyalty."

"Of course, Francis. You had that anyway." He turned to leave.

"One last thing, Geoffrey."

"Yes?"

"Give me back my fountain pen."

SEVEN

Some people prefer to pour oil on troubled waters. I prefer to throw a match.

The sun blazed fiercely outside the window, and the coffee on the table in small cups was dark and thick; in all other respects the office with its stylishly simplistic furniture and modern art trimmings might have been found on the Skeppsbron overlooking the harbor in Stockholm. Yet most of the books along the light oak bookshelves were in Turkish, and the two men in the room were of dark complexion, as were the faces in the family photographs standing behind the desk.

"Now, what brought you in such a hurry to Nicosia?"

"Only a fool tarries to deliver good tidings."

There was an air of formality between them, two Presidents, one Yakar, chief of the Turkish National Oil Company, and the other, Nures, political head of the Republic of Turkish Cyprus. It was not simply that the oil man was a homosexual of contrived manner and the politician a man of robust frame, language, and humor; there was often a distance between metropolitan and islander that reflected more than their separation by fifty miles of sea. It had been a century since the Ottomans had ruled Cyprus, and differences of culture and perspective had grown. Mainlanders patronized and shepherded the islanders—had they not delivered their cousins from the clutches of Greek extremists by invading and then annexing one third of the island in 1974? At one moment during those confused days the Turkish Cypriots had found themselves on the point of a Greek bayonet, the next they had been in charge of their own state. Except the Government in Ankara kept treating it as though it was *their* state.

Time to get rid of them, Mehmet Nures told himself yet again. For a thousand years mainland Turks and Greeks and the imperialist British had interfered and undermined, using the island as a well at which to quench the thirst of their ambitions. They'd sucked it dry, and turned an island of old-fashioned kindnesses and a million butterflies into a political desert. Perhaps they couldn't step through the looking glass, back to the ways of old, with bubble-domed churches standing alongside pen-nib mosques, but it was time for change. Time for Cypriots to sort out their own destiny, time for peace. The question was—whose peace?

"I have the honor to present to you a draft of the formal report that Seismic International will publish in a few days following their recent survey of the offshore waters." The oil man removed a folder from a slim leather case and deposited it in front of Nures, who proceeded to rustle through its pages. The file contained many colored maps and squiggles of seismic cross sections with much technical language that was quite beyond him.

"Don't treat me like a tortoise. What the hell does all this mean?"

Yakar tugged at his silk shirt cuffs. "Very little. As expected, the seismic survey has revealed that beneath the waters of Cyprus there is much rock, and beneath the rock there is… much more rock. Not the stuff, I fear, of excited headlines."

"I sit stunned with indifference."

Yakar was playing with him, a reserved smile loitering around his moist lips. "But, Mr. President, I have a second report, one which neither Seismic International nor anyone else has—except for me. And now you." He handed across a much slimmer file, bound in red and bearing the TNOC crest.

"Not the Greeks, you mean?"

"May my entrails be stretched across the Bosphorus first."

"And this says…?"

"That there is a geological fault off the coast of Cyprus that has tilted the subsurface geology of the seabed to the north and west of the island. That the structure in that area does indeed contain oil-bearing rock. And that the fault has tipped all the oil into a great big puddle about—there." He stretched and prodded a bejeweled finger at the map Nures was examining.

"Shit."

"Precisely."

The tip of Yakar's manicured nail was pointing directly at what had become known as "Watling Water"—the sea area contested between Greek and Turkish Cypriot negotiators and currently the subject of arbitration by the British professor's panel.

Nures felt a current of apprehension worm through his gut. It had taken him years to balance the scales of peace, feather by feather, he didn't know if he wanted tons of rock thrown at it right now, oil or no oil. The peace deal was important to him; by giving up so little to the Greek side he could gain so much for his people—peace, international acceptance, true independence, prosperity—and possibly a Nobel Peace Prize for himself. All in exchange for a little land and a stretch of water that was worthless. Or so he had thought.

A thick hand rasped across his dark chin. "How much oil?" he asked, as if every word had cost him a tooth.

"Perhaps a billion barrels."

"I see," he said, but clearly didn't. "What does that mean?"

"Well, the international spot price for oil is around twenty dollars a barrel at the moment. Cost of extraction about five. In round terms—approximately fifteen billion dollars."

The oil man was whimpering on about Turkish brotherhood and TNOC getting preferential access, teasing out the deal he wished to cement. Nures closed his hooded eyes as though to shut himself away from such squalor, but in truth to contemplate temptation. He had an opportunity—had created the opportunity—to turn a tide of history that had forced poison between the lips of Cypriots and had condemned his own son to be raised in a land of fear. For his grandson it could be different.

Would the world forgive him for endangering the peace process? Would his people forgive him for missing out on fifteen billion dollars' worth of oil? But could he forgive himself if he didn't try to grab both?

No contest.

"President Yakar, I think we want those rocks."

"President Nures, I rather think we do."

Yaman Hakim felt conspicuous. He had put on his best suit but it was modestly cut and he looked clumsy and otherworldly amid the style and self-assertiveness on the rue St. Honoré. Still, he reminded himself, he was not here for a fashion show.

He'd first thought of making the exchange in Istanbul with its cloudburst of humanity beneath which one solitary soul might disappear, but even among the labyrinth of *souks* and smoky bazaars the authorities had their men, the informers, and there was always the danger of his bumping elbows with someone he knew. He didn't trust his luck in such matters; he'd once gone off to Antalya on the excuse of an energy symposium in order to spend two nights with Sherif, a nubile young girl from Personnel who was into older men, only to discover that a neighbor had booked into the next room. Praises to God, the man had been engaged on a similar mission of deceit, allowing them to share the solidarity of sinners. Yet he felt the presence of prying eyes everywhere in his homeland, and this was worth so much more than a quick scramble between the sheets.

He had chosen Paris because he had once visited it as a student many years before, because there was no chance of his being recognized—and because the French understood what was required. The English were too stuffy and of constricted sphincter, while the Americans were all cowboys. If he were to survive, Hakim needed discretion, a partner who could be trusted to keep his mouth shut and not be found after two drinks and an encouraging smile bragging about it in the bar of the Hilton. In matters of corporate espionage, tax evasion, and fraud the French had all the necessary finesse, they also had bank accounts untraceable by the Turkish authorities; pity about their limp coffee.

Anxiety had made him early and he sat in the sidewalk café swirling the dregs in his cup, waiting. His mind danced with thoughts—of drowsy islands set in mystical seas that shimmered as though studded with a treasury of diamonds; of bougainvillea-clad villas overlooking the sacred Bosphorus and tinkling to the sound of female laughter; of oil wells trembling in the Mediterranean breeze beneath their plumes of black gold—and of the fetid rat-filled walls of Istanbul's notorious Yedi Giile prison, echoing with the cries of those who had come too late to repentance. It was not too late for him, not yet, he could still get out, go home, be back in the office tomorrow. Back to being Hakim the Forgotten. The man whose skill and experience had single-handedly uncovered one of the great natural treasure troves of his lifetime—without whom none of this great adventure in exploration would have been possible! But even as he had handed them his report and analysis, his chest heaving with pride, they had told him it was all in a day's work, what TNOC paid him for, he shouldn't expect any recognition or thanks. And he had received none.

An executive Citroën with immaculate black paintwork drew up on the roadway beside him and a window of darkened glass wound down.

"Mr. Hakim, over here. Quickly, please!"

Already the Volkswagen behind was sounding its horn impatiently. They had told him about the café, said nothing about a car. Disconcerted, untrusting, but seemingly with little option, the Turk scurried across the pavement. The rear door opened and he settled into the deep leather seat. A hand extended, cuffed in a timepiece of Swiss gold.

"Delighted to meet you at last, Mr. Hakim."

He had insisted on meeting the top man, face-to-face, not being fobbed off with aides and underlings. He needed decisions; he wanted to deal with the man who made them.

"Forgive the caution. Couldn't be sure you didn't have—how can I put it?—somebody else watching us at the café. A news photographer. A competitor, perhaps? I thought a little privacy might assist our discussions."

Hakim grunted. The man reeked of authority, money; Hakim was well out of his league.

"We were very interested in the material you sent us, Mr. Hakim"—carefully selected pages from the report, crumbs to whet the appetite but not enough to chew on—"interested enough to check you out. You're genuine. But is your report?"

In response Hakim took a single folded sheet of paper from his suit pocket and, with only the slightest hesitation for a final thought, passed it across. It was the report's summary page, giving the estimates of the potential beneath the seabed.

"Fascinating. And I assume there is a price for this material."

"A heavy price," Hakim growled, snatching back the single sheet. "But a very fair price."

"How much?"

"For the entire report?" He chewed his thumbnail. "A million dollars."

The other man didn't flinch. His stare was direct, examining Hakim as if some clue to their business might be found in his leathered face; defiantly the Turk stared back.

"This matter is very simple, Mr. Hakim. Your information is of no value to anyone unless it is accurate, and of no value to my company unless we get the license to drill."

"When the time comes you will buy the license. With this report you will know how much to pay—and who to pay."

"That time is some way off."

"Sadly for you, I am not a patient man."

"Then let me get to the point. My proposal—which is also my final proposal—is this." An envelope had appeared in his hands. "Here is fifty thousand dollars, for sight of the report. If after studying it we believe its contents to be genuine, there will be another two hundred thousand dollars." He held up a hand to stay the objection beginning to bubble within the Turk. "And if my company succeeds in obtaining the license and striking oil, there will be a payment to you of not one, but two million dollars. Worth that, if what you say is true."

It was the Turk's turn to consider, agitatedly squeezing his salt-streaked mustache as though wishing to pluck it from his lip. "But how can I trust you?"

"Mr. Hakim, how can I trust you? How am I to know you're not hawking this same document around every one of my competitors? There has to be a measure of mutual trust. And look at it this way, what would be the point of my trying to cheat you of millions when there are potentially billions at stake?"

The Turk was breathing heavily, trying to encourage the supply of oxygen to his thought processes.

"If your document is genuine, I shall be giving you a quarter of a million dollars with only your word that it's the sole copy in circulation. A costly mistake for me if your word is false." The Frenchman paused. "But it would be a still more costly mistake for you."

"What?" Hakim mocked. "You are threatening to break my legs?"

"Not at all, my friend. I would simply let the Turkish authorities know of your activities. I imagine your legs would be the least of your problems."

The Frenchman smiled, raised the envelope with its fifty thousand dollars, and gently proffered it.

Hakim stared, debated, twisted, and tore at himself, but the exercise was pointless. It was too late now, neither conscience nor caution could argue with fifty thousand dollars and more, much more, to come. From within his briefcase of imitation crocodile he extracted his report and handed it across.

EIGHT

What is the point of conquering mountains? It's bloody cold, the food is appalling, and who wants to do everything roped helplessly to some stumbling idiot?

No, not mountains. Better to conquer men.

A glorious spring dawn brimming with rose-tinged enthusiasm had advanced across London, delighting most early risers. Mortima Urquhart could not know her husband shared none of the collective spirit.

"Good morning, Francis. The weather gods seem to be smiling in celebration. Happy birthday."

He didn't move from his position staring out from the bedroom window and at first offered only a soft "Oh, dear" and a slight flaring of the nostrils in response. He lingered at the window, captured by something outside before shaking his head to clear whatever pest was scratching at his humor. "What have you got for me this year? Another Victorian bottle for the cabinet? What is it—eighteen years of bloody bottles? You know I can't stand the things." But his tone was self-critical, more irony than ire.

"Francis, you know you have no interests outside politics and I'm certainly not going to give you a bound copy of *Hansard.*

Your little collection has at least given you something for the hacks to put in their profiles, and this particular piece is rather lovely. A delicate emerald green medicine bottle that is supposed to have belonged to the Queen herself." She puckered her lips, encouraging him along. "Anyway, I like it."

"Then, Mortima, if you like it, so shall I."

"Don't be such a curmudgeon. I've something else for you, too."

At last he turned from the window and sat opposite her as she held forth a small package with obligatory ribbon and bow. Unwrapped, it teased from him the first sign of pleasure. "Burke's *Reflections on the Revolution in France.* And an early edition." He fingered the small leather-bound volume with reverence.

"A first edition," she corrected. "The pioneer volume for the Urquhart Library, I thought."

He took her hands. "That is so typically thoughtful. And how appropriate that our Library should start with one of the finest anti-French tirades ever written. You know, it might inspire me. But…I have to admit, Mortima, that this talk of birthdays and libraries smacks all too much of retirement. I'm not yet ready, you know."

"The young pretenders may seem fleeter of foot, Francis, but what's their advantage if you are the only one who knows the route?"

"My life would be so empty and graceless without you." He smiled, and meant it. "Well, time to give the ashes a rake and discover whether the embers still glow." He kissed her and rose, drawn again to the view from the window.

"What *is* out there?" she demanded.

"Nothing. As yet. But soon there may be. You know the Thatcher Society wants to erect a statue to the Baroness on that piece of lawn right out there." He prodded a finger in the direction of the carefully manicured grass that lay beyond the wall of the Downing Street garden, opposite St. James's Park. "You know, this is a view that hasn't much changed in two hundred and fifty years; there's a print hanging in the Cabinet Room and it's all there, same bricks, same doors, even the stones on the patio are original. Now they want to put up a bloody statue."

He shook his head in disbelief. "And the erection fund is almost fully subscribed." He turned sharply, his face twisted by frustration. "Mortima, if the first thing I'm going to see every morning of my life when I draw my bedroom curtains is that bloody woman, I think I shall expire."

"Then stop it, Francis."

"But how?"

"She doesn't merit a statue. Thrown out of office, betrayed by her own Cabinet. Is the statue going to show all those knives in her back?"

"Yet almost all of them are hacked from office, my love. By their colleagues or the electorate. Like Caesar, taken from behind by events they hadn't foreseen. Ambition makes leaders blind and lesser men bloody; none of them knew when the time had come to go."

"There's only one Prime Minister who should have a statue there, and that's you!"

He chuckled at her commitment. "Perhaps you're right—but flesh and blood turn to stone all too soon. Don't let's rush it."

He turned himself to stone two hours later, as fixedly as if he had spent the night wrapped in the arms of the Medusa. It was his press secretary's habit to arrange on a regular basis a meeting with representatives of charities—ordinary members, not experienced leaders—inviting them to the doorstep of Number Ten but not beyond, a visit too brief to allow for any substantial lobbying but long enough to show to the cameras that the Prime Minister cared—the "Click Trick," as the press secretary, a hockey player and enthusiast named Drabble, termed it. Having been at his desk since six collating the morning's press, extracting from it selected articles he thought worthy of note and preparing a written summary, he met Urquhart in the entrance hall shortly before nine thirty.

"What is it today, Drabble?" Urquhart inquired, striding briskly down the red-carpeted corridor from the Cabinet Room.

"A birthday surprise, Prime Minister. This week it's pensioners, they're going to make a presentation."

Somewhere inside Urquhart felt part of his breakfast liquefying. "Was I told of this?"

"You had a note in your box last weekend, Prime Minister."

"Sadly, kept from me by more pressing letters of state," Urquhart equivocated. Damn it, Drabble's notes were so tedious, and if a Prime Minister couldn't rely on professionals to sort out the details…

The great door swung open and Urquhart stepped into the light, blinked, smiled, and raised a hand to greet the onlookers as though the street was filled with a cheering crowd rather than a minor pack of world-weary journalists huddled across the street. A group of fifteen pensioners drawn from different parts of the country were gathered around him, arranged by Drabble, who was giving an advanced simulation of a mother hen. The mechanics were always the same: Urquhart asked their names, listened with serious-smiling face, nodded sympathetically before passing on to the next. Soon they would be whisked off by one of Drabble's staff and a junior Minister from an appropriate department to be plied with instant coffee and understanding in a suitably impressive Whitehall setting. A week later they would receive a photograph of themselves shaking hands with the Prime Minister and a typed note bearing what appeared to be his signature thanking them for taking the trouble to visit. Their local newspapers would be sent copies. Occasionally the discussions raised points or individual cases that were of interest to the system;

almost invariably the majority of those involved went back to their pubs and clubs to spread stories of goodwill. A minor skirmish in the great war to win the hearts and votes of the people, but a useful one. Usually.

On this occasion Urquhart had all but completed the ritual of greeting, moving on to the last member of the group. A large package almost five feet in height was leaning against the railings behind him and, as Urquhart swung toward him, so the pensioner shuffled the package to the fore. It turned out to be a huge envelope, addressed simply: *To the Prime Minister.*

"Many happy returns, Mr. Urquhart," the pensioner warbled.

Urquhart turned around to look for Drabble, but the press officer was across the street priming the cameramen. Urquhart was on his own.

"Aren't you going to open it then?" another pensioner inquired.

To Urquhart's mind the flap came away all too easily, the card slipped out in front of him.

"*We are for you, FU*" was emblazoned in large red letters across the top. Across the bottom: "*65 Today!*"

The group of pensioners applauded, while one who was no taller than the card itself opened it to reveal the message inside.

"*Welcome to the Pensioners' Club,*" it stated in gaudy script. "*OAP Power!*" The whole thing was decorated with crossed walking sticks.

Urquhart's eyes glazed like marble. Rarely had the photographers seen the Prime Minister's smile so wide, yet so unmoving, as if a chisel had been taken to hack the feature across his face. The expression lingered as he was drawn across the street, more to lay his hands upon the wretched Drabble than to go through the ritual of bantering with the press.

A chorus of "Happy Birthday!" mingled with shouts of "Any retirement announcement yet, Francis?" and "Will you be drawing your pension?" He nodded and shook his head in turn.

The mood was jovial and Drabble enthusiastic; the fool had no idea what he'd done.

"Are you too old for such a demanding job at sixty-five?" one pinched-faced woman inquired, thrusting a tape recorder at him.

"Churchill didn't seem to think so. He was sixty-five when he started."

"The American President is only forty-three," another voice emerged from the scrum.

"China's is over ninety."

"So no discussions about retirement yet?"

"Not this week, my diary is simply too full."

Their slings and arrows were resisted with apparent good humor; he even managed to produce a chuckle to indicate that he remained unpricked. Politics is perhaps the unkindest, least charitable form of ritualized abuse allowed within the law; the trick is to pretend it doesn't hurt.

"So what do you think of today's poll?" It was Dicky Withers of the *Daily Telegraph*, an experienced hand known for concealing an acute instinct behind a deceptively friendly pint of draft Guinness.

"The poll."

"Yes, the one we carried today."

Drabble began an unscheduled jig, bouncing from foot to foot as though testing hot coals. He hadn't included the poll in his digest, or the intemperate editorial in the *Mirror* titled "*It's Time to Go.*" Christ, it was the man's birthday, one day of the year to celebrate, to relax a little. And it wasn't that Drabble was an inveterate yes-man, simply that he found it easier to accept the arguments in favor of circumspection. All too frequently messengers who hurried to bring bad news from the battlefield were accused of desertion and shot.

"Forty-three percent of your own party supporters think you should retire before the next election," Withers elaborated.

"Which means a substantial majority insisting that I stay on."

"And the most popular man to succeed you is Tom Makepeace. Would you like him to, when the time comes?"

"My dear Dicky, when that time comes I'm sure that Tom will fight it out with many other hopefuls, including the bus driver."

"*Makepeace = Bus Driver,*" Withers scribbled, noting the uncomplimentary equivalence. "So you intend to go on, and on, and on?"

"You might say that," Urquhart began, "but I wish you wouldn't. I'm enjoying a successful career and, though I'm not greedy for power, so long as I have my wits and my teeth and can be of service..."

"What do you intend to do when eventually you retire, Mr. Urquhart?" Pinch Face was thrusting at him again.

"Do?" The creases of forced bonhomie turned to a rivulet of uncertainty. "Do? Do? Why, be anguished and morose like the rest of them, I suppose. Now, you'll excuse me, ladies and gentlemen. I have a Cabinet meeting to attend."

He turned and embarked upon what he hoped was a dignified retreat back across the street—like a lion regaining his den, Drabble decided, tail thrashing ominously. He declined to follow.

Urquhart brushed into his wife as she was emerging from the lift to their private apartment. "Everything went well?" she inquired before she had noticed his eyes.

"They say it's time for a change, Mortima," he spat, grinding his teeth. "So I'm going to give 'em change. Starting with that bloody fool of a press secretary."

"Astonishing," Urquhart thought to himself as the Cabinet filed in around the great table, "how politicians come to resemble their constituencies."

Annita Burke, for instance, an unplanned Jewish suburb full of entangling one-way systems. Richard Grieve, a seedy run-down seafront (which he had once plastered with election posters stating "*Grieve for Rushpool*" and had somehow managed to live it down). Arthur Bollingbroke, a no-frills Northern workingmen's club with a strong tang of Federation bitter. Colin Catchpole, the member for the City of Westminster, a ruddy face with the redbrick architectural style of the Cathedral, while other parts of his anatomy were rumored to linger in the backstreets of Soho. Geoffrey Booza-Pitt—yes, Geoffrey, an invented showman for the invented show town of New Spalden. Middle class and entirely manufactured, lacking in roots or history—at least any history Geoffrey wished to acknowledge. He had been born plain Master Pitt to an accountant father with a drinking problem; the schoolboy Geoff had invented an extended name and some mythical South African origin to explain away untidy gossip about his father that had been overheard by friends across a local coffee shop. And it had stuck, like so many other imaginative fictions about his origins and achievements. You could fool some of the people all of the time, and Geoffrey reckoned that was enough.

Then there was Tom Makepeace, with the flat humor of the East Anglian fens, the stubbornness of its clays, and the moralizing tendencies of its Puritan past. He was an Old Etonian with a social conscience Urquhart ascribed to an overdeveloped sense of guilt, unearned privilege in search of unidentified purpose. The man had undoubted talent but was not from Urquhart's mold, which is the reason he had been dispatched to the Foreign Office where his stubbornness and flat humor could bore for Britain and help fight the cause in the tedious councils of Brussels, and where his moralizing could do little harm.

Urquhart's Cabinet. "And few of you seem to be keeping your eye on the ball, if I may be frank." The mood was all flint; Drabble had gone missing, the ghost of his folly not yet exorcized.

"We must finish in ten minutes; I have to be at the Palace for the arrival of the Sultan of Oman." He looked slowly around the long table. "I trust it will be rather more of a success than the start of the last state visit."

His gaze set upon Annita Burke, Secretary of State for the Environment. She was both Jew and female, which meant that the doors of power started off double-locked for her. She had stormed the drawbridge by sheer exuberance but now she sat rigid, head lowered. Something on her blotter appeared to have become of sudden importance, monopolizing her attention.

"Yes, it was a great pity, Environment Secretary. Was it not?"

Burke, the Cabinet's sole female, raised her head defiantly but struggled for words. Had it been her fault? For months she had planned a great campaign to promote the virtues and dispel the tawdry myths surrounding the nation's capital; from their corners and quiet tables in some of London's finest restaurants the publicity men had examined the runes and pronounced; a press conference and brass band had been organized, a fleet of billboards assembled, and seven million leaflets printed for distribution around the city on launch day.

"Making a Great City Greater."

What they had not foreseen—could not have foreseen, no matter how many slices of corn-fed chicken and loch-reared salmon they had sacrificed—was that launch day would also coincide with the most catastrophic failure of London's sewer system, a progressive collapse of an entire section of Victorian brickwork that had flooded the Underground and shorted the electrical control network. Points failure, and humor failure, too. A million angry commuter ants had erupted onto the streets, creating a gridlock that had extended beyond the city to all major feed roads. On one of those feed roads, the M4 from Heathrow Airport, had sat the newly arrived President of Mexico, expecting a forty-minute drive to the royal and political dignitaries already assembled for him at Buckingham Palace. But nothing had moved. The truck-borne poster hoardings had been stuck and defaced. Most of the leaflets had been dumped undelivered in backstreets. The press conference had been canceled; the brass band had not arrived. And neither had the Mexican President, for more than three hours.

It was a day on which the dignity of the capital died, swept away in a torrent of anger and effluent. Failure required its scapegoat, and "Burke" fitted the tabloid headlines so well.

"Great pity," she concurred with Urquhart, her embarrassment exhumed. "The Ides were against us."

"And you've come up with a new idea for reestablishing our reputation for caring environmentalism. The Fresh Air Directive. Article 188." He made it sound like a charge sheet.

"Health & Safety at Work. Sensory pollution."

"Smells."

"Yes, if you like."

"And we're against them, are we?"

"The European Commission has proposed that all urban workplaces be monitored for excessive sensory pollution with a strict enforcement code for those sites that don't meet the set standards."

"You know, there's a curry shop at the end of my street..." Bollingbroke began in his usual homespun fashion, but Urquhart drove right through him.

"Clean up or close down. And you approved of this."

"Wholeheartedly. Cleaner air, better environment. Honors our manifesto commitment and gives us a ready answer to those who claim we've been dragging our feet on Europe." She tapped her pen on her blotter for emphasis, betraying her unease. He seemed in such acid humor.

"Have you ever been to Burton-on-Trent, Environment Secretary?"

"I visited for two days when I was sixteen, for a sixth-form symposium." Her dark eyes flashed; she wasn't going to let him patronize her.

"And it hasn't changed very much in the many years since.

Still five breweries and a Marmite factory. On a hot summer's day the High Street can be overpowering."

"Precisely the point, Prime Minister. If we don't make them clean up their act they'll not lift a finger themselves."

"But the entire town lives on beer and Marmite. Their jobs, their economy, breakfast and tea, I suppose. And far be it from me to remind you that the brewers are among the party's staunchest corporate supporters."

The Environment Secretary became aware that the two Ministers seated on either side, though still in the same claret leather seats, had yet managed to distance themselves physically from her, as though fearful of getting caught by a ricochet.

"And you'd close them down. Wipe the entire town off the map. My God, not even Göring was able to do that."

"This is a European proposal that we are obliged to..."

"And how many towns will those ill-begotten French close down? In August the whole of Paris reeks when the water level drops. Small wonder they all flee to the seaside and abandon the city to the tourists."

"This is a collective decision arrived at after careful study in Brussels. Our future lies in Europe and its..."

There she was, driving up her one-way street again, in the wrong direction. "Bugger Brussels." He could no longer contain his contempt but he did not raise his voice, he must not seem to lose control. "It's become nothing more than a bureaucratic brothel where the entire continent of Europe meets to screw each other for as much money as possible."

Bollingbroke was rapping his knuckles on the table in approval, tapping out his fealty. The curry shop could stay.

"If you had spent as much time there as I have, Prime Minister, you would realize how"—she reached for a word, considered, weighed the consequences and compromised—"exaggerated that description is." One day, one day soon, she promised herself, she would no longer hold back the strength of her views. She wouldn't let herself be emasculated like most of the men around the table. She was the only woman, he daren't fire her. Dare he? "This directive is about chemical plants and refineries and..."

"And fish markets and florists' shops! Environment Secretary, let me be clear. I am not going to have such Euro nonsense pushed through behind my back."

"Prime Minister, all the details were in a lengthy position paper I put to you two weeks before the Council of Ministers in Brussels approved the measure. I'm not sure what more I needed."

"Instinct. Political instinct," Urquhart responded, but it was time to back off, move on. "I can't be expected to take note of every tiny detail buried in a policy document," he parried, but the effect was ruined as he fumbled for his reading glasses in order to locate the next item on the agenda.

What motivated Makepeace to join the fray even he had trouble in identifying. He was by nature an intervener. A friend of Annita and strong supporter of Europe, he didn't care for Urquhart's arguments or attitude. Perhaps he felt that since he occupied one of the four great offices of state he was in a strong position to conciliate, lighten the atmosphere, pour oil on troubled waters.

"Don't worry, Prime Minister," he offered lightheartedly as Urquhart adjusted his spectacles. "From now on we'll have all Cabinet documents typed in double space."

The oil exploded. It was as if he had offered an accusation that Urquhart was—what? Too old? Too enfeebled for the job? Fading? To Urquhart, deep into humor failure, it sounded too much an echo of the demands for change. He rose with such sudden venom that his chair slid back on the carpet.

"Don't deceive yourself that one opinion poll gives you special privileges."

The air had chilled, grown exceptionally rarefied, thinned by rebuke. Makepeace was having difficulty breathing. A tableau of deep resentment had been drawn in the room, growing in definition for what seemed several political lifetimes. Slowly Makepeace also stood.

"Prime Minister, believe me I had no intention..."

Others grasped the opportunity. Two Cabinet Ministers on their feet must indicate an end to the meeting, a chance to bring to a close such extraordinary embarrassment. There was a general rustling of papers, and as rapidly as seemed elegant they departed without any further exchange of words.

Urquhart was angry. With life, with Drabble, Burke, and Makepeace, with them all, but mostly with himself. There were rules between "the Colleagues," even those whose ambition perched on their shoulders like storm-starved goshawks.

"Thou shalt honor thy colleagues, within earshot."

"Thou shalt not be caught bearing false witness."

"Thou shalt not covet thy colleague's secretary or job (his wife, in some cases, is fair game)."

"Thou shalt in all public circumstances wish thy colleagues long life."

Urquhart had broken the rules. He'd lost his temper and, with it, control of the situation. He had gone much further than he'd intended, displayed insufferable arrogance, seeming to wound for the sake of it rather than to a purpose. In damaging others, he had also damaged himself. There was repair work to be done.

But first he needed a leak.

It was as he was hurrying to the washroom outside the Cabinet Room that, near the Henry Moore sculpture so admired by Mortima, he saw a grim-faced Makepeace being consoled by a colleague. His quarry had not fled, and here was an opportunity to bind wounds and redress grievances in private.

"Tom!" he summoned, waving to the other who, with evident reluctance, left the company of his colleague and walked doggedly back toward the Cabinet Room. "A word, please, Tom," Urquhart requested, offering the smallest token of a smile. "But first, a call of nature."

Urquhart was in considerable discomfort, all the tension and tea of the morning having caught up with him. He disappeared into the washroom, but Makepeace didn't follow, instead loitering outside the door. Urquhart had rather hoped he would come in; there can be no formality or demarcation of authority in front of a urinal, an ideal location for conversations on a basis of equality, man-to-man. But Makepeace had never been truly a member of the club, always aloof, holding himself apart. As now, skulking around outside like a schoolboy waiting to be summoned to the headmaster's study, damn him.

And damn this. Urquhart's bladder was bursting, but the harder he tried the more stubborn his system seemed to grow. Instead of responding to the urgency of the situation it seemed to constrict, confining itself to a parsimonious dribble. Did all men of his age suffer such belittlement, he wondered? This was silly—hurry, for pity's sake!—but it would not be hurried. Urquhart examined the porcelain, then the ceiling, concentrated, swore, made a mental note to consult his doctor, but nothing seemed to induce his system to haste. He was glad now that Makepeace hadn't joined him to witness this humiliation.

Prostate. The old man's ailment. Bodily mechanics that seemed to have lost contact with the will.

"Tom, I'll catch you later," he cried through the door, knowing that later would be too late. There was a scuffling of feet outside and Makepeace withdrew without a word, taking his resentment with him. A moment lost, an opportunity slipped. A colleague turned perhaps to opponent, possibly to mortal enemy.

"Damn you, come on!" he cursed, but in vain.

And when at last he had finished, and removed cuff links and raised sleeves in order to wash his hands, he had studied himself carefully in the mirror. The sense inside was still that of a man in his thirties, but the face had changed, sagged, grown blemished, wasted of color like a winter sky just as the sun slips away. The eyes were now more bruised than blue, the bones of the skull seemed in places to be forcing their way through the thinning flesh. They were the features of his father. The battle he could never win.

"Happy birthday, Francis."

Booza-Pitt had no hesitation. In many matters he was a meticulous, indeed pedantic, planner, dividing colleagues and acquaintances into league tables of different rank that merited varying shades of treatment. The First Division consisted of those who had made it or who were clearly on the verge of making it to the very peaks of their professional or social mountains; every year they would receive a Christmas card, a token of some personal nature for wife or partner (strictly no gays), an invitation to at least one of his select social events and special attention of a sort that was logged in his personal secretary's computer. The cream. For those in the Second Division who were still in the process of negotiating the slippery slopes there was neither token nor undue attention; the Third consisted of those young folk with prospects who were still practicing in the foothills and received only the encouragement of a card. The Fourth Division, which encompassed most of the world who had never made it into a gossip column and were content in life simply to sit back and admire the view, for Geoffrey did not exist.

Annita Burke was, of course, First Division but had encountered a rock slide that would probably dump her in the Fourth, yet until she hit the bottom of the ravine there was value to be had. She was standing to one side in the black-and-white-tiled entrance hall of Number Ten, smoothing away the fluster and composing herself for the attentions of the world outside, when Geoffrey grabbed her arm.

"That was terrible, Annita. You must be very angry."

There were no words but her eyes spoke for her.

"You need cheering up. Dinner tonight?"

Her face lit at the unexpected support; she nodded.

"I'll be in touch." And with that he was gone. Somewhere intimate and gossipy, he thought—it would be worth a booth at Wiltons—where the flames of wounded feelings and recrimination might be fanned and in their white heat could be hammered out the little tools of political warfare, the broken confidences, private intelligences, and barbs that would strengthen him and weaken others. For those who were about to die generally preferred to take others with them.

Dinner and gossip, no more, even though she might prove to be vulnerable and amenable. It had been more than fifteen years since they'd spent a romping afternoon in a Felixstowe hotel instead of in the town hall attending the second day of the party's youth conference debating famine in the Third World. They both remembered it very keenly, as did the startled chambermaid, but a memory it should remain. This was business.

Anyway, Geoffrey mused, necrophilia made for complicated headlines.

NINE

I will trust him when I hold his ashes in my hand.

It stood in a backstreet of Islington, on the point where inner city begins to give way to north London's sprawling excess, just along from the railway arches that strained and grumbled as they bore the weight of crowded commuter trains at the start of their journey along the eastern seaboard. During the day the street bustled with traffic and the bickering and banter from the open-air market, but at night, with the poor street lighting and particularly when it was drizzling, the scene could have slipped from the pages of Dickens. The deep shadows and dark alleyways made people reluctant to pass this way, unless they had business. And in this street the business after dusk was most likely to be Evanghelos Passolides's.

His tiny front room restaurant lay hidden behind thick, drawn curtains and a sign on the grimy window that in loud and uncharitable voice announced that the establishment was closed. There was no menu displayed, no welcoming light. It appeared as though nothing had been touched for months, apart from a well-scrubbed doorstep, but few who hurried by would have noticed. Vangelis, as it was known, was unobtrusive and largely unnoticed, which was the point. Only friends or those recommended by friends gained access, and certainly no one who in any life might have been an officer of the local authority or Customs & Excise. For such people Vangelis was permanently closed, as were his accounts. It made for an intimate and almost conspiratorial atmosphere around the five small tables covered in faded cloths and recycled candles, with holly-covered paper napkins left over from some Christmas past.

Maria Passolides, a primary school teacher, watched as her father, a Greek Cypriot in his midsixties, hobbled back into the tiny open-plan kitchen from where with gnarled fingers and liberal quantities of fresh lemon juice he turned the morning's market produce into dishes of fresh crab, sugar lamb, suckling pig, artichoke hearts, and quails' eggs. The tiny taverna was less of a business, more part hobby, part hideaway for Passolides, and Maria knew he was hiding more than ever. The small room was filled to chaos with the bric-a-brac of remembrance—a fishing net stretched across a wall and covered in signed photographs of Greek celebrities, most of whom were no longer celebrities or even breathing; along cluttered shelves, plates decorated with scenes of Trojan hunters fighting for control with plaster Aphrodites and a battalion of assorted glasses; on the back of the door, a battered British army helmet.

There was an abundance of military memorabilia—a field telephone, binoculars scraped almost bare to the metal, the tattered and much-faded azure blue cloth of the Greek flag. Even an Irish republican tricolor.

In pride of place on the main wall hung a crudely painted portrait of Winston Churchill, cigar jutting defiantly and fingers raised in a victory salute; beneath it on a piece of white card had been scrawled the words that in Greek hearts made him a poet the equal of Byron: *I think it only natural that the Cypriot people, who are of Greek descent, should regard their incorporation with what may be called their Motherland as an ideal to be earnestly, devoutly, and feverishly cherished...*

It was not the only portrait on the wall. Beside it stood the photograph of a young man with open collar, staring eyes, and down-turned mouth set against a rough plaster wall. There was no sign of identity, none needed for Michael Karaolis. A promising village boy educated at the English School. A youthful income tax clerk in the colonial administration, turned EOKA fighter. A final photograph taken in Nicosia Jail on the day before the British hanged him by his neck until he was dead.

"Vangelis."

Since he had buried his wife a few years before, Evanghelos Passolides had been captured more than ever by the past. Sullen days were followed by long nights of rambling reminiscence around the candlelit tables with old comrades who knew and young men who might be willing to listen, though the numbers of both shrank with the passing months. He had become locked in time, bitter memories twisting both soul and body; he was stooped now, and the savagely broken leg that had caused him to limp throughout his adult life had grown noticeably more painful. He seemed to be withering even as Maria looked, the acid eating away inside.

The news that there was to be peace within his island only made matters worse. "Not my peace," he muttered in his heavy accent. He had fought for union, *Enosis*, a joining of all Greeks with the Motherland—one tongue, one religion, one Government no matter how incompetent and corrupt, so long as it was our Government. He had put his life on the line for it until the day his fall down a mountain ravine with a thirty-pound mortar strapped across his back had left his leg bones protruding through his shin and his knee joint frozen shut forever. His name had been on the British wanted list so there was no chance of hospital treatment; he'd been lucky to keep his leg in any condition. The fall had also fractured the spirit, left a life drenched in regret, in self-reproach that he and his twisted leg had let his people down, that he hadn't done enough. Now they were about to divide his beloved island forever, give half of it away to the Turk, and somehow it was all his fault.

She had to find a distraction from his remorse, some means of channeling the passion, or sit and watch her father slowly wither away to nothing.

"When are you going to get married?" he grumbled yet again, lurching past her in exaggerated sailor's gait with a plate of marinated fish. "Doesn't family mean anything to you?"

Family, his constant refrain, a proud Cypriot father focused upon his only child. With her mother's milk she had been fed the stories of the mountains and the village, of mystical origins and whispering forests, of passions and follies and brave forebears—little wonder that she had never found a man to compare. She had been born to a life illuminated with legend, and there were so few legends walking the streets of north London, even for a woman with her dark good looks.

Family. As she bit into a slice of cool raw turnip and savored its tang of sprinkled salt, an idea began to form. "*Baba.*" She reached out and grabbed his leathery hand. "Sit a minute. Talk with me."

He grumbled, but wiped his hands on his apron and did as she asked.

"You know how much I love your stories about the old days, what it was like in the village, the tales your mother told around the winter fires when the snow was so thick and the well froze. Why don't we write them down, your memories. About your family. For *my* family—whenever I have one." She smiled.

"Me, write?" he grunted in disgust.

"No, talk. And remember. I'll do the rest. Imagine what it would be like if you could read the story of *Papou,* your grandfather, even of his grandfather. The old way of life in the mountains is all but gone, perhaps my own children won't be able to touch it—but I want them to be able to know it. How it was. For you."

He scowled but raised no immediate objection.

"It would be fun, *Baba*. You and me. Over the summer when school is out. It would be an excuse for us to go visit once more. It's been years—I wonder if the old barn your father built is still there at the back of the house, or the vines your mother planted. And whether they've ever fixed that window in the church you and your brothers broke." She was laughing now, like they had before her mother died. A distant look had crept into his eyes, and within them she thought she saw a glint of embers reviving in the ashes.

"Visit the old family graves," he whispered. "Make sure they're still kept properly."

And exorcize a few ghosts, she thought. By writing it all down, purging the guilt, letting in light and releasing all the demons that he harbored inside.

He sniffed, as though he could already smell the pine. "Couldn't do any harm, I suppose." It was the closest he had come in months to anything resembling enthusiasm.

TEN

I see no point in compromise. It's rather like suggesting jumping as a cure for vertigo.

Mortima despaired of trying to check her face in the flicker of passing street lights as the car made its way up Birdcage Walk. "So what kind of woman is Claire Carlsen?" she asked, snapping away her compact.

"Different." Urquhart paused to consider. "Whips don't much care for her," he concluded, as though he had no identifiable opinion of his own.

"A troublemaker?"

"No. I think it's more that the old boys' network has trouble in finding the right pigeonhole for a woman who is independent, drives a fifty-thousand-pound Mercedes sports car and won't play by their rules. Has quite a tongue on her, too, so I'm told."

"Not something of which you as a former Chief Whip would approve. So why are we going to dinner?"

"Because she's persistent, her invitation seemed to keep creeping to the top of the list. Because she's different."

"Sounds as if you *do* approve, Francis," she probed teasingly, her curiosity aroused.

"Perhaps I do. As Chief Whip I welcomed the dunderheads and do-nothings, but as Prime Minister you need a little more variety, a different perspective. Oh, and did I say she was under forty and extremely attractive?" He returned the tease.

"Thinking of giving her a job?"

"Don't know. That's why we're going this evening, to find out a little more about her. I could do with some new members of the crew."

"But to make room on the life raft you have to throw a few old hands overboard. Are there any volunteers?"

"I'd gladly lash that damned fool Drabble around the fleet. And Annita Burke was born to be fish bait."

"I thought she was loyal."

"So is our Labrador."

"Go further, Francis. Much further. Bring it back."

"What?"

"Fear. They've grown idle and fat these last months, your success has made things too easy for them. They've found time to dream of mutiny." They were passing Buckingham Palace, the royal standard illuminated and fluttering proud. "Even a King cannot be safe on his throne."

For a moment they lost themselves in reminiscence.

"Remind them of the taste of fear, the lash of discipline. Make them lie awake at nights dreaming of your desires, not theirs." The compact was out again, they were nearing their destination. "We haven't had a good keelhauling for months. You know how those tabloid sharks love it."

"With you around, my love, life seems so full of pointed opportunity."

She turned to face him in the half light. "I'll not let you become like Margaret Thatcher, dragged under by your own crew. Francis, you are greater than that."

"And they shall erect statues to my memory…"

She had turned back to her mirror. "So make a few examples,

get some new crew on board. Or start taking hormone therapy like me."

❖ ❖ ❖

The door of the buttermilk stucco house set in the middle of Belgravia was opened through the combined effort of two brushed and scrubbed young girls, both wearing tightly wrapped dressing gowns.

"Good evening, Mrs. Urquhart, Mr. Urquhart," said the elder, extending a hand. "I'm Abby and this is Diana."

"I'm almost seven and Abby is nine," Diana offered with a lisp where soon would be two new teeth. "And this is Tangle," she announced, producing a fluffy and much-spotted toy dog from behind her back. "He's very nearly three and absolutely..."

"That's enough, girls." Claire beamed proudly from behind. "You've said hello, now it's good-bye. Up to bed."

Stereophonic heckling arose on either side.

"Pronto. Or no Rice Pops for a week."

Their protest crushed by parental intimidation, the girls, giggling mischievously, mounted the stairs.

"And I've put out fresh school clothes for the morning. Make sure you use them," their mother called out to the retreating backs before returning to her guests. "Sorry, business before pleasure. Welcome, Francis. And you, Mrs. Urquhart."

"Mortima."

"Thank you. I feel embarrassed knowing your husband so much better than you."

"Don't worry, I'm not the jealous type. I have to share him with the rest of the world. It's inevitable there should be a few attractive young women among them."

"Why, thank you," Claire murmured, acknowledging the compliment. In the light of the hallway's chandelier she seemed to shimmer in a way that Mortima envied and which she had thought could only be found in combination with motherhood between the pages of *Vogue*. Was Claire also the type that had herself photographed naked and heavily pregnant, just to show the huddled, sweating masses with backache and Sainsbury's bags just how it was done?

Claire introduced her husband, Johannis, who had been standing back a pace; this was his wife's event and, anyway, he gave the impression of being a physically powerful man who was accustomed to taking a considered, unflustered view of life. He also had the years for it, being far nearer Urquhart's age than his wife's, and spoke with a distinctively slow though not unpleasant accent bearing the marks of his Scandinavian origin. Carlsen's self-assured posture suggested a man who knew what he wanted and had got it, while she displayed the youthful vitality of a woman with ambitions still to be met. Contrasts. Yet it took only a few moments for Mortima to become aware that in spite of the superficial differences, somehow the Carlsens seemed to fit, have an understanding, be very much together. Perhaps she hadn't married him simply for the money.

Claire led the way through to a reception room of high ceiling and pastel walls—ideal for the displayed works of contemporary European artists—in which the other eight guests had already assembled. Urquhart knew only one of them, but knew of them all; Claire had provided him with a short and slightly irreverent written bio of every diner, including Johannis. She'd made it all very easy, had chosen well. A bluff Lancashire industrialist who did extraordinary things with redundant textile mills that kept his wife in Florida for half the year and in racehorses for the rest. The editor of *Newsnight* and her husband, a wine importer who had provided the liquid side of the meal, which he spiced with spirited stories of a recent trip to vineyards in the mountains of Georgia where, for three nights, he had resided in a local jail on a charge of public drunkenness until he had agreed to take a consignment of wine from the police chief's brother. The wine turned out to be excellent. There was also an uninhibited Irishman-and-American-mistress partnership who had invented the latest departure in what was called "legal logistics"—"profiling alternative litigation strategies," he had explained; "Lawyers' bullshit, it's witness coaching and jury nobbling," as she had offered.

And Nures. Urquhart had known he would be there, a relatively late addition to the guest list while on a private visit to London for dental treatment; his family's fruit firm had used Carlsen freight facilities for more than a decade. The Foreign Office would normally have expressed qualms about his meeting the President of Turkish Cyprus in this manner, without officials present, but Nures was no longer an international pariah. Anyway, the Foreign Office couldn't object because Urquhart hadn't let them know; they would have felt obliged to parley with Nicosia, Ankara, Athens, Brussels, and half a dozen others in a process of endless consultation and compromise to ensure no one was offended. Left to the Foreign Office, they'd all starve.

Claire thrust a malt whiskey into Urquhart's hand—Bruichladdich, she'd done her homework—and propelled him toward the *Newsnight* editor and the developer, neither of whom would be sitting next to him during the meal.

"Pressure groups are a curse," Thresher, the developer, was protesting. "Am I right, Mr. Urquhart?" He pronounced it Ukut, in its original Scottish form, rather than the soft Southern Urkheart so beloved of the BBC, who at times seemed capable of understanding neither pronunciation nor policy. "Used to be there was a quiet, no-nonsense majority, folks that mowed their lawns and won the wars. But now everyone seems to belong to some minority or other, shouting t'odds and lying down in t'road trying to stop other folk getting on with life. Environmentalists"—Thresher emphasized every syllable, as though wringing its neck—"will bring this country to its knees."

"We have a heritage, surely we must defend it?" Wendy the *Newsnight* editor responded, accepting with good grace the fact that for the moment she had been cast in the role of lonesome virtue.

"Green-gabble." Urquhart pounced, joining in the game. "It's everywhere. Knee-jerk nostalgia for the days of the pitchfork and pony and trap. You know, ten years ago the streets of many Northern towns were deserted, now they're congested with traffic jams as people rush to the shops. I'm rather proud of those traffic jams."

"Could I quote you, Prime Minister?" Wendy smiled.

"I doubt it."

"Here's something you might quote, but won't, lass." Thresher was warming to his task. "I've got a development planned in Wandsworth centered around one old worm-eaten cinema. Neither use nor ornament, practically falling to pieces it is, but will they let me knock it down? The protesters claim they prefer the knackered cinema to a multimillion-pound shopping complex with all the new jobs and amenities. Daft buggers won't sit in t'cinema and watch films; no, all they do is sit down in t'street outside, get up petitions and force me to a planning inquiry that'll take years. It's a middle-class mugging."

"Not in my house, I trust." Claire had returned to usher them to the dining room. As they followed her bidding, Urquhart found himself alone with Thresher.

"So what are you going to do, Mr. Thresher?"

"Happen I'll take my money away, put it in some Caribbean bank and buy myself a pair of sunglasses."

"A great pity for you. A loss for the country, too."

"What's Government going to do about it then, Prime Minister?"

"Mr. Thresher, I'm surprised that a man of your worldly experience should think the Government is capable of doing anything to help." Urquhart had a habit of talking about his colleagues in the manner of a world-weary headmaster confronted with irresponsible schoolboys who deserved a thrashing.

"So it's off t'Caribbean."

"Perhaps the answer might lie a little closer."

"How close?"

"Brixton, perhaps?"

"You interest me."

"I was merely wondering why, if the protesters want a cinema, you don't give them a cinema."

"But that's not the game. Anyway, nobody comes."

"You're obviously showing the wrong films. What do you think would occur if, for instance, you started showing cult films with a strong ethnic flavor? You know, Rasta and dreadlocks?"

"I'd have to start giving the tickets away."

"Lots of them. Around the black community, I'd suggest."

"God, the place'd start swarming with 'em. But what would be the point?"

Urquhart plucked the other's sleeve to delay him at the entrance to the dining room, lowering his voice. "The point, Mr. Thresher, is that after four weeks of Bob Marley and juju, it wouldn't surprise me if the good burghers of Wandsworth changed their minds about your cinema; indeed, I harbor the strongest suspicion they'd crawl to you on hands and knees, begging you to bring in the bulldozers." He raised a suggestive eyebrow. "It's a pathetic fact of middle-class life that liberalism somehow fades with the nightfall."

Thresher's jaw had dropped; Claire had appeared once more at their side to organize them. "This is a decent house. So whatever you two are plotting had better stop," she instructed genially. "Otherwise no pudding."

"I think I've just 'ad that, pet. You know, your boss is a most remarkable man." Thresher's voice vibrated with unaccustomed admiration.

"I'm glad you agree. Does my feminine intuition sense a

substantial check being written out to party headquarters?" she inquired, twisting his arm as she led him to his place.

"For the first time in my life, I think I might."

Claire found her own seat at the head of the table, flanked by Urquhart and Nures. "I'm impressed, Francis. I've been trying for five years to get him to open his wallet, yet you did it in five minutes. Did you sell the whole party, or just a few principles?"

"I merely reminded him that among the grass roots of politics are to be found many weeds."

"And in the bazaar there are many deals to be done," Nures added.

"A touch cynical for someone who's off duty, Mehmet," she suggested.

"Not at all. For what is the point of going to the market if you are not intending to deal?" he smiled.

"Window-shopping?"

His eyes brushed appreciatively over her, taking in the subtle twists of silk—she had no need of excessive ornamentation—not lingering to give offense, before running around the dining room, where modern art and soft pastel had given way to Victorian classic displayed upon bleached oak paneling. "You do not leave the impression of one who spends her life with her nose pressed up against the window, Claire."

"That's true. But at least it enables me to lay my hand on my heart and deny any ambition of grabbing your job, Francis."

"How so?" he inquired, in a tone that suggested he wouldn't believe a word.

She puckered her nose in distaste. "I couldn't possibly live in Downing Street. It's much too far from Harrods."

And the evening had been a great success.

It was as Urquhart and his wife were preparing to leave that Nures took him to one side.

"I wanted to thank you, Prime Minister, for everything you

have done to help bring about peace in my island. I want you to know we shall always be in your debt."

"Speaking entirely privately, Mr. President, I can say how much I have admired your tenacity. As we both know to our cost, the Greeks have never been the easiest of people to deal with. Do you know, the Acropolis is falling down around their ears yet still they demand the return of the Elgin Marbles? Intemperate vandalism."

"The Greek Cypriots are different, of course."

"Accepted. But Balkan blood runs thicker than water. Or logic, at times."

"And oil."

"I beg your pardon?"

"You know the seismic report of the offshore waters has been published?"

"Yes, but it didn't show any oil, did it?"

"Precisely." Nures paused, a silence hung between them. "But I wanted you to know that if there were any oil, and if that oil were under my control, I would very much want my British friends to help us exploit it."

"All this talk of oil, you sound as if you expect it. But there was nothing in the report."

"Instinct?"

"I hope for your sake those instincts are right. But it would then depend upon the outcome of the boundary arbitration."

"Precisely."

"Oh, I think I begin to see."

"I have very strong instincts in this matter, Mr. Urquhart. About the oil."

Urquhart was clear that his feet were now standing directly in the middle of the bazaar. "I cannot interfere, even if I wanted to," he replied softly. "The arbitration is a judicial process. Out of my hands."

"I understand that completely. But it would be such a pity

if my instincts were right yet the arbitration went wrong, and the Greeks gave all the exploitation rights to their good friends the French."

"A tragedy."

"Great riches for both your country and mine"—why did Urquhart feel he really meant "for both you and me"? Instinct, that was it—"great riches lost. And I would lose most. Imagine what would happen to me if my people discovered that I had given away a fortune in oil? I would be dragged through the streets of Nicosia."

"Then we must hope that fortune smiles on you, and wisdom upon the judges."

"I would have so many reasons to be exceptionally grateful, Mr. Urquhart."

Their confidences balanced carefully on a narrow ledge; any move too swift or aggressive, and they would both fall—would Urquhart attempt to run, or would he push? They spoke in whispers, taking care to maintain their poise, when suddenly they were joined by a new and uninhibited voice. "Such a rare commodity in politics, don't you think, gratitude?" It was Mortima who, farewells indulged, had been hovering. "You'd rather be flayed alive than let the French run off with anything, Francis. You really must find a way of helping Mr. Nures."

"I shall keep my fingers crossed for him." And, nodding farewell to the Turk, Urquhart crept back off the ledge.

Claire was waiting for him by the front door. "A truly exceptional evening," he offered in thanks, taking her hand. "If only I could organize my Government the way you organize your dinner parties."

"But you can, Francis. It's exactly the same. You invite the guests, arrange the menu, decide who sits where. The secret is to get a couple of good helpers in the kitchen."

"As it happens I've been thinking of rearranging the table,

playing a bit of musical chairs. But you make a good point about the backstage staff. What do you think?"

"You want me to be indiscreet."

"Of course. Drabble, for instance?"

"A disaster."

"Agreed. And Barry Crumb?"

"So aptly named."

"No Crumbs in the kitchen Cabinet, you think?" He laughed, enjoying the game.

Barry Crumb was the Prime Minister's Parliamentary Private Secretary. The PPS is a Member of Parliament but in the view of many the lowest form of parliamentary life. The job is that of unofficial slave to a Minister, performing any function the Minister may request from serving drinks to spying on colleagues. As such it is unpaid, but the cost to the individual is high since the PPS is deprived of any form of independence, being required to follow the Government line on all matters of policy. Thus it is an excellent means of shutting up a backbencher who is becoming troublesome.

Yet the job is more, and much sought after, for it provides privileged insights into Ministerial life and is regarded as the first step on the ladder, the training ground from which new Ministers are plucked. Those involved in the process liken themselves to a "Tail End Charlie," a rear gunner who with luck may survive and move forward through the ship to become a navigator, perhaps one day even the captain. Those of more cynical disposition suggest that it is merely the start of the process whereby a backbencher is deprived of the capacity for independent thought and action, thereby making him suitable to be selected for higher office.

A PPS dwells in the shadow of the Minister and has no independent existence. But that shadow may be long, and the PPS has rights of access, both in the Palace of Westminster and at the Department of State, even at times in the Minister's private life.

And to have access in abundance to a great Minister, let alone a Prime Minister, to hover at the right hand and to sit in the rear seat, is one of the most fascinating opportunities available to any young parliamentarian, which is why so blithely they trade their independence for insight and opportunity, and the rudimentary beginnings of influence.

It was a pity about Barry Crumb. He jumped when he should have tarried, hovered when he should be gone, an enthusiast but a man so afraid of getting it wrong that self-consciousness deprived him of initiative and any ability to read Urquhart's mind or moods. The man had no subtlety, no shade. No future.

"He's not up to it, is he?" Urquhart stated.

"No. But I am."

He took his coat and chuckled at her impudence. In the whole of Christendom there had never been a female PPS, not to a Prime Minister. The boys wouldn't like it, lots of bad jokes about plumbing and underwear. But, Urquhart reflected, it was his intention to shake them up, so what if it upset a few, all the better. Remind them who's in charge. He needed a fresh pair of legs, and at the very least these would be a young and extremely attractive pair of legs, far easier to live with than Crumb's. And he had the feeling she might prove far more than merely a mannequin.

"Would you get rid of the Mercedes and start buying your suits at Marks & Spencer?"

"No. Nor will I as your PPS shave my head, grow hair on my legs, or allow myself headaches for three days every month."

He waved good-bye to the rest of the guests, the business of departure replacing the need to reply. "Time to depart." He summoned Mortima who was bidding Nures farewell, but Claire was still close by his shoulder, demanding his attention.

"I am up to it, Francis."

He turned at the door. "You know, I do believe you are."

ELEVEN

All politicians are cuckoos. I betray, therefore I am.

There was no longer pleasure for her, nothing but dark childhood memories dragged from within by the rhythmic protest of a loose bedspring. She couldn't hide it, he must have noticed, even as his frantic climax filled the bedroom with noise.

That is much how she remembered them, the childhood nights in a small north London duplex with Victorian heating and walls of wafer, filled with the sounds of bodies and bedsprings in torment. When the eight-year-old had inquired about the noises, her mother had muttered sheepishly about childish dreams and music. Perhaps that's what had inspired Harrison Birtwistle, although by preference she'd rather listen to the torturing of bedsprings.

Did anybody still sleep in those classic cast-iron bedsteads full of angry steel wire and complaints, she wondered? It had been so many years since she had, and no regrets at that. Nor did she miss the sitting room carpet, a porridge of cigarette burns and oil blots and other stains for which there had never been any explanation. "I'll go down to Hardwick's and get you another," her father had always promised her mother. But he never did.

Claire Carlsen had left so much behind, yet still the distant echoes tugged at her; she remembered the fear more than the physical pain and abuse, the disgust where later she learned there might have been love, the tears made scarcely easier to bear by the fact they were shared among all three children. She had escaped, as had her sister, but not her younger brother, who still ran a small fish wholesalers around the street markets of south London in between extended bouts of hop-induced stupefaction and wife beating. Like his father. He'd probably go the same way, too, unless his drunken driving intervened. Their father had come home late for Sunday dinner as usual, had cursed them all and thrown his overcooked food away, slumped on the floor in front of *The Big Match*, belched and closed his eyes.

The doctor later declared it had been a massive coronary. "No pain, Mrs. Davies," he had assured. Better than the bastard deserved. They had burned the sitting room carpet on the same day they'd burned him.

The memories sprouted like weeds and she knew that no matter how much she hacked and raked, the roots would always remain buried deep inside.

"Where were you?" Tom Makepeace, still breathless, raised his flushed head from the pillow.

"Oh, a million miles away and about thirty years ago. Sorry," she apologized, gently levering his weight off her.

"In all the years I've known you I don't think I've ever heard you talk about your childhood. Locked doors." With a finger he began rearranging the blond hair scattered across her forehead. "I don't like you having secrets from me. When I'm with you like this, I want to have you all. You know you're the most important thing to happen in my life for a very long time."

She looked at him, those kind, deep, affectionate eyes, still retaining a hint of the small stubborn boy that made both his politics and personality emotional and so easy to embrace. And she knew now was the moment, must be the moment, before too much damage was done.

"We've got to stop, Tom."

"You've got to get back to the House?"

"No. Stop for good. You and me. All this."

She could see the surprise and then injury overwhelm his face.

"But why…?"

"Because I told you from the start that falling into bed with you did not mean I was going to fall in love with you. I can't fill the gaps in your life; we've got to stop before I hurt you." She could see she already had.

He rolled onto his back and studied the ceiling, anxious that she should not see the confusion in his eyes; it was the first time in many years he wished he still smoked. "You know I need you more than ever."

"I cannot be your anchor." Which was what he so desperately needed. As the currents of politics had swirled ever more unsteadily around him, some pushing him on, others enviously trying to snatch him back, the lack of solid footing in his private life had left him ever more exposed. His youngest son was now twenty and at university, his academic wife indulging in her new freedom by accepting a visiting fellowship at Harvard that left her little more than a transient caller in his life with increasingly less to share. He was alone. Fifty had proved a brutal age for Makepeace.

"Not now, Claire. Let's give it another month or so, talk about it then." He was trying hard not to plead.

"No, Tom. It must be now. You have no marriage to risk, but I do. Anyway, there are other complications."

"Someone else?" Pain had made him petulant.

"In a way. I spent an hour with the PM this morning. He wants me to be his PPS."

"And you accepted?"

"Don't make it sound like an accusation, Tom. For God's sake, you're his Foreign Secretary."

"But his PPS, it's so…personal."

"You're jealous."

"You seem to have a weakness for older men," he snapped, goaded by her observation.

"Damn you, leave Joh out of this!" Her rebuke hit him like a slap in the face and hurt more.

"Forgive me, I didn't mean…It's just that I'm concerned for you. Don't get too close to Francis, Claire. Don't lash yourself to a sinking ship."

"Dispassionate concern for my welfare?"

"I've never advised you badly before."

Which was undeniable. Makepeace had guided Claire in her first political steps, sustaining her when successive selection committees had determined that her looks were too distracting or that her place was with the children. When she had persevered and her persistence paid off, he'd helped her find her feet around the House and prepared her for its sexual bombast, had even tried to gain her entry to one of the exclusive dining clubs that generate so much useful contact and mutual support around the House of Commons—"like smuggling an Indian into Fort Apache," he had warned. He'd been a constant source of encouragement—although, she reflected, he had never suggested that she become his PPS.

"PPS to Francis Urquhart," he continued, "is such a compromising position. Politically."

"We all have to compromise a little, Tom. No point in being the virgin at the feast."

"Moral ends justifying compromising means?" He was accusing again.

"Do you mind if I get out from between the damp sheets of your bed before we discuss morality? Anyway, you know as well as I do that politics is a team game, you have to compromise to have any chance of winning. No point in pretending you can score all the goals by yourself. I want my chance on the team, Tom."

"Some of the games Urquhart wants to play I have no desire to join, let alone help him win."

"Which is another reason why we have to stop seeing each other like this. There's so much talk about the two of you being set on collision course, you must have heard the whispers."

"Drumbeats accompanied by a native war dance, more like. Tony Franks on the *Guardian* bet me that either I or Urquhart would be out of Government within a year. He's probably right." His face hovered above hers, creased in pain. It would hurt, losing his place in politics. He came from a long line of public servants; his great-grandfather had been a general who had insisted on leading from the front, and in the mud of Flanders had died for the privilege. But politics was so much more dangerous than war; in battle they could kill you only once. "Is that the real reason you want us to stop? Divided loyalties? Are you backing Urquhart against me?"

She took his head in her hands, thumbs trying to smooth away the lines of distress. "I am becoming his PPS, Tom, not his possession. I haven't sold my principles, I haven't suddenly stopped supporting all the things you and I have both fought for. And I haven't stopped caring about you."

"You mean that?"

"Very much. In another life things might have been much closer between us; in this life, I want to go on being friends."

She kissed him, and he began to respond passionately.

"One last time?" he whispered, running his hand from neck to navel.

"Is that what we've been about? Just sex?"

"No!" he retorted.

"Pity," she replied, and kissed him again.

❖ ❖ ❖

Passolides put down his cup with a nervous jolt, caught unawares by the high double beep of the electronic pager that summoned them. Maria leaned across the table to mop up the spilled coffee with her napkin.

"That's us, *Baba.* It's time."

They had been waiting a little more than half an hour in the small coffee shop of the Public Record Office in Kew, Evanghelos refusing to take his eye for one instant off the red-eyed pager issued to all searchers after truth—at least, what passed as truth in the official British archives. Anything that smacked of British officialdom made him nervous and aggressive, a habit he'd not lost since the old days in the mountains. Even in Islington they had always wanted to snoop, to control him, sending him buff-colored envelopes that demanded money with menaces. Why should he, of all people, pay the British when they owed him so much? A health inspector had once spent an entire week spying on his front door, convinced Passolides was running a business, refusing to give up his vigil until he was dragged away by influenza and other more pressing hazards to the health of the citizens of Islington. He hadn't known about the back door.

While he'd been suffering on the cold dank street, behind the tightly drawn curtain the friends of Evanghelos Passolides had spent their evenings toasting his victory over the old enemy. "To Vangeli!"

The aging Cypriot had little faith that the enemy would help him now. It had been Maria's idea, something to pursue his interest in the old days, to refresh his memories, an excuse to get him out from behind the drawn curtains by suggesting they might see what information, explanation, or excuse the British documents of the time might offer. So they had traveled across London to the PRO in Kew, a concrete mausoleum of the records of an empire gained, grown, and ultimately lost once more.

The amiable clerk in the reference room had not been optimistic. "The EOKA period in Cyprus? That'll have a military or security classification. Used to be a standard fifty-year embargo on those. You know, anything marked SECRET and vital to the continued security of the country. Like old weather forecasts or if the Greek President picked his nose." He shrugged. "But they review the records every ten years now, and since the cutbacks at the Ministry of Defense I think they're running out of bomb shelters to store all the boxes. So when they can they throw them away or throw them at us. You might be lucky."

And they were. In Index WO 106. Directory of Military Operations and Intelligence. "7438. Report on security situation and EOKA interceptions in Troodos Mountains, April–October 1956."

Passolides stabbed his finger at the entry. "They chased us across the mountains for two days, with me on a stretcher and rags stuffed in my mouth to stop me screaming," he whispered. "That's me."

They had entered their order for the file on the reference computer terminal. And waited.

And been disappointed.

The PRO at Kew is not all that it seems. Away from the reference room, behind the scenes in the repository, computerization hands over to dusty fingers and cardboard boxes. Nearly a hundred miles of them. In a temperature- and humidity-controlled environment and to the strains of Roy Orbison and Lulu blaring over the loudspeakers (the whole point of the PRO is that it is not up to date) a young man had sorted through the vast banks of shelving in search of one file among the millions. Once found, it had been transported slowly on a system of electric trolleys and conveyor belts to the general reading room, when Maria and her father had been summoned.

But it was not there. Beneath the air-conditioned hush and white lighting they had searched WO 106/7438 for any reference to the pursuit of Evanghelos and his EOKA comrades during those days of high summer. How they had hidden in an underground hide with British soldiers less than six feet away and where one grenade would have killed them all. How he had begged his comrades to shoot him rather than abandon him to the clutches of the enemy. How they would have done it anyway, to avoid any risk of his betraying what he knew.

There was nothing. The tired manila folder was stuffed with individual sheets of paper secured with a string tag, mostly fuzzy carbon copies that appeared to have been retained at random rather than with any sense of logic or in an attempt to preserve a comprehensive record of events. Particularly difficult period, the clerk had explained. The Suez War had erupted in October and everything had been chaos as the British Army turned its attention from the defense of Cyprus to the attack on Egypt. Entire regiments had been transferred and the island had become a churning transit point for the armies of invasion. Paperwork, never the greatest strength of soldiers at war, in many cases had simply been abandoned. For the British, it seemed, Passolides didn't exist, had never existed.

But there was something else. A memory. His finger was once again pointing at the single sheet index at the front of the file.

Item 16. May 5. Above the village of Spilia.

The date. The location. He had difficulty scrambling through the file to locate the reference; when he had done so, he trembled all the more. A single photocopied sheet of paper, an intelligence report of an action in the mountains near to where it was believed an extensive EOKA hideout was located. Two unidentified terrorists intercepted while transporting weapons and other supplies. An exchange of fire, the loss of a British private. The killing of the two Cypriots. Burning and burial of their bodies to reduce the risks of reprisals. No further indication as to the location of the hideout. A recommendation that further sweeps be conducted in the area. Signed by the officer in charge of the operation.

The officer's name had been blanked out.

"That's why it's photocopied. To protect the identities of British personnel," the clerk had explained. "Not a cover-up, just standard procedure. No way the name will be released, not while he's still alive. After all, imagine if it had been you."

But it had been me, and my brothers!

Passolides had tried to explain, to insist, to find out more, but his voice and clarity were cracked by emotion and the clerk was bemused by the old man's talk of murder on a mountainside. In any event, there was nothing more to be found. No other archive, no other records. Whatever the British system had to offer was all here; there was nothing more to be found, except the name. And that he couldn't have.

"They were only boys, buried in those graves," Passolides groaned.

"You don't need Records," the clerk had offered, convinced the old man with tears in his eyes was a little simple. "You need a War Crimes Commission."

"But first I need a name."

TWELVE

Never sleep with a politician. When they turn their back on you, they take the duvet with them.

"Damn it! D'you think they've got a new editor or something, Mortima?"

She looked up from her crispbread and letters.

"*The Times* crossword has become so"—he searched for the word—"elusive. Impenetrable. They must've changed the editor."

No, she thought, it's not the crossword that has changed, Francis. It's you. There was a time when you would have slain the allusions and anagrams before porridge.

Irritably he threw the newspaper to one side. The front page was miserable enough, now the back page, too. He searched around the crowded breakfast table and retrieved another sheet of paper. "Fewer problems with this one," he muttered with considerably more enthusiasm, and began marking off items like so many completed clues. He paused in search of inspiration. "Four or five down, d'you think?"

"Give me a hint of what we're talking about, Francis."

"A bit of Byng. Time to shoot a few admirals in full view of the fleet to encourage the others, I thought. Just as you recommended—to bring back a bit of fear?"

"I see. A reshuffle."

"Four or five to go, I thought. Enough to cause a real stir, yet not so many as to look as though we're panicking."

"Who are you volunteering?"

"The Euro drones and iron wits. Carter. Yorke. Penthorpe—he's so abrasive that every time he opens his mouth he all but sharpens the blade for his own throat. And Wilkinson. Do you know he actually spends almost as much time in France as he does in his constituency? Judgment's addled by cheap wine and fraternizing." With a decisive thrust he ran another name through with his pen.

"What about Terry Whittington? I never know whether he's half-cut or simply sounds it."

"Yes, a problem when the Minister in charge of the Citizens' Charter can't even pronounce the words without drenching the interviewer. Dull dog but, oh, such a sparkling and well-connected wife. Haven't I told you?" He looked over his glasses in remorse. "It seems she's been indulging in what are known as continental conversations with the Industry Commissioner in Brussels while dear old Terry's been lashed down in all-night session with nothing more diverting than his fellow Ministers."

"*Quelle finesse.* Be a pity to lose such an interesting point of leverage within the Commission."

"Particularly with harsh words on car quotas coming up."

She bit into the crispbread, which crumbled and fled, and for several seconds she distracted herself with reassembling the pieces.

"So who else?"

"Annita, of course. I know she's the only woman, but she sits twittering at the end of the Cabinet table and I can barely hear a word." He shook his head in exasperation. "It's not me, is it, Mortima?"

"Francis, selective hearing is not only a Prime Minister's

prerogative but also one of his most useful weapons. You've had years of developing it to a fine art."

It was more than that, she thought, but he seemed reassured. She picked up a knife and, with a deft flick of the wrist that seemed unnatural on a lady, sliced off the top of a soft-boiled egg. "And what of Tom Makepeace?" The yolk flowed freely.

"Dangerous to get rid of him, Mortima. I'd prefer to have him on board with his cannon firing outward than on another ship with his sights trained on me. But there might be some"—he waved his hand in the manner of a conductor encouraging the second violins—"rearrangement around the deck. Find him a new target. Environment, perhaps."

"Kick him out of the Foreign Office? I like that."

"Let him struggle with the wind and waters of our green and pleasant land. Purify the people, that sort of thing. What greater challenge could a man of conscience want?" He was already practicing the press release. "And meanwhile remind the buggers in Brussels we mean business by giving the foreign job to that hedgehog Bollingbroke. He suffers from flatulence. Late nights locked in the embrace of our European brethren seems the obvious place for him."

"Excellent!" She stabbed at the heart of the egg with a thin sliver of crispbread.

"And put Booza-Pitt into the Home Office."

"That little package of oily malevolence?" Her face lit in alarm.

"And so he is. But he's crass and vulgar enough to know what the party faithful want and to give it to them. To touch them where it matters."

"As he does half the Cabinet wives."

"But I in turn am able to touch him where it matters. I hold his loyalties in the palm of my hand and all I have to do is squeeze. There will be no trouble from Geoffrey." Suddenly he sat bolt upright in his chair, sniffing the air, as a ship's captain senses the arrival of new weather from disturbed skies.

"Francis…?"

"That's it! Don't you see? Eight down. 'European emergency.' Twelve letters."

"What, 'Bollingbroke'?" She was counting off the letters on her fingers, bewildered by his sudden switch of priorities.

"No. *Nein. Nein. Nein!*" He gave a triumphant chortle and swooped once more upon his newspaper, filling in blank spaces on a flood tide of enlightenment. "You see, Mortima. Old Francis still has what it takes."

"Of course you do."

Just in case, however, she decided a measure of insurance might be in order.

The corridors of power resemble a Gordian knot of interwoven connections—relationships matrimonial, familial, frequently carnal, bonds of blood, school, and club (beware the man who has been turned away by the Garrick), ties of privilege and prejudice that run far deeper than the seasonal streams of professional acquaintance or achievement. The nectar of tradition sipped at birth or grudges indulged during afternoons on the playing field or evenings in the dorm may provide a framework for a life, sometimes even a purpose. The British Establishment is no accident.

In unravelling these inner mysteries and tracing the origins of influence, no tool is of more use than a copy of *Who's Who.* Most of the gossamer threads of acceptability are to be found within its pages, as well as the raucous buzzing from the occasional brash interloper who, like the insect charging the spider's web, rarely lasts.

Mortima's copy was a couple of years old, but still gave her most of what she needed to know. It told her that Clive Watling was going to be a problem. He had no family of note, no schooling of eminence, no breeding, merely endeavor and honest accomplishment. Which, for Mortima's purposes, wasn't enough. He was proud of his humble origins in the small community of Cold Kirby, which lay at the edge of the Yorkshire Moors; his primary school had been given a place of honor in the list, as had his presidency of the Cold Kirby Conservation Society and membership of other local groups. This was a man whose booted feet were stuck very firmly to the moors, where gossamer threads were as rare as orchids. Yet…

As luck—no, the fortune of family connection—would have it, a second cousin to the mother of Mortima Urquhart (*née* Colquhoun) still owned substantial Northern acreages in the vicinity of Cold Kirby, along with the hereditary titles pertaining thereto, and Mortima had engaged her noble cousin to extend an invitation to drinks on the terrace.

The terrace of the Palace of Westminster fronts the northern bank of the great river where once had strolled Henry VIII, through the blossom trees and hedging of what at that time had been his palace garden. It was always a problem site, being immediately adjacent to the medieval City of London with its teeming humanity and overflowing chamber pots. Perhaps it was on some fetid summer's day while walking through the overpowering air that the King grew envious of the sweet-scented palace that stood further upstream at Hampton Court, where his Lord Chancellor lived, Cardinal Wolsey, a man whose fortunes and grasp on his home were to decline as the tidal flow of the Thames washed its noisome waters beyond, and then back again, past the King's door. In any event, the spot never achieved great popularity until those mightiest of urban redevelopers, the Victorians, built both sewers and solid embankment and thereby transformed its attractions. By the side of the river the architects Barry and Pugin erected a great orange-gold palace for Parliament in the manner of a sand castle by the beach, complete with flags and turrets. On its fringe they formed a terrace where on warm summer days members of either House of Parliament might sit and sup, the lapping waters easing the passage of time and legislation instead of launching, as in days of old, an assault on their senses.

Major the Lord "Bungy" Colquhoun traveled to London infrequently, but when he did he found the House of Lords a most convenient club. He had therefore been amenable to his cousin's prompting that he should hold a small drinks party on the terrace and invite a few carefully selected guests. He did not know his near-neighbor and soon-to-be-noble brother from Cold Kirby, but was happy to meet him. As was Mortima.

Watling was an affable man, courteous but cautious, feeling his way on uncertain soil. He was not a man to rush. For a while on the terrace he stood quietly, staring across the silt-brown river to where an army of worker ants were transforming what had been St. Thomas's Hospital into what was to become an office and shopping complex with multiscreen cinema.

"Progress?" she inquired, standing at his elbow.

"You mean the fact that if my heart were to stop right now they'd take an additional fifteen minutes to get me to treatment?" He shook his head. "Since you ask, probably not."

"But it wouldn't, you know, not in the House of Lords. Every Gothic nook and cranny in the place seems to be stuffed with all sorts of special revival equipment. Every closet a cardiac unit. You're not allowed to die, you know. Not in a royal palace. It's against the rules."

He chuckled. "That's reassuring, Mrs. Urquhart. I suppose as a judge I'd better stick to the rules."

"I don't profess to understand the legal system..."

"You're not supposed to. Otherwise what'd be the point of all us lawyers beavering away at the taxpayers' vast expense?"

He was shy, mellowing a little; it was her turn to laugh. "And are you taking the King's shilling at the moment?"

"The Cyprus shilling, to be precise."

"Oh, that one's yours?" She allowed the breeze to ruffle through her hair, anxious not to appear—well, anxious. "Is the case a difficult one?"

"Not unduly. The areas of difference are clear and not especially large; it's a finely balanced matter. So the panel sits in judgment for about twelve hours a week, the rest of the time we go off and...compose our thoughts." He raised his glass of champagne in self-mockery.

"So there's a panel? For some reason I had the idea it was an entirely British affair."

"And it would have been all the better for it. Sometimes I find the Entente Cordiale neither an *entente* nor particularly *cordiale*." The previous day Rodin, the Frenchman, had been at his most persistently illogical and truculent. But then he usually was.

"So the French are involved, too?"

"And a Malaysian, an Egyptian, and a Serb. In theory the heat we generate is supposed to reforge swords for the service of a better world, although in practice the plowshares often have edges like razors."

"I suspect you're secretly very proud of what you do. But—forgive my ignorance—doesn't having such a mixture of nationalities, and particularly the French, in this case make your task a little...awkward?"

"In every case," he agreed with vehemence. "But why especially in this?"

"I mean, with the oil..."

"Oil? What oil?"

"Don't you know? Surely you must. They will have told you."

"Told me what? The seismic showed no oil."

"But apparently there's another report, very commercially confidential, or so I've heard—perhaps I shouldn't have?—which says the place is floating on a vast reservoir of oil. And if it goes to the Greek side, the French have been promised the exploitation rights." She looked puzzled. "Doesn't that make it difficult for a French judge?"

So that's what the bastard Breton's been up to. Watling's face clouded with concern, while the great River Thames, and Mortima beside it, rushed on.

"Forgive me. Forget everything I've said. It was probably something I overheard and shouldn't have—you know, I never really take much notice of these things, whether I should know or shouldn't know." She sounded flustered. "I'm a silly woman stumbling into areas I don't understand. I should stick to dusting and *Woman's Hour*."

"It is probably something we shouldn't be talking about," he conceded, his face soured as though his drink had been spiked. "I have to deal with the facts that are presented to me. Impartially. Cut myself off completely from extraneous material and—forgive me—gossip."

"I hope I haven't embarrassed you. Please say you'll forgive me."

"Of course. You weren't to know." He spoke softly but had become studiously formal, the judge once more, gazing again across the river, at nothing. Working it out.

Mortima held silence for a moment as she fought to recompose herself, twirling the long stem of her glass nervously. It was time to occupy new territory, any new territory, so long as it wasn't sitting on oil. She offered her best matronly smile. "I'm so glad you could bring your mother; I understand Bungy gave you both tea."

He nodded gently. "My mother particularly enjoyed the toasted tea cakes. Couldn't stand the Earl Gray, though. Said she was going to bring her own tea bags with her next time." Watling experienced a sudden twinge of anxiety—"next time." Had the baron-to-be let slip a confidence by appearing to assume too much? Would the Prime Minister's wife know about New Year? But surely the invitation to tea and the terrace was simply a means of easing him into The System?

"And your father?"

"No longer with us, I'm afraid. Indeed, to my enduring regret I never knew him, nor he me."

"How very sad." Once more she was ill at ease, flushed, seeming incapable of finding the right topic, distressed by her clumsiness. She took a deep breath. "Look, all my nonsense about oil, please don't think I was implying that it might affect the opinion of the French judge. I respect the French; they're a nation of brave and independent spirits. Don't you agree?"

Watling all but choked on his champagne. She took his arm, fussing with concern. His eyes bulged red, his complexion bucolic. She began to wonder about the revival equipment.

"My apologies," he coughed, "but I'm afraid I don't entirely share your opinion about the French. A little personal prejudice."

"So, you're a Yorkshire-pudding-and-don't-spare-the-cabbage man, are you?"

"Not quite, Mrs. Urquhart. You see, my father died in France. In 1943."

"During the war...?" Her face had become a picture of wretchedness but this was not a subject from which, once engaged, he was to be easily diverted.

"Yes. He was an SOE agent, parachuted behind the lines. Betrayed to the Gestapo by the local French mayor who was a quiet collaborator. Most of them were, you know. Until D-Day. The French got back their country, and in return my mother got a small pension. Not much on which to bring up four children in an isolated Yorkshire village. So you will understand and forgive, I hope, my little personal prejudice." There was no mistaking the restrained hint.

But there was more. The oil. The French. The Breton bastard. Now Watling knew why Rodin was being so stubborn. Suddenly it was all a mess. How could he impugn the integrity of a fellow judge? He had no proof, nothing but suspicions, which some would call prejudice. In any event, the smallest reference to oil would throw the proceedings into chaos. No, he would have to resign, wash his hands of it, his own judgment undermined by gossip and private doubt. But that would also cause chaos. Inordinate delay. Endanger the peace, perhaps. And he could kiss the barony of Cold Kirby-by-the-edge-of-the-Moors good-bye.

"But I know your reputation for impartiality, Professor Watling," he heard the silly woman protesting. "I feel certain none of this will affect your views..."

There was one other way. He could stay quiet. Pretend he hadn't heard. Get the job done, as everyone was begging him to do. Dispense justice, in spite of the French.

"And your father—I'm so sorry," she continued. "I had absolutely no idea."

At least, no more idea than had been supplied by *Who's Who* and a few minutes spent perusing Watling's press cuttings.

He crossed himself in the laborious manner of the Orthodox and knelt in the new-cropped grass beside his wife's grave, positioning his bones like a man older than his years. "*Eonia mnimi—may her memory live forever*," he muttered, running his hand along the lines in the marble, ignoring the complaints of his splayed leg. At his elbow, Maria replaced the fading flowers with fresh, and together they reached back with silent thoughts and memories.

"This is important," he said, "to do honor to the dead."

Greek legend is built around the Underworld, and for a man such as Passolides who knew he must himself soon face the journey across, the dignities and salutations of death were matters of the highest significance. Throughout the history of the Hellenes, life has been so freely cast aside and the dark ferryman of the Styx so frequently paid that elaborate rituals of passage have been required in order to reflect a measure of civilization in a world that was all too often uncivilized and barbaric. Yet for George and Eurypides there had been no ritual, no honor, no dignity.

Since their metaphorical stumble across the brothers' graves an appetite for his own life seemed to have been conjured within Passolides. He had gained a new fixity of purpose, and if for Maria it seemed at times to be excessively fixed, at least it was a purpose, a mission, a renewed meaning, which had produced within him a degree of animation she had not witnessed since the happier times before her mother had passed away. Even his leg seemed to have improved. During the day he had begun to leave the shadows of his shrine, taking frequent walks on a limp leg through Regent's Park, often muttering to himself, relishing the open green spaces once again, the arguments of sparrows along the hawthorn paths, the rattle of limes beside the lake. It was as close as he could get in the center of London to the memories of a mountainside.

As Maria polished the cool marble headstone she examined her father carefully, sensing how much he had changed. His small round face was like a fruit taken too long from the tree, wizened, leathered by age and ancestry, his hair sapped steel white, cheeks hollowed by the pain of his clumsy and uncomfortable body. Yet the eyes glowed once more with a renewal of purpose, like an old lion woken from sleep, hungry.

"What was the point, *Baba*? What were the British hiding?"

"Guilt."

He knew his subject well. Guilt had filled his own life to exclusion, the feeling that somehow he had failed them all, comrades and kin. He had failed as the eldest son to protect his younger brothers, failed again as a cripple to pick up the banner of resistance dropped by them. He would never admit it to anyone and only rarely to himself, but secretly he resented his martyr brothers, even as he loved them, for George and Eurypides were the honored dead while Evanghelos was inadequate and miserably alive. He struggled in their shadow, unable to live up to his brothers' memory, uncertain whether he could have found the same courage as they had, and deprived of any chance to try. He would never be a hero. He'd spent a lifetime trying to prove to the world that his dedication was the equal of his brothers', even while in his cups blaming them. He blamed them and in turn blamed himself for the worm of envy and unreason that turned inside him. Yet now, it seemed, and at last, there was hope of relief, somebody else to blame.

"Guilt," he repeated, rubbing his leg to help the blood circulate. "What else does a soldier hide? Not death, that's his business. Only guilt has to be buried away. Burned."

She plucked a few stray strands of grass from around the grave as she listened. He thought she knew nothing of his hidden shame but she had lived with it all her life and understood, even though she could do nothing about it. "Go on, *Baba*."

"They had a right to kill my brothers, under the British law. George and Eurypides had guns, bombs; who but a few toothless Greeks would have complained? The British once hanged an eighteen-year-old boy, Pallikarides, because he was found carrying a gun. It was their law. Mandatory." He had trouble with the word, but not its meaning. "No, it was not their death they tried to hide. It must have been the manner of their dying."

"So that's why they burned the bodies, because of what they had done to them. Torture?"

"It happened." He stopped, his eyes focused on a land and a point in time far away. "Maybe they weren't bodies when they burned them. Maybe they were still alive. That happened too." On both sides, although he didn't care to remember and it was something else he would never admit to his daughter. But even after all these years it had proved impossible to wipe his memory of the figures soaked in gas and vengeance. *"Prodótes!"*

Traitors, Greek convicted of informing on Greek, stumbling down the village street, still screaming their innocence through charred lips, eyes no longer sighted, burned out, their bodies turned to bonfires that branded a terrible message of loyalty into all who saw. But George and Eurypides had betrayed no one, weren't *prodótes*, hadn't deserved to die like that.

"You know what this means, *Baba*? There may be more hidden graves."

For the Greeks of Cyprus, on long winter's nights when the womenfolk stoked the fires of remembrance and told stories of the life of old, no memory cut so deep as that of "the missing ones." In 1974 Greek extremists in Athens, frustrated at the lack of progress toward *Enosis*, union between island and mainland, had conspired to overthrow the Nicosia Government of Archbishop Makarios. It was a fit of madness from which Cyprus would never recover. Five days later the Turks had retaliated and invaded the island, dividing it and breaking up the ethnic jigsaw in a manner that ensured it could never be remade. During that time a thousand and more Greek Cypriot men had disappeared, swept up by the advancing Turkish Army and swept off the face of the known world. Their suspected fate had always been a source of unfeigned outrage to the Greeks and embarrassment to the Turks—such things happened in war, misfortunes, examples of isolated barbarity, even wholesale mistakes, but who the hell liked to admit it afterward? Yet in the quest for peace the Turks *had* admitted, surrendered all they knew about "the missing ones," which after nearly a quarter century was painfully little—a few scattered graves, old bones, fragmentary records, faded memories—but even a small light shining upon the island's darkest hour brought understanding and helped ease the suffering, had allowed families to mourn and do honor to the dead. *Myrologhia*. Yet now it seemed there were more graves. Dug even earlier, by the British.

For Maria, who had never known her uncles and could therefore not share fully in their loss, the issue was a matter of politics and of principle. Yet for her father it was so much more. A matter of honor and of retribution. Cypriot honor. Vangelis retribution.

"We must find out what we can about these hidden graves, *Baba*."

"And about the crimes they tried to bury in them." He heaved his bent body up straight, like a soldier on parade. "And which bastard did the burying."

THIRTEEN

Trial by ordeal is a system of feudal torture that has been done away with everywhere, except in Westminster.

At the south-facing entrance to the Chamber of the House of Commons stands an ornate and seemingly aged archway, the Churchill Arch. Its antiquity is exaggerated, the smoky pallor having been produced not by the passage of time but by its presence so close to one of Reichsmarshall Göring's bombs, which razed the Chamber to the ground on 10 May 1941. On either side of the archway stand bronze statues of the two great war leaders of modern times, David Lloyd George and Winston Churchill. Lloyd George's pose is eloquent, Churchill's more aggressive, as though the old warrior were hurrying to deliver a booted blow to the backside of the enemy. A little further along is a plinth bearing no statue, perhaps left as an act of encouragement to all those who pass and who hope, by dint of endeavor and great achievement, to join the rank of revered statesmen.

Roger Garlick would not, in any passage of lifetimes, number among them. Of course, he had a high opinion of himself that fit his role as a Junior Whip, one of those whose task it was to round up Government MPs and herd them through the voting lobbies. Garlick was a man of considerable girth but limited oratorical ability; he recognized that his chances of achieving high public acclaim were thereby limited and relished the opportunity to exercise his influence more privately, through the dark arts of whipping. He feasted on abuse, his favorite diet being new members and any woman.

"Roger!" The cry of recognition came from Booza-Pitt, making his way through the Members' Lobby where MPs gather to collect messages and exchange gossip and other materials necessary to their work. Booza-Pitt reached out and squeezed the Whip's arm in greeting but didn't stop. Garlick was a useful contact, a man who was willing in private and under pressure from a second bottle of claret to share many of the personal secrets he had unearthed about his colleagues, but the middle of the Members' Lobby was not the place. The Transport Secretary made off in search of other indiscretions.

The Lobby was crowded, as was always the case in the half hour before Prime Minister's Question Time when Members assembled for the ritual spilling of blood—occasionally Urquhart's, more frequently that of the questioner and particularly that of Dick Clarence, the youthful and ineffectual Leader of the Opposition who had a tendency to appear as a schoolboy attempting to be gratuitously rude to his long-suffering headmaster. There had to be order in class, and it was Garlick's job as one of the form prefects to impose it. Thus, when he spotted Claire entering the Lobby, his eyes extended like the glass beads on the face of a child's bear.

"Missed you at the vote last night, my dear. I stood up for you, of course, but the Chief Whip threw a terrible tantrum. Took me half a bottle of whiskey to calm him down." He pinned her up against the base of Lloyd George.

"Sorry, Roger. Pressing engagement, I couldn't get out of it."

"Not good enough, you know, old girl. I put my arse on the line for you, now you owe me. How about saying sorry over dinner tomorrow night?" He leaned his thick arm on the statue behind her, bringing them closer together, an intimacy he claimed by right as a Whip. He reeked of Old Spice and other things less sweet. She was searching the Lobby for someone else—anyone else—to distract her attention, but he did not notice, his own eyes were clamped firmly upon her blouse.

"Sorry, Roger, can't do tomorrow. I'm having my hair done. Following night's out, too, I'm hoping to go to assertiveness class. If my husband lets me." She smiled, hoping he might take the hint.

"Next week, then," he persisted. "It'd be fun. There's a hint of a reshuffle coming up, new jobs going, we could discuss your future. Might even be able to get you added to the Whip's List of new stars."

As he spoke, a fellow Member squeezed past and Garlick took the opportunity to move his body still closer, trying to brush against her. Claire voiced no objection; in this hothouse of stretched emotions and endless nights it was not uncommon for her to be propositioned, particularly after Members had indulged in a good dinner, and alienating every colleague who had put a hand on her knee or an amorous arm around her waist would leave her a member of a drastically reduced party. Boys' club rules, and she had asked to join. But she didn't have to take Garlick's crap.

"Not next week, Roger. I'm having a new kitchen fitted." She continued to smile, but with great firmness she placed her fingers on his chest and pushed him away.

Both his attitude and the corner of his lip turned with the rejection. "Bloody women! You're all the same in this place. Useless. How the hell can we run the country with you crying off every time you get a migraine or one of the kids goes down with mumps." Other Members standing nearby had begun to tune in; he was aware he had acquired an audience and raised his voice. "It's about time you got something straight. This isn't a knitting class or a crèche, it's the House of Commons, and you're here to do as you're told. Leg up. Lie down. Roll over. Adopt as many different positions as a missionary in a pot. You were elected to support the Government, not to wander through the voting lobbies as though you're picking and choosing underwear at Marks & Spencer. You turn up when we tell you and do as you're told!"

The blood was flowing early today; from among the colleagues gathered around came a shuffling noise, a mixture of embarrassment and expectation, like the sound of a butcher's apron being passed.

"I am very sorry I missed last night's vote, Roger. I had no choice." She took great care to squeeze out any tremble or trace of emotion that might have crept into her voice.

"What was so important, then, that you had to let us all down? For God's sake don't tell me you had a pressing engagement with your bloody gynecologist."

"No, I wasn't on my back, Roger. I was with Francis. You know, the Prime Minister? He asked me to become his PPS."

The audience around them stirred and Garlick's jowls began to take on a deeper hue of crimson. He appeared to be having trouble controlling his lower jaw. "The Prime Minister asked you to become his…" He couldn't finish.

"His Parliamentary Private Secretary. And you know what kind of girl I am, Roger. Couldn't possibly say no."

"But the Chief didn't know anything about it," he stammered. He prayed he was being wound up.

Of course the Chief Whip didn't know, couldn't possibly have been brought in on the discussion. He was one of those marked to end up in the pot beside the missionary. Along with several of the Junior Whips.

"FU was planning to mention it to him over lunch today. It obviously hasn't come down the line yet. At least, not as far as you."

A senior member of the audience plucked at Garlick's sleeve. "Game, set, and testicles, I'd say, old boy," and walked off chortling.

Garlick appeared like a punctured Zeppelin, arms flapping uselessly, making gushing noises, deflating, half the man he had just been yet, as she knew, more than the man he was shortly to be. She had come upon the privilege of access and inside information, and Claire realized how much she loved it. Incapable of speech, all communications facilities shot away, Garlick turned and shuffled off in the direction of the Whips' Room and its bottle of whiskey.

"I'm really delighted, Claire, always thought you were overdue for recognition. Put a word in for you with the Boss some time ago. Glad to see it helped." Out of nowhere Booza-Pitt was at her elbow; his antennae were awesome.

"I can't believe all the good words that have been put in for me recently," she replied cryptically.

"I hope I can be one of the first to congratulate you. Let's have dinner. Soon."

The invitation. Which would be followed by solicitous inquiries about her husband and a small gift for the kids. In one bound she had jumped from Division Three straight into Division One, leapfrogging over the heads of some two hundred—mostly male—colleagues. It filled Geoffrey with unease. She had short-circuited his system, the system he had designed to protect him and promote his cause. She didn't fit and he didn't understand her, couldn't control her. He might have the authority of Ministerial office but she had the influence of access—she'd practically be living at Number Ten. She was competition, raw and naked—talking of which, there was no point in trying to get her to bed, he'd already tried.

The whispered news had already circumnavigated the Lobby and Geoffrey became aware that many eyes were upon them. In proprietorial fashion he took her by the arm. "You and I are going to have so much fun," he said, and led her into the Chamber.

Urquhart stumbled into his place on the Government Front Bench, clutching his red folder. He would have preferred to stride into the Chamber, making a grand entrance from behind the Speaker's Chair, but the place was always packed for his appearances and he had to squeeze past bodies, elbows, legs, and other outstretched impedimenta of Members who hadn't seen him coming. He'd almost made it to his seat, stepping high like a dressage exercise, leaning on Tom Makepeace's shoulder for support, when a Junior Treasury Minister experienced a cramp spasm and kicked his Prime Minister in the shin. Another volunteer for the view from the backbench gods.

In spite of it, Urquhart felt good, very positive. Over lunch he had informed the Chief Whip that his services as bosun would no longer be required on the voyage. The man had understood what it portended. The great ship of state rarely stopped to pick up those who had fallen overboard, let alone any who had been deliberately dropped; he'd've been better off as a barnacle. Yet at his point of greatest misery he had been thrown a life belt, the promise of a peerage after the next election if he kept his mouth shut and caused no trouble in the meantime. So with that he had sat down and made a reasonable show of enjoying his final meal, in between the soup and fish helping his Prime Minister complete the final tally of those who would join him over the side. The sense of duty and discipline is instilled sufficiently deep within the psyche of most Whips that the sight of blood, even their own, does not appear to affect their appetite.

As he sat in his seat by the Dispatch Box, gazing at the army of Opposition assembled in layered ranks before him, Urquhart was struck by how much like a fairground shooting gallery it all appeared. Row upon row of ducks who in good order would flutter to their feet and present themselves for—well, dispatch, with the umpires of the press lobby gazing down in impartial anticipation as they waited to count the scorched feathers. He intended they should have a busy day. His eyesight might be going, but not his instinctive aim.

The first duck to squawk and break cover was a Welshman whose voice conveyed the gentle lilt of the Clwyd coastline and a wit of solid coal. With vigor and at seemingly interminable length, he was expressing his concern that the Prime Minister cared too little for matters European. Urquhart drew a deep breath of boredom and raised his eyes to examine the ceiling, his thoughts passing through it to the roof terrace above... Quickly he wrenched himself back to the business of the House.

"Finally, the Prime Minister says he believes in a single economic market, and so do I. But if he truly does believe, why oh why does he turn his back on a single currency? All these pounds, schillings, and pesetas are so w-w-wasteful."

He says it beautifully, Urquhart thought, practically eisteddfod standard. All Welsh wind. He rose and leaned an elbow on the Dispatch Box to give himself better aim.

"If I might be allowed to intervene in the Honorable Gentleman's soliloquy..." He smiled to show there were no hard feelings. Then with a decisive flick he closed the red folder in front of him, which contained his civil service briefing. Apparently this was not to be a civil service answer. "I would like him to know that I entirely agree with him."

There was a buzz of consternation. Since when did Urquhart agree with the Opposition?

"Well, almost entirely, on his main point. Which I take to be"—adroitly and without the Welshman being fully aware of it, Urquhart was moving the goal posts, wanting to play an entirely different game—"which I take to be what we have to do in order to bring about an effective single market in Europe? Although I fail to see why he should be so keen to do away with the British pound and banish the King's head from the coin of our realm."

The Welshman was flapping his wings; that's not what he had meant at all. And who the hell was Francis Urquhart to put on the armor of Royal champion?

"But let me tell him." Urquhart's finger was pointing, taking aim. "If we want to build a single market, get rid of waste and inefficiency, there is something far more important than a single currency. And that's a single language."

There was a stunned silence as the House digested this entirely new morsel. In the box reserved for civil servants to the side of the Speaker's Chair, an aide began riffling through the pages of his brief like a prompter desperately trying to return the play to the lines of its script.

"Oh, yes," Urquhart continued, raising his voice and preparing to hit the adverbs and adjectives. "There is nothing more wasteful and expensive for business than having to deal in a multitude of different languages. The cost runs into billions every year, measure it in whatever currency you will. The economic logic is indisputable, our first priority must be to talk with one voice." He shrugged his shoulders as if confronted with a problem he could do nothing about. "I suppose it is simply an accident of history that the only language capable of meeting that bill is English."

From his position along the Front Bench, Bollingbroke gave a roar of delight—his Saturday night special, as Urquhart termed it, a noise several octaves above steak and kidney pudding and more appropriate to celebrating a victory by Manchester United. Urquhart was grateful nonetheless and turned to acknowledge the cheer, which was being picked up widely behind him. He noticed that Tom Makepeace displayed little desire to join the celebrations.

"So, when the Europeans come and start talking to me about a single currency in English, that's when I'll start listening," he declaimed. He was enjoying himself thoroughly. Sod the diplomatic etiquette. Was it his fault if Brussels had no sense of humor? "And I shall expect the Honorable Gentleman's unflinching and Welsh-hearted support." A nice touch; that'll go down in his constituency like a slut on a slide.

Urquhart beamed at the uproar all around and resumed his seat. Even before he had done so, the Opposition Leader was on his feet, stretching at his Armani seams, his face flushed with outrage. Urquhart nestled back on the leather. Having seen his colleague blown away in a flurry of feathers, only a complete turkey would be so eager to take his place. But Clarence was a complete turkey, practically oven-ready.

"I have rarely heard views expressed in this House that have been so unworthy and un-European. The Prime Minister's performance today has been a national disgrace. In a few days' time he is to fly to a meeting with the French President. Does he not realize the sort of greeting he will have to endure? What will it do to the reputation of this country to have its Prime Minister booed through the streets of Paris?" Paradoxical cheers came from his supporters behind, which quickly died in confusion as Urquhart accepted them graciously. Clarence battled on. "When will the Prime Minister realize how much damage he is doing to the interests of this country with his stubbornness, his constant veto of new ideas, his abject refusal to be a good European?"

Tumult. It took a considerable time and the repeated intervention of the Speaker before Urquhart had any chance of being heard. He saw no reason to rush.

"Perhaps it's the Right Honorable Gentleman's youth that makes him so impetuous. Perhaps, too, it explains his apparent willingness to come to this House every week and learn by the good old Victorian method of a sound thrashing. But youth alone isn't enough to excuse ignorance." Urquhart eased back the sleeves of his suit in the manner of a teacher preparing to chalk a blackboard. "He seems to have climbed so high up his European Tower of Babel that he's become giddy and disorientated. Once more I shall have to bring him down to earth. Remind him of the other times when the world had cause to be grateful that we in Britain set our face against the fashion in Europe. When we exercised our veto. Said 'No,' 'No,' and 'No' again. Showed ourselves stubborn and utterly unwilling to bend. As we did in 1940. We stood alone, backed only by God and the seas when all the rest"—he dismissed them with a broad wave of his hand—"had capitulated."

Bollingbroke was going all but berserk, determined that his support should be heard above the volleys of disorder being fired from the benches around. As he paused in the din, Urquhart was reminded of the pose adopted by the statue of Churchill beyond the doors of the Chamber and he decided to give it a try, left foot to the fore, jacket sides swept back, hands grasping hips, leaning forward to face the sound of gunfire.

"Our *stubbornness*—I believe that was the word he used—our stubbornness saved Europe then. And the British Prime Minister wasn't booed in the streets after we'd liberated Paris, they got down on their knees and gave thanks!"

God, that would cause chaos in France, but he could live with that. The French had not a single vote that counted on election night. Overhead he could see eager faces in the press gallery leaning out for a better view; more importantly, the benches behind him had become a raging sea of white Order Papers, as though to a man the Government Party was preparing to ward off another threat of invasion. Well, almost to a man. Makepeace was sitting, legs stiff and outstretched, dour expression cast in cement. He would be a problem when he unthawed. But Urquhart thought he had the solution to that.

❖ ❖ ❖

Urquhart strode briskly down the corridor leading to his office in the House of Commons, composing headlines.

"What d'you think? 'FU Blasts Brussels Babble'? 'Francis 6, France 0'? How about 'To Be or Not to Be—That is the Language'? Yes, I like that."

Claire struggled to keep up. He had left the Chamber with the zest of a soprano buoyed by a dozen curtain calls, motioning her to follow. Normally he would have been surrounded by a pack of civil servants but they had decided to fall into a protective huddle and linger while they counted their dead. He swept into his room, held the heavy oak door for her then slammed it shut with the crash of an artillery barrage. He stood to attention, facing her, presenting himself for inspection.

"How was I?"

"You were completely..." She searched for the word. What could she say? His mastery over the House amazed and inspired her in the same measure as the rabid jingoism of his words offended all she held dear. But her views, for the moment, didn't matter; she was here to learn. "Francis, you were completely bloody impossible."

"Yes, I was, wasn't I? Feathers everywhere. Best pillow fight in ages." He bounced on his toes, a younger man by forty years, unable to contain his enthusiasm.

"Francis, were you serious? About a single language?"

"Course not. It'll never happen. But it'll bugger up all this nonsense about a single currency for a while, and our voters will love it. Worth another three percent in the polls by the end of the month, you wait and see."

He was unusually animated, the adrenaline still pumping. Question Time was trial by ordeal, when the most powerful man in the land was dragged to the edge of a great cliff and made to look down upon the fate that must one day await him on the rocks below. She had heard that in order to endure the ordeal some Prime Ministers had drunk, others had been physically sick beforehand, but in the Chamber Urquhart seemed always in control, almost nerveless. Yet here behind closed doors she could feel the tension flooding through his pores. His blood was hot, his passions high, a lover at orgasm. She was being permitted to share a moment of great intimacy.

"You are my lucky charm, Claire. I can feel it."

He reached out, held her by the arms, claiming her, and at the same time seeking support from her as the fire within him slowly began to subside. She tried to pretend there was nothing sexual in the moment but in vain—here was power, the most potent of forbidden fruit, and authority, passion, vulnerability, all mixed as one, every indulgence she had ever dreamed about in politics and of which she was now part. She stared into his eyes, awed by the privilege of the moment, knowing that her political life would never be as simple again.

The moment was broken by the sounds of protest coming from outside the door and the hurried and unannounced entrance of a figure in a state of considerable agitation. It was Tom Makepeace. His agitation seemed only to grow as he caught the wake of the intimate moment between his leader and his former lover. He had been about to offer a cursory apology for bursting in but decided to dispense with any of the tattered formalities, glaring first at Claire before turning on the Prime Minister.

"Francis, that performance was little short of a disgrace. An insult to our European partners. In one afternoon you've managed to unravel everything I've achieved in my time as Foreign Secretary. And all for the sake of gratuitous parliamentary fisticuffs."

"You've got to learn, Tom, that it's not all Queensberry Rules in Europe. Occasionally you need a bit of pepper on the gloves."

"You can't go screwing around with foreign policy without having the courtesy to consult me first, I won't have it. How can you expect me to deal in good faith with my counterparts after that?" He tossed back the forelock that had fallen across his brow, trying to recompose his temper.

"Ah, good point. I don't."

Claire took a step back. She knew what was coming and felt as if she were intruding. She experienced a strong twinge of embarrassment, too. Was it because Makepeace had until a few days previously been her lover, or because she was as yet unaccustomed to the rituals of humiliation? His gaze of suspicion followed her.

"Tom, you are one of my most capable and pious of Ministers, a great source of strength. Potentially. You are also the Government's most passionate Euro-enthusiast, a source of considerable confusion. Potentially. So—I'm moving you to Environment, where your piousness can find its reward and your enthusiasm can inflict less harm."

The blow had been landed but the effect was not instantaneous. By degrees the forelock tumbled forward once more and his expression turned to confusion. Stiffly, his head began to shake from side to side as though trying to shake itself free from sudden confusion and disbelief.

"Think about it, Tom. You're a man of great administrative ability and considerable social conscience in a Government believed by most to be utterly heartless. That must cause you as much distress as it does me. So where better to display your personal credentials and the Government's best intentions than in the field of Environment? Good for you, good for us all."

The head was still shaking. "I'll not accept."

"It's not a matter for debate."

"Environment or Out?"

"If that's the way you want to put it."

Makepeace drew a deep breath, struggling for composure that, after a few moments, he found. "Then I resign."

Claire looked afresh at him; God, he really meant it. He wouldn't compromise. He was wrong, but she found herself appreciating more than ever that streak of stubbornness, both noble and naive, which was the most endearing and aggravating feature of Tom Makepeace. Urquhart, however, seemed less impressed. His euphoria had gone, to be replaced by unadorned exasperation.

"Tom, you can't resign! For God's sake stop being so petulant and look at what it means. It won't be so very long before I decide to retire and the party starts looking for a new leader. My guess is they'll go for a change of style, too. Someone with a little less stick and a bit more sugar than me. Someone who has a different bias to his politics, just for the joy of a change. Sounds like a pretty good description of Tom Makepeace. Environment is a great opportunity for you—grab it with both hands!" He allowed the thought to take root for a moment. "What the party won't do, Tom, is to hand over its destiny to someone who's spent the last couple of years sulking on the backbenches."

Makepeace was wound tight as a piano wire, feet spread apart for support, his arms knotted lest his hands betray the trembling emotions inside, his features set rigid as he struggled for control. Slowly, at the very edges of his mouth, Claire noticed the traces of a wistful smile beginning to appear, the picture of a man saying farewell to something of great importance to himself. But what? Position? Or principle?

"Francis, your logic is almost impeccable. It has only one small fault."

"And what is that?"

"You underestimate how much I have come to dislike you." And with that he was gone.

The silence he left behind grew oppressive. "I suppose that meant no," Urquhart muttered at last.

"Shall I go after him?"

"No. I'll not beg." Nor would he forgive. "And it was threatening to be such a pleasant day."

❖ ❖ ❖

It might, perhaps, have made a difference if Makepeace had been allowed a few quiet moments for thought and reflection, an opportunity to set practicality alongside his sense of wounded pride in order to discover which would finish the day stronger. But the wind of fate blows capricious in Westminster, and it was not to be. The corridor from the Prime Minister's House of Commons office emerges directly beside the stairwell leading down from the press gallery. In his careless anger Makepeace all but bowled over Dicky Withers as the pressman emerged from the stairs.

"Arrest this ruffian, Sergeant!" Withers demanded of the policeman who guarded this sensitive section of palace corridor.

"Not likely, Dicky. I've just put five quid on him becoming the next Gaffer."

"A pity," Makepeace responded as he dusted down the pressman in apology. "You'd have got much better odds in the morning."

Withers eyed his assailant carefully, noting the unusually discomfited expression. "That's one hell of a hurry, Tom. Tell me, are you flying or fleeing?"

"Does it make a difference?"

"Sure. When a Foreign Secretary is caught charging around like that it must be either a woman or a war. Which is it? You know you can confide in me. I'll only tell about a million people."

Makepeace finished straightening the carnation at the pressman's lapel. Everything in its order. "Get the boys together for me, Dicky. Lobby Room in fifteen minutes. Then we can tell the whole bloody world. Can't give you an exclusive, but you'll get the first interview afterward."

"Sounds like war."

"It is."

MAKEPEACE DECLARES WAR ON URQUHART
FOREIGN SECRETARY "QUITS IN DISGUST"

BY RICHARD WITHERS, POLITICAL EDITOR

Foreign Secretary Thomas Makepeace left the Government yesterday amid bitter recriminations with Downing Street over the direction of Government policy. There was also controversy as to whether he had resigned or been sacked.

"I've walked out on him in disgust," Makepeace told a hurriedly convened Westminster press conference.

Downing Street sources later went to considerable effort to deny this, stating that he had been "consistently out of step" with Government policy on Europe, and the Prime Minister had no choice but to dismiss him. One Government loyalist last night described Makepeace as "a Euro crank."

It was a day of extraordinary excitement at Westminster. The sensational resignation/dismissal followed immediately upon scenes of uproar within the House of Commons after the Prime Minister Francis Urquhart had denounced great rafts of European orthodoxy.

Last night Makepeace announced the formation of a new pro-European group within the Government party called "the Concorde Club." "It will be modern, progressive, and entirely up-to-date. It will be opposed to political Neanderthalism," he said. Observers were left in no doubt that the political Neanderthal he had most in mind was Francis Urquhart.

It is unclear how much support the Concorde Club will gain but if the widely respected Makepeace is able to gain a substantial following, it will represent a most serious threat to the Prime Minister and his chances of continuing long in office.

One senior party source commented that it "was nothing less than a declaration of war."

FOURTEEN

Beware the politician who talks about his political principles. He is usually picking your pocket.

She rapped at the door. "He's on, Francis."

From within the bathroom there was the sound of water being swirled and agitated as Urquhart eased himself back to the present. "Leave the door open, would you? And switch it up."

She did as he asked, and also refilled his glass. They made such a balanced team, she mused, with their instincts so intertwined, facing the world and its foibles practically as one. She couldn't remember the last time they had indulged a serious difference of opinion. Was it the redecoration of the apartment at Downing Street or the sacking of his first Chancellor? He'd played both in traditional fashion, while she had encouraged him to be more adventurous with both the decor and the ax. They'd compromised; she'd changed the furniture and he'd kept his Cabinet colleague (but only for another six months, she remembered. Francis had sacked him on her birthday—beneath it all he could be such a romantic).

He wasn't often wrong—hadn't been that morning when he'd offered a few predictions over breakfast. "It'll be a busy weekend for Tom," he had forecast. "Standard rules of engagement for poor losers. Friday they run to the arms of their constituents for a show of moral support. Saturday it's a walk in the garden with the wife and waifs for a display of family values, then off on Sunday to the vicar to parade the conscience—a personal and intensely spiritual odyssey that somehow always seems to be accompanied by a makeup man and the mongols of the camera pack. Lord, how it must turn the stomach of picture editors, but somehow they seem to manage."

"His wife's buried away in America, isn't she?"

"True. Maybe he has a girlfriend tucked away somewhere. You know, I think we should keep an eye on young Tom. Perhaps he has hidden depths."

Now, as the early evening news announced that the once-and-maybe-future Cabinet Minister had been greeted enthusiastically by his Women's Luncheon Committee meeting, a shout of derision and the noise of parting waters came from the bathroom. Urquhart emerged wrapped in a towel.

To the apparent excessive interest of the pursuing news crew, Makepeace was shown purchasing a bag of oranges in his local market.

"Nice touch. From high ministry to lowly market place—our man of the people," Urquhart reflected.

"Bet he pays with a twenty-pound note. He won't have the slightest idea how much they cost," Mortima muttered less charitably.

"Mr. Makepeace, what are your plans now?" a breathless interviewer pressed as Makepeace produced his wallet.

"To go home and relax. It'll be the first weekend in almost ten years I haven't been surrounded by red boxes; I'm rather looking forward to it."

"But you'll miss being in office, surely? Do you want to return to Government at any time?"

"I'm only fifty. I hope there'll be a chance to serve again sometime."

"But not under Francis Urquhart. Yesterday you called his Government unprincipled. Do you think it's time for the Prime Minister to step down? Or be pushed?"

Makepeace made no immediate response. He stood with his hand extended, waiting for his change. It came in a great handful of coins, which he did not bother to count.

"Mr. Makepeace, should the Prime Minister be forced to go?" the interviewer pressed.

He turned to face his interrogator and the nation, his brow darkened as though considering a dilemma of enormous consequence. Suddenly he broke into an impish grin.

"You might say that," he offered. "But at this stage I wouldn't care to comment..."

Urquhart reached for the remote control and silenced his tormentor. "I've handled this matter badly," he reflected. "Should've handled him better. Never wanted him out. But... politicians of principle. They're like a hole in the middle of the motorway."

"This morning's press was fine," she added supportively.

"It was no better than a draw, Mortima. A Prime Minister should do better than merely a draw."

He was being so ruthlessly honest with himself. But could he also be honest about himself, she wondered? Clad in nothing more than a bath towel he looked so vulnerable, and she began to ruminate yet again on his passing years, the glorious days of summer turned fading autumn, a time when even a great oak tree must lose its leaves and stand bare before the pitiless winds. He had given so much, they had both given so much, yet as the seasons of their lives changed they would have so little to look forward to. There was no joy in watching him grow old.

Approaching winter. A patchwork of creases and crevices. Thin emaciated finger-twigs, parchment skin of bark, when the sap begins to wane and the nights grow longer in a landscape covered with axmen.

"Why do you want to go on, Francis?"

For a moment he looked startled. "Because it's the only thing I know. Why, do you want me to stop?"

"No, but it may cost you more than ever to continue, and I think you should know why you continue."

"Because I honestly believe I am the best man for the job. The only man, perhaps. For the country—and for me—I must go on. I'm not ready to spend the rest of my days looking back. There are too many memories, those things we ought not to have done."

"You won't be able to go on forever, Francis."

"I know. But soon I shall become the longest-serving Prime Minister in modern times. Francis Urquhart's place in history will be secure. Not a bad thing for us to have achieved, Mortima. Something for us to share, I suppose, after all this has been put by."

"To justify the sacrifices past."

"As you say, to justify the sacrifices past. And those still to come."

"Mummy, why didn't Mr. Urquhart lock up Toad?"

Claire put down the book and gave her youngest daughter, Abby, a cheerful hug. "I don't think Mr. Urquhart was around then, darling."

"But he's been around forever."

It dawned on Claire that Francis Urquhart had been Prime Minister since before either Abby or Diana had been born. A long time. A lifetime.

"I think Mr. Urquhart is Toad," the oldest child joined in from the other side of the sofa.

"Don't you like Mr. Urquhart?" her mother inquired.

"No. He's not very kind and never listens. Just like Toad. And he's so *old*."

"He's not that old," Claire protested. "Only a little older than Daddy."

"A very little older than Daddy," Johannis commented wryly. He was examining the financial pages of the evening newspaper while managing to watch the news and eavesdrop at the same time.

"Did your Mummy read *The Wind in the Willows* to you when you were a girl?" Diana inquired.

"No, darling. She didn't."

"Did you have an unhappy childhood, Mummy?" Diana was beginning to pick up so many of her mother's unspoken thoughts, much as Claire had when she was a child. Her own mother had spoken so little to her, not wanting to share the pain, trying to protect her from the truth. But the pain had come, even when there had been no beatings, for when there was no abuse there was silence. That's how it had been for Claire and how it would never be for her own children. Screaming matches, hysterical argument, voices and fists raised until she thought her heart would crack. Then long periods of silence. Complete silence. Meals that were spent in silence, long days in silence, even her mother weeping in silence. The silence of the hell cupboard beneath the stairs where on occasions she was locked and more frequently she hid. A childhood of abuse and silence, the noise of wounding and the yet more wounding sound of silence—perhaps it all evened out in the end. She had survived. She was a survivor.

"Buy shares in him, d'you think?" Joh asked, his attention now upon the television news. "Or has he gone the way of all flesh?"

Tom Makepeace paid for his oranges.

She wondered how much Joh knew, or guessed. Before they had married they'd discussed openly his fears that a husband twenty-three years older than a wife would inevitably be found deficient, lacking in some important respects, that one day he would be a pensioner while she was still in her prime and in almost all such relationships there was bound to develop a gulf that could only be bridged by trust and immense understanding. "You cannot keep a marriage warm if both sides of the bed go cold," he'd said. How well he had foreseen. But that had been a long time ago; had he in the years since made the crossover in his mind from abstract theory to fact? If he had, as she suspected he had, he'd offered no hint of it. Loyal knight, husband, guide, father-confessor, never inquisitor. It made her respect and love for him all the stronger.

"No," she responded to her husband's question. "Not yet at least."

"But Tom Makepeace could be a danger."

"Do you really think so?"

"I am a businessman, my love, not a politician. But make your own market analysis. How long do most Prime Ministers last—three, four, five years? He's already lasted more than ten. No one can defy the odds forever; the chances of your Francis still being in office in two years' time are very small. Age, accident, ill health, unpopularity. Time has many unpleasant allies."

"But he seems at the height of his power."

"So was Alexander when he fell from his horse."

"What are you saying, Joh?"

"I suppose I'm saying be careful. That there's every likelihood of Francis Urquhart falling beneath the chariot wheels while you are his PPS—correction, not falling, more likely being thrust beneath by a baying mob. And all his handmaidens with him. Don't tie yourself too closely."

"And you think that Tom Makepeace will do the thrusting?" She found the terminology peculiarly uncomfortable.

"Makepeace, or someone like Makepeace. You should keep an eye on him."

His logic was, as always, impeccable; a shiver of distress passed down her spine.

"How would you do that, Joh? Keep an eye on him?"

He appeared not to have heard, setting aside his newspaper in order that he could embrace his daughters before sending them off to bed accompanied by the normal chorus of complaint. Only when Abby and Diana had departed, towing soft toys and endearments, did he turn once again to his wife. "How? Depends how important it was."

"According to you, very."

He massaged his hands, a vizier warming them above a campfire on some damp, starless night, his lips moving as though sucking at the pipe he used to love before he met Claire and loved her more. "A talkative friend. Close colleague, perhaps. Nothing electronic or illegal. That sort of thing, you mean?"

She stared at him, afraid to acknowledge what she meant, even to herself.

"A driver. Drivers know all the secrets. They could've abolished the CIA in exchange for one driver in the Kremlin motor pool. I'd get a friendly businessman to offer him a driver with big ears inside the car and a big mouth out of it."

"Not illegal?"

"More an accident."

She bit her bottom lip, puckering her face as though tasting lemons. "Suppose, Joh, just suppose for the sake of argument that a businessman was impressed by the Concorde Club and wanted to offer Tom some gesture of support—a small donation for administrative support, the loan of a car and driver to replace the Ministerial car he's just lost..."

"A driver of incontinent tongue and divided loyalty."

"What would you say, Joh?"

"I'd say that would alter the odds significantly in Mr. Urquhart's favor. For a little while."

"How might that be done?" she asked softly.

He examined her closely, probing, hypothesis spilling into resolution. He needed to be certain.

"Rather easily, I would guess. But I'm sure a busy girl like you wouldn't want to be bothered with such detail."

"I suspect you're right."

He paused, contemplating the new door that had opened up on their lives. "Seems it's not only your job that's changed."

"What do you mean?"

"I thought you rather liked Tom Makepeace."

He knew, she was sure. At times he seemed to have a mirror into her mind and she had no hiding place from him, even inside.

"I did. I suppose I still do."

"But?"

"But..." She shrugged, grown suddenly weary. "But politics." It seemed to explain everything. Yet it excused nothing.

FIFTEEN

The Mediterranean is a full, confused sea, littered with wrecks and old ruins.

Evanghelos Passolides sang a song of ancient honor as he invoked the miracle of the mallet, beating short strips of pig into what by later that evening would have become cuisine. Thud—squish—smash, and another thousand bygone warriors were tossed to the Underworld.

Maria prepared the evening tables. She'd turned up again after another long day's teaching for no better purpose than to watch over him and to indulge her growing concern. His moods had become increasingly capricious, occasionally malevolent, an appearance of determination followed by outbursts of bitterness when it seemed that the forces of authority were once again standing guard over his brothers' graves, fending him off with their rules of silence. They'd tried to find out more about the unknown officer and the precise location of the burial site, but no one in authority displayed any spark of interest. It was all so very long ago, miss, by now there'd be nothing to dig up but problems. Put the details in writing and we'll see what can be done. So Maria had written but there had been no reply, the letter left to circulate through the corridors of power until it dropped from exhaustion.

Meanwhile Passolides cooked, sang mournful songs, and grew ever more resentful.

And it was her fault. She had interfered with his silent grief, stirred his hopes and, with them, dark memories. She couldn't drop it now, any more than he could.

Family. The bonds of loyalty. Bondage. Links that had chained her for so many years, the finest hour of her womanhood, first to a dying mother then to a grieving father. And for him, a ligature tied so tight it had all but strangled the life from him. For both their sakes, she had to find help from somewhere. From someone who could break through the artifice and excuses, someone who could find out about the brothers' graves, and whether there were any other graves. But who?

As the television news flickered on the small monochrome screen perched above the coatrack, she saw a man of authority and responsibility, a man who talked of principle and his determination to defend the rights of ordinary men and women against insensitive and arrogant Government, even as he bought his oranges…

Clive Watling looked around the lunch table and wondered why he had been so naive. He'd swallowed the Ponsonby line that it would be an easy task, the issues simple, the evidence direct, the conclusions all but self-evident. Yet they couldn't even agree on what to eat. Two Muslims, one of whom had an ulcer, a vegetarian, a native of Yorkshire who liked his food like his law—ample in quantity and unambiguously honest. And then, of course, there was Rodin, who insisted on kosher food and scowled upon whatever was presented on the plate with a look of Jacobin condescension. About most things in this world, it seemed, Rodin had already formed his inflexible opinion.

There was so little certainty to international law; so much was left to textual interpretation, to confusing precedent, hopefully to common sense and fundamental principle. How it could be left to unreconstructed tribalists like Rodin he would never fathom.

For weeks the academics, geologists, politicians, historians, maritime experts, and professional lobbyists garbed as lawyers had trooped before their sittings and expounded on the matter, which in essence was simple. Beyond the breeze-kissed beaches of Cyprus lay two disputed areas of continental shelf, east and west. Hand them to the Greeks, or to the Turks, or find some means of division that could be dressed in a cloak of equity and natural justice. Miles of salt water, sea anemones, and sand.

And oil.

Watling was sure of it now. And he was sure the Frenchman knew. Whatever else could explain his utter unreason? Any proposal that the Turks might gain a substantial proportion of the continental shelf was resisted with vehemence, even the suggestion that they draw a straight line down the middle and split it in equal halves was disparaged and denounced. The "share of lions," as he put it, must go to the Greeks. While they waited in the private dining room for their first course Rodin had been pressed for his defense—what new principle of international justice could he possibly invoke to justify such an imbalance of objectivity?

"It is simple and irrefutable," he had pronounced, swirling the water in his glass as though inspecting a dribble of English wine. "The Turks invaded, took their territory by force. At the cost of many lives and in defiance of the United Nations. It would be appeasement of the worst kind to offer them reward for their bloody actions."

"We are not here to deliberate upon the war," Osman the Egyptian had scolded.

"That is exactly what we are doing!" Rodin spat. "If we show favor to the Turks we sanctify future acts of international terrorism. What would we be saying to the world—grab territory, rape and pillage the inhabitants into exile, and in twenty years' time the international courts will offer you congratulation and confirm the spoils?"

"That's how frontiers have been fixed throughout the ages, for goodness' sake," the Malaysian muttered.

"I'd hoped we could find a rather less medieval means of settlement," Rodin replied icily. "Oh, don't quote me your Bering Seas and Beagle Channels, why should we hide behind ancient precedent?"

"Because it's the law," Osman responded quietly.

"But it isn't justice."

Justice, Watling mused to himself, he talks of justice. And this the man who had so vehemently argued the case of French fishermen in their attempt to force themselves upon the fishing grounds of Guernsey, quoting in his public cause Napoleonic treaty and national honor while arguing grubby compromise behind closed doors. Now compromise of whatever kind that left the Turk within a hundred miles of oil shale he condemned with the mock virtue of a *tricoteuse* hearing the clatter on cobbles of approaching tumbrels.

Watling eyed the Frenchman. Of course Rodin knew! Watling found himself wondering whether Rodin actually took money for his views, or was the merest sniff of French national interest sufficient to turn him? Whichever, it mattered little, the result would still be the same. If Watling allowed it.

French justice. Of the type that had been meted out to his father. For a few mouthfuls Watling fought the urge within that was attempting to drench his own views in prejudice—but there was no conflict here, he decided, no contradiction, his sense of principle was entirely in accord with his antagonism. French bigotry and self-interest was not to be confused with fair play, not in Watling's court. Rodin spoke glibly of justice, so on the stake of justice the Frenchman would be impaled. Watling would see to it. As a matter of high principle. And pleasure.

SIXTEEN

All politics are the search for advantage.

Cabinet Government frequently resembled a herd of pigs flying in close formation, he thought. In the Orwellian world of Westminster there was one prerogative above all accorded to the Chief Pig, that of choosing his companions for the flypast, and it was something of a pity that the resignation of Makepeace had taken the edge off the reshuffle, implying an element of enforced necessity instead of presenting it as unadulterated Urquhart. Makepeace was an overweight boar, he'd insisted, fattened to excess on a diet of Brussels and scarcely capable any longer of liftoff let alone the aerial gymnastics required for public esteem on the British side of the Channel. Market time. "Should remind others of the constant need to remain lean and hungry," he'd told his new press officer, Grist. "And the blessings of the bacon slicer."

Grist had made a good start to such a significant day, suggesting that the Prime Minister conduct a brisk walk around the lake in St. James's Park in order to supply appropriate images for the benefit of photographers, a mixture of purpose and vigor. One of the cameramen had suggested the Prime Ministerial hands might be placed around the neck of a domesticated goose, "just to give the public an idea of how it's done, Mr. Urquhart." He declined.

By the time he returned to Downing Street an impatient flock of reporters and lobby correspondents was perched along the barriers, waiting upon first prey. Blood was about to be splashed over their boots and they squabbled among themselves, fighting for the first morsel, launching thrusts at the Prime Minister from across the road. He responded with nothing more than a wave and a look of sincerity practiced to perfection before retreating toward the glossy black door.

"Cry God for England and St. George?" It was Dicky Withers. The wise old bird was saving his energies and his thoughts to hang upon a special moment.

Urquhart turned in the doorway to look once more upon the scene, and nodded in Dicky's direction. Dicky knew what this was all about.

"And warm beer, white cliffs, and flying pigs," Urquhart muttered. He said no more before disappearing inside. There was work to be done.

It would be a long day. With long knives.

For Geoffrey Booza-Pitt, the day had started in admirable fashion. He'd gone fishing at the Ritz, casting champagne and scrambled egg upon the familiar waters until she had risen innocently for the bait. Breakfast with Selina would in any event have been a pleasure, but the attractions of her body were as little for the Transport Secretary compared with those of her mind—or, more specifically, her memory. She was a secretary in the office of the Party Chairman and was one of several in similar political employment whom Geoffrey regularly fed and flattered. In all such cases he preferred breakfast to bed, being cautious about sleeping with women of naive years where sex could be seen as a prelude either to emotional entanglement or to the insinuations of a gossip column, neither of which Geoffrey could countenance. Sharing breakfast offered much more robust reward, pillow talk without the cigarette ash and mascara smears, information *sans* ejaculation.

Booza-Pitt's political philosophy was unorthodox. He did not believe, for instance, that information attracted ownership, at least the ownership of anybody who was lax enough to let it slip. So Geoffrey would acquire a little bit here and a little bit there, not wholesale robbery, but in the end it all added up—as it had done when he was a student. He'd written to every Jewish charity he could find explaining that he was a devout student struggling to make ends meet, that he was £200 short on his tuition money. He'd work nights, of course, for his living expenses, but he did want to make sure of his tuition and could they please help? And, with a little bit here and a little bit there, the trickles of help had become a flood. If he'd had a conscience it certainly wasn't of Jewish origin since both his parents were casual Methodists. Anyway, he'd slept well in a bed of considerable comfort.

Information was wealth around the labyrinths of Westminster, of a value greater than money, and Selina had paid for breakfast in generous fashion. She'd typed every draft of the new campaigning document being prepared at party headquarters, every addition and amendment, every thought and rethought, the paragraphs of analysis and argument, all the conclusions. And her recall was stupendous, even as the bubbles tickled her nose and made her giggle. The new campaign, it seemed, would not be radical in approach—a little direct mail, a lightweight slogan—but it had been based on new opinion research and, like Selina, was attractively packaged. She was ebullient, unsuspecting, and tender enough to believe he really wanted to help.

Geoffrey had smiled, poured, and committed it all to his excellent memory.

The car ferrying them back to their separate offices was stuck in the morning snarl. The fool of a driver had decided to take the rapid route to nowhere around Trafalgar Square, where ranks of one-eyed pigeons stood morose and diseased on guard duty. The Transport Secretary wound up the window and settled back into his seat, for once in his life content to remain obscure, trying to avoid the attentions of fellow jammers with their acrid fumes and equally corrosive tempers. Beside him on the backseat Selina was rearranging her elegant legs, causing him to undertake a rapid reassessment of his priorities—he was a fool for thighs, perhaps he should suggest dinner next time?—when the phone began to burble. From the other end of the line came the voice of his House of Commons secretary. The guest list for his box at the Albert Hall. The promenade concert late next week. A late cancellation, the Trade Secretary off trying to pluck leaves from the tree of Japanese abundance, where he would surely discover like all his predecessors that when it came to promises of freer trade, in the Orient it was always autumn.

The interruption soured Booza-Pitt's mood, distracting him from his scrutiny of delicate ankles and contemplation of indulgence. He hated last-minute cancellations that disturbed what was often months of planning; he went into a sulk, like the Duke of Wellington receiving a scrap of paper informing him that Blücher wouldn't make it in time for Waterloo. He decided to shoot the messenger.

"So what have you done?" he demanded querulously.

"Well, I assume we'd like another top-level politician, so I've been checking the list. You've done every other member of the Cabinet in the last twelve months apart from Tom Makepeace..."

"This is a box at the Albert Hall, not a bloody crypt."

"And Arthur Bollingbroke. I've already called his secretary to check, she thinks he and his wife might be free on that evening."

"Bollingbroke! The man's a bloated bore, why the hell do you think I haven't invited him to anything else? I can't sit him down next to the American Ambassador and Chairman of ITN, he'd fart all through the overture while swilling down vast quantities of my champagne. Have you any idea how much that'd cost me?"

The secretary was trying to justify herself but Booza-Pitt was in no mind to listen. The motorist stuck in the next vehicle had recognized him and was offering a two-fingered salutation; the Transport Secretary struggled to balance discretion against a sudden compulsion to get out of the car and rearrange the guy's nasal passages.

"Perhaps we'd better wait until tomorrow, anyway," he heard her suggest.

"What on earth for?"

"Until the reshuffle is finished."

"Reshuffle…?" He choked. Selina wondered if a stray salmon bone had become lodged in his throat.

"Didn't you know? It's on television right now."

Reshuffles had always had an adverse effect on Booza-Pitt, they made him twitch. That first time, he'd been in Parliament less than eighteen months and had refused to stray more than twenty yards from the phone throughout the day, even though his second wife had told him there was no credible chance of his finding promotion so early in his career. Yet the phone had rung while he was out in the garden—"Downing Street," his wife had announced in awe through the kitchen window. He had run—rushed, tripped, fallen, broken his finger, and ripped the knee from his trousers, yet nothing would stop him from taking the call. The Prime Minister's office. Wondering whether he could help. *Of course, of course I can!* A speaking engagement in a neighboring constituency the Prime Minister had planned to undertake, yet which he must now sadly decline. The reshuffle, you understand. Could Geoffrey fill in, tomorrow night? His eyes blurred red with pain, Geoffrey had expressed his unencumbered delight at having been asked, while his soon-to-be former wife had collapsed in convulsions.

You couldn't keep him down, though. He'd been involved in every reshuffle since and now the hounds of hazard had slipped the leash again. Alarms would be ringing all around Westminster, causing grown men to cringe. He studied the telephone in his hand, his features drenched in disbelief. He hadn't known it was today, right this minute, with calls reaching out from Downing Street to summon the good and the gone while she jammed the line with waffle about how it was such a pity because she truly admired Tom Makepeace and…

"Get off the bloody phone!" he screamed.

SEVENTEEN

Loyalty is like instant coffee: it's cheap and ultimately unsatisfying.

He was still in his shirt sleeves when he opened the front door. By the lack of subtlety in the creases, she suspected he might have ironed it himself.

"You're going to hate me for pestering you at home."

From two steps up Tom Makepeace studied her, still munching his toast. She was tossing her dark hair nervously, the morning sun catching colors of polished coal. The lips were full, puckered in concern, her arms clutched around her in a troubled manner that seemed to lift her breasts toward him. Her coyness was a rarity in Westminster, so were the jeans.

"I hope it's something important, Miss…?" He'd noticed the lack of a ring.

"Maria Passolides. A matter of life and death, in a way."

But, damn it, this was the middle of his breakfast. "If you have a problem, perhaps it would be best if you wrote to me with the details."

"I have. I got a letter in return from an assistant saying thanks but you were too busy to deal with individual predicaments at the moment. He couldn't spell 'predicaments.'"

"We've had an enormous number of letters in the last few days. Mostly supportive, I'm glad to say, but far too many for me to handle personally. I apologize. Perhaps you'd care to telephone my office to arrange an appointment." He brushed his hands dismissively of the crumbs.

"Done that, too. Five times. You're always engaged."

He was losing this game to love, and on his service. "It seems I'm likely to spend the whole morning apologizing to you, Miss Passolides. Tell me briefly how I might be able to help." He did not forsake his high vantage point or invite her inside; there were so many troubled individuals, so little politicians could do, and already too many distractions from the extraordinary pile of unopened envelopes that had taken over his dining table. Yet as she talked, she touched something inside him, a pulse of interest. It was several minutes before he recognized it as lust.

"You must understand, Miss Passolides, it's a difficult time for politicians to get into the matter of missing graves, just when we seem to be on the point of peace in Cyprus."

"That's where you couldn't be more wrong." As she talked her diffidence had completely disappeared. "It's not openness that will threaten peace but continuing uncertainty and any hint of a cover-up. Even the Turks have recognized that."

He reflected on the force of her argument, his energies still weighed down by the thought of the unopened letters and unanswered calls that would pursue him for weeks to come. Life without the Ministerial machine was proving extraordinarily tiresome, with little scope for new crusades. "It's all a long way from my constituency," he offered weakly.

"Don't be so sure. There are nearly three hundred thousand Greek Cypriots in this country and a kebab shop or taverna in every high street. Overnight a politician could have an army at his side."

"Or at his throat."

"Beware of Greeks bearing grudges." She stood laughing

on the pavement. There was an unhewn energy, enthusiasm, impatience, passion, commitment, the raw edge of life in this woman. He liked that, and he liked her.

"It seems that the only way I'm going to get you and your army off my doorstep is to invite you in for a cup of tea. Then perhaps we can discuss the matter of whose side." He stood aside to let her pass. "And whose throat."

He declined his head as Urquhart strode across the threshold of Number Ten. Over the years the doorman had noticed that what had started as his brief nod of respect had developed into something closer to a cautious bow; as a good trade unionist he'd fought the tendency but found it irresistible, built upon generations of inbred class attitudes that instinctively recognized authority. Damn 'em all. The atmosphere had changed in Downing Street, especially when Mortima Urquhart was around, growing more formalized with the passage of time and Parliaments, a royal court dressed in democratic image. One day, the doorman reassured his wife, the great unwashed would stir and shake like a million grains of sand beneath Urquhart's feet and he would slip to his knees and be gone, buried beneath the changing tide of fortune. One day, someday, maybe soon. But in the meantime the doorman would continue to smile and bow a little lower, the better to inspect the shifting sands.

The door closed, shutting out the cries of inquisitive hunger from the press corps. They'd be thrown a few bones later. Before then, there were dishes to carve. Urquhart studied his watch. Good, the timing was perfect. He'd've kept Mackintosh waiting for exactly twenty minutes.

Jasper Mackintosh was standing in the corner of the hallway, tapping his handcrafted shoe on the black-and-white floor tiles, trying with little success to hide his irritation. As the owner and publisher of the country's second largest and fastest-growing newspaper empire, he was more accustomed to being waited on than waiting, and after a lifetime of building and breaking politicians he was left in no undue awe by his surroundings. Several months previously he'd concluded that the time had come to start pulling the plug on Francis Urquhart—not that the Prime Minister had done anything politically damaging or offensive, simply that he'd been around so long that stories about him no longer sold newspapers. Change and uncertainty sold newspapers, and business dictated it was time for a little turmoil. Mackintosh was on a high, and in a hurry. Only last week he'd finally agreed to the terms of purchase for the *Tribune* chain of newspapers, a lumbering loss-making giant staffed by worn-out journalists working in worn-out premises for a worn-out readership, yet which offered well-known titles and great potential. The journalists could be paid off, new premises could be constructed, a new readership bought through heavy advertising and discounting, but the cost was going to be high, many tens of millions, and there was no room in Mackintosh's world for standing still. He had to get the money men off his back. That meant headlines, happenings, histrionics, and new heroes. Sentimentality was a sin.

Mackintosh had already decided that Urquhart had lost this morning's game, and not simply for starting it twenty minutes late. He assumed the Prime Minister wanted to rekindle the relationship, perhaps give him an exclusive insight into the reshuffle in exchange for sympathy. No chance. In Mackintosh's world of tomorrow, Francis Urquhart didn't feature. Anyway, where was the courtesy, the deference he expected from a supplicant? Urquhart simply grabbed him by the elbow and hustled him along the corridor.

"Glad you could make it, Jasper. I haven't got a lot of time, got to dispatch a few of the walking wounded, so I'll come straight to the point. Why have you directed your muck spreaders into Downing Street?"

"Muck spreaders?"

"Driven by your editors."

"Prime Minister, they are souls of independent mind. I have given countless undertakings about interfering…"

"They are a bunch of brigands and whatever the state of their minds, you've got them firmly by the balls. Their thoughts tend to follow." Suddenly Urquhart called a halt to the breathless charge down the passageway. He hustled Mackintosh into the alcove by the Henry Moore and looked him directly in the eye. "Why? Why are you writing that it's time for me to go? What have I done wrong?"

Mackintosh considered, and rejected the option of prevarication. Urquhart wanted it straight. "Nothing. It's not what you've done, it's what you are. You're a giant; your shadow falls across the political world and leaves others in the shade. You've been a great man, Francis, but it's time for a change. Let others have a chance to grow." He smiled gently; he'd put it rather well, he thought. "It's business, you understand. The business of politics and of newspapers. Nothing personal."

Urquhart seemed unaffected by the obituary. "I'm obliged to you, Jasper, for being so direct. I've always thought we had a relationship that was robust and candid, which could withstand the knocks of changing times."

"That's extremely generous of you…" Mackintosh began, but Urquhart was talking straight through him.

"And speaking of the knocks of changing times, I thought it only fair—in equal candor and confidence—to share with you some plans the Treasury is proposing to push forward. Now you know I am not a man of high finance, I leave that to the experts like you. Extraordinary how the nation entrusts the fate of its entire national fortune to politicians like me who can scarcely add up." He shrugged his shoulders, as though trying to slough off some unwelcome burden. "But as I understand it you've undertaken to buy the *Tribune* and are going to pay for it all by issuing a large number of bonds to your friends in the City."

The newspaper man nodded. This was all public knowledge, a straightforward plan to raise the money by huge borrowings, with the interest payments being set off against his existing company's profits. Overall his profits would plummet but so would his tax bill, and in effect the Inland Revenue would end up paying for the expansion of the Mackintosh empire, which in a few years' time would be turned into one of the biggest money spinners in the country. Debt today, paid for by the tax man, in exchange for huge profit tomorrow, paid directly to Mackintosh. Creative accounting and entirely legal. The money men loved it.

"The point is," the Prime Minister continued, "and this is just between the two of us, as old friends…"

Somewhere inside, at the mention of friendship, Mackintosh felt his muesli move.

"…the Treasury is planning to make a few changes. As from next week. Something about the losses of one company no longer being able to be set off against the profits of another. I don't profess to understand it, do you?"

Of course Mackintosh understood. So well that he grabbed the wall for support. It was a proposal to slash the canvas of his creative accounting to shreds. With those rules his tax bill would soar and even the dullest underwriter would realize he'd no longer be able to repay the debt. He was already committed to buying the *Tribune*, no way out of it, yet at the slightest hint of a rule change the money men would wash their hands of the whole plan, walk away to their champagne bars and Porsches, leaving him with…

"Ruin. You'd ruin me. I'd lose everything."

"Really? That would be a pity. But the Treasury button counters are so very keen on this new idea, and who am I to argue with them?"

"You are the bloody Prime Minister!"

"Yes, I am. But, apparently, one not long for this world. On the way out."

"Oh, God." Mackintosh's shoulders had slumped, the tailored suit seeming to hang like sacking. A man reduced. He raised his eyes in search of salvation but all he could find were the long drapes that stood guard beside the tall sash windows of the hallway, colored like claret, or blood. His blood. Time to swallow pride, words, self-respect. He cleared his throat with difficulty. "It seems my editors have badly misjudged you, Prime Minister. You appear to have lost neither your acumen nor your enthusiasm for office. I shall inform them of their error immediately. And I think I can assure you that no editor who holds anything but the highest regard for your many and varied talents will ever work for one of my newspapers."

For an endless breath Urquhart said nothing. The lips closed, grew thin, like the leathered beak of a snapper turtle, and the eyes ignited with a reptilian malevolence and a desire to do harm that Mackintosh could physically feel. It was the stuff of childish nightmares; he could taste his own fear.

"Good." At last the lips had moved. "You can find your own way out." Urquhart had already turned his back and was a step away from the dejected Mackintosh when he spun around for one final word, the features now bathed in a practiced smile.

"By the way, Jasper. You understand, don't you? All this. It's business. Nothing personal."

And he was gone.

EIGHTEEN

The Greeks have a history of heroic failures. No one has yet discerned what their future might be.

It was a night out for the boys. Loud, rumbustious, earthy, scarcely diplomatic, not at all ecclesiastical. Hardly the place one expected to find His Grace the Bishop of Marion and the High Commissioner of the Kingdom of Great Britain and Northern Ireland. But the Cypriot Bishop was one of the new breed of clerics who sought orthodoxy only in their religion.

"Welcome, most high of high commissioners." The Bishop, clad in the black of the clerical cassock, spread his arms in greeting and chuckled. As Hugh Martin, the British diplomat, entered, three of the four men who had been sitting alongside the Bishop rose and melted to the sidelines. The fourth, who was as broad as the Bishop was tall, was introduced as his brother, Dimitri.

"I'm delighted you could come and enjoy what, with God's grace, will be a night of momentous victory for my team," the Bishop continued, while two girls who said nothing through enormous smiles offered trays of wine and finger food.

"*Your* team, your Grace?" Martin inquired lightheartedly.

"Indeed," the Bishop responded in his most earnest of tones. "I own the team. In the name of the bishopric, of course. A fine way of extending God's bounty to the masses, don't you think?"

On cue the thousands of ardent football supporters packed into Nicosia's Makarios Stadium erupted into a stamping war cry of delight as twenty-two players filed onto the pitch. The Cyprus Cup Final was about to get under way.

In the corner of the private box high up in the stadium a mobile phone warbled and one of the besuited assistants began muttering into the mouthpiece. Martin looked afresh at the scene. He was new to the posting in the Cypriot capital yet already had heard of the extrovert Theophilos, still only in his forties, who controlled an empire that covered not only hearts and souls, but also pockets—a newspaper, two hotels, several editors, still more politicians, and a vineyard that was arguably the finest on the island. But Martin hadn't known about the football team. Clearly there was much to learn about this Harvard Business School–educated, well-groomed cleric.

The Englishman was grateful for the whirring fans that spilled the air around the box. Nicosia was one of those capitals that seemed to be in the wrong place, tucked behind the Kyrenia Mountains on the wide plains of Mesaoria, touched by neither rippling sea breeze nor fresh mountain air, where even as early as May the heat and exhaust fumes built to oppressive levels. The Makarios Stadium had become a concrete cauldron nearing the boil, bringing sweat and fanatical passion to the brows of the packed crowd, yet beneath his ankle-length bishop's robes Theophilos remained cool. Elegantly he dispatched instructions via the assistants who sat behind him, all of whom were introduced as theology teachers yet who, judging by their frequent telephone conversations, were equally at home in the world of Mammon. Only his brother Dimitri, a highly strung man of fidgeting fingers whose tongue ceaselessly explored the corners of his cheeks, sat alongside the Bishop and the High

Commissioner; the others remained in a row of chairs behind, except for a single man who neither spoke nor smiled but stood guard beside the door. Martin thought he detected a bulge beneath the armpit, but surely not with a man of the cloth? He decided that the sweet, heavy wine they were drinking must be affecting his imagination.

The game proceeded in dogged fashion, the players weighed down by the heat and the tension of the occasion. Martin offered diplomatic expressions of encouragement but Dimitri's hand language betrayed his growing impatience, his cracking knuckles and beaten palms speaking for all the Cypriots in the box as, down on the field, nervous stumble piled upon wayward pass and slip. Only the Bishop expressed no reaction, his attentions seemingly concentrated on the shelling of pistachios and the flicking of husks unerringly into a nearby bowl. A dagger pass, sudden opportunity, raised spirits, a waving flag, offside, another stoppage. Then stamping feet. Jeers. Irreverent whistles. From within the plentiful folds of the Bishop's cassock a finger was raised, like a pink rabbit escaping from an enormous dark burrow.

"Fetch the manager" were the only words spoken; with surprising haste for a man whose spiritual timing was set by an ageless clock, one of the students of theology disappeared through the door.

It was more than fifteen minutes to halftime, yet less than five before there was a rapping at the door and a flushed, tracksuited man was permitted to enter. He immediately bowed low in front of the Bishop. To Martin's eye, unaccustomed as he was to the ways of the Orthodox, there seemed to be a distinct and deliberate pause before the Bishop's right hand was extended and the manager's lips met his ring.

"Costa," the Bishop addressed the manager as he rose to his feet, "this is God's team. Yet you permit them to play like old women."

"My apologies, *Theofiléstate*, Friend of God," the manager mumbled.

The Bishop's voice rose as though warning a vast crowd of the perils of brimstone. "God's work cannot be done without goals, the ground will not open to swallow our opponents. Their left back has the tinning speed of a bulk carrier, put Evriviades against him—get behind him, get goals."

The manager, scourged, was a picture of dejection.

"There's a new Mercedes in it for you if we win."

"Thank you. Thank you, *Aghie*, Saintly One!" He bowed to kiss the ring once more.

"And you'll be walking to the bus stop if we don't."

The manager was dismissed in the manner of a waiter who had spilled the soup.

Martin was careful to conceal his wry amusement. This was a theater piece, although whether put on for his benefit or that of the manager he wasn't completely sure. He had little interest in football but a growing curiosity in this extraordinary black-garbed apparition who appeared to control the destiny of souls and cup finals as the doorkeeper of hell controls the hopes of desperate sinners. "You take your football seriously," Martin commented.

The Bishop withdrew a packet of cigarettes from the folds of his cassock; almost as quickly an aide had ignited a small flame thrower and the Bishop disappeared in a fog of blue smoke. Martin wondered if this were a second part of the entertainment and he was about to witness an Ascension. When the cleric's face reappeared it was split with a smile of mischief.

"My dear Mr. Martin. God inspires. But occasionally a little extra motivation assists with His work."

"I sincerely hope, your Grace, that I never have cause to find myself in anything other than your favor."

"You and I shall be the greatest of friends," he chortled. One of the young girls refilled their glasses; she really was very pretty. Theophilos raised his glass. "Havoc to the foes of God and Cyprus."

They both drank deep.

"Which reminds me, Mr. Martin. There's a small matter I wanted to raise with you…"

"And there's another small matter I wanted to raise with you, Max."

Maxwell Stanbrook thought he truly loved the man. Francis Urquhart stood framed against the windows of the Cabinet Room, gazing out like the admiral of a great armada about to set to sea. Stanbrook had arrived less than twenty minutes before at his office in MAFF, the Ministry of Agriculture, Fisheries, and Food, to be told by his agitated private secretary that he was wanted immediately at Downing Street.

"So what is it, Sonia?"

"I don't know, Minister—no, really I don't."

Stanbrook was firmly committed to the proposition that Government was a quiet conspiracy of civil servants who pulled all of the strings and most of the wool, and he took an active and incredulous dislike to those who claimed they didn't know or suggested there was no alternative. He was notorious throughout Whitehall for throwing—literally hurling—position papers back at civil servants wrapped in a shower of uncivil expletives. The Mobster in the Mafia, as he was known. It was no secret that many in the corridors of power desperately wanted to see his comeuppance; had that time arrived?

A year earlier he'd thought he might have cancer. He remembered how he had walked into the consultant's office trying to mask his dread, to still the shaking knee, to put a brave face on the prospect of death. Somehow it had been easier than this; the fear of mortal illness was nothing compared to the wretchedness he felt as he had walked into the Cabinet Room. Urquhart was there alone. No pleasantries.

"I've had to let Annita go," the Prime Minister began.

God, he was on the list…

"I want you to take her place. Environment Secretary. Put a bit of stick about. You know, Max, the drones in the department fancy themselves as the new thought police. An environmental watchdog here, a pollution inspectorate there. And what's the point? No sooner had they given every school child nightmares about global warming than we had to send in the army to dig hypothermic pensioners out of the snow. Next it was a paper demanding billions of pounds to combat drought fourteen days—fourteen days!—before North Wales and an entire cricket season were washed away in floods. Pipe dreams, nothing but pipe dreams they conjure up over long lunches in Brussels to keep themselves in jobs. Sort it out for me, will you, Max?"

"Be a pleasure, FU."

"One thing in particular. This Fresh Air Directive—you remember? Brussels trying to make British factories smell like a French bordello. Bloody nonsense, I'll not have it."

"But I thought the directive had already been approved."

"Yes, it'll be carved on Annita's headstone. She didn't like it, not at all gracious about going; suspect I'll have to watch my back for knitting needles. But although it's European policy, domestic governments are responsible for implementing it."

"They've turned us into odor officers. Pooper snoopers."

"Precisely. Now, there's been a lot of loose criticism about us being poor Europeans, you can imagine how distressing I find that. So I want you to ensure that the monitoring arrangements are implemented meticulously. I suggest once a year, usually in January. Preferably during a gale."

"On the windward side of town."

"Max, you could go far."

"I shall certainly do my best."

Urquhart chuckled benevolently, wondering if he had just spotted a new potential rival. He would watch him, as he watched them all. He rose from his chair and walked to the window from where he could see the trees of St. James's.

"There's another small matter, Max. Tricky. One of the first things you'll be asked to do is to sign an order permitting the erection of a statue to the Blessed Margaret—just out there." He waved in the direction of the park. "The money's been raised, a sculptor commissioned, they're ready to go." He turned. "And I want you to find some way of stopping it."

"Do you have any suggestions, FU?"

"I'd rather hoped you might come up with some. It would be embarrassing if I'm seen to oppose it, they'd say I was motivated by envy, which of course is not the case. It's the principle of the thing. This is not a Government of idolatry and graven images. I want you to know there is no thought of personal advantage in my position on this matter..."

"And I insist that you understand, my dear Mr. Martin, there is no thought of personal gain for me in all this. Many new jobs will be created for poor farmers in a desperately undeveloped part of our island."

"But Cape Kathikas is a nature reserve. It's meant to be undeveloped. To preserve the orchids and other rare plants."

The Bishop gesticulated extravagantly, the loose sleeves of his cassock slipping back to reveal surprisingly well-muscled forearms. "There are a hundred thousand hillsides for the orchids. But only one Cape Kathikas. Let me tell you of my vision..."

Cape Kathikas, it seemed, was an ideal spot not only for the indigenous and exceptionally scarce orchid *Ophrys cypria* Renz, but also for a twin-hotel resort complete with helipad, golf course, conference center, and marina. The local inhabitants of this westerly cape, after generations of isolation and impoverishment and fueled by stories of unimagined riches, were enthusiastic to the point of uprising that their small and fruitless plots of land should be transformed into approach roads, sand traps, water hazards, staff quarters, and the other accumulated clutter of a Costa del Kypros. And if the Church in the person of Theophilos who owned most of the land were also to benefit hugely, it seemed merely to bestow God's blessing upon their venture.

There was only one other obstacle, apart from the orchids. That was the fact that the Cape was a field firing range for the British military, designated as such under the Treaty of Establishment, which had given Cyprus its independence and where for twenty-one days a year the coastal rocks and its offshore environs were peppered with Milan and Swingfire antitank missiles. Bound to play merry hell with a high-rise hotel and marina.

"Do you really need a firing range?" Theophilos asked.

"As much as we need an army."

"Then we shall find you another area for your operations. There must be so many other parts of the island that might be suitable."

"Such as?"

"The British surely wouldn't stand in the way of us Cypriots developing our economy," the Bishop responded, ducking the direct question. "It would raise so many unpleasant memories."

"I thought the objections were being led by Cypriots themselves, the environmentalists. Those who value the area as a national park."

"A handful of the maudlin and the meddling who have small minds and no imagination. Lunchtime locusts who know wildlife only from what they eat. What about our poor villagers?"

"What about the orchids?"

"Our villagers demand equality with orchids!"

There was no answer to that. Martin offered a conciliatory smile and subsided.

❖ ❖ ❖

Booza-Pitt was gabbling. He did that when he was nervous, to fill in the spaces. He didn't like spaces in a conversation. As a boy they had tormented him, fleeting pauses in which his mother drew breath before continuing with her ceaseless tirade of complaint about her lot in life. So, as a means of defense, he had learned to launch himself into any conversation, talking across people and above people and about anything. He was an excellent talker, never at a loss for words. Trouble was, he'd never really learned to listen.

Urquhart had been alone at the great Cabinet Table when Geoffrey had entered the room. The Prime Minister said nothing but as Geoffrey walked to his chair on the opposite side of the table Urquhart's eyes followed him closely, almost as if he were still trying to make a judgment, uncertain, unsettled. And unsettling. So Geoffrey had started talking.

"I've had this idea, Francis. A new set of campaigning initiatives for the Party. Thought about it a lot. Build on the reshuffle, get us going through the rest of the year. I've talked it through with the Party Chairman—I think he's going to put it all in a paper for you. The main point is this…"

"Shut up, Geoffrey."

"I…" Geoffrey shut up, uncertain how to respond.

"The Chairman has already told me about his campaigning ideas, just before I fired him. I have to say you are an excellent peddler of other people's ideas."

"Francis, please, you must understand…"

"I understand all too well. I understand you. Perhaps it's because we are a little alike."

"Are you going to fire me after all?" Geoffrey's tone was subdued; he was trying hard not to beg.

"I've thought about it."

Booza-Pitt's face, depleted by misery, sank toward his chest.

"But I've decided to make you Home Secretary instead."

A curious gurgling noise emerged from the back of Booza-Pitt's throat. The prospect of being translated into one of the four most powerful posts in Government at the age of thirty-eight seemed to have snapped his control mechanisms.

"They'll say I'm grooming you for the leadership when I've gone. But I'm not. I'm putting you there to stop anyone else using the post to groom himself for the leadership. And to do a job. Using your talents at peddling other people's ideas. My ideas."

"Anything you say, Francis," Booza-Pitt managed to croak, throat cracked like the floor of an Arabian wadi.

"We shall soon be facing an election and I've decided to move the goal posts a little. A new Electoral Practices Act. A measure so generous and democratic it'll leave the Opposition breathless."

Booza-Pitt nodded enthusiastically, with no idea what his leader was talking about.

"I want to make it easier for minority candidates to stand. To allow for"—Urquhart dropped his voice a semitone, as though making a speech—"a fuller and more balanced representation of the views of the general public. To ensure a Government more firmly rooted in the wishes of the people." He nodded in self-approval. "*Yes*, I like that."

"But what does it mean?"

"It means that any candidates who get more than two thousand votes will have all their election expenses paid by the State."

The face of the new Home Secretary had suddenly turned incredulous. "You're winding me up, Francis. With that on offer every nutter and whiner in the land is going to stand."

"Precisely."

"But..."

"But who else would these minorities and malcontents vote for, if not for themselves?"

"Not for us, not even if you lobotomized every single one of them."

"Well done, Geoffrey. They'd vote for the Opposition. So by encouraging them to stand we'll suck away several thousand votes from the Opposition in practically every constituency. Worth at least fifty seats overall, I reckon."

"You, you…"

"You're allowed to call me a deviously scheming bastard, if you want. I'd regard it as a compliment." For the first time in their interview, Urquhart's features had cracked and he was smiling.

"You are a devious, scheming, brilliant bastard, Francis Urquhart."

"And a great champion of democracy. They will have to say that, all the newspapers, even the Opposition."

"The updated version of divide and rule."

"Exactly. We ran an empire on that principle. Should be good enough for one little country. Don't you think, Home Secretary?"

A spotlight had been thrown on the box and Theophilos held his arms up high to acknowledge the attentions of the halftime crowd, his robes cascading like dark wings. A great raven, Martin thought, and with similar appetites.

"So may I expect your cooperation and support, Mr. Martin?" the cleric continued, casting the question over his shoulder as he offered the sign of the cross in blessing. "This is a rare opportunity."

"So are the orchids."

For a moment the Bishop's arms seemed to freeze in impatience; Dimitri had begun to develop a distinctive lopsided scowl as the conversation turned in circles. He was examining his broad and heavily callused knuckles as though the answer to every problem could somehow be found in the crevices.

"I don't wish to appear unsympathetic," the Englishman

continued, glad that his pedigree as a Diplomatic Service Grade 4 enabled him to control most of his outward appearances, particularly those that might convey any measure of disagreement or displeasure. It was not the task of the Foreign & Commonwealth Office to be seen saying no. "Your problem is not with the British, it's with your own Government. And with the environmentalists."

"But this is ridiculous." The Bishop's voice grew sibilant with exasperation. "When I approach our stubborn donkey of a President he claims the problem lies with you British. And the environmentalists. The British military climbs into bed with the goddamn greens while our poor peasants starve." He swung around suddenly, like an unwanted visitor of the night appearing at a bedroom window. The blue enamel adorning his heavy crucifix gleamed darkly in the light; his eyes, too. "Do not underestimate how important this is to me, Mr. Martin."

"My regrets. The British Government cannot become involved in a domestic dispute in Cyprus."

"But you are involved!" Theophilos slumped angrily into his seat as the second half commenced. "You have two military bases on our island, you have access rights across it, and you fire your missiles and bullets upon it. The only time you choose not to become involved is when we most need you. Like when the Turks invaded."

Conversation ceased as the Bishop struggled to regain his humor and the young women served more wine. Martin declined; he made a mental note never to drink again while in the presence of Theophilos, a man whose attentions required all of one's wits in response. When the Cypriot spoke again, his voice was composed, but seemed to contain no less passion.

"Many Cypriots find it unacceptable that you British should continue to have a military presence on our soil."

"The two bases are sovereign British soil, not Cypriot. That was clearly agreed in the Treaty of Establishment."

"The soil is Cypriot, the blood spilled upon it for centimes has been Cypriot, and the treaty is unjust and unequal, forced upon us by British colonial masters in exchange for our independence. I advise you, Mr. Martin, not to base your arguments upon that treaty, for ordinary Cypriots will neither understand nor approve. Encourage them to think about such matters and they will demand it all back. You might end up having no firing range, no bases, nothing."

The warning had been delivered in the manner of a wearied professor lecturing a dullard, the tone implying no room for argument, brooking no response. There seemed nothing more to discuss, a silence hanging uncomfortably between them until their mutual discomfort was thrust aside by a shout of jubilation from all around. Evriviades had scored.

"You've just lost a Mercedes."

"And you, Mr. Martin, might just have lost the friendship of the Cypriot people."

"Who's there?"

"A friend."

"There are few friends about on days like these."

"Count me as one."

The door of the back room in L'Amico's restaurant, tucked away behind Smith Square, slid open to reveal the large figure of Harry Mendip. He'd heard Annita Burke and Saul Wilkinson were lunching privately, sharing sorrows and anger at having been sacked, unwilling to face the whispers and stares of a more public place. Mendip knew how they felt; he'd been one of the victims last time around.

"Will you eat with us, Harry?"

"My appetite's not for food."

"Then what?"

"Action."

"Revenge?"

"Some might call it so."

A third glass of wine was poured, another bottle ordered.

"Everything is Urquhart. Damn him."

"Little Caesar."

"He acts like a Prince, not a Prime Minister."

"And we bow and bend the knee as his subjects."

"Abjects."

"Yet what, apart from ruthlessness, has set him so high?"

"And what, apart from ruthlessness, will bring him down?"

They paused as the waiter collected a few scattered dishes.

"He's grown so lofty that his feet scarcely touch the ground."

"But when they do, the ground is soaked with blood. Slippery soil. He is vulnerable."

"Butchered too many, over the years."

Annita Burke refilled the glasses. "Are we of the same mind?"

The other two nodded.

"Then who is to lead this enterprise?"

"How about Yorke? He's fit for stratagems and treasons."

"A happy blend of mischief."

"But there's no harmony in his soul. Nothing to lift the hearts and sights of others."

"Then Penthorpe."

"With those fearsome ferret eyes that make a man think he's volunteering for the gallows? I think not."

"You, Annita."

She shook her head. "No, this one is not for me. Harsh words in a woman are always dismissed as hormones at war. And in my case no one would forget they are Jewish hormones. Anyway, I lack that sharpness of foot and wit necessary to lead the dance."

"Then there is only one."

They all knew the name.

"Makepeace."

"He will be hard to convince."

"All the better once he is so."

"To challenge for the leadership?"

"What is the point? Urquhart has filled the party machine with placemen whose spirits are dead and who've sold their souls."

"Then if we cannot take Urquhart away from the party, we must take the party away from him."

"Meaning?"

"A new leader, and a new party."

Mendip sucked in his breath. "That is a dangerous enterprise," he said slowly.

"An honorable one, too. At least, Makepeace would make it seem so."

"And I'd rather be torn apart as a dog of war than stay to be slaughtered like a sheep."

Burke raised her glass. "A toast. Let's be masters of our own fate."

"All the way to the door of hell."

As Booza-Pitt stumbled out of the Cabinet Room in a haze of elation he all but bounced off the portly figure of Bollingbroke, who was admiring the white marble bust of William Pitt that nestled in a niche on the wall.

"He had it right, don't you think?" Bollingbroke inquired, eyes raised in admiration. The homespun accent stretched vowels as though he were chewing a mouthful of black treacle toffee.

Booza-Pitt tried to adjust his profile to match that of the eighteenth-century Prime Minister, wondering what on earth the other was prattling about.

"Prime Minister at the time of Trafalgar, you know. When we blew apart Napoleon's fleet. Heard some crap that he was a relative of yours. Stuff 'n' nonsense. Not true, is it?"

Faced with such a direct challenge, Booza-Pitt was loath to

lie. He shrugged his shoulders inconclusively. Damn the man, he was gibbering when all Geoffrey wanted to do was to flaunt his new eminence and be gone, leaving the other splashing and waterlogged in the wake.

"What were his words, Geoff, can you remember?"

He shook his head, lost in the labyrinth of the Bollingbroke mind. He suspected it was some test of his family credentials.

"'England has saved herself by her exertions, and Europe by her example.' That's what he said, did Pitt. Heck, not a bad motto for today, neither. You know, Froggies never change. I'll have to remember that. Now I'm Foreign Secretary."

He poured the news deftly into Booza-Pitt's lap where it landed much like a bucketful of pond life.

"You—are Foreign Secretary?" Booza-Pitt squeaked. "Arthur, I'm so delighted for you. You must come and split a bottle of Bollinger with me."

"Can't stand the stuff. Best bitter man, meself."

Booza-Pitt began to gain the impression that he was being wound up. "I've been given the Home Office," he responded weakly, deflated by the prospect of being forced to share the day's headlines with Bollingbroke.

"Yes, I know," the Foreign Secretary responded, practicing one of those looks with which he would convey to the French the full depth of his disdain without uttering a single undiplomatic word. "I'm off. Got to go and sort out all those bloody Bonapartists." He turned away brusquely. "Hello, pet," he greeted an approaching figure cheerfully, and was gone.

Claire appeared, or might have been there all the time, Geoffrey was not sure which.

"Congratulations, Home Secretary."

God, had everyone heard about his promotion before him?

"But a word of advice," she continued. "The tie."

"You like it?" he said, running his finger down the vibrant silk motif. "Australian. An aboriginal fertility symbol, I'm told."

"It's a little too"—she sought the appropriate term—"courageous."

"What's wrong with my tie?" he demanded defensively.

"Remember, Geoffrey, the job of Home Secretary is to share miseries and explain away disappointment. Why policemen are towing away shoppers' cars instead of cutting off football hooligans' goolies, that sort of thing. You're not supposed to look as if you're enjoying it." She smiled mischievously and headed for the Cabinet Room door.

Hell, would no one allow him to relish the moment? "That's not all a Home Secretary might do," he countered. "Francis and I have got plans." His tone suggested a conspiracy of friendship and great secrets, an alliance which no one dare mock. And it had stopped her in her tracks, he was pleased to note.

She turned to face him. "If you're going to screw the electorate, for pity's sake don't wear a tie advertising the fact." Then she was gone, entering through the Prime Minister's door without knocking.

COURT OF ARBITRATION

For the Delimitation of Maritime Areas between the Republic of Cyprus and the Provisional Republic of Northern Cyprus.

DECISION

PRESIDENT: Mr. Clive Watling. MEMBERS OF THE COURT: Mr. Andreas Rospovitch, Mr. Michel Rodin, Mr. Shukri Osman, Mr. Farrokh Abdul-Ghanem…

The Court, composed as above, makes the following decision…that while Greek Cypriot fishermen have traditionally fished in these waters, and the two sides have agreed to quotas enabling those Greek Cypriot fishermen currently engaged in fishing these waters to continue so as to ensure that their livelihoods may be protected, such traditions of access and the other "special circumstances" raised by the Greek Cypriot side cannot override the geographical features that lie at the heart of the delimitation process…

Moreover, notwithstanding the fact that independent seismic surveys have indicated little potential exploitable mineral resources on the continental shelf, there is in any event no reason to consider such mineral resources as having any bearing on the delimitation…

In the view of the Court there are no grounds for contending that the extent of the maritime rights of either side should be determined by matters of equity as they relate to the past history of the island. The legality of the Turkish invasion of 1974 is not a matter for consideration by this tribunal, which recognizes the long-standing de facto jurisdiction of the Turkish Cypriot authorities in the northern portion of the island…

Both Parties, in rebutting their opponent's claims, tend to contradict the very principles they have invoked in support of their respective positions. The Court must assure itself that the solution reached is both reasonable and equitable, and to that end, bearing in mind the legally binding assurances provided to Greek Cypriot fishing interests by the Turkish Cypriot authorities…

For these reasons:

THE COURT OF ARBITRATION: by three votes to two, being in favor President Watling and Judges Osman and

Abdul-Ghanem, and against Judges Rospovitch and Rodin, draws the following line of delimitation…

With a final check of the wording, Watling signed the definitive document. It pleased him more than he could describe. A historic agreement that would help cement both peace in a troubled corner of the world and his place among textbooks and precedents that would be passed down to future generations of international jurists. There was also the peerage. His mother could enjoy toasted tea cakes on the terrace any time she wanted now, while he would never more want for invitations to California, anywhere for that matter, including test matches. They'd be proud of him, back in Cold Kirby-by-the-edge-of-the-Moors. The Judgment of Watling Water. A fine judgment—a fair one, too, which couldn't always be said about such matters. Now it was done and whether they discovered oil, antiques, or the bones of the Minotaur didn't matter a damn—and should never have mattered. This was a judgment of law, not a poker game with drilling licenses.

Justice. British justice. And if it entailed screwing the French into the bargain, then the bargain was all the better for it. Rodin could rot in hell.

NINETEEN

The fundamental skill of diplomacy is all about give and take. And take. And take. And take...

It had developed into a silent tussle of wills. The BBC cameraman kept adjusting the angle repeatedly in order to gain an uncluttered view of the Prime Minister and his announcement in front of Number Ten—it was, after all, Urquhart's moment—but the new Foreign Secretary was intent on basking in the sunshine of television lights and the reflected plaudits. With the persistence of an outbreak of measles the rotund outline of Bollingbroke kept insinuating itself into the picture until he was standing to attention, suit buttons straining, immediately behind the Prime Minister's right shoulder. Urquhart's Praetorian Guard.

One of the private secretaries had suggested that perhaps the statement should have been made to Parliament rather than to the media, but Grist—good Grist, whose instincts were so sound—had captured Urquhart's mood. On the doorstep of Downing Street there was no Leader of the Opposition to throw up supercilious questions and comment, no former-and-recently-fired Minister to claim part of the credit, nothing to prevent Urquhart from occupying the top slot on the lunchtime news all by himself. Except for Bollingbroke. Maybe next time they would truss him to a chair.

Thus had a grateful nation been given the opportunity to witness FU expressing his delight at turning closed minds into the open hands of friendship, accepting the accolade of Statesman. Formally inviting the leaders of both Cypriot republics to fly to London in eight weeks' time for the signing of the final and definitive peace accord—and thus providing him with another glorious media binge and guaranteed victory in an arena where no other British politician could even enter.

Francis Urquhart. Man of Peace.

In a small floral-patterned room on the top floor of 10 Downing Street, at the eastern end of the living quarters that are so small, so unbefitting the head of a major Western government, and so very English in their understatement, Mortima Urquhart sat at the Regency desk that had once been her grandmother's. She pushed aside the letters she had been answering and with a small key unlocked the drawer, taking from it her private address book. There was a slight tremble to her fingers, the sense of anticipation she had known when riding to hounds as they were about to down a great stag. An inward struggle between excitement, fear, and—conscience? The hand reached out, no longer for crop or reins but the telephone, the one she'd installed many years before when they had first moved in. The telephone that did not go through the switchboard. Her phone, for her purposes. The quarry had been cornered, there was good news she wished to share. But not with too many people.

"I regret, Mr. President, that the air-conditioning plant has broken down again."

A knot of anxieties had tangled around the aide who was

soaked in sweat from his recent spittle-scattered brawl with the engineering supervisor. It had been to no effect, the temperature was still rising rapidly into the eighties. The two fans he had placed in the corners of the room seemed to have negligible impact on the heavy Nicosia air, which smelled and tasted as though it had been breathed many times before.

Nures, a man of passion and varied temper, seemed to bear no trace of ill will. He had removed jacket and tie, sipped sweet mint tea and was mopping his receding brow with a large red handkerchief. He was also poring over a map, and exulting.

"Soon we shall have new air conditioning—all of us. And new roads. Schools. Homes. A new airport, even. No longer to be outcasts." His dark eyes shimmered with hope. "A fresh start."

"We have much to be grateful for," the aide offered damply, trying to push along the unexpected tide of good humor.

"And good friends," Nures responded, "to whom we owe more than gratitude."

Theophilos wrenched the towel from around his neck and with an impatient wave of his hand dismissed the barber.

"What's your problem?" Dimitri badgered as the door closed. He was seated at the monitor on the Bishop's ornate mahogany desk, his thick fingers tapping out instructions on the keyboard. The screen sprang to life. "Market's up, it likes all this talk of peace. And Swiss interest rates rose the other day. It's been a good week for us."

"Political capital, that's what we must watch, little brother," Theophilos replied, scratching the roots of his newly trimmed beard. "If we are to rid ourselves of this fool of a President we need a taste of chaos. Peace at his hand is about as welcome as an outbreak of cholera." He glanced at his watch. A television interview in ten minutes. He exchanged the Rolex for a plain leather band and climbed back into the dark bishop's cassock, hanging around his neck the heavy crucifix, once more the simple man of God.

"So what are we to do?"

"Pray. To God in Heaven and any other gods you can find in the back of your closet. Get down on your knees. Humble yourself. And beg that the Turks will be caught trying to fuck us up once more."

The telephone warbled. From the rear seat of the Citroën limousine on the congested streets of Paris, the businessman stretched to answer it, listening carefully. He said nothing, his attention focused absolutely on the message and its consequences, which were clear. The quarter of a million dollars he'd already handed to—what was the name of that Turkish quisling? He'd already forgotten—had been thrown away, the gamble had been lost. And it hurt. Even in the oil business, a quarter of a million unreceipted dollars makes a heavy hole in the petty cash account. Yet that was the least of the pain, for it seemed certain that he was about to lose more, far more. Thousands of millions of dollars' worth of lost opportunity. Oil by the seaful. It seemed he would never get to drill his wells.

He replaced the receiver without a word, hearing it latch gently into place. The darkened glass and heavy noise insulation of the limousine cocooned him from the chaos on the street beyond. This was a sheltered world, a world of privilege and security, protected from the outside. Except for the phone. And the messages it brought.

He was a controlled man, emotionally desiccated, with his appetites reserved for only one thing. Oil. The Earth's milk. More precious to him than his own blood. With a rage as silent as the engine at idle and his fist balled like a mallet, he began pounding the leather armrest, heedless of the pain, until it broke.

❖ ❖ ❖

She rolled to one side and, as the sheet slipped across the contours of her body, he felt himself shaking inside once more. Until he had met Maria he hadn't been sure quite where his loins were, now they seemed to be everywhere, vibrating with an extraordinary energy every time he undid a button or clasp. In Maria he had found an ideal partner, a woman of natural curiosity and wit who was not afraid to acknowledge the shortcomings of her experience and was anxious to overcome them. They were explorers, trekking together through new territories and relishing the joys of discovery.

He was surprised he felt no guilt, for he knew now that his marriage was over. It was form with no substance, his wife the absentee landlord of his loyalties, his house no longer a home, and it was not enough. He had tried many things to fill the void in his life—ambition, esteem, endeavor, achievement—but nothing would work while he was alone. The presence of Maria Passolides in his world—and in his bed—had made him realize that.

As she propped herself up on the pillow, he watched transfixed as a bead of sweat trickled its way from around her neck past the creases of olive skin between her breasts. "What are you thinking, white man?" she asked, amused.

With the point of his little finger he traced the passage of the droplet, which had made a sudden rush for her navel. "I'm thinking about what I can do for you."

Her eyes closed as his finger slid slowly past her belly button, her breath quickening. "Christ, what did you have for breakfast?" she panted. The blood was beginning to rush once more, her body desperate to make up for so much lost time.

Reluctantly his finger sidetracked, diverted to the outside of the thigh and then was gone. "Not this," he muttered. "You came to me for help. About the graves."

"Sure," she said, "but why the sudden hurry?" She sought

his hand but he rolled back to give them both some breathing space.

"We have little time left," he continued. "If we don't get an answer during the next eight weeks, before the peace agreement is signed, it will never happen. After that no one will be interested, not in this country. Something else will be in the news. They'll say they've done their job, wash their hands. Cyprus will go back to being a faraway island where it might be nice one day to take a holiday in search of young wine and old ruins. Nothing more. It must be now, or we'll never find the answer."

"So what do we do?"

"We make a fuss. Put on some pressure. Try to stir up a few old memories."

Instinctively, as she thought about his words, she pulled the sheet up to her neck. Over the last few days she'd tended to forget the reason why she had originally sought his help, distracted by the discovery of how versatile his help could be. They had made love in his kitchen chair that first time and in her exuberance she had torn off the arms. After they had finished laughing she had volunteered to take it back to Habitat, but then she changed her mind, deciding she would never be able to keep a straight face when inevitably they asked how it had happened. Somehow she felt sure everyone would guess simply by the way she smiled. So they'd pushed the pieces into the corner and tried the other kitchen chair, and the Chesterfield in his study where her damp skin stuck to the leather and made a ripping sound as it peeled off. He'd only invited her to bed—his wife's bed—when it seemed there was something more than sweating flesh behind his willingness to see her. He'd not offered help in exchange for sex any more than she had offered sex for his help, but their separate motives were becoming more intertwined and confusing, so much so that she'd had to be reminded of her original purpose in knocking on his door. She felt a pang of guilt, but orgasms could be so distracting. And such fun.

"If only I'd met you while I was still Foreign Secretary this might have been so much easier," he said wistfully. "I could've unlocked some doors from the inside rather than having to kick them down from out in the street."

"But then you would be deceiving me officially instead of personally."

"What do you mean deceiving you personally?" He sounded affronted.

"That cup of tea you offered me the first day we met and you invited me into your kitchen? I still haven't had it." She leaned over and kissed him before rolling out of bed.

"Now get up, Makepeace. There's work to be done."

Evanghelos Passolides sat alone in his darkened restaurant. The last diner had long gone and he'd made a perfunctory effort at cleaning up, but had been overcome with melancholy. He felt deserted by everything he loved. He hadn't seen Maria for days. And his own Government in Nicosia was about to give away a large chunk of his beloved homeland to the Turk. Was this what he had fought for, what George and Eurypides had died for?

He sat among all the memorabilia, drunk, an empty bottle of Commanderia at his elbow. A glass was lying on its side, the tablecloth stained red with droplets of what many years before might have been blood. He sobbed. In one hand he held a crumpled photograph of his brothers, two tousle-haired boys, smiling. In the other he held a much burnished Webley, the pistol that had been taken from the body of a British lieutenant and with which he had always promised to exact his revenge. Before he had become a cripple.

Now it was all too late. He had failed in everything he had

touched. Others were heroes while life had stripped him of honor and all self-respect. He sat alone, forgotten, an old man with tears coursing down his cheeks, remembering. Waving a pistol. And hating.

TWENTY

Leadership is about change. Breaking things. Breaking people. Their hearts, their backs, and, when necessary, their lives.

A man's place in history is no more than that—one place, a single point in an infinite universe, a jewel that no matter how brightly it may be polished will eventually be lost among a treasury of riches. A grain of sand in the hourglass.

For Urquhart, this was a hallowed scene: the shiny leather bench scuffed by the digging of anxious nails, the Dispatch Box of bronze and old buriri polished by the passing of a thousand damp palms, the embellished rafters and stanchions that, if one listened carefully and with a tuned ear, still echoed with the cries of great leaders as they were hacked and harried to eclipse. Every political career, it seemed, ended in failure; the verdict of this great Gothic court of judgment never varied. Guilty. Condemned. A place of exhortation, passing approbation, and eventual execution. Only the names changed.

In recent days, whenever he turned away from the lights, there were voices in the shadows that whispered it would one day be his turn to fall, a matter only of time. As he sat on the bench they were at it again, the whispers, growing assertive, impertinent, almost heckling him. And through them all he could hear the voice of Thomas Makepeace.

"Is my Right Honorable Friend aware"—the constitutional fiction of friendship passed through Makepeace's lips like vinegar—"that the Greek Cypriot community in this country is deeply concerned about the existence of graves that still remain hidden from the time of the war of liberation in the nineteen fifties...?"

Old memories like embers began to revive, to flicker and burn until the crackle of flames all but obliterated the words with which Makepeace was demanding that the British Government lay open its files, reveal all unreported deaths and burial sites, so that the tragedies of many years ago could finally be laid to rest?

For a moment or two the House observed the unusual sight of the Prime Minister sitting stiffly in his seat, seeming unmoved and unmoving, lost in another world before cries of impatience caused him to stir. He rose stiffly to his feet, as though age had glued his joints.

"I am not aware," he began with an uncharacteristic lack of assertiveness, "of there being any suggestion that graves were hidden by the British..."

Makepeace was protesting, waving a sheet of paper, shouting that it had come from the Public Record Office.

Other voices joined in. Inside his head he heard contradiction and confusion, talk of graves, of secrets that would inevitably be disinterred with the bones, of things that must remain forever buried.

Then a new voice, more familiar. "Fight!" it commanded. "Don't let them see you vulnerable. Lie, shout, wriggle, abuse, rabbit punch on the blind side, do anything—so long as you fight!" And pray, the voice might have added. Francis Urquhart didn't know how to pray, but like hell he knew how to fight.

"I believe there are great dangers in opening too many old cupboards, sniffing air that has grown foul and unhealthy," he began. "Surely we should look to the future, with its high hopes, not dwell upon the distant past. Whatever happened during that ancient and tragic war, let it remain buried, and with it any evils that were done, perhaps on all sides. Leave us with the unsullied friendship that has been built since."

Makepeace was trying to regain his feet, protesting once more, the single sheet of paper in his hand. Urquhart silenced him with the most remorseless of smiles.

"Of course, if the Right Honorable Gentleman has anything specific in mind rather than suggesting some stampede through old archives, I shall look into the matter for him. All he has to do is write with the details."

Makepeace subsided and with considerable gratitude Urquhart heard the Speaker call for the next business. His head rang with the chaos of voices, shouts, explosions, the ricochet of bullets; he could see nothing, blinded by the memory of the Mediterranean sun reflecting off ancient rock as his nostrils flared and filled with the sweet tang of burning flesh.

Francis Urquhart felt suddenly very old. The hourglass of history had turned.

"Go for it, Franco," the producer encouraged. He sat up in his chair and dunked his cigarette in the stale coffee. This could be fun.

Behind a redundant church that had found a new lease of life as a carpet warehouse in a monotonous suburb of north London lies the headquarters of London Radio for Cyprus, "the voice of Cypriots in the city," as it liked to sign itself, ignoring the fact that the four miles separating it from the City of London stretched like desert before the oasis. Describing the basement of Number 18 Bush Way as a headquarters was scarcely more enlightening—LRC shared a peeling Edwardian terrace house with a legitimate travel agency and dubious accounting practice. It also shared initials with a company manufacturing condoms and an FM wavelength with a Rasta rock station that fractured ears and heads until well after midnight. Such are the circumstances of community radio, not usually the cradle for budding radio magnates and media inquisitors. LRC's producers and interviewers struggled hard to convey to their small but loyal audience an air of enthusiasm even while they did daily battle with second- and thirdhand equipment, drank old coffee, and tried hard to remember to turn on the answering machine when they left.

Yet this item had legs. The girl was good, somewhere behind those lips and ivories was a brain, and the old man was a fragment of radiophonic magic, his voice ascending scales of emotion like an opera singer practicing arias. Passion gave him an eloquence that more than made up for the thick accent; what was more, in its own way the story was an exclusive.

"Remember, you're hearing this first on LRC. Proof that there are graves left over from the EOKA war, which are buried deep within the bowels of British bureaucracy..."

The producer winced. Franco was an arsehole from which a stream of incontinence poured forth every Monday and Wednesday afternoon, but he was cheap and his uncle, a wine importer, was one of the station's most substantial sponsors.

"So what do you want?" Franco asked the pair.

"We want as many people as possible to write in support of Thomas Makepeace and his campaign to have the full facts made public. We can prove the existence of two graves, those of my uncles. We want to know if there are any more."

"And you, Mr. Passolides?"

There was a pause, not empty and mindless but a silence of grief, long enough to capture the hearts of listeners as they imagined an old man rendered speechless by great personal tragedy. Even Maria reached over to touch his hand; he'd been behaving so oddly in recent days, morose, unshaven, digging away within himself, changes that were ever more apparent since she'd been spending more time away from him. When finally his voice emerged the words cracked like a hammer on ice.

"I want my brothers."

"Great, really great," Franco responded, shuffling his papers in search of the next cue.

"And I want something else. The *bastardos* who murdered them." The voice was rising through all the octaves of emotion. "This was not war but murder, of two innocent boys. Don't you see? That is why they had to burn my brothers' bodies. Why they could never admit it. And why this miserable British Government continues to cover it up. Wickedness! Which makes them as guilty as those men who pulled the trigger and poured the gas."

"Yeah, sure," Franco stumbled, scratching his stubble, unused to anything more heated than a weather report. "So I suppose we'd all better write to our MPs and give Mr. Makepeace a hand."

"And crucify the bastards like Francis Urquhart who are betraying our island, selling us out to those Turkish *poustides*..."

The producer was second generation, not familiar with all the colloquial Greek covering the various eccentricities of human anatomy, but the intonation was enough to cause him alarm, especially with license renewal coming up. Uttering a prayer that no one from the Radio Authority was listening, he made a lunge for the fade control. And missed. The cup of stale coffee tipped everywhere, over notes, cigarettes, his new jeans. Havoc. Evanghelos Passolides, after an armistice of almost fifty years, was back at war.

TWENTY-ONE

All opposition requires retaliation. I prefer to get my retaliation in first.

The French Ambassador had begun to feel a strong sense of kinship with General Custer. Since the elevation of Arthur Bollingbroke to the Foreign and Commonwealth Office, business had degenerated into bloody war, waged by the Frenchman against insuperable odds and a foe who had dispensed with diplomatic trimming in favor of wholesale scalping. Monsieur Jean-Luc de Carmoy had no illusions about the fact that the Court of St. James's had become distinctly hostile territory. The Ambassador preferred to pursue his campaign with strawberries and champagne rather than the .44 caliber Winchesters of the U.S. cavalry but, like the blond American general, he had made the deeply personal decision that if he were going to die he would do so surrounded by friends. They milled about him as he stood directing maneuvers from the lawn of his official residence overlooking Kensington Gardens.

"Enjoying the quiet life, Tom?"

Makepeace cast his eyes at the garden crowded with guests. "As much as you."

"Ah, but there are differences between our lives," de Carmoy sighed, lifting his eyes in search of the sun that shone over his beloved Loire. "I feel at times as though I have been sold into slavery, where every rebuke must be met with a smile and every insult with humility." He paused as a butler with hands resembling black widow spiders supplied them with full glasses before taking Makepeace by the arm and leading him toward the seclusion of a nearby lime arbor. There were obviously things to discuss.

"I envy you, Tom."

"The freedom of the wilderness. You envy that?"

"What would I not give at times to share with you the liberty to speak my mind."

"About what in particular?"

"Your Mr. Urquhart." His face had the expression of a leaking milk carton.

"Scarcely *my* Mr. Urquhart."

"Then whose, pray?"

Around them the branches of the pleached limes twisted and entangled like a conspiracy. They were both aware that the Ambassador had crossed beyond the frontiers of diplomatic etiquette but, caught in the crossfire between Bollingbroke and the Quai d'Orsay, de Carmoy was in no mood for standing still.

"Tom, we've been friends for a long time now, ever since the day you summoned me to the Foreign Office to administer a formal mutilation"—the Frenchman brushed some invisible piece of lint from the sleeve of his jacket—"after that confidential computer tape went missing from British Aerospace."

"Along with two French exchange technicians."

"Ah, you remember?"

"How could I forget? My first week at the Foreign Office."

"You were frightfully severe."

"I still suspect the clandestine hand of some official French agency behind the whole thing, Jean-Luc."

The shoulders of the Ambassador's well-cut suit heaved in a

shrug of mock Gallic confusion. "But when you'd finished you sat me down and plied me with drink. Sherry, you called it."

"Standard Foreign Office issue. For use only on open wounds and Africans."

"I think I tried to get Brussels to reclassify it as brush cleaner."

"Didn't stop you finishing the whole damned decanter."

"My friend, but I thought it was meant to be my punishment. I remember I was swaying like a wheat field in an east wind by the time I returned home. My wife consoled me, thinking you'd been so offensive I'd had to get drunk."

Like old campaigners they smiled and raised glasses to toast past times and dig over old battlefields. The Frenchman took out a cigarette case packed with Gauloises on one side and something more anodyne on the other; with a quiet curse Makepeace took the Gauloise. He'd started smoking again, along with all the other changes in his personal habits. God, he'd left her only an hour ago and knew that in spite of the aftershave he still reeked of her. Pleasure and pain. So much was crowding in on him that at times he had trouble finding space to breathe. Slowly the trickle of humor drained from his eyes and died.

"How is Miquelon?" he asked.

"Blossoming. And yours?"

"Teaching. In America." He gave his own impression of the Gallic shrug, but without the enthusiasm to make it convincing.

"You sound troubled. Let me ask…"

"As Ambassador? Or as an old friend?"

"About politics. I have no right to pry into personal matters." In any event, the Ambassador didn't have to. At the merest mention of his wife, Makepeace's face had said it all. He'd never make a diplomat, no inscrutability, all passion and principle. "I hear many expressions that the era of Francis Urquhart is drawing to its close, that it is only a matter of time. And much discussion of who, and how. Many people tell me it should be you."

"Which people?"

"Loyal Englishmen and women. Friends of yours. Many of the people here this afternoon."

Makepeace glanced around. Among the throng was a goodly smattering of political correspondents and editors, politicians and other opinion-formers, few of whom were renowned as Urquhart loyalists. From a distance and from behind a tall glass, Annita Burke was staring straight at them, not attempting to hide her interest.

"You've been getting pressure," de Carmoy stated, knowing it to be a fact.

"Nudges aplenty. I suppose I'm meant to be flattered by so much attention. Now's the moment, they say, step forward. But to be honest, I don't know whether I'm standing on the brink of history or the edge of a bloody cliff."

"They are your friends, they respect you. Virtue may be a rare commodity in politics; it may speak quietly at times, but no less persuasively for that. It sets you apart from others."

"Like Francis Urquhart."

"As a diplomat I couldn't possibly comment."

Makepeace was in too serious a mood to catch the irony. "I've thought about it, Jean-Luc. Thinking about it still, to be precise. But did any of these friends of mine suggest to you how their…ambitions for me might be achieved? Or are these no more than slurpings through mouthfuls of Moët?"

"My assessment is that this is not idle talk. There's a desperate sense of longing for a change at the top. I've heard that not just within your party but from across the political spectrum."

"And from Paris, too, no doubt."

"*Touché*. But you can't deny there's a great moral vacuum in British politics. You could fill it. Many people would follow."

Makepeace began running his index finger tentatively around the rim of his crystal glass as though he were tracing the cycles of life. "For that I need a vehicle, a party. I might be able to grab at the wheel, force Urquhart off the road, but it would probably do so much damage that it'd take years to get it working again. The party's scarcely likely to offer the keys to the man who caused the accident."

"Then create your own vehicle. One that's faster and better built than Urquhart's."

"No, that's impossible," Makepeace was responding, but they were interrupted by another guest, the Minister for Health who was seeking to bid farewell to his host. Felicitations and formal thanks were exchanged before the Minister turned to Makepeace.

"I've got only one thing to say to you, Tom." He paused, weighing both his words and the company. "For God's sake keep it up." With that he was gone.

"You see, you have more friends than you realize," the Ambassador encouraged.

"In his case not a friend, merely a rat hedging his bets."

"Perhaps. But they are edgy, waiting to jump. The rats, too, believe the ship is sinking."

Makepeace was back with the rim of his glass, which was vibrating vigorously. "So often we seem to go around in empty circles, Jean-Luc. What's necessary to make it more than noise, to get the whole universe to shatter?"

"Action."

The Ambassador reached for the finely cut crystal, taking it from his guest's hand and holding it aloft by the stem, turning it around until it had captured the rays of the afternoon sun and melted into a thousand pools of fire. Suddenly he appeared to fumble, his fingers parted and before Makepeace could shout or move to catch it the glass had tumbled to the lawn. It bounced gracefully and lay, undamaged, on the grass.

Makepeace bent his knee to retrieve it, stretching gratefully. "That's a stroke of..."

In alarm he snatched his fingers back as, with the heel of

his elegant handmade shoe, the Frenchman crushed the glass to pieces.

The helicopter swept low along the black sand coastline of Khrysokhou Bay in the northwest of the island, past the tiny fishing villages they had known as boys. Those days of youth had been long, summers when the octopus had been plentiful, the girls had eager eyes and much to learn, and sailing boats had bobbed in the gentle swell beside clapboard jetties. Not so long ago the road back through the mountain had been little more than a rutted track; it had since turned into a swirling tar highway that bore on its back thousands of tourists and all their clutter. The fishing villages now throbbed to the beat of late-night discos, the price of fish had soared, so had the price of a smile. Progress. Yet the sailing boats were still moored inside ramshackle harbors, which collected more flotsam than jetfoils. Opportunities unfulfilled, yet Theophilos's marina on the nearby cape would change all that. Once he'd got the British off his back.

The helicopter banked. "Bishop's Palace in five minutes," the pilot's metallic voice informed them through the headphones. Dimitri reached for the hand grip; he hated flying, regarding it as an offense to God's law, and would only submit to such folly so long as God's personal messenger were by his side. Trouble was that his brother traveled everywhere by helicopter, often flying the machine himself, which served only to exaggerate Dimitri's congenitally twitchy disposition. He'd give his life for his brother but prayed it wouldn't be necessary at this precise moment. He sat upright in his seat, relieved that the noise of the engine precluded conversation.

Theophilos, by contrast, displayed an exceptional degree of animation. He'd been studying a newspaper, repeatedly stabbing his finger at it and thrusting it in Dimitri's face. Dimitri was sure this was done deliberately in the knowledge that any activity other than rigid concentration on the horizon would induce in him an immediate and humiliating attack of sickness. In many ways they were still kids back on the rocks by the beach, playing, planning new and greater adventures, testing each other's courage, bending the rules. Dimitri recalled the first day his brother had returned to the family house as a priest, clad in his robes, clutching his crucifix and bible, a dark apparition in the doorway surrounded by all the panoply of holy office. Dimitri, overawed and uncertain, had fallen immediately to his knees, head bowed in expectation of a blessing; instead Theophilos had raised a leg, placed his boot squarely upon his brother's shoulder, and sent him spiraling backward to the ground. That night they'd got bladder-bursting drunk on homemade wine, just like old times. Nothing had changed. Theophilos was always the bright and ambitious brother, honed by a year at Harvard's Business School, who would lead the family Firm. Dimitri was a man of linear mind, reconciled to following. Even in helicopters.

They had landed on the helipad behind the palace and Dimitri, having cheated death once more, came back to the world of the moment. His brother was still absorbed in the newspaper, *The People's Voice*, a leading Cypriot newspaper in London. This in itself was not unusual since the Firm had well-watered business contacts among the expatriate community and Theophilos took considerable care to ensure that his press coverage was high in both profile and praise, but this item was not about him. It appeared to be an extensive report concerning missing graves, many column inches, which the Bishop kept caressing with the tips of his fingers, yet his words were inaudible, sent spinning away in the wash from the rotors. As they clambered from the cabin instinctively they ducked low, Dimitri wanting to kiss the ground in relief while the Bishop struggled to secure the flowing *kalimachi* headpiece. He continued to cling to the newspaper.

"What? What did you say?" Dimitri roared in his brother's ear as the noise behind them began to subside.

Theophilos stood to his full height, his holy garb adding further inches and authority. He was smiling broadly, the gold cap of his tooth much in evidence.

"I said, little brother, that you should brace yourself. We're about to catch a bad dose of bone fever."

TWENTY-TWO

Westminster is the type of place that on occasion makes Chernobyl attractive as a holiday destination.

The nudges aplenty applied to Makepeace and about which he had complained to de Carmoy had grown to outright body blows. Telephone calls, snatches of passing conversation, journalists asking The Really Serious Question, all seemed to conspire to push him in a direction he was reluctant to take.

But why the reluctance? Not for lack of ambition, nor fear of the probable suicidal consequences of taking on the Urquhart machine. Surrounded by more self-professed friends than ever before, nevertheless he felt more isolated than at any time he could remember, almost adrift. He'd been shorn of his Ministerial support machine for the first time in a decade—its secretaries, advisers, tea makers, ten thousand pairs of hands, and most of all the daily decisions that made him feel so much part of a team. Even for a man so long in political life he had been mortified to discover that for all the new supporters he appeared to have gained, others he had counted as friends now turned the other way, found things with which to busy themselves whenever he appeared. Friendship within a divided party may be Honorable by the compulsion of parliamentary etiquette, but it is far from Reliable.

Then there was his marriage. It was empty and hollow but it had had form, a regularity that was comforting even if for so many months of the year it amounted to no more than a phone call a week. He hadn't called for more than two, and she hadn't inquired why.

Exhilarating as he found such freedoms, they were also confusing and, when he was left alone to brood, almost frightening, like a climber reaching across a crevasse for his first mountain top. And behind him they kept pushing, pushing, pushing, Annita Burke in particular. She was sitting beside him in the rear of the car, Quentin Digby the lobbyist in front. Digby was going on about how the media adore fresh faces and a new story, and this would be the biggest and newest for years. Annita, her black eyes witchlike in the glow of the dashboard, sat stirring. "The logic is overwhelming," she was saying. "The support is there. For you. I've talked to a posse of people in recent days. They'd follow you all the way, given half a chance."

"The chance of anonymity, you mean," Makepeace responded acerbically. "Any support short of actual help for fear FU might find out what they're up to."

"No, not a clandestine coup, no attempt to take over the sweetshop by stealth. It probably wouldn't work and it's not your way."

"Then what?"

"A rival sweetshop. A new party."

God, this had all the echoes of his conversation with Jean-Luc. He remembered Annita's display of interest at the garden party and began to wonder whether she had put de Carmoy up to it. She was a cynic and natural conspirator, perhaps too much so; how many of the other nudgers, winkers, and pushers had she organized, cajoled, perhaps persuaded to imply support just to get her off their backs?

"You'd dominate the headlines for weeks. Build a momentum," Digby was encouraging. "After all these years of Urquhart people want a change. So give it 'em."

"I've twelve former Cabinet Ministers telling me they would back you, and even one present member of the Cabinet," Annita continued.

So she *was* organizing. "Who?"

"Cresswell."

"Ah, the soft white underbelly. A man whose only fixed opinions seem to center on puddings and port."

"But worth a week of headlines."

"Publicly?" Makepeace demanded. "He'd come out and say so publicly?"

"Timing is everything." Digby was at it again, leaving the question unresolved. "Once the first few are out of the trap, others will follow. Momentum is everything. It's catching, like mumps."

"Safety in numbers," Makepeace muttered, almost to himself. "It makes that first step so vital."

"Timing *is* everything," Burke echoed, delighted that Makepeace's observations appeared to be focusing on the definitive and practical. His mind was on the move, three parts there, just one last push…"You can go all the way, Tom, if we retain the initiative. We must start organizing now, but for God's sake don't reveal your hand too soon, until everything is ready. The trouble with you is that once you make your mind up about something you're too impatient, too emotional. Too honest, if you like. It's your biggest fault."

True enough. Exactly what Claire had told him. He could handle himself, but there were other problems. "To fight and win an election we need a machine, grass roots in the constituencies, not just a debating society in Westminster," Makepeace reflected.

"That's why we need time."

"And timing."

The car had stopped outside Vangelis, where he had invited them to eat. And, it seemed, to plot. It sparked a memory of something Maria had said at their first meeting by the milk bottles. About a ready-made headquarters in every high street and overnight an army at his side.

The ghost of a smile hung on his lips. The various strands of his life seemed to be drawing together, or at least entangling themselves. Urquhart. Ambition. Maria. Passion. All pushing him in the same direction. Suddenly there seemed to be no point any longer in reluctance or resistance, he'd better lie back and enjoy it. And as Maria had said only the previous night, his timing was usually immaculate.

They disembarked from the car. "I guess about eleven o'clock, Mickey," he told his driver. "Not earlier, I'm afraid. I've a feeling this dinner is going to be a long one."

Mickey tipped his cap. This new job was proving to be most stimulating. The pay was better than sitting around the corporate car pool; Makepeace was a kind and considerate passenger. And the gossip was a hell of a lot more entertaining than listening to businessmen wittering on about ungrateful clients and their wives' muscle-minded tennis coaches.

Others were being pushed and jostled. Hugh Martin was in his forties, once fleet of foot and a former rugger wing-forward who was more than accustomed to the elbows and abuse of a line-out. He hadn't expected to find the same tactics used outside the Nicosia Cyprus Folk Art Museum. The museum, which lay among the labyrinths behind the city's ancient fortified walls, was promoting its most recent exhibition, and invitations had been issued to the city's erudite and elevated, the British High Commissioner among them. He had counted on a pleasant stroll around the stands with Mrs. Martin, greeting old friends and making some new, perhaps even finding something to inspire his wife, who had started a small collection of ceramics. Instead he found a group of almost twenty people gathered outside the hall distributing leaflets. He had no chance to discover what the leaflets said because as soon as they saw his official Rover draw up the group turned its full attention and considerable volume in his direction.

His bodyguard, Drage, was out of the front seat first. "I'll check it, sir."

But Martin was both curious and amused. If the capital's demonstrations were anything like its plumbing, the noise would far exceed the efficiency. Anyway, this was Nicosia, courteous, civil, archetypically Cypriot, not Tehran or bloody Damascus. So he followed. It was a move he would soon regret.

"British murderers," one old crone hissed through purple gums, propelled to the fore by younger hands behind her. A banner appeared, something about graves and war crimes, and as the protesters gathered around someone behind her shoulder spat. It missed, but the swinging fist didn't. It came from too far back to inflict any real damage but the surprise caused him to gasp. Drage was at his side now, pushing and shouting for him to retreat to the car, but in turn they were being pushed back by far greater numbers and the High Commissioner, still disorientated and clutching his stomach, stumbled. Drage caught him, lifted him up and tried to move him toward the car. Martin thought the blow must have done him more harm than he had realized for he was seeing lights; to his dismay he discovered they were the lights not of mild concussion but of a television crew. Every part of the demonstration—every part, that is, which occurred after the landing of the blow—was being caught on video. The anger of aged mothers. Waving banners demanding an end to British colonial cover-up. Ban the Bases. The stumbling retreat of a High Commissioner, carried like a child in the arms of his bodyguard, fleeing into the night from the wrath of old women. The first spark of Cypriot defiance. Such an unhappy coincidence that the news crew should have found itself in the right spot at precisely the wrong time. Bone fever had broken out.

TWENTY-THREE

To offer compromise is like suggesting to a shark that he lick you first.

The tea room's infested."

"Mice again? I understand Deirdre all but jumped out of the window into the Thames last week when she found two of the little brutes staring up at her. They're rampant behind the paneling. Time to bring back the cat, d'you suppose?"

"Not mice. Rumor." Booza-Pitt was exasperated with his leader's apparent flippancy. "Tom's up to something, but no one seems to know precisely what."

In the background the squealing serenade of children at play came from around the pool area where a dozen of them, all offspring of senior Ministers, were indulging in the rare delights of a summer Sunday at Chequers. Out on the sweeping lawn the Environment Secretary was running through a few golf shots as a policeman in blue sleeves and bulky flak jacket passed by on patrol cradling a Heckler & Koch semiautomatic; on the patio, in the shade of the lovely Elizabethan manor with its weathered and moss-covered red brick, an air force steward served drinks. The atmosphere was relaxed, lunch would be served shortly, and Urquhart seemed determined not to be pushed. This was his official retreat; he'd handle matters in his own way.

"A leadership challenge in the autumn," the wretched Booza-Pitt was persisting, trying so hard to impress that his eyebrows knitted in concern like a character out of Dostoyevsky.

"No. Not that. He'd lose and he knows it." Claire sipped a mint julep—the bar steward had recently returned from a holiday in New Orleans—and subsided. She was leading the Home Secretary on; Urquhart knew and was amused by it, only Geoffrey was too blind to realize. For him, the conversation had already become a competition for Urquhart's ear.

"Even so, he might. Out of spite. Inflict a little damage before he fades into the shadows."

"No. He has other ideas." She subsided again.

Urquhart was himself by now intrigued. She had an air of such confidence, and a voice that brushed like fresh paint on canvas, but he couldn't yet see the picture.

"Like what?" Geoffrey threw down a challenge.

Claire looked to Urquhart; she'd intended to keep this for a more private moment but he was of a mind that she should continue. A golf ball clattered around their feet, followed by a belated cry of warning from the lawn; evidently the Environment Secretary was in considerable need of his practice. Urquhart rose from the wooden garden seat and began to lead them around the pathways of the garden, out of earshot and driving range of others.

"A new party," she began once again. "A big media launch with some prominent names in support. Then more to follow over the weeks ahead. Several from within our own party. Perhaps one or two even from within the Government."

"Madness!" Booza-Pitt snorted.

But Urquhart's eyes had grown fixed, his frame stooped in concentration as he walked, studying the ground as though peering through a trap door into a personal hell. "He'd hope for a couple of by-elections where they'd buy anything new on the shelf. Bite after bite, taking mouthfuls out of my majority. Making it ever more difficult for me to govern."

"One step building on the next."

"He wants to bleed me. Death by a thousand cuts."

"Could he do it? Could he really?" Booza-Pitt had at last caught the changing wind. "Sounds like a party no one but women's magazines would take seriously."

"Even women take time off from painting our nails to vote, Geoffrey. We're not all hot flushes and flower arranging."

A sense of urgency crept into the Prime Minister's step; Booza-Pitt felt he was being left behind. "But where'd he get the money for it all?" he demanded breathlessly. For Geoffrey, the practicalities of life all came down to a question of money. He'd once found a shortcut on the school cross-country run and, much to his annoyance, had made the team. He'd found consolation by selling the shortcut to his friends.

"Money's not his problem, it's time," Claire responded. "Time to build momentum. Time to build an organization before the next election and to establish that he's more than merely a figment of the media's fevered imagination. Time to encourage our sweaty band of galley slaves to jump ship."

"It'd be no more than a dinner party at prayer," Booza-Pitt all but spat in contempt. Then his expression altered as though refashioned with a mallet. "Good God. What does that mean for my Bill? *I'd* be giving him all the money."

Urquhart came to a sudden halt under the limbs of a spreading cedar tree. "Not quite what I had in mind," he conceded quietly.

"I've…I've got to withdraw it. Somehow." Booza-Pitt's voice trailed away, his mantle as defender of democracy in tatters even before it had been woven.

"There is another way," Claire offered.

"One that would keep my reputation?"

"Keep the Government's reputation, Geoffrey," she corrected. "Your Bill will sponsor as many different groups as possible. Fine. We mustn't give Tom a clear run."

"Nibbled to death by a thousand minnows, that was always my thinking," Geoffrey exclaimed, wondering whether the time had come to reclaim authorship of the plan.

"And meanwhile make damn sure our own supporters have got something to get their teeth into. Let's fly the flag for them. Give them something that reminds them what we're all about, and how much they'd lose if it all went wrong."

"Like what?" Geoffrey pleaded.

"I thought you were the one with all the bright campaigning ideas." It was Urquhart, his tone sharp, back among them. "Geoffrey, why don't you go and have a wander through the Long Library before lunch? Fascinating collection of first editions—Sartre, Hemingway, Archer. Right up your street."

"Maybe a little later, FU?" he suggested, determined not to be written out of the plot.

"Geoffrey. Be a good fellow and bugger off."

"Yes, right—Long Library. See you at lunch then."

She marveled at his resilience to insult. Even now, she suspected, he was working on how he would divulge to others the privilege of the PM's personal invitation to inspect his rare editions.

"He'll not love you for that," she commented.

"Geoffrey is incapable of love for anyone except himself. His adoration of his own inadequacies is as total as it is astounding and leaves no room for anyone else. I suspect I shall survive, as will he."

In the distance a lunch gong was being beaten and the squeals of children echoed with renewed impatience, but he ignored the summons, instead gripping her arm and leading her through French windows that brought them from the terrace into the house. They were in his study with the windows firmly closed behind them, shutting them off. Suddenly she felt claustrophobic, the rules had changed. This was no longer a summer stroll around the garden making sport with Booza-Pitt, but one-on-one, she and Urquhart, in an atmosphere of personal intensity she'd never felt with him before.

"I'm sorry, Francis. Did I offend you, talking about the possibility of defeat?"

"No. You managed to express, and most eloquently, something that"—he was going to say "voices inside my own head"—"my own thoughts have been telling me all too sharply."

"So you think it could happen?"

"I'm not a fool. Of course it could happen. We're no more than passengers on a tide; even as we are rushed along by it, only one small slip could sweep us under."

"And if we were to slip and he were to win, just once, there would be no way back for us. Tom's always been committed to proportional representation—he'd change the election law himself, skew it in favor of the small parties, the minnows."

"Who would grow into great pikes and tear any Government apart. This country would be turned over to chaos. By legislative order of Booza-Pitt and Makepeace, destroyers of civilization. Hah!" To her alarm he sounded as if he found ironic pleasure in the prospect of the Apocalypse.

"You would be history," she warned.

"And favored by it all the more!"

She realized why she had begun to feel so claustrophobic. She was standing beside not just a man, but a political Colossus whose deeds would be writ large. Yet she had known that from the very start; wasn't that why she had agreed to join him, for her own selfish place in his shadow, the thrill and experience of standing beside a great chunk of that story? Up so close, so privately, it left her not a little in awe.

"There is one major gap in his armor," Urquhart continued in a state of considerable animation, "his point of greatest vulnerability. He must keep his momentum going, appear irresistible before enough people will take their courage in their hands and march with him. But to raise an army he needs time. Time that is ours to give, or to deny. We must keep an eye on young Tom."

"I already am," she responded a little sheepishly. She'd intended to keep it secret, in case he disapproved, but the atmosphere of intimacy overcame her caution. "He has a new driver who is—how shall I put it?—extremely keen to share his experiences, especially when he picks up his weekly paycheck. From a very close friend of my husband."

"Really? How splendid. I should have thought of that. I'm slipping."

"Or perhaps I'm learning."

He began to look at her quizzically, in a new light. "I do believe you are—turning out to be a truly remarkable find, Claire, if you'll allow me to say so." He had turned to her, taken her hands, his voice dropping to a softer register. He'd already invited her to share so much, yet there was a new and pressing intimacy in this moment. "One thing I have to ask. You've been pretty tough about Tom Makepeace. Politically, I mean. Yet from the way you understand him so well I get the impression—a sense, perhaps—that once you and he were… close. Personally."

"Would it have mattered?"

"No. Not so long as I could be sure of your loyalty."

Loyalty tied by bonds at least as secure as any she had shared with Makepeace.

"Francis, you can. Be sure of my loyalty."

She felt herself being pulled by the enormous force of gravity that surrounded him. She panicked, realizing she was losing control, her lips reaching up toward him. Suddenly she was afraid, of both him and her own ambitions. She was falling, yet couldn't find it within her to resist, even in the knowledge that coming so close to him was likely to leave her burned up and scattered like cinders. As had happened to others. She was on fire.

Then there was ice. Urquhart drew back, allowed her hands to fall and deliberately broke the spell that tied her to him. Why, she would never know, and Urquhart would never admit, even to himself.

For how can a man admit to such things? The guilt he felt for others he had taken in such a way, used, discarded, left utterly destroyed. With the passage of time he felt himself being drawn toward the day of his own judgment and such things bore more heavily on his mind. Some might even mistake it for conscience. Or was it merely the knowledge that in the past such entanglements had caused nothing but grief and turmoil, confusion he could do without in a world that, thanks to Thomas Makepeace, had suddenly grown far more complicated?

Yet there was something else that turned his blood cold. The gnawing dread that Francis Urquhart the Politician had been constructed on the ruins of Francis Urquhart the Man. Incapable of children, denied immortality. A desert, a barrenness of body that had infected the soul and in turn had been inflicted upon Mortima, the only woman he had ever truly loved. The others had all been pretense, an attempt to prove his virility, but in the end a pointless exercise, a scream in a soundproof chamber.

And, as she stood before him, desirable and available, he was no longer sure he could even raise his voice. The end of Francis Urquhart the Man.

Francis Urquhart the aging Politician stepped back from temptation and torment.

"Best that we keep you as my good luck charm, eh?"

In the Cypriot capital the crowds streamed through the entrance gates for an evening with Alekos, a young singer of talent from the mainland who had built a remarkable following among Greeks of all ages. The young girls swayed to the rhythm of his hips, old women fell for the voice that dripped like honey on dulled ears, the men were won over by the manner in which he crafted the images and emotions of Hellenism into music of the Greek soul more powerful than a first half hat trick by Omonia. He had flown from Athens for a special concert in support of the Cyprus Defense Fund. Few of the several thousand enthusiasts at the open-air auditorium gave a thought to how a concert could raise money for the CDF when all the tickets had been given away, as had the large number of banners being waved above the heads of the emotion-gripped crowd. *We Shall Not Forget*, the refrain in memory of the victims of Turkish invasion, was thrust high alongside other soul slogans such as *Let Us Bury Our Dead With Honor, British—Give Back Our Bases* and, yes, even *Equality With Orchids.*

The Bishop was much in evidence, cloaked dark in the seat of honor and surrounded by a hardworking team of his theological students. Theophilos was well pleased. Even the occasional outbreaks of alcoholic excess brought on by the heat and the ready supply of beer he bore with paternal fortitude. For three hours Alekos and his supporting musicians stirred, scratched, tickled and whipped their passion; as the night grew deeper, he reached for the refrain of *Digenes Akritas*, a tale of heroic defiance against the foreign foe, of cherished memories from the mists of time and, above all, of victory. They sang and swayed with him, lit matches and candles, their faces illuminated by hope in the darkness as the tears flowed freely from men and women alike. Alekos had them in his palm.

"Have *you* forgotten?" he breathed into the microphone, his voice stretching out to touch every one of them.

"No," they sobbed.

"Do you want to forget those who died?"

"No…"

"Who gave their lives for a free Cyprus? Some of whom lie buried in unknown graves?" His voice was firmer now, goading.

(Later when he heard the reports, Hugh Martin was to wince at how Alekos in one emotional sweep had entangled together the subject of British graves with the Turkish invasion.)

"No, no," they replied, with equal firmness.

"Do you want your homeland given away for British military bases?"

He stirred the muddy waters of old hatreds like a shark's tail. In the darkness they began to lose their individual identities and become as one. Greek. Full of resentment.

"Then will you give your homeland away to bastard Turks?"

"No! Never!"

"Do you want your sisters and daughters to be screwed by bastard Turks, like your mothers were when the bastards invaded our country?" His clenched fist beat the night air, his bitterness transmitting to others.

"NO."

"Do you want your President to sign a treaty that says it's all right? All forgotten? All over? That they can keep what they stole?"

"NO," they began to shout. "NO. NO. NO."

"So what do you want to say to the President?"

"N-O-O-O-O!" The cries lifted through the Nicosia night and spilled across the city.

"Then go and tell him!"

The doors were thrown open and thousands swarmed out of the auditorium to find buses lined up to take them the two kilometers to the Presidential Palace, whose guards they taunted, whose gates they rocked, and whose wrought iron fencing they festooned with their banners. By the light of a huge pink Nicosia moon, the largest demonstration in the city since the election came to pass, and twenty-three unwise arrests ensured that the stamping of angry feet would continue to grab headlines for days afterward.

Like every other detail of the concert, even the encore had gone according to plan.

TWENTY-FOUR

The game of politics usually proceeds by a succession of afterthoughts.

"Gaiters and gongs again tonight." Urquhart sighed. He had lost count of the number of times he'd climbed into formal attire on a summer's evening in order to exchange inconsequential pleasantries with some Third World autocrat who, as the wine list rambled on, would brag about his multiple wives, multiple titles, and even multiple Swiss bank accounts. Urquhart told himself he would much rather be spending his time on something else, something more fulfilling. But what? With a sense of incipient alarm, he realized he didn't know what. For him, there was nothing else.

"I see they're pegging out the lawn for that wretched statue." Mortima was gazing out of the bedroom window. "I thought you'd told Max Stanbrook to stop it."

"He's working on it."

"It's preposterous," she continued. "In a little over a month you will have overtaken her record. It's you who should be out there."

"She wasn't supposed to lose, either," he reflected softly.

She turned, her face flecked with concern. "Is all this Makepeace nonsense getting you down, Francis?"

"A little, perhaps."

"Not like you. To admit to vulnerability."

"He's forcing my hand, Mortima. If I give him time to organize, to grow, I give him time to succeed. Time is not on my side, not when you reach my age." With a silent curse he tugged at his bow tie and began again the process of reknotting it. "Claire says I should find some way of calling his bluff. Fly the flag."

"She's turning out to be an interesting choice of playmate."

He understood precisely what she was implying. "No, Mortima, no distractions. In the past they've caused us so much anguish. And there are voices everywhere telling me I shall need all my powers of concentration over the next few months."

"People still regard you as a great leader, Francis."

"And may yet live to regard me as a still greater villain."

"What is eating at you?" she demanded with concern. "You're not normally morbid."

He stared at himself in the mirror. Time had taken its undeniable toll; the face was wrinkled and fallen, the hair thinned, the eyes grown dim and rimmed with fatigue. Urquhart the Man—the Young Man, at least—was but a memory. Yet some memories, he reflected, lived longer than others, refused to die. Particularly the memory of a day many years earlier when, in the name of duty and of his country, he had erred. As the evening sun glanced through the window and bathed the room in its rich ocher light, it all came back. His hands fell to his side, the tie unraveled again.

"When I was a young lieutenant in Cyprus"—the voice sounded dry, as though he'd started smoking again—"there was an incident. An unhappy collision of fates. A sacrifice, if you like, in the name of Her Majesty's peace. Tom Makepeace today wrote to me, he knows of the incident but not my part in it. Yet if it were ever to be made public, my part in that affair, they would destroy me. Ignore everything I have achieved and strip me like wolves."

He turned to face her. "If I give Makepeace any of what he wants, he will pursue the matter. If I don't, he'll pursue me. Either way, there is an excellent chance I shall be destroyed. And time is on his side."

"Then fight him, Francis."

"I don't know how."

"You've plenty of strings to your bow."

He joined her by the window, took her hands, massaged her misgivings with his thumbs, gently kissed her forehead. "Strings to my bow. But I'm not sure I have the strength anymore to bend the bloody thing." He laughed, a hollow sound she chose not to share. "We must have one more victory, one more successful election behind us. The Urquhart name, yours and mine, written into history. The longest-serving Prime Minister this century."

"And the greatest."

"I owe that to you even more than I owe it to myself. I must find some way of beating him, destroying him—any way! And quickly. Everything I have ever achieved depends on it."

"And what then, Francis?"

"Then perhaps we can think about stepping back and I can become an intolerable old man in carping retirement, if that's what you want."

"Is that what you want?"

"No. But what else is there? Apart from this I have nothing. Which is why I'm going to fight Tom Makepeace. And all the others. So long as I breathe."

For Mortima it sounded all too much like an epitaph; she held him close in a way they'd not embraced for a considerable time, nuzzling into loose flesh and afraid she was falling into the deep pit of his empty old age.

Suddenly he stiffened, measurably brightened. Something over her shoulder had caught his eye. The workmen had finished laying out the stakes—miniature Union flags, would you believe—and a large lawn mower was lumbering toward them. It approached hesitantly, its progress obstructed, forcing it to slow, to stop and swerve to avoid them. It did so with considerable difficulty, chewing up the neat turf and knocking over several flags as the gardener wrenched at the wheel. Clearly it was not a machine designed to mow in such confined circumstances. Urquhart observed all this with growing interest.

"Anyway, my love, a great general doesn't need to bend his own bow, he gets others to do that for him. All he needs are ideas. And one or two have just come knocking at my door."

"Max!" he summoned.

Ministers were trooping into the Cabinet Room where they found him at its far end, slapping his fist like a wicket keeper waiting for the next delivery, rather than in his accustomed chair beneath the portrait of Walpole.

Stanbrook made his way over as the others milled around, uncertain about taking their seats while he was still standing.

"Max, dear boy," Urquhart greeted as the other approached. "Our little conversation about the statue. You remember? Haven't signed the Order yet, have you?"

"I've delayed it as long as I possibly could, FU." Stanbrook tried to make it sound like a substantial victory of Hectorian proportion. Then, more sheepishly, "But I can't find a single damned reason for turning it down."

Urquhart chastised with a glance, then laid an arm upon his colleague's shoulder and turned him toward the window. "There's only one reason for turning down such a worthy project, Max, and that's because they haven't raised enough money."

"But they have. Eighty thousand pounds."

"That's just for the statue. But what about its maintenance?"

"What's to maintain with a statue, FU? An occasional scrub for pigeon droppings is hardly likely to run up bills of massive proportions."

"But it's not just the birds, is it? What about terrorists?"

Stanbrook was nonplussed.

"Home Secretary," Urquhart called to Geoffrey, who came scampering. The others, too, began to draw closer, fascinated by what was evidently some form of morality play or possibly bloodletting of the new Environment Secretary—either way, no one wanted to miss it.

"Geoffrey, wouldn't you say that a statue of our Beloved Former Leaderene situated just beyond the gardens of Downing Street would be an obvious target for terrorist attack? A symbolic retribution for past failures? Theirs, not hers. Let alone a target for the more obvious attentions of petty vandals and graffiti goons."

"Certainly, Prime Minister."

"And so worthy of steps to ensure its—and our—security. Twenty-four hours a day. Perhaps a specially dedicated video security system. How much would that cost?"

"How much would you like it to cost, Prime Minister?"

"Splendid, Geoffrey. To install and maintain—at least ten thousand pounds a year, wouldn't you think?"

"Sounds very reasonable to me."

"Then, of course, there's the monitoring of that system. Twenty-four hours a day. Plus a visual inspection of the site every hour during the night by the security watch."

"No change from another twenty thousand pounds for that," Geoffrey offered.

"You see, Max. There's another thirty thousand a year that will have to be found."

Stanbrook had grown pale, as though hemorrhaging. "I think the fund will just about run to that, FU."

"But you haven't thought of the grass, have you? A surprising omission for a Secretary of State for the Environment."

"The grass? What's the bloody grass got to do with it?" Both his perspective and his language had collapsed in confusion.

"Everything, as I shall explain. Come with me."

Urquhart flung open the doors to the patio and, like Mother Goose, led all twenty-five of them in file down the stairs, into the garden, through the door in the old brick wall, and in less than a minute had brought them to the site of the stakes. Startled Special Branch detectives began scurrying everywhere in the manner of cowboys trying to round up loose steers.

"Away! Away off my grass!" he shouted at them. "This is most important."

Security withdrew to a nervous distance, wondering whether the old man had had a turn and they should send for Smith & Wessons or Geritol.

"Observe," Urquhart instructed, hands spread wide. "The grass. Beautifully manicured, line after line. Until"—he made a theatrical gesture of decapitating a victim kneeling at his feet—"here."

They gathered around to inspect the scuffed and torn turf on which he was standing.

"You see, Max, the lawn mower can't cope. It's too big. So you're going to have to get another one. Transport it here twice a week throughout the summer, just to mow around the statue."

"Take a bit of strimming, too, I've no doubt." Bollingbroke had decided to join what was evidently a glorious new summer sport.

"Thank you, Arthur. A strimmer as well, Max. The whole bally production line we have created to keep the green spaces of our gracious city shorn and shaven—disrupted! Put out of gear. Ground to a halt. For your statue."

"Hardly my statue," Stanbrook was mumbling, but already there was another player on the field.

"Chief Secretary, what would be the cost of a small mower and strimmer, their storage and transportation from said storage about fifty times a year, plus an allowance for all the chaos to the maintenance schedule that is likely to ensue?" He made it sound as if the center of London was sure to grind to a halt.

"I'd say another ten thousand," a youngish man with lips that operated like a goldfish pronounced. "Minimum."

"So that's ten, and ten, and twenty. Makes another forty thousand pounds, Max."

"I'll tell the Society."

"Not just forty thousand pounds, Max. That's forty thousand pounds a year. We'll have to ensure that a fund is available to generate that sort of money for at least ten years; otherwise the taxpayer will end up footing the bill. We couldn't have that."

"Not when I'm just about to announce a freeze on nurses' pay," the Health Secretary insisted jovially.

"And where's the Chancellor of the Exchequer? His Prime Minister wants him. Ah, Jim, don't be bashful."

The Chancellor was thrust by many willing hands from seclusion at the rear of the assembly amid a chorus of laughter.

"Chancellor. A fund sufficient to generate forty thousand pounds a year for a minimum of ten years. How much are we talking about?"

Jim Barfield, a rotund Pickwickian figure with a shock of hair that made him look as though his brains had exploded, scratched his waistcoat and sucked his lower lip. "Not used to thousands. Throw a few noughts on the end and I'd have no trouble but..." He scratched once more. "Let's say a quarter of a million. Just between friends."

"Mr. Stanbrook, has the Society got a quarter of a million pounds? In addition to the eighty for casting said statue?"

Stanbrook, not knowing whether to laugh along with the rest, to fall to his knees and kiss the grass, or to crawl away in humiliation, simply hung his head. "No graven images!" a voice from the west flank of Whitehall insisted. The others applauded.

"Then it is with much regret…"

He had no need to finish. The Cabinet to a man, even Stanbrook, applauded as if on the green trimmed sward of Westminster they had been watching one of the finest conjuring tricks of the decade. Which, perhaps, they had.

He felt good. He had shown he was still the greatest actor of the age; it had been as important to remind himself as to remind the others. His view had been salvaged, the past exorcized. Now to exorcize the future.

TWENTY-FIVE

Ambition should be strong enough to take a hard polish. And a damned good kicking.

Claire ran into him as she was scurrying out of the House of Commons Library. She was clutching papers and he had to reach out to prevent her from toppling.

"Hi, stranger."

"Hello to you." The voice was soft, the old chemistry still at work. Reluctantly Makepeace withdrew his supporting arm and let her go. "Running errands for the boss?" he inquired, indicating the papers and regretting it immediately. Urquhart had already come too much between them.

"Would it seem silly if I suggested I'd missed you? I've thought about you a lot."

"I'm sure that's true," he retorted, hurt male pride adding a sharper edge than he'd intended. "I suppose coming from an acolyte of Urquhart I should take such attention as a compliment."

She searched for his eyes but they remained elusive, darting along the corridor, falling at his feet, unwilling to allow her to inspect the wounds she had inflicted on him. He was acting more like a secret and bashful lover than when they'd shared something to be secretive about.

"I'd like to think that we could still be friends," she offered, and marveled immediately at her own hypocrisy. She meant it; she retained a strong sense of affection and respect for him, a man with whom she had shared so much. Yet she was also the woman who was trying to bring him to his knees. For the first time she began to be aware of how far she had moved, had strayed perhaps, from her own image of herself. She'd become two people, political animal as well as woman, in two worlds, one black, the other white, and the dark world where she stood in the shadow of Francis Urquhart was tugging her away from her roots and those she had loved.

"Claire, there are only two sides in this place right now. Those who stand with him, and those who don't. There's no room in the middle anymore."

A colleague passed by and they both stood in embarrassed silence as though their past secrets had been betrayed to the evening press.

"I've not sold out," she began again, anxious to reassure herself as much as him.

Disdain sharpened his eye. "Spare me that sweet talk about means and ends, Claire. Like curdled milk, I'll only swallow it once. With him, there is but one end. Francis Urquhart. And any means will do. Face up to it. You've sold out."

"I wasn't born to all this like you, Tom. I've had to fight and scratch for every little thing I've achieved in this place. I've taken all the jibes, the patronizing, the gropers, the men who preach equality yet only practice it when they go a Dutch treat for dinner. Perhaps you can afford to, but no way am I going to pack up and walk away at the first sign of trouble."

"I haven't walked away. Not from my principles."

"Great. You preach, and in the meantime Big Mac wrappers will inherit the Earth. We both have our ideals, Tom. Difference between us is that I'm prepared to do something about them, to take the knocks in pursuing them, not simply sit on the sidelines and jeer."

"I'm not sitting on the sidelines."

"You ran off the bloody pitch!"

"There are some games I simply don't want to play." His tone implied that in politics, at least, she was nothing more than a tart.

"You know, Tom Makepeace, you were a better man in bed. At least there you knew what the hell to do." She didn't mean it, was covering up for her own pain, but she'd always had a tendency to a phrase too far and this one tore across their respect like a nail across silk.

She knew she'd cut him and watched miserably as a bestockinged messenger handed Makepeace an envelope bearing a familiar crest. As he wrenched it open and read she began to frame an apology, but when his eyes came up once more, inflamed no longer with wounded pride but unadulterated contempt, something told her it was already too late.

"Those who stand with him, Claire. And those who don't."

He turned on his heel and strode away from the ruins of their friendship.

❖ ❖ ❖

10 Downing Street

Dear Thomas,

I am replying to your recent letter. I have nothing to add to the reply I gave in the House last week, or to the policy adopted by successive Governments that security considerations prevent such matters being discussed in detail.

Yours sincerely,
Francis

It had been couched in terms intended to offend. His name had been typed, not handwritten; the dismissal of his request was as abrupt as was possible for an experienced parliamentarian to devise. Perhaps he should be grateful, at least, that the letter had dispensed with the hypocrisy of the traditional endearment between party colleagues that suggested that the author might be "Yours ever."

As Makepeace entered the Chamber, the letter protruding like a week-old newspaper from his clenched hand, he trembled with a sense of his own inadequacy. There was a time, only days gone by, when a word from him would have had the System producing documents and reports by the red box load; now he couldn't raise more than a passing insult.

Claire, too, had made a fool of him—not simply because he'd said things in a clumsy manner he'd not intended, but because he hadn't realized how much of his affections she continued to command, in spite of Maria. He should know better, have more control, yet she'd left him feeling like a schoolboy.

If he was flushed with frustration as he sat down to listen to the debate on the European Union Directive (Harmonization of Staff Emoluments), within moments his resentment had soared like a hawk over Saudi skies. The House was packed, the Prime Minister in his seat with Bollingbroke at the Dispatch Box, holding forth on matters *diplomatique* with the restraint and forbearance of a bricklayer approaching payday.

"Emoluments!" he pronounced with vernacular relish. "Wish I 'ad some of them there Emoluments. It says in this Sunday newspaper"—he waved a copy high above his head—"that apparently one of the Commissioners took a personal interpreter with him on a ten-day visit he made recently to Japan. By some oversight, 'owever, the young lady turned out to be qualified only in Icelandic and Russian." He shrugged as though confronted with a problem of insurmountable complexity. "Well, I dunno, they probably all sound the same and

I'm sure she had her uses. But it's a bit much when they come back and start asking for more."

Mixed shouts of encouragement and objection were issuing from all sides when, in a stage whisper everyone in the Chamber (with the exception of the scribe from *Hansard*) had no trouble in hearing, he added: "Wonder if I could get it on expenses?"

The debate was rapidly turning into music hall, much to the annoyance of several members of the Opposition who attempted to intervene, but Bollingbroke, as though standing defiant watch from the cliffs of Dover, refused to give way.

"And for what purpose are we being asked to pay the good burghers of Brussels more, Mr. Speaker?" he demanded, waving down several who wanted to offer an answer. "I'll tell you. One of their latest plans is to issue a standard history of Europe that can be used in all our schools. Sort of...give our kids a common perspective. Bring them together."

Several members of the Opposition Front Bench were nodding their heads in approval. They should have known better.

"A visionary epistle. Apparently, the Germans never invaded Poland, the Italians never retreated, the French never surrendered, and we never won the war."

Pandemonium had erupted in every corner of the Chamber, the noise being so great that it was impossible to tell who was shouting in support and who in condemnation of the Foreign Secretary. But Makepeace had sprung to his feet, the flush on his face indicating beyond doubt the depths of his outrage. Bollingbroke, always willing to plumb such depths, gave way.

"In all my years in this House I have never heard such an ill-tempered and bellicose performance by a Foreign Secretary," Makepeace began. "When all the rest of Europe is looking for a common way forward, he seems intent on acting like an obstinate child. And his Prime Minister, who likes to pretend he is a statesman, sits beside him and cheers him on."

Makepeace had become confused with his targets. In the seat beside Bollingbroke, Urquhart was chatting with Claire, who was leaning down from her guard post in the row behind to whisper something in his ear. From where Makepeace stood, it looked almost like an affectionate nuzzle. His sense of personal betrayal grew.

"When the rest of Europe is as one, for God's sake shouldn't we be joining with them rather than scratching over old wars?"

"In my Dad's day they called that appeasement," Bollingbroke shouted, but did not attempt to reclaim the floor; he was enjoying the sight of Makepeace being wound tight like a spring.

"This Government is picking foreign quarrels for the sole purpose of covering its failures at home. It has lost all moral authority to continue in office…"

Nearby, Annita Burke was nodding her head in approval, urging him on, while several others around her were also trying to listen, their heads inclined in sympathy rather than joining the general commotion. Through it all, Bollingbroke could be heard scoffing: "So he's found morality since he was kicked out of office, has he? Convenient."

"As the bishops themselves have recently said in General Synod, this country needs a change in direction and a new sense of moral leadership—a leadership that this Government and this Prime Minister doesn't even attempt to provide."

That was enough for Bollingbroke, who sprang to his feet and started thumping the Dispatch Box. "What have you achieved compared with Francis Urquhart?" he was shouting. "Compared with him you're like a pork-scratching on a pig farm. Francis Urquhart has brought prosperity to this country, peace to Cyprus…"

The mention of Cyprus arrived like a slap across the face to Makepeace. It seemed to have galvanized Urquhart, too, who was tugging at the sleeve of his Foreign Secretary. Bollingbroke, startled at this unusual intervention from his Prime Minister, subsided into his seat, his place at the Dispatch Box taken by Urquhart. The House fell to silence, fascinated to catch the next turn of the carousel.

Urquhart cleared his throat. "I hate to interrupt my Right Honorable Friend—I was rather enjoying his contribution—but all this talk about morality and bishops. So muddled and misleading. You know, Mr. Speaker, I find it extraordinary that those who spend so much time warning about the dire consequences of wrongdoing in the afterlife are often so silent about it in this life. Turn the other cheek, they suggest." He sighed. "But if that's the self-appointed role adopted by the bishops, that cannot be the role for Government—at least not my Government. Our job is not to forgive those who have done wrong. Our job is to protect those who haven't."

If Makepeace had thrown down the gauntlet of morality, Urquhart seemed intent on retrieving it and using it as an offensive weapon.

"Don't misunderstand me, I have a high regard for the contribution made to the success of my Government by the Right Honorable Gentleman while he was a member of it." He offered a slow smile soaked in derision. "Although I don't recall sitting around the Cabinet table hearing him expound on how we were making such a mess of things. Not until I sacked him. But loss of office can have such a distorting effect on a man's perspective and memory."

The gauntlet struck again. Slap!

"I don't doubt the sincerity of his personal values, but I do find them odd. Odd when he says we must do this or that, simply because the bishops say so. Even more extraordinary that we should follow this or that course of action because the rest of Europe says so. Where's the morality in that? In secondhand opinions that follow the herd like dogs follow a dust cart?"

Slap.

"Morality is about deciding for yourself what's right. Then

doing something about it. Let me have around me men of action, not moralizers with empty words. I've nothing but scorn for those"—Urquhart's eyes lashed in the direction of his former colleague—"who sit back and carp at the efforts of others. Who descend from their high moral vantage points after the battle is over and tell the wounded and dying how they got it wrong…"

Makepeace tried not to flinch, but inside he hurt. Claire's taunt still echoed in his ears—sitting on the sidelines, she'd accused—and now this. They were out to humble him, together. He looked around him as the blows rained down. Those he regarded as supporters were shifting uncomfortably in their places while Annita's expression urged him on—do something! He rose to his feet, asking for the floor.

"No, no," Urquhart slapped him down. "I've heard enough theology from him to last me a good long while."

Makepeace held his ground, demanding to be heard, his clenched hand raised—it still gripped Urquhart's letter—while Urquhart loyalists were jeering, shouting at him to resume his place. Slap, slap, slap! Makepeace stood alone, defying the blows, but was he simply to stand there—doing nothing, as Urquhart had taunted—allowing himself to be gouged and mauled? Annita's eyes brimmed with sorrow as his own brimmed with the injustice of it all.

"Since he lost office," Urquhart was saying, "his attitude has become so critical, so negative, so personally embittered and destructive that I sometimes wonder what he's doing in the same great party as me."

SLAP!

So there it was. The public challenge. He had no choice but to respond. All around him those with whom he had discussed and conspired were examining him, wondering whether he was up to the duel. Makepeace against Urquhart. He knew that if he ducked the challenge at this moment it would be all but impossible to persuade some of the conspirators to join with him at a later time. Yet it was too soon, too early, he wasn't fully prepared. Don't be too impatient, emotional, Annita had warned...but even eagles must fly with the wind. And if he played the politician then he had also been born a man, and that man was hurting inside, his cheeks smarting, his thoughts misted by a dark and deepening fury that demanded satisfaction.

Satisfaction. For the humiliations delivered publicly on the floor of the House. Satisfaction for the insults delivered more privately in the letter in his hand. Satisfaction for denying Maria and her father. And for stealing away Claire.

Satisfaction for it all. Now!

From his position on the benches three rows up, Makepeace stepped sideways into the gangway. Was he running away? The prospect brought the House to instant and observant silence. He stepped down toward the floor of the great Chamber, to the red lines drawn on the carpet that separated Government side from opponents by the measure of two swords, the boundary between friend and unremitting foe. Then he stepped across. Not a heartbeat anywhere, not a sound to be heard, a Chamber so packed with emotion yet as though frozen. They watched as Makepeace mounted the steps through the benches of Opposition, one, two, three rows, and took a vacant seat.

The House exhaled with a single breath as life returned and tumult was restored. They had witnessed a slice of parliamentary life so rare it would fill their chronicles and be retold to grandchildren around the fire. Makepeace had crossed the floor, abandoned his party, torn up the rule book, and declared war on Urquhart, to the last breath.

Yet as he looked across the Chamber to the benches from which he had fought for so many years, Makepeace thought he saw the shadow of a faint, fugitive smile cross Francis Urquhart's lips.

TWENTY-SIX

The Greeks invented democracy. Little wonder that since then they have caused nothing but chaos.

The eye of an inhospitable Levantine sun stared down upon the Cypriot capital, baking the narrow streets of the central city like bricks in a kiln. Hugh Martin was relieved to reach the air-conditioned sanctuary of the Power House, a former electricity generating station that had been turned with considerable imagination into one of the old quarter's most exclusive restaurants. Works of fine contemporary art competed with menus and wine lists for the attention of the well-heeled clientele, one of whom, Dino Nicolaides, was editor of the *Cyprus Weekly* and intent on conducting an in-depth interview with his guest. For that purpose he had commandeered the seclusion of the table by the door, which led to the rear courtyard.

Martin apologized to the editor for the presence of Drage—the atmosphere in Nicosia in recent days had soured like uncollected rubbish, and demonstrations of one sort or another had become a daily occurrence, with the demonstrators becoming increasingly confused about whether the target of their protest was the Turks, the British, or the Cypriot Government itself.

"Summer madness," the editor agreed, and Drage was deposited on a stool by the bar.

If the furniture and decor were fashionable, the hospitality was in best Cypriot tradition and Martin was soon relaxed. Drage, however, could afford no such luxury, having been inducted by his superiors into the Order of Toasted Testicles with crossed pokers after the fiasco outside the museum. "Never again," his superiors had admonished. "Better a widow's pension for your wife than you make a complete ass of yourself on the main evening news." Never again, Drage had vowed. He sat eagle-eyed on his stool, the innocuous flight bag in which he carried "the necessary" perched on the bar beside him, fingers tapping nervously upon his knees. He offered a perfunctory smile but no conversation to the two Cypriots who stood beside him at the bar ordering drinks.

The incident, when it arrived, did so with extraordinary speed. Halfway through the meal a guest from a nearby table rose and crossed to greet the editor and diplomat, an action that in itself aroused little suspicion in such a small community. Drage, however, was immediately on his guard, cursing that the bright sunlight streaming through the window was burning into his retina as he stared, turning all those around the table into silhouettes. He blinked, blinked again, searching the profile of the new arrival for any sign of the unusual. Drage did not notice—could not have noticed in the circumstances—the eyes of the High Commissioner growing large with alarm and searching in his direction. Martin's arms remained motionless on the table, as he had been ordered. It was in the same moment when Drage thought he might have detected the outline of a small barrel protruding from beyond the far side of the intruder that the door immediately behind the table and leading to the courtyard began to open. Fear began to rise through his veins. Drage made a grab for his bag.

Impossible! As he reached for the zip that secured the flight bag he discovered that it had been smeared with superglue. Child's play! Yet so extraordinarily effective. The fastener was stuck solid, the revolver and alarm transmitter inside as inaccessible as though they were still locked in the High Commission's vault.

Two men—Drage's companions from the bar—had now entered through the rear door. One was waving what appeared against the glare to be some form of submachine gun while the other helped hustle the High Commissioner up and out. The submachine gun had stopped waving and for several seconds the attacker was pointing it fixedly in Drage's direction. Then he, too, was gone. Not even a scream, it had all happened so quickly and most guests in the restaurant were still enjoying their food, their first thought of alarm arriving only as Drage kicked over the bar stool in his lunge for the door. It was, as he knew in every fiber it would be, locked. By the time he had made it out through the restaurant's main entrance and around the side into the chrysanthemum-covered courtyard, the getaway car was speeding off and already lost in the narrow streets of the carpenters' quarter. He didn't even get a make, let alone a number.

He had lost the British High Commissioner.

TWENTY-SEVEN

Life is too short to learn the rules.

He sat behind the drawn curtains of his Commons room, eyes closed. The storm was about to break around him and there could be no retreat. Fate, destiny, the games of gods, call it what he might, had contrived to bring him to a time of great decision; if he failed the test they would say he lacked not the opportunity, only courage.

Less than twenty minutes after Makepeace had crossed the floor and changed the face of parliamentary politics, Urquhart had heard of the kidnapping of Martin. Havoc wherever he looked. And in havoc, opportunity. For war had been declared against him on two fronts, the first upon a parliamentary field where his skills and sagacity were matched by none, the other in a distant arena that was one of the handful in the world where British troops were still stationed. An arena he knew so well, where the long journey of his manhood had started, and might yet finish. Where Makepeace would have trouble following, and wouldn't even know what the spoils were.

There was a knock on the door, a secretary's head appeared. "Prime Minister, the Cabinet have all assembled."

"A moment more. Ask them to give me a moment more."

A final moment, a last listen to the voices inside that spoke of tempests and terrible trials. These were skies of blood that foretold men's doom and which others dared not walk in. But Francis Urquhart dared. He had wars to fight, and without delay. For in war, timing was everything.

And that time had come.

He had sent the wheel of fortune spinning and there was nothing to do but relish the exhilaration of the risk. He felt better than he had done in months. There was a lightness to his step as he walked the few yards from his room back into the Chamber, clutching his piece of paper, a single sheet with a simple portcullis crest and in his own hand, a note that would end up in the Urquhart Library. Or in the Tower. That reminded him, perhaps he should get Booza-Pitt to add a simple amendment to his Bill providing tax breaks for companies who contributed to educational funds. Like the Urquhart Library or the Endowment. There was still time.

The Chamber was full, aware that such an extraordinary and impromptu gathering of Cabinet Ministers betokened considerable drama. MPs rustled like leaves in a drying autumn wind as Urquhart placed the single sheet upon the Dispatch Box, smoothing its cream edges, and began.

"Mr. Speaker, with your permission I would like to make a statement. This afternoon in the House, a Member crossed the floor in an act that not only reduced this Government's majority, but also threatens a period of damaging uncertainty..." Others would say it, would already be shouting it as they prepared the morning newspapers, so there was nothing to be lost by the admission. "Such uncertainty can only do harm to the good governance of this country. Moreover, claims were made that my Government had lost its moral authority to govern. That is a challenge no Government can ignore."

He leaned back from the Dispatch Box so that he could survey his audience and, more importantly, keep them dangling, impatient upon his words.

"This Government prefers to take its authority not from self-appointed moralists but from the people. It is the people to whom we listen and in whom we trust; it is for them to say who should sit on these benches and who among the Opposition. It is the people who must decide."

From the corner of its collective eye the whole House was looking at Makepeace, who sat impassive, aware that Urquhart was challenging every line of his credentials, and awkward on a crowded bench where not a single one was numbered among his friends or supporters. He looked isolated; he'd jumped too soon.

"In order to bring an end to the uncertainty, it is my intention to ask His Majesty for a dissolution and a general election at the earliest practicable moment, after the passage of certain essential pieces of parliamentary business. That moment should be in four weeks next Thursday. Thank you."

Picking up his piece of paper, Urquhart left the Chamber.

For several long moments the House reacted in the manner of some prehistoric beast under attack. A bemused silence, before sounds of confusion began to rattle among many throats. Then a sustained bellow as the creature finally became aware that its tail had been torn away. Cries of determination and rage rose on all sides.

"Good God, I never thought I'd see it. The day when Francis Urquhart ran up the white flag of surrender." A young scribe in the press gallery tore at his notebook, infected by the air of anarchy that prevailed.

Beside him Dicky Withers appeared unmoved, eyeing the scene below him with no apparent display of heat, drawing in his cheeks as though sucking on his favorite pipe. "Bloody fool."

"What, Urquhart?" his junior colleague inquired.

"Not Urquhart. You. He's not running away, he's called Makepeace's bluff."

"But he's behind in the polls, now his party is split..."

"You watch 'em. Faced with an electoral drowning, not many will be keen to join Makepeace in jumping ship."

He nodded toward the former Foreign Secretary, who was walking alone out of the Chamber. In an arena where everyone was shouting, rebuking, gesticulating, only he seemed to have nothing to say, and no one to say it to.

TWENTY-EIGHT

A Greek life is built around ruins and rumor.

Nicosia swelters by day; by night, life is lived on the street, in the open-air eating places, on corners, at coffee shops, in parks beneath the stars. The hot pavements chatter, gossip flows along every gutter; at traffic lights young men lean out of their car windows or from mopeds to exchange banter and cigarettes with passersby, for everyone seems to be connected either by business or by blood. But, since the Turks invaded, mostly by blood.

And in the stifling atmosphere the soft wind of rumor sweeps through the backstreets, is passed from balcony to bus queue like a mistral of mistruth. Blow your nose by the Famagusta Gate and it has become a full-scale epidemic by the time, an hour or so later, it has reached Makarios Avenue. One day, perhaps, television may rescue the Cypriots, replacing febrile excitement with numbing uniformity and squeezing conspiracy into the commercial breaks. One day, perhaps, but until then, the Cypriot will believe anything.

Except politicians.

Beneath a roof of woven palm fronds in the shadow of the great Venetian walls of the old city, a waiter served two British tourists, patiently explaining the menu, imploring them to try the boiled brains that were a specialty of his cousin, the cook, and warning them off the squid. "Last week's. Too old." He shook his head as though at a graveside.

A young boy, no more than ten, passed between the tables distributing leaflets. He stopped before the couple, clearly identifying them as British. "Good mornings," he offered, along with a full smile and a leaflet each, before continuing with his task.

"What does it say?" the woman inquired of the waiter.

"It says we want the British out of Cyprus," he responded cheerfully, before spying the look on her face. "No, not you, Madams. The bases. Only the bases. We want the British to stay, we love you. But as our friends in our homes and our tavernas. Not in the bases." His cheerful clarification suggested not a trace of rancor. "Now, how about some suckling pig, freshly butchered...?"

Suddenly a scooter, underpowered and hideously over-throttled, squealed to a halt at the curbside and the waiter exchanged greetings with the driver. The noise grew, however, as did the animation of both waiter and driver, who were gesticulating as though warding off an attack of ravenous vampire bats. Then the waiter turned to his cousin who was leaning from the window of the kitchen. More shouts—the waiter abandoned his pen, pad, and corkscrew on the tablecloth—and the battle with the bats continued as he backed away in the direction of the scooter. Pursued by cries from his cousin that clearly fell well short of endearments, he climbed on the back of the scooter and disappeared into the night.

The cousin appeared at the guests' table carrying an expression of wearied forbearance, wiped his hands on his apron, and reclaimed the pad.

"But...what was all that?" Madams inquired.

He shrugged. "Bones. They've found more bones. So

there's another demonstration at the Presidential Palace. Don't worry, ladies, he's only gone for a quick shout. Be back in half an hour. Now, what can I get you? Has he told you about the squid…?"

There were bones, uncovered in the hills behind Paphos beneath a pile of rocks in an olive grove. They weren't of an age that matched with graves from either the British or Turkish wars, and it turned out they weren't even human. But it would be days before forensic analysis established the facts and in the meantime there would be protests, rumors, inventions, and outright lies.

Through dragging Cypriot days and beneath hard blue skies, truth rots like a gangrenous limb.

The Presidential Palace in Nicosia is an unlikely affair. Built to house the imperial trappings of an early British Governor after the old headquarters were wrecked by a popular uprising, it was in its own turn burned to the ground by the coup against Archbishop Makarios, which opened the door to the Turkish invasion. This would have been an opportunity to erase the British stamp upon the presidential home once and for all, and to create a palace of entirely modern Cypriot design. "But the British are our history," the Archbishop was supposed to have said. "They are our friends." So, along with the Archbishop, the Palace was restored in the old style, complete with the dominant British coat of royal arms carved in sandstone above the main entrance. *Dieu et Mon Droit.* An unlikely affair.

Aristotle Nicolaou was a similarly unlikely affair. Tall, stooped, of uncomfortable construction, the President had a leanness and a blue intensity in his eyes that set him apart from most Cypriots. He was a philosopher rather than a politician, a man who had encountered no greater pleasure in his life than teaching economics at the London School of Economics and marrying an English wife. His happiness had disappeared with the Turkish invasion that had torn the island apart, and he had returned for no better reason than to assuage his sense of guilt at missing the hardships being endured by his fellow Cypriots. It was not a sense of guilt shared by his wife. Nicolaou was a man of broad ideals who had never fully reconciled himself to the tactics and daily concessions required of political life, any more than he had to those required in his marriage. As he sat at the small desk in his office, surrounded by family photographs and the paraphernalia of power, he felt adrift. Through the great Moorish stone-arched windows came the sound of protest from beyond the palace gates—louder than ever tonight—and from the telephone came the sound of protest from the British Prime Minister. He didn't know how to handle either.

"Ari, I must emphasize how seriously I take this business. I'm not going to allow people to start kidnapping my High Commissioners and get away with it."

"Francis, I'm committing everything to this. We'll find him."

"But you haven't. Have you even found out why he was taken?"

"A radio station received a telephone call about two hours ago. Untraceable, naturally. Called itself 'The Word.' Gave the position of Mr. Martin's birthmark. Said it will give the rest of him back in exchange for all files concerning hidden war graves and a commitment from your Government to withdraw from your 'outposts of imperialism,' as it called them. Bones and bases."

"Bloody blackmail."

In a bowl in front of Nicolaou were piled fresh lemon leaves from the garden; he crushed a few between his fingertips, savoring the sharp fragrance, as was his custom at times of stress. "Can we at least encourage them to talk about it?"

"Ari, I've got an election campaign about to start. I've no intention of kicking that off by dickering with terrorists."

"It's more than that, I'm sure. It's aimed at me, too. They want to prevent me signing the peace treaty. Even now I have a mob beating at my door."

Beneath the canopy of a hundred thousand stars, another wave of protest drifted across the grounds—God, had they broken in? For once he was glad his wife was away on yet another trip to Paris. More culture. Shopping again.

"How seriously should we take these people?"

"Have you British not yet learned to take Cypriots seriously?" Nicolaou sounded caustic. "We may be a nation of tavern keepers and taxi drivers, but you'll remember we saw off the British military machine with little more than a handful of homemade bombs and stolen rifles."

"I remember."

"Above all, *I* cannot afford to forget. Throughout the ages we Cypriots have been betrayed by those who let in the Turks and other invaders through the back door. Now some believe I'm inviting them in through the front, putting out the welcoming mat. The arch deceiver, they call me. It's my head they want, not that of Mr. Martin."

"I hadn't realized things were so difficult for you. I'm sorry," Urquhart said, and didn't mean it.

The President crushed more lemon leaves and gazed across his office to where, against the soft pastel walls above the fireplace, hung a large oil portrait of his daughter, an only child born five months after their return to Cyprus. Elpída, he had called her—*Hope.* "So long as we have peace for our children, Francis, little else counts."

The maudlin fool. Matters appeared to be getting out of control in Cyprus; Urquhart could not have been more content. "And you believe these bone grinders who oppose the peace are the ones holding my High Commissioner?"

"I do."

"Then who in God's name is behind it all?"

Nicolaou sighed wearily. "I wish I knew."

She was twenty-three, extended in leg and lip with an adventurous, uncomplicated outlook. That's why she had become an air stewardess, to see something of the world and its charms, and particularly its men. She hadn't counted on meeting a man like this. Within ten minutes of their encounter in first class he'd offered her a job—better pay, more regular hours, no more anonymous hotel rooms and shabby, sweaty nights with men trying desperately to forget they were over forty and heavily married. At least this one wasn't married. But she hadn't expected to be looking down the barrel of a revolver.

Her hand went to her throat in alarm. From six feet away the barrel waved, fell, once, twice, three times, indicating the buttons on her blouse. He nodded as her fingers found them; she was nervous, trembling, had trouble unfastening the first. The others came away more easily.

The barrel flicked to the left, then the right as though brushing her shoulders, and her bra straps fell. The whole garment dropped to the floor to join the blouse. She shivered as a breeze from off the sea, soaked in the scent of jasmine, crept through the open window and across her bare skin. Her nipples tightened, and so did the lines of his mouth.

Remorselessly the barrel continued its march across her body. She stepped out of her skirt and was left standing in only her underwear, her arms crossed around her as though in penitence.

Again, the barrel. She didn't answer its call this time, hesitating at the final barrier, but the barrel beckoned again, more impatiently, violently. And she did as it commanded, her breasts falling generously forward as she bent to obey. She stood, her feet apart, her legs and all his thoughts leading to but one carefully shaven point.

He stared for a long while; she felt as though she were melting inside. Then he gave an epic grunt.

"You want the job?"

"*Yes,* Kyrie."

"Good. My brother Dimitri says you're imaginative. Come and prove it. Then we're going to go and smash the Government."

TWENTY-NINE

Loyalty is for dogs.

Claire's journey had been tiring, its purpose—Jeremy Critter—tiresome. He was one of life's natural critics, the diminutive and fortyish Member of Parliament for South Warbury, who found it impossible even for a moment to hide his ambitions, still less his frustration at not having achieved them. He was a natural focus for media conjecture that he might join the Makepeace rebellion and it was speculation he encouraged since he could never resist having something new to say about himself. To pained inquiries from Downing Street he had replied in his usual blustering manner that his constituency association was applying considerable pressure and he was honor-bound to listen; in their view, he said, the Government of Westminster, of Francis Urquhart, seemed to be all too distant from the mist-filled reaches of South Warbury and lacking in concern. Perhaps if the Prime Minister had made some gesture of recognition for the loyal support that both the constituency and its Member had given over the years, they might have concluded otherwise, but in the circumstances, when loyalty was not repaid…

This was no more than Critter's usual bumptiousness. His

constituency association amounted to little more than a superannuated branch of the union of rural seamstresses sprinkled with a few old bowlers who hadn't raised stumps in years; they'd do anything he cajoled them into, including, it seemed, jumping ship. With the desertion of Makepeace, Critter had seen his chance to squeak; Claire had volunteered as rat catcher.

She'd got herself invited as guest speaker to the association's annual general meeting, a collection of fewer than thirty souls gathered in the back room of a pub. Beyond the partition wall behind her she could hear the ribald commentaries that accompanied a frame of snooker as, beside her, the association chairman rose to address the faithful. A gangling, stooped former colonel, he took a large brass fob watch from the top pocket of his jacket and laid it on the table in front of him as though waiting for the evening artillery barrage to commence.

Business began. Reports on the state of association finances—"a balance of fourteen and threepence. I beg your pardon, ladies, that should be fourteen pounds thirty *pee*...deteriorated...further deteriorated...may have to consider closure of the office and we were all very sad to see Miss Robertson go." And a row about whether the ladies' luncheon club should allow in gentlemen members. "At our age, don't make a lot of difference," one progressive soul offered. "And since there are no nominations for new holders of office," the Chairman was continuing, raising his voice above the unsavory language that was beginning to filter through from the snooker table next door, "I'd like to suggest that the present office holders simply continue."

"Can't do that," a voice objected from behind an active pile of knitting.

"And why not, pray?" the Chairman inquired.

"Miss Tweedie, our Vice President," the knitting continued. "She passed away last week."

"Oh, I'm sorry to hear that. Does make it difficult, I suppose..."

On Claire's other side, Critter beamed at them all like a dutiful son. No wonder he had them in his pocket. Could buy the lot for forty quid a year and a bus outing to Minehead. And this was the hotbed of rebellion that threatened to make national headlines by pulling behind Tom Makepeace? "Not inevitable," Critter explained to her as the meeting almost came to blows about the projected car boot sale. "But they feel so isolated, unappreciated. If only the Government could find some way of showing its concern for this constituency..."

"Like making you a Minister," she whispered.

"Are you offering?"

"No."

His jaw—what there was of it—hardened. "I value what Francis has been able to do in his many years most highly, of course. Pity he doesn't seem to value me. But this isn't personal, you understand. My association is genuinely disaffected."

"So tell them to stop it," she demanded. "A word from you and they'd get straight back to crocheting tea cozies."

"I shall listen, not instruct," he muttered pompously. "My association is very traditional. Likes to make up its own mind. On principle."

The Chairman was drawing to the end of his remarks. Soon Critter would be on his feet. His body had turned half away from her, its language spoke of defiance, of a man preparing to leap. And he had never been able to resist jumping into a headline.

"Such a pity for you," she whispered.

"What is?"

"Your association and its principles."

"What d'you mean?"

"I was simply wondering, Jerry, how these dear little old ladies will react to the fact that their conscientious Member takes so much work home with him."

"What are you going on about, woman?"

"That new secretary of yours. Taking her home with you, to your apartment in Dolphin Square. Every lunchtime."

"For work. Nothing else." He was staring straight ahead, talking out of the corner of his mouth, unwilling to meet her eyes.

"Of course. It's simply that you men don't understand the problem. You make so little provision for women at Westminster and force us into such overcrowded surroundings that all we have to do while we're queuing to wash our hands is gossip. You'd be amazed at the rumors that get around."

"Like…what?" His teeth were gritted, his complexion draining like a chicken on a production line.

"You know, mostly missed periods and missing Members. Like why you missed Standing Committee last Wednesday. And why a pair of your monogrammed boxer shorts fell out of her handbag while she was searching for her lipstick. We all laughed; she said you'd been in something of a hurry…"

"For God's sake!"

"Don't worry. I can think of very few circumstances in which I would be tempted to betray the secrets of the ladies' locker room. Very few. It's like a confessional."

He swallowed hard.

"Just as I'm sure, Jerry, you can think of very few circumstances in which you would be tempted to betray our party."

The Chairman was finished now, was tapping the glass of his watch, while the flock applauded for its Member to rise and speak.

As Claire made the long and lonely drive back to London, she reflected that rarely had she heard such a comprehensive and carefully argued endorsement of the need for party loyalty than the one delivered that night by her colleague, the Honorable and Missing Member for South Warbury.

The ninety-nine square miles of British sovereign territory located within Cyprus and deemed vital to the security of Old Blighty consists of a number of fragments, like a mosaic left incomplete by a bored artisan. Within the two main bases of Dhekelia and Akrotiri lies a host of facilities central to the defense effort, from radar-based intelligence-gathering operations and an airfield capable of accommodating the largest military transport and reconnaissance planes, to a full-sized cricket pitch, a Royal Military Police jail, seven schools, and several pubs. Each is separated from the other, some facilities are surrounded by barbed wire, some are not. In between there are many other facilities, including terraces of neat cubicle houses, fruit farms, ancient ruins, and several Cypriot villages.

There are no signposts or other markers to indicate the frontier between British and Cypriot territories, except for Catseyes. The British seem to have a passion for marking the middle of their roads in this manner, the Cypriots do not. There it begins, and ends.

The aspect of the bases is beautiful, the duty is dull. And security is a nightmare. In the event of civil unrest, the British resort to cordoning off a few of their facilities as best they can, leaving by far the greatest area without guard or protection, and trusting in the traditional moderation and common sense of the Cypriots. Such trust is usually well-founded.

Thus, when confrontation ensued at the gates of the British airfield that lies adjacent to the salt flats of Akrotiri, the proceedings had an inevitable air of unreality. Security at the gates to the airfield, which is otherwise surrounded by a double fence of chain link topped with barbed wire, was provided by two poles, painted red and white, acting as traffic barriers and swung from a central control point, flanked on either side by two small concrete guard posts that were usually unoccupied, with a sign advising that a "Live Armed Guard" (sic) was on duty. Additional defenses were provided by several well-watered rosebushes. In normal circumstances the security would not have slowed, let alone stopped, a speeding rabbit, so on this day the system was augmented by a springy coil of razor wire swung in front of the gate, a tripling of the guard (to six), and the drawing up of an ancient white Land Rover with canvas roof and languid blue lights. Far smoother, less dated Mitsubishi patrol vehicles were available, but this was deemed to be an essentially British occasion.

The confrontation commenced with the arrival shortly after eight in the morning of the entire population of the village of Akrotiri, not a difficult logistical challenge since the village lay only some two hundred yards from the gates of the base. The village economy was dominated by the base, for which it supplied a variety of eating and drinking establishments including a Chinese takeout, a grocery store, and a unisex hairdresser.

"*Elenaki mou*, what the hell are you doing here?"

"I am protesting against British exploitation."

There was a pause in the interrogation as the questioner, a corporal who was standing guard behind the razor wire, considered the implications of what he had just heard. He was confused. He and Eleni, an attractive doe-eyed girl of nineteen, had spent the previous evening at the Akrotiri Arms pub and she had mentioned nothing of such matters then. In any event, they were engaged to be married as soon as he had finished his tour of duty. He was looking forward to it; he'd already put on five pounds.

"No talking on guard duty!" the Station Warrant Officer snapped, who seemed to have eyes in his arse. "The natives may be hostile."

Three young boys, one of them Eleni's younger brother, who had occupied the branches of an olive tree next to the guard hut, roared their defiance, their faces covered in huge grins and smears of aniseed.

Eleni seemed less impressed. Perhaps she took that from

her mother, who stood directly behind her shoulder and who was never impressed. She spoke no English, never smiled but stared. At least, after much investigation, Billy, the corporal, assumed she stared, but it was difficult to be certain since her eyes faced in different directions and made him nervous. Yet in whichever direction, they never seemed to waver. He felt constantly under her scrutiny, wherever he stood. Billy balanced his SA80 automatic nervously in his hands as his beloved addressed the NCO.

"You've stabbed us in the back, Sergeant," Eleni accused.

"It's Station Warrant Officer, if you don't mind, miss."

"Then you have stabbed us in the back, *Station Warrant Officer*." Her italics had an uncharacteristically sharp edge.

"If I 'ave, it's been with me checkbook, miss."

"You sell us to Turks!" The cry came from an aged man seated on top of an equally aged tractor, whose passion far exceeded his command of English. A solitary front tooth gave him a ferocious aspect. Many of the forty or so protesters raised their voices and waved arms in agreement.

The SWO marched slowly along his narrow front line, ten paces, turn and repeat, his boots beating a steady cadence on the tarmac, steadying his troops. "If they give you a hard time, remember, lads," he growled. "Stick it in. Give it a twist. Then pull it out."

"Billy doesn't even get that when I'm being nice to him, Sergeant," Eleni shouted across to him.

The soldier to Billy's right snickered while Billy considered throwing himself upon the razor wire. The SWO turned on studded heel to face the protesters. Eleni's mother stared directly at him, without taking her eye off Billy. She hadn't got her teeth in, her gums were in constant motion as though still finishing her breakfast.

"Station Warrant Officer," he insisted once more in a throaty voice. "Let's have a little proper respect with this riot of yours, miss. Otherwise I might find myself forced to retaliate."

"How?"

"Me and the lads might have to stop visiting your uncle's pub, miss. Be a great pity, that."

But he had lost the initiative once more. Shouts and gesticulations broke out among the Cypriots, their eyes raised skyward. The SWO looked up to see, a few hundred feet above him, the fierce yellow wings of a hang glider. It was a sport much practiced from the cliffs of Kourion a few miles along the coast, and this glider was pushing his luck. Not only was he well into unauthorized territory but he was also, except for his harness, completely naked, his golden-olive body clearly detailed against the outstretched wings.

"Now that is what I call a real man," Eleni mouthed in a stage whisper. "I wonder if he has trouble steering."

"That'll bugger up Billy's private life," a guard muttered.

"And bugger up our radar ops, too," the SWO added. "What the hell will they make of that?"

As the glider made a lower pass the young girls giggled while the older women shook their heads in memory of times past. The atmosphere had deteriorated to good-natured farce as everyone gazed into the sky, except for Eleni's mother, who still maintained a wary eye on the freely perspiring Billy.

"But you're still all right for tonight?" Billy ventured hopefully to her daughter.

"Not if I catch that one first," Eleni announced loudly, her thoughts still floating aloft in the cloudless sky.

The confrontation had been defused, for the moment, but for how long the SWO was not sure.

"What d'you reckon, sir? Dickhead at—what?—two hundred meters? Vertical shot. Into the sun. Want me to give it a try?"

The SWO had suddenly lost his humor. "You might well have to try, lad. Soon you might well have to try."

Billy's future mother-in-law munched on.

THIRTY

The crowds who greet a Prime Minister on his first day in Downing Street are doing little more than practicing for the day when they will cheer him all the way to the gallows. The public loves a good hanging.

Damn."

A brace of sapphire-tipped peacocks echoed the cry. He stood on the terrace of his chateau, set in the heart of the golden hills of Burgundy, and cursed again. The great house, all turrets and echoes of tumbrels, stood overlooking some of the finest vineyards in the world, row upon row of liquid gold. On a distant escarpment stood an old fortified abbey, ancient stone glowing in the melting evening sun; in between lay nothing but the thousand acres of his empire. Early tomorrow morning the first of nearly two hundred friends and business associates, drawn by the prospect of the view and the vintage, would start arriving to pay gentle homage and to savor the restored imperial splendors of his home. An empire built on oil.

But now there was too much oil, a whole drumful of it that had been poured over, across, around, everywhere on the cropped lawn leading down to the carp lake. Vandalism as grotesque as a morning raid on the Bourse.

He shouldn't have fired the gardener. He should've sliced off his balls and any other vital part of him then thrown the rest down one of the wells. And he'd still do it, if ever he laid hands on the little bastard.

"It's appalling," his wife was complaining at his elbow, "how much damage a little oil spread in the wrong places can do…"

Suddenly his nostrils dilated, sniffing the wind like a fox approaching a familiar copse. He smelled oil, cloying crude as it spurted like virgin butter, as it would spurt one day from rigs off the coast of Cyprus. It was a deal he had lost. But which hadn't yet been signed.

"Could be worse," he consoled his wife. "Might even get better," he reflected, wondering what vandalism might be inflicted on the peace agreement by a little oil spread across its neatly trimmed edges.

"This is scarcely going to help." Claire thrust a copy of the latest wire report across the desk at Urquhart. He read it quickly.

Industry sources revealing the existence of oil in the waters off Cyprus. The Turkish waters off Cyprus. Exploitation rights expected to go to British companies…

"Excellent," he pronounced, throwing it back across the desk. "More jobs for Britain." He picked up his pen and continued writing.

"But it will infuriate the Greeks."

"Why?" He stared inquisitorially across the tops of his half-moon glasses.

"They're losing out."

"Even if these reports are true, they'll be no worse off tomorrow than they were today."

"Even so, they won't like it. Wounded pride."

"I suppose you're right. They'll probably go right over the top. There's no accounting for the excitability of Cypriots, is there?"

"And a British judge, too. This will make everything more complicated. We've jumped from a row about a few graves to one about several billion barrels of oil. Instead of hundreds of protesters there'll be…thousands. The peace deal. The election. Everything. Suddenly much more complicated."

"As usual, Claire, you display a remarkably agile and perceptive mind behind those inspiring eyes of yours." He went back to his writing.

Sensing the end of his interest—had it ever started?—she reclaimed the sheet of paper and began to leave. "I wonder who leaked it?" she inquired, almost to herself, as she crossed the room.

"I've no idea," he whispered as the door closed behind her. "But it has saved me the trouble of doing it myself."

"CYPOS HIT OIL," the *Sun* screamed.

"*Billions of barrels of oil have been found off the tiny Mediterranean island of Cyprus. The discovery is expected to bring a smile to the face of the sun-kissed tourist haunt—and to the British oil companies who are queuing up for exploitation rights…*"

By its second edition the reporter had made further inquiries and rewritten the piece under the headline: TURKISH DELIGHT.

The *Independent* took a more cautious line.

"*Large deposits of oil are reported by industry sources to have been discovered off the island of Cyprus that could amount to the largest such find anywhere in the Mediterranean…*

"*The reported discovery comes at a delicate time in the peace process between the two Cypriot communities who are due to sign a final accord in London soon. The oil deposits are believed to be exclusively within the continental shelf areas reserved by the Watling arbitration tribunal to the Turkish Cypriot sector.*

"*Last night Greek Cypriot sources in London were demanding to know if Britain, whose deciding vote awarded the disputed area to the Turkish side, knew beforehand of the likely existence of oil.*"

The response of the leading daily in Nicosia was far less

conditional. In a banner headline across its front page, it announced simply: "BETRAYED!"

They had organized a demonstration outside the Turkish Embassy in Belgrave Square. The call had gone out that morning on London Radio for Cyprus and even at short notice a band of nearly two hundred had gathered, even tried to get inside to deliver a letter of protest, but the entrance to the embassy was guarded by bombproofed security that saw them coming before they'd begun to cross the road. They were orderly; a single armed policeman from the Diplomatic Protection Group turned them back and they spent the morning staring sullenly and shouting sporadic protests from behind security barriers. By the weekend their numbers would have grown tenfold.

Passolides was not among them that morning. As so often in his life he'd plowed a lonely furrow, taking himself not to the house of the hated Turk—what was the point?—but to the gates of Downing Street, where the source of this latest betrayal could be found.

Had not the British betrayed his people more consistently than any other conqueror? Stealing the whole island for almost a century, stealing the bases for even longer. Stealing his brothers. And their graves. Now taking the oil. You knew what to expect from a thieving Turk, they made no pretense at their nature. An absolute, uncomplicated enemy who would spit in your eye as they sliced through your throat. You could trust them to be what they were. But the British! They showered you in hypocrisy, fought with weasel words. Smiled and talked of the rules of cricket as they shafted you and sold your homeland into slavery.

He'd been gripping the barrier by the great iron gates of Downing Street for nearly half an hour when a policeman, wondering at the intensity of the old man's concentration and whitened knuckles, approached him.

"What are you doing, granddad?"

"Minding my own business."

"If you're standing there, it's my business too. What are you doing?"

"Waiting to see your Prime Minister."

"You're in luck. He's just on his way out."

As the Daimler rushed through the gates it slowed before entering the traffic of Whitehall, and Urquhart looked up from his papers to see an old man staring at him from across the barrier. Their eyes met, held each other for no more than a moment, but in that short time the force of those eyes burning ruby in hate had scorched across Urquhart's mind. And dimly, through the blastproof windows, he heard the one word the man's cracked voice hurled at him, and remembered its meaning.

"*Prodóte-e-e-es!*"

He recollected the first time he had encountered it—how could he forget? Carved into the chest of an eighteen-year-old boy they had dragged from the side of his family in the middle of his sister's marriage service and shot as he cringed against the church wall like a rat in a barn.

Traitor.

THIRTY-ONE

Asking a Greek to talk about democracy is like asking an American to teach table manners.

There were few obvious targets for an anti-British protest in Nicosia. British Leyland no longer existed; British Rail didn't run that far, even intermittently. The British High Commission provided an exceptionally unpalatable opportunity, being stuck by the accident of invasion on a finger of land barely a hundred meters wide that squeezed past the armed watch towers of Nicosia Jail on one side and the still more heavily armed watch towers of the Turkish Cypriot border patrols on the other. The chances of surprise were nil, the chances of success even poorer, the chances of a bullet from one side or the other excellent, so most Nicosian dissidents searched for other options.

The British Council down from the Paphos Gate was scarcely more welcoming. Since the last riot on its doorstep it had been heavily fortified behind steel shutters from which bricks and bottles bounced pointlessly, even when the sentries in the barracks at the end of the street cooperated by turning a blind eye.

So Dimitri, who had responsibility for the organization but

who had little concept of the Britishness of institutions such as Marks & Spencer and Barclays Bank, opted for British Airways and its glass-fronted operational headquarters that lay on Archbishop Makarios III Avenue.

The vanguard arrived soon after dusk, transported from the now-permanent camp of protest outside the Presidential Palace aboard a convoy of mopeds, vans, even taxis. Soon they were joined by many others on foot or using their own resources. The Word had spread.

An exceptional degree of discipline was evident in the early proceedings. Banners were handed out, instructions and advice issued. It helped, of course, that the stewards were theological students, many of whom were from the same village as Dimitri and his brother. An extended family. The Firm had been carefully constructed on foundations of rural solidarity and tribal loyalties; it wasn't going to fail its most famous son.

It also helped that the demonstrators far outnumbered the police, who seemed content to stand back and monitor proceedings. Several were smiling.

More demonstrators were arriving, the avenue was blocked. The police contingent began to concentrate its effort on diverting the traffic. One of the stewards chattered into a mobile phone, listened attentively, then nodded. Slowly his hand began to circle around his head, stirring the cauldron. The crowd, peaceful up to that point, began chanting, waving their banners, surging forward like a human oil slick on a flowing tide, lapping around the building and clinging to its plateglass windows. The sound of oil was everywhere.

"*British Out! Bones and Bases!*" they shouted; not very creative, perhaps, but there is little originality in anti-imperial protest. "*Make War, Not Peace*" was also much in evidence.

The windows, great sheets of glass set between concrete pillars, were pounded—they bent, buckled, bowed, but did not break, not until a sledgehammer had materialized and one by one they were all systematically shattered. Even then, the control was exceptional. They didn't ransack the offices; instead, the steward exchanged his mobile phone for a can of spray paint and covered the walls and display units with slogans.

By the time he had stepped outside again, two barrels of oil had been positioned either side of the shattered doorway; from the lintel above was hanging a spittle-drenched effigy of Nicolaou. A placard around his neck stated simply: "*Turk Lover*."

The shouting reached a crescendo, the pressure of numbers was growing, it would be difficult to control for much longer. It was time. Into each of the barrels was dropped a flare, and out of each began to pour vast quantities of choking black smoke. Oil smoke, which gushed into the night air, smearing the faces of those standing nearby, infesting every corner of the shattered building and burning itself into the morning's headlines.

As soon as he saw the smoke, the senior police inspector on the scene began issuing his first substantive orders. Lights flashed, sirens moaned, a fire tender began to edge through the crowd. But already the protesters were beginning to melt away into the Nicosian night, mission accomplished, message delivered.

Not a single arrest was made.

Dark spots of hate were breaking out across the Cypriot night.

Three streets away, in the back of his official Mercedes, Theophilos replaced the phone. A good evening's work. Exceptional work. God's work.

Francis Urquhart, when he heard about it, was of the same opinion.

Amid the stormy seas of stratagem devised by man, outcrops of nonsense stick defiantly above the waves. None stuck more defiantly than the case of Woofy.

Woofy—in fact, his full name was Woofer—was a three-year-old King Charles spaniel, the pet *in loco infantis* of Mr. and

Mrs. Peregrine Duckin who lived in comfortable retirement in a white stucco villa overlooking Coral Bay, a sand-strewn corner in the south west of the island. Their Greek was fragmentary, as were their relations with the indigenous population, which amounted to little more than a nodding acquaintance with several local traders, but a substantial number of the five thousand or so civilian Britons who lived in Cyprus did so in this area and they did not want for friends.

The Duckins were to need them. For when they returned from a bridge party organized by one of their more distant neighbors they discovered that their cherished villa had, inexplicably and without warning, burned to the ground.

What was worse, there was no trace of the still more cherished Woofer. All night long they searched, crying his name, calling out across the bay, cursing for the fact that the Cypriot fire brigade seemed to have taken an unconscionable time to arrive, then crying some more. But Woofer was nowhere to be found.

Dawn rose as the Duckins stood amid the smoking ruins of their home, imploring all passersby for news of their beloved dog. One of those passersby happened to be a freelance journalist enjoying a few days' break but, wherever intrepid journalists tread, disaster is sure to be found. He sympathized, listened carefully, took photographs, shared with them their inexplicable loss—although, in light of other anti-British outrages, the loss was perhaps—no, surely—less inexplicable than at first seemed. A story for its time, lacking nothing but raped nuns.

It duly appeared the following morning, splashed across the front page of Britain's leading tabloid. A forlorn British couple standing amid the ruins of their shattered Cypriot dream. Caught between the growing crossfire.

And beneath a blazing headline.

"CYPOS ATE MY WOOFY."

The effect of halogen lights spraying across old black brick at night gave the scene a distinctly monochrome cast. A little funereal, perhaps, Urquhart mused, but appropriately melodramatic. He adjusted his tie. Behind him, the Secretary of State for Defense stood starchly to attention. News cameras flashed as the Prime Minister stepped, stern of mouth, to the Downing Street microphones.

"Ladies and gentlemen, I have an important announcement to make. Events in Cyprus have taken a further turn for the worse. Not only has our High Commissioner still not been returned, but it is obvious that the Government in Nicosia is unable to guarantee the safety of British assets or personnel. Clearly the situation is being exploited by people of ill intent, and I have a duty to protect British citizens and military personnel. Therefore, with great reluctance and purely as a precautionary measure, I have been forced to place the British bases on a state of alert and restrict Cypriot access to them. British lives and property must be protected, and our troops will have full authority to do precisely that. This is a sensitive matter, and I ask you to treat it with the seriousness it deserves."

The scrum of reporters in front of him swayed as they pushed in unison, hands thrust forward waving microphones, tape recorders, and assorted electronic tendrils like a harvest of triffids. One scribe who looked as if he had only moments before clambered out of bed was all but bent double over the security barrier in his attempt to get as close as possible. "Prime Minister, what does this all mean?"

"It's a message to troublemakers. Keep off our patch."

"Doesn't this rattle sabers, raise the stakes, though?"

"The stakes have already been raised by others. Those who have kidnapped our High Commissioner. Who attacked British property and placed British lives in peril. I have a duty to respond."

"To attack?"

"This is an entirely defensive measure."

"Will the Cypriots see it that way?"

The expression around Urquhart's mouth grew yet more stiffly grim; he couldn't betray the ironic smile that played around the paths of his emotions. He knew the Cypriots, their passions—and their polemicists, in whose hands a state of alert would be turned into something akin to a force of invasion. This was going to get much, much worse before it got better. He couldn't smile, so he simply shrugged.

"Do you have the permission of the Cypriot President for this move?"

"I don't need it. Our bases in Cyprus are British sovereign territory. I no more need permission to put our troops there on alert than I would to move tanks across Salisbury Plain. I have, of course, informed him."

"How did he react?"

In agony. With pleading. Said it would inflame the hotheads. Would play into the hands of those who opposed the peace deal, increase the pressure on British bases. Begged to be given a few more days to obtain the release of the High Commissioner. But he'd already had several days…

"He regretted the necessity for this action. As do I. But men of goodwill everywhere will understand and must support this action. My first duty is to protect British interests."

"Play hell with the island's tourist trade, Prime Minister."

"Sadly, yes." Threatens to knock it on the head.

"Where does this leave the peace deal?"

"That's for the Cypriots to decide. I cannot help bring peace to Cyprus if they will not bring peace to themselves."

"And where does this leave the election?"

"On course. This is a move in the national interest, not for party purposes. I expect the support of all responsible politicians, all sides of the political debate. I don't expect this to become an issue in the election."

No, not an issue, mused Dicky Withers, *the* issue. I'm watching a piece of banditry, the hijacking of the election campaign as Urquhart casts himself in the role of statesman, defender of the national interest, the British way of life, the rules of cricket, warm beer, sunny afternoons, Blackpool beaches, morality, virginity, and any other -inity to which votes might be attached. And Makepeace, he's got Makepeace trussed up as tight as a gutted chicken. As tight, presumably, as is our High Commissioner. Francis, you old bastard.

"And Tom Makepeace?" Withers prompted. "Where does this leave him?"

The smile was demanding to emerge, as much in recognition of Dicky's perceptiveness as in self-congratulation. Makepeace was shafted. Adrift. Nowhere to go except to hell and back. A journey for which he would find few companions.

"Where does it leave Mr. Makepeace? I have no way of knowing. Perhaps you'd better ask him."

THIRTY-TWO

There is so much history stuffed into Cyprus that it has given them stomachache.

As the first rays of dawn spilled slowly across the salt flats of Akrotiri, a battered Bedford bus coughed its way uncertainly toward the entrance of the base. It sounded very sick. In better days it had carried children from the village to their schools and produce to the local market, but for almost a year had been languishing behind the pizza bar, its rust levels having been pronounced terminal. The arrival of the bus before the entrance to the base was heralded by a noxious belch of oil smoke and a groan in the manner of some disemboweled dragon. Then it slewed, fell and died, blocking the entire entrance. By the time the smoke had cleared and the guard had crept forward to inspect the prehistoric monster, it was empty.

They took more than an hour to move it. Attempts at restarting the engine failed, and it was difficult to get a tow truck hooked to either end. They tried to raise it on jacks but the suspension collapsed and the beast retaliated by rolling onto its side. Eventually they were forced to bring along an earthmover and push it out of the way.

But not before, in an envelope attached to the steering wheel and addressed to Billy, they had found Eleni's ring.

They were outside again, in greater number than ever. What, less than two weeks before, had begun as sporadic demonstrations by handfuls were now constant and too large to estimate accurately.

They were also intensely personal. Nicolaou was the name—the target—on everyone's lips. They displayed as much logic, perhaps, as when the mob had come to condemn Christ in the marketplace, but condemn him they did.

The head of presidential security had demanded an audience, interrupting Nicolaou in the first floor living room where he was listening to his daughter, Elpída, play the piano. Beethoven. Something loud and long, to block out the insistent noise coming from beyond the gates.

"We must disperse the protesters, sir. They're a danger to traffic, to themselves. To you."

"And how would you propose to accomplish that, Commander?" He was seated, his eyes closed, fingers pinching the bridge of his nose in both concentration and anxiety.

"I'd have to call in troops; there are too many of them for my guard."

Nicolaou was wide awake now. "I can scarcely believe my ears. You want me to set the army against the people?"

"These *people*—sir—are nothing short of a dangerous mob. They've already burned buildings, their numbers are growing, their demonstrations have been playing havoc all over Nicosia. My duty is to preserve peace around the presidential palace."

"And it is my duty, Commander, to secure the peace throughout our country. That's what is at stake here, nothing less. I will not permit you to use troops and tear gas against them."

"But I don't have enough men to guarantee the security of the grounds or this building. That means you, sir."

"I have no concern for my own safety."

"And your family?"

Nicolaou turned toward his daughter, who was still at the piano. She meant everything to him. When he was lonely because his wife was once more absent, Elpída was there as companion. When he grew outraged at his wife's indulgences, she was there to remind him of what he owed to his marriage. When he was uncertain, she acted as inspiration, raising him above the short-term and trivial to the Cyprus of tomorrow. Elpída's Cyprus. Balm for his every wound.

"It is precisely for her that I must say no. I can't sign a peace treaty with the Turks if there is blood on the streets of Nicosia."

"Sir!" The commander was pleading now. His voice dropped to prevent Elpída from hearing. "As an old friend. The choice you're facing is not so much *if* there will be blood, but *whose* blood it will be."

The President walked over to the window, from where he could see out over the floodlit statue of Makarios and the cypress trees to the impressive panorama beyond. "Panayoti, come here."

The Commander walked to the President's side. Nicolaou opened the window.

"What's out there?"

"A rabble. Baying at your doorstep."

"But what do you see out there?"

"The lights of the old city."

"And beyond that, in the darkness, is the other half of our country. Isn't it time, Panayoti, to bring those two halves back together again? After all these years and so much blood?"

"That's politics, sir. Your job. My job is security. And I tell you we've got to do something about those people out there."

With the window open the howl of protest had become unrelenting.

"Then I shall talk to them."

"This is no time for humor."

"Let a few of them in. I'll talk to them from the steps."

"Madness!"

"Perhaps so. But I shall do it nevertheless."

"At least talk to them from the balcony."

"The balcony where hangs the British Royal Standard? Peeking out from behind the imperial lion? I think not. No, let it be from the steps."

"But I can't guarantee your safety!"

"Then leave that task to God."

And Panayotis, as he had been trained throughout his career, no matter how unacceptable or unreasonable the command, had obeyed. They had planned on perhaps two dozen but numbers are impossible to control when thousands are pressing against the gates, and nearer two hundred had crowded their way in by the time the gates were forced shut once more. They gathered on the driveway before the main entrance, guarded by two ornamental cannons, assorted gargoyles, a couple of flower tubs, and a cohort of the palace guard.

Shouts of fury erupted as Nicolaou appeared, waving his hands above his head for calm.

"Cypriots, countrymen. Allow me to be heard. Allow yourselves to hear."

"Turk lover!" came the cry.

"I love only one thing. Cyprus!"

"Then why give it to the filthy Turks?"

"And the British!"

"No one has suffered more than I from the thought that our country is divided. I weep for those who have lost families. Homes. Everything."

"And won't lift a finger to help them."

Panayotis was growing increasingly nervous. It was already clear that Nicolaou had failed to gain control of the crowd, was entering into a dialogue of the deaf. His logic and sincerity stood no chance against the raw emotions of a mob.

"My friends, remember what split our island. What brought the Turkish Army to our shores. It was when we Greeks fell out among each other. When Makarios stood here on these very steps and they refused to listen to him." His hands stretched up one of the sandstone columns that stood to either side. "See these holes. Where the bullets struck. When they tried to kill our Archbishop."

A scattering of neat cylindrical holes and craters had been gouged from the columns, bullet holes, relics of the coup Makarios had ordered to remain, like the royal standard, as part of the heritage. Stigmata in stone. Now Nicolaou's fingers crept toward them, stretching out, reaching for the mantle of Makarios. The tips of his fingers were almost there when another hole appeared, accompanied by a cloud of dust. Only then did he hear the gunshot.

The effect on the crowd was immediate, as though a starting pistol had been fired. They began to surge forward, pushing against the cordon of guards in front of the steps like dogs at a deer. Nicolaou, bewildered and still only at the early stages of fear, found himself borne aloft in the arms of Panayotis and hustled through the main door, which was slammed shut behind them. Within seconds from the other side there came a primitive baying and a barrage of blows against the wood. At the same time the gates to the palace grounds that had been holding back the main body of protesters were swept aside as anger turned to rage at the sound of gunfire and thousands came streaming up the long driveway.

"For God's sake, now will you go?" Panayotis barked.

"Elpída," pleaded Nicolaou.

But his daughter was already running down the circular staircase from the private quarters, past the antiquities, the stone heads and torsos, a small harvest of the island's ancient heritage that would soon lie smashed and strewn upon the ground.

Father and daughter tried to embrace, but Panayotis was already pulling them apart and dragging them down the long corridor with its Moorish arches and youthful tapestries that led through the heart of the U-shaped building. Running beside them was the sound of shattering windows, raised voices, wrecking. Then more gunshots.

Panayotis led them to a part of the palace Nicolaou had never visited, at the back of the kitchens. A door. Stone steps. Another door for which Panayotis had a large key. Then they were in a tunnel hacked from the bare rock.

"Makarios Avenue," Panayotis whispered grimly. "His escape route at the time of the last coup."

It was cool, dimly lit, at least two hundred meters long, perhaps longer—Nicolaou had lost all sense of proportion in the confined space. His thoughts were befuddled, still worrying about his commander's words. "The last coup." Was this, too, a coup?

They emerged through another door at the far side of the swimming pool, beyond the amphitheater where Nicolaou had entertained groups of schoolchildren and where, in a previous time of trouble, the British had played tennis. Then they were in the woods, vast stands of eucalyptus that glowered in the moonlight. Behind them the noise of wreckage was growing ever more relentless.

They crossed the shale and loose rocks of a dried riverbed—Nicolaou lost his footing and was once more hauled aloft by the ready arms of his commander—and they came upon the chain-link fence that separated the palace grounds from whatever lay beyond. There were no protesters here; they were too busy in the Palace. They heard the sound of a muffled explosion. Panayotis dragged them on.

Another lock on the gate through the fence. Another key.

Panayotis seemed well prepared. Then they scrambled up a bank and were standing on an empty road.

"Where to, sir? A British base?" That was where Makarios had fled, to Akrotiri, into the arms of the old enemy and away from the waving fists of his own people, but Nicolaou decided he had already that evening donned too much of the Archbishop's mantle.

"No. Not to the British. To the mountains."

Then there were headlights advancing upon them. Panayotis drew a gun.

"Stay in the bushes, sir," he instructed, and stood in the middle of the road, waving his arms.

The car stopped. No rioters, only an elderly couple driving home after an evening meal. A German couple who spoke neither Greek nor English, but who understood all too well the unmistakable language of Panayotis's gun.

With a cry of alarm the man put his foot to the floor and sped off into the night. Panayotis shrugged his shoulders in despair. What was he supposed to do, shoot a couple of elderly and unarmed tourists?

"Leave it to me," Elpída instructed and pushed him aside.

The next car contained an accountant, who stopped and listened with growing incredulity to the pretty girl. He apologized, he was almost out of gas and his mother was expecting him home, but he would be happy to take them as far as he was going. The President of the Republic of Cyprus, his daughter, and the Commander of the Palace Guard thanked him as one and climbed into his battered Renault. They'd argue about distance and destination later.

Nicolaou looked behind him in the direction of his home. An angry orange moon shone down like a celestial torch, brushing the treetops and sprinkling them with fire. The view brought tears to the President's eyes as they drove away. It was only when he had dried them and was gripping the hand of his daughter that he realized it wasn't moonlight at all. He was watching the glow as, once again, the palace was being burned to the ground.

THIRTY-THREE

Honesty is not a policy. It is merely an excuse for moral idleness.

The battered Renault and its increasingly disorientated driver got them as far as a Hertz parking lot. There Panayotis acquired an alternative vehicle. It had no ignition key but the full tank of gas seemed more compelling since the few coins Panayotis kept in his trouser pocket for the cigarette machine proved to be the only money they had between them. Nicolaou found comfort in the knowledge that Panayotis hadn't thought of everything; somehow it made him feel less of a fool.

As soon as they were beyond the city limits of Nicosia on the road to the Troodos, Nicolaou fell into a deep sleep. The tension and—yes, he admitted it—fear had drained the energy from his veins and he was overcome by a most oppressive exhaustion. They had no idea whom they could trust—was this simply a riot or a full-blooded coup attempt? And if a coup, had it succeeded? Such matters could be determined from the Presidential Lodge in the mountains from where, for a few weeks in the height of the summer and if necessary for the next few days, the country could be run.

He did not wake until they were less than ten miles from their destination and the road had begun to wind and curl its way around the mountainsides. They were among thick pine forests, the heavy trunks picked out in the headlights, standing patiently like queues of hovering tax collectors. Not until they had turned off the main road and were approaching the compound along a narrow, steeply descending lane did their spirits begin to rise as the car lights played comfortingly across the familiar picket fence of the driveway.

"Home from home," Elpída whispered, for whom the mountains had always been a place of adventure and refuge.

"And from here it's a straight drive down to Akrotiri. If necessary," Panayotis added, practical as ever.

Nicolaou remained silent, winding down the window and allowing the sweet resin air to flood in and revive his bruised soul. From beneath the wheels came the sound of pinecones being crushed. No flag was flying and there was no one in the guard hut, no welcoming flash of light or howl of dogs, but no one had known they were coming. The familiar green roofs—all corrugated iron, as was the fashion in the Troodos, to deal with the snow—flashed past as though in an old film, and behind the low wall of the vegetable garden the tomato plants were flourishing, waving gentle welcome in the breeze. The car circled slowly around the drive and approached the front of the Lodge. The moon, so angry above the skies of Nicosia, here in the mountains was the color of ripe melon and surrounded by a million shy stars. It gave greeting, dusting the front of the house and lighting their path to the green double door. Everything was as it should be.

"It's open," Elpída muttered in relief as she tried the handle.

"Let me, miss," Panayotis insisted, and led the way into the dark hallway. He was fumbling for the light switch when he noticed a chink of light coming from under one of the doorways leading off the hall. Some fool of a maintenance engineer, leaving doors open and lights…

They entered the sitting room and looked around in numb amazement. It was busy with armed men, all standing, and pointing guns in their direction. Only two people were seated.

In one corner, bound to his chair and with a mouth taped beneath glassy, exhausted eyes, sat the British High Commissioner.

And by the fireplace directly in front of them, casually sucking at a small cigar, his lips twisted in a smile of greeting, sat Theophilos.

"*Kopiáste.*"

"Sit down and join us."

"Little wonder we couldn't find your lair."

Theophilos raised a tumbler of Remy in salutation of the compliment. "You didn't think to look in your own backyard, let alone your bedroom. Nor will anyone else. I have it all here—communications, security, food. Now, by the hand of God, even you."

Nicolaou tested the bonds that tied him, like the High Commissioner and the other hostages, to a chair. It was, as he knew it would be, a futile gesture. "How did you know I would come here?"

"He moves in a mysterious way." His deep voice had a lilt, as though he were singing the Eucharist. Then he laughed, raucously. "And He gave you only three choices." He counted them off on his fingers. "Death in the ruins of the Palace. A political burial with our British enemies in one of their bases, which is what I would have preferred—your memory would have been kicked like a manged dog from every coffeehouse in the country. Or, thirdly, deliverance unto me here. For that, too, I prepared; obviously you did not see my lookout at the edge of the compound."

"There are many things I appear not to have seen," Nicolaou

remarked with evident distress. He looked across the room to where his daughter was bound. "Do you intend to harm us?"

"If need be."

"In God's name what do you hope to achieve?"

"Why, in God's name, everything. First, we shall blockade the bases until the British are forced to pack their bags and go home. In the meantime, I fear, you will be too preoccupied to fly to London for the signing ceremony with the Turks. Too many pressing engagements here. Such as signing a decree nationalizing all British assets in Cyprus. Then, I suggest, you are likely to find yourself too exhausted to continue with the strains of office. You will hand over the presidency."

"To you? Never."

"No, my dear Nicolaou. I am but a humble cleric. It is possible in time that I might become Archbishop of Cyprus, but I have no wish to hold your office. So much strain and uncertainty, don't you find?" He settled back in the simple rustic furniture scattered around the small room; Nicolaou noticed that beneath his cassock he was wearing yellow socks. "Anyway, I have too much other…business, yes, business, to concern myself with."

"Then who?"

"Why, my brother Dimitri."

Dimitri smiled, an awful jagged expression.

"Then he'd better get his teeth fixed unless he wants to give the babies nightmares," Elpída spat.

The smile went out.

"You can't possibly hope to get away with it," Nicolaou challenged.

"But of course I shall. I have every advantage. The company of the British High Commissioner. The ear of the Cypriot President…"

"I'll not lift a finger to help you."

"And not only his ear," Theophilos continued unruffled,

"but also his arse. And, perhaps more importantly, his daughter's arse."

Dimitri had moved across to Elpída with the apparent threat of thumping the insolence out of her, but had changed tactics and instead was stroking her hair, moving his finger slowly down her neck to her shoulder. He was smiling again.

A strangled cry of protest racked through Nicolaou's throat.

"I think I hold all the aces," Theophilos said, without a trace of compassion.

THIRTY-FOUR

A manifesto is like a well-cut suit. Its function is to hide a politician's nakedness.

Every step of his arrival had been greeted with a loud cry of "Huzzah!" from his troops. He had paraded before them, stiffening sinews, summoning up the blood. He could all but hear the impatient stamp of horse and the whisper of swords settling into well-oiled scabbards. An army ready to do battle.

The business was done, the Electoral Reform Bill passed, the sun setting on another Parliament. On the morrow they marched. All lungs were filled with courage, all nostrils with the scent of death—of others hopefully, perhaps of their own.

Urquhart's troops took their farewells, hearts gladdened by the propitious omens. Every hour seemed to bring news of further polls and press barons marching to their support, and already several of the enemy's generals had made it known they would be heading not to the sound of battle but only to the Chiltern Hills and, if favor shone upon them, to the House of Lords. As for the hapless Clarence, Leader of the Forces of Opposition, the soothsayers were already gathering outside his tent, their speculations vivid as to whether he would fall on his sword or have to be hacked. If, indeed, he managed to survive the battle. Three weeks on Thursday.

And of Makepeace there had been no sound, and scarcely sight. A general without troops.

Time to let slip the dogs of war.

She began to shiver and yelp, a noise like a beaten dog, her cries filling the room and tumbling through the open window, but still he did not stop.

Makepeace had called her, said he needed her, and she had jumped. And so had he, as soon as she came through the door and dropped her bag, but it was not an exercise of adventure, more in the manner of a savage reprisal and experimentation in pain. When it was over, he buried his head in the pillow, ashamed of her silent tears.

"You've never been like that before," she mourned. She thought she could taste blood in her mouth.

When eventually his face rose from the pillow, his eyes were also rimmed red. "I don't expect you to forgive me. I've never done anything like that before. I feel such a bloody fool. Sorry."

"You ought to be."

For a while she plotted retribution, thought she might hit him, take a bread knife and split him in two, but their relationship was more than sex, more even than love. Somehow she sensed that he was the victim. Instead of rushing for the kitchen she stared at the confusion in his eyes. "Rough day?"

"The bloodiest. Ever. Like I want to destroy the last thing that's important to me. Before, like everything else I cherish, it turns and destroys me."

She raised herself on an elbow, ready to listen. It was the moment to reach for a cigarette.

"It was the final Question Time. I arrived early but the bench was already crowded. They'd deliberately squeezed up to leave no room for me. So I shoved myself in, right at the end, all elbows and shoulders and nudging. Like a prep school bus trip. Then Marjory appeared—you know, the one who looks like a moulting orange squirrel and throws up barricades before breakfast? She just stood there, waiting to get past. So I… moved. Got up to let her past. Then they simply pushed again. Pushed me right out. They were all laughing, mocking me." He cringed with the humiliation—"No room for me on either side of the House. I had to sit on the bloody floor."

Slowly she began to gurgle with mirth.

"You too?" His eyes flared in accusation but already the truth was beginning to dawn. "It was so bloody childish." An expression of self-ridicule trickled from between reluctant lips. "And so very effective." He had the grace to look embarrassed.

Her lips brushed at the creases.

"But there was more. The frustration of knowing there was nothing I could do or say. Urquhart stood there accepting the plaudits of his acolytes and the rest of us were left like a crowd at a coronation."

"Didn't you try to say anything about Cyprus?"

"And give him the chance to play his Churchill impersonations? Didn't you hear what he said in his speech last night? 'Wherever an Englishman stands, there we shall stand also. Wherever an Englishman falls, there we shall be to raise him up…'" His fingers began to twist at the loose ends of her hair. "I'm facing the most important battle of my life and I don't have a single ally. Except for you. Even Annita can't look me in the eye."

The rage was gone; the brutal man had become no more than a little boy lost.

"There were so many who promised to walk with me. Now not one of them seems able to find their feet. All I have is the hope that I might be able to hold on to my own seat. Otherwise…" He deflated into his pillow.

"There are plenty of people who will walk with you, ordinary people outside of Westminster. You're not alone."

"Truly?"

"You know it's true."

"But I've no time. No party. No friends. No issue anymore. Urquhart's like some malevolent magician, he's made them all vanish."

"Go over Urquhart's head. Stand up for fair play. Give people an excuse to march with you."

"Without a political machine it'd be a damn long march."

"That's a great idea."

"What is?"

"A Long March. Instead of burying yourself in your constituency, take your cause to the people in the country. Walk with them. Talk with them. Show the world your strength."

He sat up. "What would be the point?"

"It's a means of showing how much support you have. A way to become a figure of real power and authority after the election, even if you don't yet have a party and a hundred parliamentary seats. Be a voice for all those who feel disillusioned and left out of the present system. A one-man revolution."

He curled up his legs, placing his chin on his knees while he considered. "Great media possibilities. A march from—where, Manchester to London via Birmingham?—the country's three greatest cities with speaking stops and interviews on the way."

"Surrounded by supporters, real people, not ancient party hacks. Something fresh, a total contrast to all the other campaigns."

"Best way of beating the Government machine in my own constituency, by showing national support." He was beginning to bounce on the mattress, inflated by enthusiasm, when suddenly the air began to escape.

"Do we have time? It would need a big start. And would need to grow, momentum to keep it going."

"I'll provide the start. Give me three days and I'll deliver two thousand Greek Cypriots anywhere in the country, with posters in every high street and organizational support in every town. After that it's up to you and a lot of luck."

"If it fails, peters out, my political career will be ruined."

"If you don't try it, you're ruined anyway. What have you got to lose?"

"Nothing, I suppose. Apart from you."

She pulled him toward her. "Come and show me how it's done properly. Before we go out and do it to Francis Urquhart."

"If I'm to do all this walking, hadn't I better preserve my strength…?"

But already his protests were too late.

"Come, Corder, it's a warm day. Into the garden."

Superintendent Corder of the Special Branch followed his Prime Minister through the Cabinet Room and down into the walled garden. Urquhart indicated a bench beneath the shade of a rowan tree and they sat down together. Tea was ordered.

The privilege of such intimacy was not lightly bestowed, but Corder had earned the trust over many years of loyalty and unquestioning service. He was unmarried, had never displayed anything other than a mechanical sense of humor, a policeman with a university education but few apparent interests apart from his work of heading Urquhart's personal security team, passing up promotion in order to remain in that task. He was an extraordinarily self-contained individual whose first name was known to very few. Mortima, who had tried to interest him in opera, occasionally speculated that the Urquharts were his only friends. But they were of different worlds. Once, while on a pheasant shoot in Northamptonshire, Urquhart had winged a bird that had crashed from the sky to lie fluttering pathetically in front of them. Before anyone could move, Corder had drawn his revolver and finished the job, the 9 mm bullet at such close range spreading pieces of giblet for several feet in every direction. As Urquhart related later to his wife, not very sporting but damned effective.

Corder had a small red file in his hand, which he opened in his lap.

"Probably not significant, but I'm not paid to take risks, sir." He spoke in a series of assaults, short, rapid bursts, rather like machine gun fire. "Over the last few days the local Greek Cypriot radio station in London has been spouting like a volcano, throwing all sorts of criticism in your direction. Getting really carried away. But the worst has come from this man." He handed across the file. "Evanghelos Passolides. About your age. Appears to own some sort of eating house in north London. We don't know much about him, apart from the fact that he appears to have connections with Mr. Makepeace. And that he's said on live radio—the transcript's at the back of the file"—in a monotone Corder began quoting from memory—"that you deserve to have the skin ripped from your lying bones, various material parts of your anatomy thrown to dogs, and the rest of you buried in a deep grave and forgotten about in the same manner he suggests you've forgotten about his brothers. He's the gentleman who…"

"Yes, Corder, I know who this gentleman is," Urquhart whispered, staring at the photograph in the file. "And I haven't forgotten his brothers."

His mouth had run dry and he longed for the tea at his side, but he knew his hand would shake and betray him, so long as those eyes of long-festered malevolence were staring up at him. Abruptly he closed the file. So now he knew the name of the brother. Had seen him, practically on his doorstep, had felt his hate, which refused to die. It was as though ghosts from all those years ago had chased him around the world.

"Probably a harmless old crank," Corder was saying, forgetting the age similarity with Urquhart, "but he has threatened you, and what with you being out and about on the campaign trail we can't afford to take chances. What would you like me to do with him? Warn him off? Lock him away for a bit? Or forget about him? As it's election time and this is all very personal, I thought this one should be your call. Even parking tickets can get political at a time like this."

"Thank you, Corder," Urquhart responded softly. A gentle breeze riffled through the honeysuckle and ran across the lawn, glancing off Urquhart's brow. He could feel prickles of sweat.

"Trouble is, if we do nothing it could simply get worse. His threats. The bilge on the radio. Do you want me to have him shut up?"

There were other voices, too, inside Urquhart's head, whispering, blowing at the mists of doubt, helping him to see more clearly and to decide.

"No, Corder, not the man, don't touch him. No martyrs. But the station..."

"London Radio for Cyprus."

"It must surely have broken all sorts of codes. Race Relations Act, election law, any number of broadcasting regulations."

"I'll bet it's probably got illegal substances hidden on the premises, too. Could almost guarantee it."

"Yes, I suspect you could. Let's pull the plug on them, revoke their broadcasting license. Silence their foul mouths. Then there would be no need to run the risk of turning Passolides into an object of public sympathy. What do you think?"

"Just tell me when you want their lights to go out, and it's done."

"Excellent. Now, Corder, tell me about the old man's links with Mr. Makepeace..."

"And it turns out he's been rogering the daughter."

Tom hadn't wasted much time, Claire mused. Rebounding like a badly sliced golf ball.

"The thing that surprises me," Urquhart was saying, "is that you'd heard nothing about it. From the driver. Apparently they've been going at it like Caribbean cats in an alley."

Surprised her, too. The driver must have known, told Joh. Ah, but there it was. Joh hadn't told her. Wouldn't have told her. All too close to home, perhaps…

"We need to know more. Does he dress up as Robin Hood? Leap from piles of *Hansard*? Nuggets like that are more precious than pieces of the cross," Urquhart continued, "in encouraging those lame mules in the press to rise up as one beast."

All this prying, probing for weaknesses. Not the best way, she was beginning to realize. Not Joh's way. He'd not been the first of the Carlsens she had known. Claire and his son, Benny, had been contemporaries at university, and had been considerably more. Their affair had begun at the start of the Trinity term in a punt moored beneath a conspiring willow on one of the headwaters of the Cherwell and had continued throughout a glorious summer of hedonism spent among the sand dimes and melon patches of Zakynthos, living in a state of self-centered lust. One evening they'd gone to watch the turtles clamber up the beach to their nesting sites; they'd taken a bottle and already had more than enough to drink. They'd met another, older man, on his own. Benny had suggested they share the drink and, later, had suggested they share her, too. And why not? Benny would've jumped at a similar chance. She'd obliged, on the warm sands of turtle beach, and after that it had never been the same between her and Benny. Up to that point they'd tried to share all their sexual experiences and appetites, but this one she hadn't afterward wanted to share. It had been a mistake, an own goal, something that made her realize she might have the body of a woman but yet lacked judgment in its use. And judgment about Benny. She didn't want to talk about it. So he'd grown jealous, obsessive, tormented by the memory of her writhing pleasurably in the moonlight, and they had bickered all the way back to their separate and final years of study.

Then, a lifetime later, she had met Joh. She hadn't wanted to fall in love with him and had tried hard to prevent it but it had happened. And, when she had met Benny again after all those years and Joh had read the tormented expressions on their faces, he had known. He blamed no one and had understood when Benny decided to go and run the Stockholm office and rarely visited. He had never asked.

How different Joh was from Francis Urquhart. Urquhart always searched for weaknesses to exploit, private pieces that would wither a man's reputation to the roots when exposed to the sun. For him, every man of stature was a threat to be cut down to the stump. She began to realize that for Urquhart there were no mountains, no glorious escarpments and swooping valleys, only a flat and desolate landscape upon which he alone cast a shadow.

She'd learned a valuable lesson today. She found Francis Urquhart hugely attractive. But she didn't very much like him.

THIRTY-FIVE

There is no democracy in Heaven. I think God has a point.

They'd discovered you couldn't organize a huge march in three days, but in five they had worked wonders. The novelty of the idea in a campaign that threatened to be squeezed of initiative by the party machines attracted several showy pieces in the press and on television, and fifty thousand leaflets were printed, their hurried and unambitious style carrying an appealing touch of sincerity. A small alternative advertising agency developed a logo for T-shirts emblazoned with the message "*FU Too.*" He sighed when he saw it, but discouraged no one—if the event were small enough for him to control, he would already have failed. Only the route was firmly within his grasp—authorities permitting. The line of march was to begin in Albert Square beside the Town Hall in Manchester and finish in Trafalgar Square, something over two hundred miles in fourteen days with the bits in between being worked on almost as they marched. But march they did.

There were considerably fewer than two thousand on that first Sunday morning and their politics were distinctly dappled—the great majority were Cypriots with their families but there were also environmentalists, militant vegetarians, a smattering from the antihunting lobby who came to present a petition and left, a woman who had been at university with Makepeace and now ran a free-love-and-alfalfa commune somewhere in Cumbria, and three candidates from the Bobby Charlton for President Party. There were also enough journalists and television cameras to make it worthwhile. They came to look, to crow, to write feature pieces dipped in condescension and cant. "*Making War with Makepeace,*" the *Telegraph* wrote opposite a photograph of three members of the Manchester Akropolis weight-lifting team persuading the candidate of the Sunshine Brotherhood to put his clothes back on. Others wrote of chaotic coalitions, of Makepeace and his coat of many colors. But they wrote. And others read. It gave Makepeace a chance.

The Battle Bus, as it was known, was a specially designed coach armored with Kevlar and mortarproof compartments that had been constructed as Urquhart's primary means of road transport for the campaign. Chauffeur-driven Daimlers were deemed too remote and untouchable for the ordinary voter—although had any ordinary voter managed to penetrate the cordon of security thrown around the Battle Bus at every stop and touched anything apart from the windscreen wiper, they would have activated an alarm system delivering almost as many Special Branch officers as decibels. In motion now, sliding through the night air on its way back to London, there was nothing to disturb the Prime Minister's peace but the whisper of air conditioning and the quiet murmurings from the front compartment of aides conducting a postmortem on the day's campaigning.

The campaign rally had been a success—no hint of hecklers getting into the hall, a good speech and, Urquhart had to admit, an even better video, although Mortima had been going on about resetting the music track. The evening had rather made up for the afternoon, an industrial visit to a factory that made agricultural equipment that included cattle prods. Some reptile from the press pond had discovered that the biggest single order for the electronic prods came not from an agricultural concern but from the National Police Headquarters in Zaire. Testicle ticklers. Urquhart had decided he'd test one on the cretin who arranged the visit.

But that had been the Six O'Clock News and now the main evening news pictures and the morning headlines would carry more sensible coverage. Not a bad day's work, he reflected as he rested, eyes closed, in the Tank Turret—the bus's fortified central compartment.

There was a tugging at his sleeve. "Sorry to disturb you, Prime Minister, there's a call from Downing Street. You'll need the scrambler."

A sense of anticipation rose through tired limbs as he picked up the phone. It was his private secretary.

"Prime Minister, shall we scramble?"

Urquhart pushed the red button. During the last campaign they'd discovered a car shadowing the route of the bus with sophisticated monitoring equipment, hoping to pick up the chatter of the mobile phones and fax machines. He'd been disappointed to discover that the eavesdroppers were from neither the Opposition nor the IRA, either of which would have doubled his majority, but simply freelancers from a regional press bureau. They'd pleaded guilty to some minor telegraphy offense and been fined £100, making several thousand by selling details of their enterprise to the *Mirror*. He held a sneaking admiration for their initiative, but it had left his civil servants as reluctant to break news as pass wind. To bother him on the campaign trail betokened a matter of some importance.

He listened attentively for several minutes, saying little until the call had finished and he had switched off the phone.

"Trouble?" Mortima inquired from her seat on the other side of the bus where she had been signing letters.

"For someone."

"Who?"

"That remains to be seen." His eyes flashed and he drew back from his thoughts. "There has been an announcement from Cyprus. It appears that our High Commissioner and their President Nicolaou are both alive, well, and being held hostage in the mountains."

"By whom?"

He laughed, genuinely amused. "By a bloody bishop."

"You've got to get them out."

Urquhart turned to examine Mortima, who shared none of his humor.

"It will be all right, Mortima."

"No it won't," she replied. Her tone had edges of razor. "Not necessarily."

In the subdued night lighting of the bus he could sense rather than see her distress; he moved to sit beside her.

"Francis, you may never forgive me..." She was chewing on the soft flesh in her cheek.

"I've never had anything to forgive you for," he replied, taking her hand. "Tell me what's worrying you."

"It's the Urquhart Library and the Endowment. I've been making plans..."

He nodded.

"Making arrangements for the funding."

"I'm delighted."

"Francis, I did a deal with President Nures. If I could help him achieve a satisfactory arbitration decision for the Turkish side, he would ensure a consultancy payment made over to the Library fund."

"Do we have a fund?"

"In Zurich."

"And did you—help achieve a satisfactory decision?"

"I don't know. I had a talk with Watling but I've no idea if it helped. The point is, neither does Nures. I told him I'd fixed it and he's delighted."

"How delighted?"

"Ten million dollars."

"A drop in an ocean of oil."

"These arrangements are normal business practice in that part of the world…"

"A finder's fee."

"…and I have a letter signed by him to confirm the arrangement. He also has one from me. One letter each, guaranteeing our good faith. No copies. Just him and me. No one else knows."

Urquhart considered all he had been told, his fingers steepled as though in communion with a higher authority. He seemed to find some answer and turned slowly to his wife.

"So what is the problem?"

"I also did a deal with the wife of President Nicolaou."

He shook his head in confusion.

"She approached me at a meeting of the Commonwealth Parliamentary Wives—we've always got on well over the years at those meetings. She'd just come from Paris—she has good contacts there, perhaps a lover, I'm not sure. Anyway, she'd heard reports of the oil, very specific reports, said how important it was to her poor country. And to some immensely rich oil concerns in Paris. How grateful both would be for any help… So, we did a deal. I would try to help, no guarantees. Payment only on result. Nothing if the Greeks lost the waters, nothing if they found no oil. On two conditions. That all dealings would be conducted through her, so I would never have to meet anyone else and my name wouldn't be revealed to the people in Paris."

"Very sensible. And the second condition?"

"Four million dollars."

"She must have been deeply disappointed at losing out on the decision."

"We cried on each other's shoulder."

"Does her husband know?"

"No. He's an unworldly academic…"

"He's a Greek politician."

"He didn't know, I'm sure. It would have raised too many questions about her—how can I put it?—friends in Paris."

"Then what is worrying you so?"

"Another letter. From me to her. Which apparently she left in a safe in the Presidential Palace. Now she doesn't know who's got it, even if it still exists."

His words were slow and solemn. "That is a considerable pity." The implications were all too apparent.

She fell silent for a moment, eyes downcast. "I've been trying to find the right moment to tell you. Do you hate me?"

He looked at her for a long time until, in the shadows of the night, her eyes came up to meet his once more.

"Mortima, all you have ever done you have done for me. As far as I have ever climbed, you have been at my side. All we have ever achieved has been achieved together. I could not feel anything for you that I do not feel for myself. I love you."

Her eyes washed with gratitude but there was still within them a cold glint of fear. "But, Francis, the letter may fall into the wrong hands. It would destroy me. And with it, you."

"*If* it fell into the wrong hands."

"Do you realize what must be done? We have to make sure the letter is safe. Grab back the President. Send in the troops. Take on the Cypriot mob. Use any means and any force necessary."

"But haven't you realized, Mortima? That is precisely what I have planned to do all along."

❖ ❖ ❖

They were prepared for the assault. Somehow they'd figured it out—perhaps it was the unexpected request for all recent program tapes, or an unwise word on the telephone from one of the officials at the Radio Authority in Holborn. For when three police vans and an RA van drew up outside 18 Bush Way, the doors were blockaded and the airwaves drenched in emotional outpourings that would have done justice to the Hungarian Uprising. Not from Franco, of course. At the first hint of trouble he'd legged it, suggesting that to get caught up in a hassle with officialdom might interfere with his Open University course. They could have used Franco, shoved him in the metal cabinet jammed up against the front door to give it more dead weight.

Resistance was never likely to be more than token; there were too many windows, too many hands on too many sledgehammers for them to hold out long. London Radio for Cyprus went off the air as a policeman kicked out the lock of the studio door and with a polite "Excuse me, sir," reached across and flicked off the power supply. Simultaneously he also managed to kneel on the producer's fingers, although whether by accident or design was never established.

But not before the excited Cypriot had succeeded in squeezing out one final phrase of defiance. The EOKA cry of resistance.

"*Eleftheria i Thánatos!*"

When Passolides returned that afternoon from purchasing fresh crab and vegetables at the market, he found the plateglass frontage to his restaurant smashed to pieces and the curtain of seclusion ripped into shreds. A neighbor told him that a car had drawn up, a man climbed out with a sledgehammer and without any evident sense of haste had calmly shattered the window with three blows.

Passolides hadn't called the police, he didn't trust them, but they arrived anyway, a man in plain clothes with an indecipherable name flashing a warrant card.

"Not a lot we can do, sir," he'd explained. "Trouble is, outspoken gentlemen like you make yourselves targets at a time like this. Lot of anti-Cypriot feeling around in some quarters, what with the High Commissioner gone missing. Wouldn't be surprised if this happened again."

He'd closed his notebook, dragging back the remnants of curtain to peer inside.

"By the way, sir, I'll tell the sales tax people you're ready for inspection, shall I?"

The French Foreign Minister sat studying papers before the start of the meeting in Brussels. It was more than the routine gathering of the Council of Foreign Ministers; indeed it had an element of drama. The British would be practicing a little crawling today, and it would force that appalling man Bollingbroke to adopt a position of vulnerability that the Frenchman was looking forward to exploiting. He'd taken enough from the Englishman in recent weeks; he relished the opportunity to show that handing out punishment was not an exclusive Anglo-Saxon prerogative.

His reverie was broken by the clamping of a large hand on his shoulder.

"Allo, Allen."

Damn him. Bollingbroke always Anglicized the name, refusing to pronounce it properly.

"Looking forward to a fine meeting today, Allen. You know, getting your support on this Cyprus matter."

"It's a complicated problem. I feel it would be inadvisable to rush…" But already the Englishman was talking through him. It was like watching a bulldozer trying to cut grass.

"It could get rough, you know. Might have to send in the

troops. But I've just thought, Allen. What you ought to do. Offer us some of your own troops, a sort of international gesture. After all, we're trying to sort out an international problem. Restoring order and democracy in Cyprus. We'd take care of 'em, make sure none of 'em got hurt."

"They can certainly take care of themselves," the Frenchman responded, ruffling with pride. "But are you suggesting that we give you French troops to help sort out this mess you English have got yourselves into?"

"That's right."

"Impossible!"

"You surprise me," Bollingbroke responded, astonishment wrinkled across his face. "I'd have thought you'd jump at it. Why, give you Frenchies a chance to be on the winning side for a change."

Another hand came down on the Frenchman's shoulder, a playful tap he suspected was intended to break his collarbone. His neck turned the color of the finest Burgundy as he threw aside the folder containing his briefing notes. He knew how to handle this meeting.

The French representative was adamant and intractable. He would not be moved and, since most of the other partners had little desire to be moved, even the traditional compromise of fudge was lost. Every request by the British Government for support was turned down. Flat. *Non!* No token troops, no selective sanctions, not even words of encouragement or understanding. Europe turned its back on Bollingbroke. Throughout the long meeting he argued, cajoled, insisted, threatened, suggested all sorts of dire repercussions, but to no avail. And when the vote was taken and he stuck out like a stick of Lancashire rhubarb, he simply smiled.

They've no idea, he mused to himself. Middle of an election campaign and Europe says No. Deserts us. With British lives at stake. It'll be the Dunkirk spirit all over again. They'll be running up Union Jacks on every council estate in the country and saying prayers in chapel in praise of Arthur Bollingbroke. And Francis Urquhart, of course. Just as FU had said they would.

Bloody marvelous.

THIRTY-SIX

If you want a camel to move you shove a stick up its arse, and the bigger the stick, the quicker he'll obey. I put a lot of stick about.

It was Thursday. Exactly two weeks to go before the election.

"I am concerned, Prime Minister, that we should not rush into things. There are lives at stake and, to be frank, we've never prepared for a contingency of this sort. Invading Cyprus, if you will."

"Don't worry, General, I've thought of that for you."

The Deputy Chief of Defense Staff (Commitments), Lieutenant General Sir Quentin Youngblood, cleared his throat. He wasn't used to having his military judgment either questioned or improved. "But with the greatest respect, Prime Minister, we've found no one who can brief us on the layout. We simply don't know what this Presidential Lodge looks like and what sort of target it will be."

"Look no further, General. I visited the Lodge several times when I was serving in Cyprus. It used to be the summer home of the British Governor. It won't have changed much; the Cypriots are sticklers for tradition. Too idle for change."

"Even so, there are so many political complications. I must ask for a little more time for preparation." He looked around the other members of the War Cabinet seeking support. The Defense Secretary was shuffling his briefing papers, about to join in.

"No!" Urquhart's hand banged down on the Cabinet table. "You're asking to give the bloody Bishop more time. Time in which he will strengthen his position and raise the costs for us all..."

Let alone increase the chances of Mortima's letter falling into the wrong hands.

"But there are logistical problems, too. We can't afford to rush in blind," Youngblood protested.

Urquhart looked around the table at COBRA, the Cabinet subcommittee gathered together to handle "Operation Defrock," as Urquhart had called it. Apart from Youngblood there sat Bollingbroke as Foreign Secretary, the Defense Secretary, the Attorney General (to pronounce on legal requirements), and the Party Chairman to help with presentation and the selling of a great victory. The defense chiefs had muttered objections to the inclusion of the Party Chairman, afraid that it would make the matter seem all too party political a fortnight before polling day. How right they were.

Booza-Pitt had asked to be included, practically begged. For however long it lasted this exercise was going to be at the top of the news and he wanted to be there with it. He'd left a pleading message with Urquhart's private office, insisting that as head of one of the three great departments of state his input and inclusion were vital. But it was a busy day; Urquhart hadn't even bothered to reply. "Life is destined to be so full of disappointments for the boy," he'd ventured to his private secretary. But at least Booza-Pitt wasn't a man of faint heart, unlike some. Urquhart stared directly at the General.

"These logistical problems. What form do they take?"

Youngblood drew breath. "Since the rather lurid reports were published of the Foreign Secretary's discussions in Europe"—Youngblood cast a reproachful look across the table, determined that blame should be shifted onto political shoulders—"elements of the Cypriot community have treated our preparations as tantamount to a declaration of war. My local commander in Cyprus tells me of a considerable increase in public hostility. It has made any initiative we might take considerably more complicated."

"And will grow more complicated the longer we leave it."

"But at this stage there are too many imponderables. I cannot guarantee success."

"You cannot guarantee that the British Army can whip a bloody bishop?" Urquhart could scarcely contain his derision.

"Success in my opinion is achieving our objectives without unnecessary loss of life."

"And it is delay that threatens disaster. Timing, timing, timing, General. For God's sake, the Presidential Lodge is barely twenty miles along good roads from our base at Akrotiri. We could be there before your tea's had time to grow cold."

"But..."

"Are there armed men waiting at the gates of Akrotiri to intercept our convoy? Is that what you are afraid of?"

"There is a blockade..."

"No, General. No more excuses. The time has come." Without taking his eyes off the military man, Urquhart had reached for the red phone that sat in front of him on the Cabinet table and raised it to his ear.

"Give me Air Marshal Rae."

"Prime Minister!" Youngblood protested in puce. "The chain of military command and communication goes through me. We cannot have politicians interfering in a military operation and..."

"General, you've already insisted that this is a political

operation as well as a military one. Are you trying to deny the Prime Minister the right to discuss matters with the local commander?"

Youngblood stared back defiantly but held silence, uncertain of his ground. Air Vice-Marshal Rae was not only the Commander, British Forces Cyprus, but had a further role as the Administrator of the Sovereign Base Areas, effectively the political governor of the British territories. Two hats. But which was he wearing at this moment…? While Youngblood pondered several centuries of constitutional etiquette and precedent, the communications chain of command that ran through operational headquarters at Northwood and onward via satellite above the Sahara had worked without flaw; within seconds Urquhart was linked with the Commander/Administrator in Episkopi at the heart of the Akrotiri base.

"Air Marshal Rae, this is the Prime Minister. I'm talking from the Cabinet Room. I understand your base is under some form of blockade."

He paused while he listened.

"I see. There are two hundred women at the gates blockading it with prams and babies' strollers." The glance he shot at Youngblood was like a viper's tongue. "In your opinion, would breaking through that blockade of prams constitute a threat to the lives of British servicemen?"

A pause.

"I thought not. That being the case, Air Marshal, my orders to you are to cordon off the Presidential Lodge. Make sure that the Bishop and the hostages cannot get out, and no one else can get in. I want it sealed tight. That is to be done immediately. You are then to wait for further instructions. Is that clear?"

Urquhart turned his attention to those in the Cabinet Room. "Gentlemen, are we in agreement?"

All eyes were turned to Youngblood. Now that the orders

had been issued, to dispute them would be professional suicide. He would have no choice but to resign. And, as Urquhart knew, he was not a rash man, likely to jump to precipitate action. The General found something of consuming interest to study among the papers in front of him.

The news cameraman knew the moment was at hand from the increased level of noise, of shouted commands, of stamping feet and revving engines that had been coming from behind the wire and outbuildings at Episkopi all through the night. He could sense rather than see a change in the activity around the gates, a quickening of pace behind the rolls of razor wire, a sharpness in the reflex, like a lumbering sumo wrestler about to hurl himself at his opponent. The women sensed the change, too, calling to their children, hugging them more closely than ever, reassuring each other even while their eyes spoke of anxiety and danger. Keep together, they whispered. Success through solidarity. And they had chained and tied the collection of prams and strollers together such that it would take an hour to untangle them all.

But "Stinger" Rae did not have an hour.

The first sign of movement came soon after dawn from two olive-painted vehicles that drove up rapidly until a squeal of brakes brought them to a halt only inches from the gates. Several of the women at the front of the demonstration stood in order to gain a clearer view; they were the first to be hit and sent sprawling by the powerful water jets of the fire tenders. The vehicles were not specifically built for riot control, the nozzles of their hoses not set for maximum force, but nevertheless the impact of these "gentle persuaders," as Rae's press officer would later term them, was devastating. Within less than a minute the demonstration in front of the gates had been washed away in a flood of children's screams. Even as they sobbed in the rushing gutters and on the grass verges around the gateway, teams of servicemen ran into action. The first removed the razor wire, dragging it roughly to one side, another team of medics fanned out among the women and their infants to minister to the minor injuries, abrasions, and bruises that had been inflicted and the vapors thereby caused. Hot coffee and milk were already at hand. A third team of military policewomen scoured through the overturned and waterlogged baby vehicles to ensure that they were all empty. One sleeping infant was lifted from a stroller and handed to his dazed mother sitting on the grass verge. Then the all clear was pronounced.

With a grumble of diesel engines, a long snake of vehicles came into view, headed by a phalanx of four-ton trucks. They hit the jumble of baby carriages at a good thirty, and left them crushed flat beneath the tires. They were followed by ambulances, Land Rovers, a signals truck, and more four-tonners, carving through the barricade like a sleigh through fresh snow. They left behind them the tears of children and the sight of sobbing women picking over the wreckage, just in case. They also left behind them a delighted news cameraman.

They took the main road into the hills, past the dam, until their progress was slowed by the serpentlike curving of the black tar as it wound its way through the pine forests. The air was noticeably cooler; the drivers could smell the pine resin even inside their cabs as they crashed their way down through the gears. They encountered no opposition. Fifty-three men in all, led by a Lieutenant Colonel Rufus St. Aubyn, which included the assault force, four specialist signals operators, a squad of diversionary troops, and medics. Just in case.

In two hours they were there. Turning off the main road beneath the gaze of the huge golf ball radar domes that dominated the highest points, dropping down a gorge strewn with the tall, mastlike trunks of pines. At the top of the gorge they left two men and a roll of razor wire, more than enough to secure the narrow entryway. At the lowest point, where the road rejoins the main highway, they did the same. And in between on a carpet of pine kernels but out of sight of the green metal roof of the Lodge, the remainder of the troops scurried around to spy out the land and secure their communications.

Within four hours it was done.

That evening Makepeace, with Maria at his side, held a rally to the south of the pottery town of Stoke-on-Trent. Five days had passed since the start of the Long March and it had come to a crucial phase. The novelty was gone, and so had many of the hangers-on, particularly those who were there to gawp or to disrupt, perhaps, the type that gathers to stare as a man stands on a ledge and threatens to jump. In Makepeace's case he had jumped and they'd been interested solely in the gruesome result. Yet he had disappointed them. He'd bounced.

Most who still walked with Makepeace were now intent on the same purpose of protest. None but a handful had followed him all the way, but many came to walk for a day, more for an hour or a mile, pushing children, carrying banners, cheerfully accepting the hospitality provided along the way by mobile kebab shops and local Greek businesses. Yet day by day the numbers had visibly diminished. The efforts of those distributing the leaflets ahead of their progress were tireless, their determination unbowed, yet there was a limit to the amount of coverage the media would give to an endless, uneventful march, and the promotional push of television news had begun to wane. Until today.

In modern warfare the greatest obstacle to military success is often not the muzzle of an adversary's gun but the lens of a camera. The scenes of women cradling babies in arms being set upon by jets of British Army water that spouted like flame-throwers dominated the lunchtime news. They were excellent action pictures that puzzled and upset many viewers; great adventures in distant lands were made of victories over panzer divisions or darkened fuzzy-wuzzies, not defenseless children. The military vehicles scythed through baby carriages like wolves through a Siberian village, leaving devastation, tears, and much anger in their wake.

And so by that Friday evening Makepeace had found new recruits to his cause. Greek Cypriots, who gathered in larger number and with still greater determination than before. Those whose politics were inspired by a European ideal came too, offended by Bollingbroke. There were pacifists aplenty, waving "Make Peace" slogans, along with those who did not regard themselves as being political but whose sense of the balance of decency had been upset by the news pictures. There were banners, speeches, babies in arms, an impromptu concert of folk songs, and a display of Cypriot dancing that carried with it a sense of renewed commitment for the cause of the Long March.

At dusk in a park they sang, joined hands, shared; they held up a thousand flickering candles whose light turned the park into a field of diamonds, jewels of hope that adorned their faces and their spirits. Before them, on a makeshift stage beneath the limbs of a great English oak, Makepeace addressed his followers and, beyond them, a nation.

"We have set out, as has a convoy in a place faraway yet a place close to all our hearts today, called Cyprus. But our intent could not be more different. Where they threaten war, we talk of peace. Where they brush aside babes in arms, we open our arms to all. Where they believe the answer lies in the strength of military force, we believe the answer lies in our conjoined and peaceful sense of purpose. And where they do the bidding of Francis Urquhart, we say, 'No! Not now, not tomorrow, not ever again!'"

And many who were watching on television or listening to his words on radio resolved to join him.

❖ ❖ ❖

Passolides watched the events unfolding on his television screen, feeling more deserted than ever. His soul boiled at the sight of women and children under fire from British Tommies, being cut down, cast aside, just in the manner he thought he remembered through the mists of time, mists that had been thickened with romantic tales of suffering until they obscured the truth. Memory and emotion play tricks on old men.

He sat alone in his deserted and ruined restaurant, the Webley in front of him in case the wreckers returned, watching Makepeace. For many Cypriots the Englishman was growing as a hero, a latter-day Byron, but this was not a view shared by Passolides. The man had taken his only daughter, had taken her in flesh and away from him. Not asked, not in the Greek way, simply taken. As the English had always taken. And who the hell was this Englishman to claim the mantle of honor borne so bravely by George and Eurypides and hundreds of others—a mantle that, but for cruel fate, should also have been Evanghelos's own?

So he drank, and spat at the name of Makepeace, even as he grew to hate Francis Urquhart the more.

Then he heard them outside, scratching at the temporary plywood sheeting that covered the damage, kicking at the remaining traces of glass, snickering. They were back! With a roar the old man made for the door, flung it open and threw himself into the street. He found not men with sledgehammers but three youths, obviously the worse for drink, spraying graffiti.

"I will kill you for this," he vowed, taking a step toward them.

"Yeah? You 'n' whose army, you bleedin' old fool?" The three turned to confront him, full of beerish bravado.

"One against three. I like these odds," one scoffed.

"Soddin' Cypos shouldn't be 'ere anyway. Not their country," another added.

They were almost upon him before, in the shadows cast by the dim street lighting, they saw the revolver he was waving at them and the gleam of madness in his eye. They didn't bother hanging around to find out whether the gun or its crazed owner were for real.

THIRTY-SEVEN

Politics are far more honest than love. In politics you expect betrayal.

At the rear of Downing Street, where the garden wall backs onto Horse Guards Parade, there is a narrow L-shaped road, at the side of which is a large wall box. Within the wall box run many yards of British Telecom wiring, and nearby is a hole in the wall through which signaling cable can be fed directly into Downing Street. Once connected—and it takes less than a couple of hours to complete the task—television signals can be received from any point on the globe.

Military engagements make for good pictures. What Cable News Network had done for the Gulf War, defense establishments around the world had decided to do for all their wars thereafter—although on a rather less public scale than CNN. On arrival in the mountains, St. Aubyn's signals operators had unloaded their large metal boxes from their four-tonner, exposed the racks of control equipment, set up two remote-control cameras at some distance on either side of the Lodge, slotted together the segmented parts of a two-meter dish, and with a compass located and locked on to the Eutelsat satellite in geostationary orbit above the equator. From there the test signals were bounced to Teleport in London's Docklands, thence to the BT Tower opposite the taverna in Maple Street, and onward to two monitors in the Cabinet Room.

Francis Urquhart was almost ready to wage war.

The screens flickered into life to reveal the solid, unpretentious, and tightly shuttered three-story Lodge set amid a tangle of tall trees, slightly comic in its bright green paintwork.

"Looks like a Victorian rectory in some down-at-heel diocese," Bollingbroke muttered.

"That's almost precisely what it is," Urquhart responded. He dismissed the technicians from the room before turning to the red phone. "Your report, please, Colonel St. Aubyn. You are on a loudspeaker to the other members of COBRA, and we have vision on the monitors."

"The area is now secure, Prime Minister. There's only one access route and we have that blocked. The ground surrounding the Lodge is pretty inhospitable, the side of a mountain covered in pines and thorn bushes. One or two men might just make it but they'd never get a whole party out. Not including a woman and a bishop, sir. We have them corked up."

"Excellent. What resistance do you expect?"

"Difficult to say at the moment. As you can see on your screens, there are various other buildings surrounding the Lodge that might give us cover; on the other hand, we're not yet sure whether there are guards in any of those buildings who might see us long before we can get to them. I'll have to wait for the cover of darkness for a full evaluation, I'm sure our night scopes will tell us all we need to know."

"Very good."

"Trouble is, Mr. Urquhart, the Lodge itself is an old solid stone structure, the type they don't build anymore."

"Yes, I remember."

"An excellent defensive position," St. Aubyn continued. "Roof made of corrugated metal that will clatter like a drum. Outhouses on one side that might contain guards, an open stretch of lawn leading to a helipad on the other. Countryside completely covered with dried pine debris that makes a sound as though you're walking on cornflakes. If they're not fast asleep they're going to know we're coming, and from quite a distance."

Youngblood gave a loud *harrumph* that bordered on, but did not quite cross, the line of insolence.

"Does your communications wizardry allow you to put me directly in touch with His Grace the Bishop?" Urquhart asked.

"It will if I get Private Hawkins here to shin up a telegraph pole and tap into his phone line. Take about five minutes."

"Do it, please."

They waited while Hawkins made his effort at earning the Distinguished Flying Cross, during which Youngblood yet again put his case. There could be no surprise, he insisted, they had no specialist assault troops on site. They must wait, delay, lower the Bishop's guard through fatigue. To push ahead trying to release the hostages by force would be folly, more likely to result in their deaths than their release.

To it all, Urquhart offered no reply.

And then he was through.

"Bishop Theophilos? This is Prime Minister Francis Urquhart."

"At last. What kept you? I have been waiting for your call."

"What kept me, my dear Bishop, was the need to put a military cordon around the Lodge where you are holding the hostages. That cordon is in place. You are now my prisoner."

A belly laugh crackled down the phone. "Forgive me, Prime Minister, I had forgotten what an excellent sense of humor you British retained in adversity."

"But time is on my side, Bishop. Those troops could stay there weeks, months if necessary."

"If you believe that, Mr. Urquhart, then you are a fool. Do you not realize what you have done by bringing your troops to this place? You have invaded Cyprus, my country. Even as we speak the tide of resistance will be flooding through this island. You will find no friends here and the longer you squat on my doorstep like some imperialist bully of old, the more you increase my power and the easier it will be to sweep you off this island for good. It is time, time to complete the unfinished business of earlier years. Why in God's name do you think I've been sitting here waiting for you? Did you not recognize the trap that I set for you?"

Evening was drawing across Cyprus, casting long shadows and suddenly giving the pictures of the Lodge a more gloomy cast. Urquhart's voice dropped to a more thoughtful register. "I hadn't looked at it in that light."

The Defense Secretary winced and quickly covered his eyes, pretending to be deep in thought. Youngblood raised himself in his chair in the manner of his ancestor, Ezekiel, saddling up before the charge at Balaclava, his eyes growing bulbous with righteousness. The Bishop's metallic but distinct voice continued to fill the room.

"I have wine enough for weeks and food for months, Prime Minister. I am in no hurry. Oh, yes, I was almost forgetting. And I have four hostages. I am a great believer in the afterlife. I shall have no compunction whatsoever in propelling them toward it at an accelerated rate if I so much as sniff the socks of a British soldier approaching this Lodge."

"Is that a Christian view?" Urquhart protested.

"We have a saying in Cyprus: The Bishop's son is the Devil's grandson. We are a nation of priests and pirates, and few can tell the difference." He chuckled.

Urquhart's voice had lost its assurance, sounded deflated. "There need be no violence, Bishop. I want no casualties."

"Sadly, I suspect there must be at least one casualty, Mr. Urquhart."

"Who?"

"You, my dear Prime Minister. You have, what—thirteen days to go before your election? I cannot believe the British people will consider reelecting a Prime Minister who, sadly, will be humiliated by a Cypriot Bishop. Because I demand that you announce before election day your intention of withdrawing from your bases."

"How can I possibly agree to that?"

"Because if you don't, I shall send to your newspapers slices of Mr. Martin's ears."

"I see."

"I hope you do."

Urquhart paused. "Bishop, is any of this negotiable?"

A pause. "The timing, perhaps. Withdrawal in five years rather than immediately. In exchange for a substantial aid package, of course. You see, Mr. Urquhart, I am not an unreasonable man."

"I need to think about this. Give me time to think."

"All the time in the world." He gave another laugh and cut the phone link.

Sitting starchly upright across the table, Youngblood was contempt made flesh. "I told you to wait," he hissed.

"And I told you time was on the Bishop's side, not mine."

"But you said you needed time to think..."

"I don't need to think, I already know what I'm going to do."

"Which is?"

Urquhart took one final look at the scene on the television monitor. "I'm going to burn that bastard out."

THIRTY-EIGHT

Death. For some it is an exquisite adventure, for others an obliteration. One's point of view depends very much on whose death it is, and whether you are inflicting it or suffering it.

Four hostages in total. Three men and a woman. All in the same room downstairs. We picked them up on the night scopes, Prime Minister. As you can see, during the day the windows of the Lodge are shuttered but at night they open some of them for air. We've counted seven hostiles inside, including the Bishop, another three posted in outbuildings on watch."

"Metal roof like a drum, solid stone walls, windows shuttered, door presumably secured," Urquhart mused. "If I asked you to gain access, Colonel St. Aubyn, how would you do it?"

On the far side of the Cabinet table, Youngblood propelled himself to his feet.

"Colonel, stand by," Urquhart instructed, closing the link. "General Youngblood. People only rise from this table in order to leave."

"But this is senseless! We *must* wait. Wear them down psychologically. Give us time to put in a specialist SAS squad.

St. Aubyn's men are ordinary infantrymen, they're not equipped for special forces work. They can't go in blind. Shouldn't go in at all."

"The blindness is yours. He wants us to wait, to delay. Even now he'll be organizing and by tomorrow an army of infant soldiers in their buggies will have arrived to give you yet another excuse for delay."

"Wait, consider. I implore you."

"Seize the time, General."

Urquhart made it clear he would not be moved, both jaw and mind set like rock. The soldier knew it was useless, the anger in his voice was replaced by a measure of considered disgust.

"What demon is driving you?"

"Political leadership demands many sacrifices."

"But of whom? One fool throws a rock into a pond and a thousand young men may drown trying to retrieve it."

"If this goes wrong, I'm the sacrifice and you can dance a jig on my grave."

"My feet are already tapping."

The insult was poured slowly, like treacle, and brought a gasp of astonishment from the military advisers who sat in a row behind Youngblood.

Urquhart's eyes offered not a flicker. "Weren't you supposed to have put that in code, General?"

"I wanted there to be no misunderstanding. I think I have your measure, Mr. Urquhart."

With that the Deputy Chief of Defense Staff (Commitments) strode from the room.

"Bishop, good morning."

"Ah, my dear Mr. Urquhart. *Kalimera.* You have had a good night's rest, I trust? No unpleasant dreams."

"Little sleep but time for much thought."

"And shall I have the privilege of knowing to where those thoughts lead you?"

"To a deal. An exchange."

"But. There's a But. I can hear the rumble of conditions already sticking in your throat. Take care not to choke."

"The terms you outlined yesterday are impossible."

A drizzle of ridicule washed across Theophilos's words. "You wish to fiddle at your own funeral?"

"I wish to survive, very much. But consider. If I let it be known that I am—how would I term it?—acknowledging the Cypriots' just claims for the return of the base areas and I were to announce my conclusions before the election, then, as you say, I shall be a casualty. Driven from office. But whose purpose will that serve? Not yours. A week on Thursday there would be a new Prime Minister who would feel no obligation to honor any undertaking given by me. Quite the contrary, he would probably have been swept into Downing Street on the promise to keep every inch of the bases."

"And I shall have kept your High Commissioner. In pieces."

"Exactly. No one would win."

The Bishop hesitated; his trump card seemed to have turned distinctly soggy and more difficult to play.

"You are suggesting that the British would act the jackal and break their word. As they have done so many times before."

"That's one way of putting it."

The sound of a hot liquid being vigorously slurped came over the line; an extended pause for thought. "You spoke of a deal. A counterproposal?"

"You release the High Commissioner, and in return I give you a written pledge about the bases."

"British paper!" the Bishop scoffed.

"And also a substantial aid package. I'm willing to be highly imaginative about that package, Bishop. And very personal."

"I understand."

"You will also understand that the agreements about aid and the bases cannot be made public until after the election. You see, you need me in Downing Street to meet these promises. You've got to help me win."

"But how will I know you will deliver afterward?"

"You will have my signature..."

"Not enough!"

"...and a substantial down payment of the aid package as a token of good faith. In cash. Delivered into your hands for safekeeping. It can be arranged within hours."

"Mr. Urquhart, I am beginning to like you. A man after my own heart."

"We have a common interest, Bishop, perhaps even a common destiny."

"The start of a splendid affair," Theophilos chuckled.

"I believe you have a saying in Cyprus that everyone pulls the quilt over to their own side."

"But at least it seems we shall be sharing the same bed..."

The voice trailed off. From the other end of the phone came sounds of interruption. The Bishop could be heard asking in a gruff voice what amid the flames of hell was happening. Confusion. Then he was back on the phone.

"Urquhart, you English bastard. What are you up to?"

The Troodos Mountains are the pine green heart of Cyprus. The towering ranges that stretch up to Mount Chionistra act as a cloud trap, sucking in the winds of the eastern Mediterranean, bringing relief from the oppressive heat of the plains and water in an abundance that is the envy of most other Mediterranean islands. But it is not always so in the Troodos. The rain falls mainly in winter while the summer months are parched. The shadow-dappled glades between the pines scorch to arid bowls of dust, the forest ferns die and desiccate while the carpet of flowers that is spread in springtime is rolled back to reveal the dried bones of once-abundant vegetation. The bracken and fallen timbers of the forests are turned to a compost of kiln-dried tinder, and cooling winds may become the harbinger of death. Disaster in a spark.

The back of the Troodos itches with the scars and scabs of old forest fires, silent charcoaled testimony to the power of flame whose noise and smoke resemble a belching express train and may travel almost as fast. Men who know the mountains fear the flame.

The first wisp of smoke began to curl into the sky from beside the roadway that runs below the Presidential Lodge at the start of the tourist trail leading to the Caledonian Falls. A cigarette end, the rays of the sun focused through the glass of a carelessly discarded bottle, the embers of a lightning strike, there might have been many explanations, but only one consequence. The gossamer thread curled into the sky like a kitten edging for the first time away from its mother's side. It was already growing rapidly when the Bishop's guard posted in the third-floor window of the Lodge spotted it. By the time Theophilos had climbed up the stairs to see for himself, it was approaching with the roar of a lion.

He wrenched the phone from its cradle. "What double dealing is this, Urquhart? How stupidly you condemn four hostages to death."

"Bishop, listen to me very carefully. You touch the hostages and both you and I are finished. I will be blamed and you will be butchered. I would have no choice but to order my troops in."

"You pretend you did not set this fire? Liar!"

"For God's sake are you telling me this is the first forest fire you've seen? It could've started in a thousand ways, the important thing is to finish it. My troops are already fighting the fire. If you wish to leave the Lodge I shall arrange safe transport…"

"We stay!"

"Then do that, but don't touch the hostages. Remember that you and I will stand or fall together in this matter. We are bound as one."

"Urquhart, I do not trust you. But you can trust me. I swear on my Holy life that at the first sight of any British soldier approaching this Lodge I shall take one of the hostages and throw him from the top-floor window. Just to show you my good faith. And if you don't keep the fire away from the Lodge, I shall accept your offer of transportation. But I shall leave another hostage behind in the ashes. Do you hear?"

"All too well. But there is no need for that. I'm told that there are already two helicopters on their way to you equipped with firefighting facilities. The Lodge will be safe."

"You'd better pray for your own soul if it is not."

The Wessex HC2 trooplift helicopters were the old workhorses of the military skies, long since phased out in most other parts of the world for larger, more sophisticated machinery better able to deal with frontline conditions. But Cyprus wasn't the front line—or hadn't been, until now. The Wessex was all they had, but it was adequate for the task. The flight from Akrotiri lasted less than fifteen minutes, even equipped with the cumbersome rainmaker buckets slung beneath Mission Three-Zero Alpha and its sister craft Bravo. They'd flown in formation up beyond the Kouris Dam, which diverted the precious emerald waters from their rush to the sea and toward the concrete oven of Limassol, the drone of the twin gas turbines bouncing back from the valley sides, extending still further the footprint of noise and declaring their imminent arrival even before the villagers of

Monagri, Doros, and Trimiklini could rise from the tending of vines and spot them in the sky. They climbed, the four-bladed rotors grabbing more urgently at the thinning mountain air, the torque increasing as the craft fought to maintain formation and speed, crewmen tightening in anticipation as, ahead of them, the malevolent swirl stood out dark against the clear skies.

They found their water supply less than two minutes from the source of the fire, the tanks of a trout farm full of fingerling and grower fish. In one mouthful each Wessex scooped up a hundred and fifty gallons of water and yards of protective netting—half a year's work for the farmer, whose cries of despair and incomprehension were lost beneath the flattening roar of whirling rotor blades. With an ironic bow of acknowledgment the two Wessex left the farmer to his tears of frustration and headed for the Lodge.

On instructions from his brother, Dimitri had checked the bonds of the four hostages, ensuring that they were immobile and had no chance of escape by tying their legs as well as their upper bodies. As always, he took particular care with Elpída, his eyes groping and hands brushing across the cotton of her blouse as he tested the bonds, running his callused palms around her thighs, squeezing, wine-sour breath falling across her cheeks. His eyes were glassy bright, pumping with adrenaline and anxiety.

"Before this is over, my beauty, I'm going to show you what a real man is made of," he smirked.

"Please, not so tight, you're cutting the circulation in my leg."

He settled on his haunches in front of her, removed the ligature, raised the dress high above her knees, and began massaging the muscles.

Elpída smiled, a look of pure plastic, then kicked him straight in the crotch.

It was only as he regained his breath and was no longer squirming in agony that the threats began to tumble forth. How he would have her, no matter what his brother said, and what he would do to her warm moist flesh. He stumbled to his feet, still bent, clutching himself with one hand while the other drew back and unleashed itself in fury across her cheek. His ring scoured a plum-colored graze; he sneered and stooped close in expectation of submission. Her father shouted in alarm.

There were tears in her eyes but again Elpída smiled, and spat in his face.

Dimitri was about to strike her once more when his collar was grabbed and he was cuffed about the head. He went sprawling in surprise and, rolling over, discovered the figure of his brother looming over him, arm raised to threaten him again.

"Fool!" Theophilos snarled. "Is there no time when your brain rises above your belt?"

Dimitri prepared to growl and snap, Theophilos to strike, when they both froze, their dispute forgotten in an instant. For in the distance they could hear the rumbling thunder of helicopters.

THIRTY-NINE

A conscience is like a rock, always waiting to trip you up.

The two helicopters came in at three hundred feet, skirting the jumble of tourist shops and cheap restaurants huddled below the mountain top and dropping down through the gorge of ancient black pines. Even at that height they could feel the cauldron of heat bubbling beneath them, the pilots struggling to maintain control as bursts of superheated air hit the underside of the fuselage. The fire had fanned out, catching the mountain air and swirling it into innumerable eddies and currents that were then thrown out in all directions, the flames following. Climbing the mountainside. Creeping nearer the Lodge.

Mission Three-Zero Alpha was the first to start its bombing run, the pilot guided by the instructions of the crewman in the rear. Even leaning out from the fuselage in the embrace of the dispatcher's harness it was difficult for him to determine a precise point of impact; from above all that could be seen was an angry swirl of thick dark smoke being blown forward above the flames. The first run would be no more than target spotting, suppressing the smoke screen to provide a clear line of sight.

Alpha hovered to get its bearings before moving decisively

forward, slicing across the leading edge of the fire. It was traveling at forty knots, the pilot throwing anxious glances at his torque meter as he was forced to use near-maximum power to cope with the unhappy combination of height, sudden heat, and heavy payload that turned the craft from a porpoise into a mother duck. He could screw up the transmission if he wasn't careful. It didn't help that he was practically blind, the limited forward vision provided by the droop-nosed Wessex all but obliterated by plumes of smoke. He was in the hands of God and his crewman, one of whom, he knew for a fact, had slipped in an extra pint of Guinness last night.

The crewman was latched firmly to the handrail and had one foot perched on the wheel of the undercart to give himself extra inches of reach and sight. "Steady. Steady. Left ten. God, it's bloody hot. Steady." The craft was in his hands, the pilots following his commands as he tried to find the right release point. A gust of wind snatched at the smoke below, carving out a gap through which he thought he could see it. It was as good a bearing as he was going to get. He yanked the cable that fired the rainmaker release. The newly liberated Wessex leaped forward as half a ton of water spread out and drenched two hundred square yards of forest. Yet already thousands were in flame.

The first Wessex was already heading back toward the trout farm when Mission Three-Zero Bravo maneuvered into position. Perhaps the rear crewman directing the approach was a shade hesitant, for from above it appeared as though he'd covered the almost identical section of forest as Alpha, a wasted run, but from below the action looked spectacular, for a passing second the rainmakers creating great rainbow arcs in the sky before the pall of smoke and new steam once again covered the sun. Hope, heat, darkness, and still more flame marked the time as the rearmed Wessex craft returned to resume the onslaught.

But still the fire was not out. The flames licked forward like the tongue of a fire serpent, enraged, defiant, setting about everything in its path, which led directly to the Lodge.

And the trout pond was empty. A new water supply had to be found, more vital minutes away.

The attack was beginning to falter.

❖ ❖ ❖

"For pity's sake, Mr. Urquhart, the fire is less than a hundred meters from the Lodge."

The Bishop's tone had altered. The bluster had disappeared, ground away by anxiety as he had watched the assault of the helicopters being repulsed by the forces of nature.

"They are doing their best. Another helicopter has been scrambled from Akrotiri." Yet even Urquhart was sounding less confident. "Their problem is finding a suitable water supply."

"Enough of your excuses, Englishman!"

"Bishop, let me evacuate you and your men. I give you my word..."

"As I have given you mine. If I am forced to leave this place, one of the hostages will remain behind. And her death will be on your hands."

"What more can I do, Bishop?"

"Pray, damn you. Down on your knees."

"I already am."

The flames were only seventy meters from the Lodge, advancing remorselessly. They had already encountered the fence of barbed wire thrown around the perimeter of the compound and reduced it to a cat's cradle of blackened shards. Glowing embers were soaring on the convection currents, thrown high into the heavens before cascading down upon the lawn in front of the Lodge and bouncing off its metal roof.

Bravo had made his final pass. The water bombing had

proved ineffective, the nearby water supplies exhausted. In a gesture that stank of defeat, the pilot pressed the jettison button and ditched the rainmaker bucket, shedding the last hope of quenching the fire.

Theophilos watched it all with growing anxiety. He had thought his plan foolproof, beyond the means of man to unravel. He hadn't counted on God getting in the way.

As he watched through the partially opened shutters of the Lodge he was gripped by a grim fatalism. Someone was going to die—had to die, he had given his Holy word on it. As the moment of decision approached, he found his hand was trembling. He hid it deep within the folds of his cassock.

Yet the play was not finished. Even as the Bishop peered from the Lodge, Bravo circled around ahead of the fire until it was almost above the Lodge. Slowly it edged forward until it hovered only fifty feet from the ground, its wheels practically brushing the pine tops, interposing itself directly between the building and the approaching fire. The rotor blades sliced through the air, hurling a downdraft of immense force against the trees. A new front in the battle had been opened. A wall of air was pushed forward from the helicopter until it met the advancing flames and the two air masses engaged in a war of great winds. Choking billows of smoke and dust were hurled in all directions, encasing the helicopter in a blinding envelope of debris. Bitter tongues of flame leaped upward, only to dash against the concentrated fury of fifteen hundred horsepower of mechanical muscle and be forced back in retreat. Mission Three-Zero Bravo did not kill the flame, which sidetracked, sought new avenues of advance, but with both courage and skill and flying almost blind amid the smoke it held the fire from the Lodge while Alpha and the newly arrived support helicopter continued with the work of the rainmakers.

Inside the Lodge the noise was deafening. The force of the

swirling blades beat down upon the corrugated metal roof like a hammer upon a drum, obliterating all other sounds and making conversation impossible. Shutters rattled, a chimney pot crashed down, corrugated roofing sheets began to flap loose, thoughts were shaken by the irresistible frenzy of sound until they fell apart.

Theophilos watched the scene from an upstairs window with a huge grin of relief. The forward march of the flames had been stopped, he felt much better now. He wasn't going to have to kill anyone after all.

They chose a small square window that led into the darker recesses of the Lodge, on the side farthest away from the fire.

The Lodge, their target, had been designed more than a hundred years before by a French poet, Arthur Rimbaud, while still in his twenties. He was a man of rich experience for his few years, a life dedicated to indulgence, drinking, and bawdy conversations, which he supported through his activities as a gun runner, explorer, trader, man of letters—and architect. His building design, however, was utterly commonplace, the Lodge owing its survival more to the stoutness of its stone than to its beauty or practicality. The kitchen, in particular, was a miserable affair, narrow and dark, so at a later stage it had been modified by adding a small extension for storage, and light for that extension was provided by a small window. It was out of character with the other windows in the Lodge, which were mostly tall with a pretense at elegance. This window was scarcely two feet square. It was also the only window into the Lodge without shutters.

They knew precisely where the hostages were held, in the sitting room at the far end of the house from the kitchen. They suspected that there were at least an equal number of the Bishop's men guarding them and another three, including the Bishop, were stationed at windows keeping watch on the progress of the fire. With luck, they could account for them all.

Captain Rupert Darwin had been placed in charge of the assault squad. Aged thirty-two, infantry, he was a man of endeavor and experience rather than notable achievement who had served in Ulster and Oman as well as United Nations duty in strife-torn Nigeria. He had also been to the same school as the Air Vice-Marshal—they were distantly related—but it was his two tours of duty on rotation with the Special Air Service in Northern Ireland rather than blood ties that in all probability had accounted for his selection to lead the assault on the Lodge. Six ordinary but experienced riflemen plus the captain, one for each hostile body, armed with the short SA80 rifle, smoke grenades, and thunder flashes. With faces blackened they had approached the Lodge from the side farthest away from and up-mountain of the fire, their camouflage smocks providing more than adequate cover among the smoke-strewn trees.

They had come to within twenty yards, each footstep sending telltale rivulets of pine needles creeping down the steep slope. They lingered behind the fissured boles of the pines until it had been confirmed that the three lookouts posted in the outbuildings had been taken out—without even a curse, as it later transpired, so distracted had they been studying the progress of the fire. Their task could only get more difficult. With a final glance at the shuttered windows and fearing a spying eye and angry muzzle behind every one, Darwin and his men had swarmed from behind their pines and tumbled down the final stretch of slope to the wall of the kitchen extension. No cry, no shout of alarm, nor sound of shot—nothing but the pounding of rotor blades that even from the far side of the building made it sound as if they were standing in the middle of an avalanche.

Darwin edged to the window, his back pressed flat against the wall. He could feel the trickle of sweat along his backbone.

Now was the worst moment, when it all started, the point of no return in the operation when your life was about to depend upon the lessons squeezed from a thousand years of military history. That and a whole pile of luck. The time when you swallowed the fear, prayed it was your day to survive. He took a deep breath, knowing it might be his last, and spun to face the window.

The kitchen was empty—of course, who would want coffee at a time like this? His luck was holding, already he felt better. But they could not risk the sound of shattering glass. They taped and cut out a section of windowpane, carving a hole with a glass cutter through which the latch could be released. In less than thirty seconds the window had swung open. In another thirty Darwin and two others were inside, the rest of the men following in quick order.

The galley kitchen was narrow, no cover, no place to run or hide, a killing field if but one of the Bishop's men confronted them in such confined quarters. They needed to get out of it as rapidly as possible. But they were through, into the dining room with its dark, formal furniture. There were dirty plates on the table, cheese and bread crumbs, fruit, several empty bottles of wine, screwed-up cigarette packets, and on the sideboard two submachine guns and boxes of ammunition. The eyes of Makarios, dark and somber in oils, stared down upon them, but no one else.

Within the house the bombardment of noise seemed still more remorseless, echoing between stone walls until the inside of their heads throbbed. There was no possibility of communicating through speech, all commands were given with a flick of the fingers to an order of battle orchestrated and meticulously scored in the hours before. Beyond the dining room they knew they would find a central hallway leading from the main door, and beside the door a half-open shutter where there should be a lookout. He'd been there all morning, damn him if he'd moved in the last ten minutes. Up the stairs from the hallway on the top floor they expected to find another lookout; the Bishop was reported to be on the middle floor, in the main bedroom with a view overlooking the fire. Beyond the hallway was the sitting room with four bound hostages and—they hoped—the four remaining hostiles. All accounted for. Perhaps. A man each.

The lookout positioned beside the main door was the key that, once turned, would open up the stairway and the approach to the sitting room. But they could afford no shots, no noise that might cause the lock to jam.

The paneled oak door from the dining room opened silently. Darwin smiled grimly. The theology student-turned-liberation fighter had been spending too much time on theory, his practical skills proving woefully inadequate. While he dragged at a cigarette his machine pistol lay on the chair a good pace away from the window, a pace he would never get the chance to take. Before he'd even turned a sergeant had the point of a bayonet pressed against the jugular and a hand forced over his mouth. The lookout froze, his eyes filled with fear, the bayonet point breaking the skin on his throat as he swallowed. Then he fell to his knees as though in prayer. One down.

In his heart, Darwin knew that the assault on the sitting room couldn't be as simple. The position of the hostages was critical; if they were all set apart from their captors, an exchange of fire might be risked. He glanced through the crack in the door, cursed. One of the guards was seated directly beside the hostages, facing the window where, silhouetted against the bright light, standing shoulder to shoulder and struggling for a better view, two others stood. There should have been three.

The male hostages were tied in a row, also facing the windows, but the young woman was behind them and turned toward the door. One cheek was raw red and two buttons on her untidy blouse were missing, torn away. Yet there was a light in her dark eyes that ignited as she saw Darwin's sooted face. He raised a finger to his lips; she closed her eyes, managed a small smile.

The rubber-soled boots made no distinguishable noise upon the carpet. The seated guard was felled with a blow from a rifle butt, offering nothing more than a low moan as he crumpled to the floor. Still there was no response from the men standing at the window, so overpowering and obliterating was the noise. Two soldiers stationed themselves as a wall of flesh between the guards and the hostages, another pair approached those at the window. Barrels to their backs. The captors stiffened in alarm. One accepted his fate in a flurry of raised hands and dropped weapons, but the other swung around, determined, hate in his eyes, his arm sweeping at the short barrel of the automatic rifle. All he got was the butt in his face, a blow that broke his nose and left him covered in blood. He fell to the floor, groaning.

The briefest of checks on the hostages assured Darwin that all were alive, although Martin in particular, captive for almost two weeks, appeared wan and exhausted. Any attempt to elicit from them the precise whereabouts of the Bishop and the other targets was frustrated; they didn't appear to know, the noise prevented any useful exchange.

It was while he was questioning the High Commissioner that Darwin's attention was aroused by the look of alarm that suddenly was drawn across the face of one of his men. He turned to discover that the freed woman had picked up one of the many small arms left lying around and was standing over the fallen guard with the busted nose. She kicked him to attract his attention. He stopped moaning, looked up, saw a special look in her eyes, held out a bloodied, pleading hand.

Elpída let him grovel until she could see fear stretched tight across his face like a piano wire. Then she fired and blew Dimitri's right kneecap into a mush of skin and bone fragments. "Next time, you bastard, you'll come crawling to me."

Dimitri's body began to jerk, trying desperately to get hands around his shattered leg while every movement sent a thousand volts of agony shooting through his body. He was screaming at the top of his voice.

As though she were handing out refreshments during a hot afternoon on the lawn of the Presidential Palace, Elpída gave the gun to Darwin and went to tend to her father.

The Captain felt sick. He'd lost control, the game plan was unraveling. It seemed certain that the gunshot and Dimitri's cries of agony would have been heard by those still unaccounted for. He had the hostages secure, but the job was not yet finished. And he'd have to do the rest on his own.

As he contemplated the stairs, his mouth went dry and his finger stiffened around the trigger. He had little idea what to expect—Urquhart's briefing had only extended as far as the ground floor—and there were too many doors leading off the landing, any of which could leap open in a blaze of gunfire. Like O'Mara Street near the river in Derry, a disheveled terraced house with peeling wallpaper and no carpet, on a miserable November day when he'd been sent to pick up an IRA suspect. At the top of a short flight of stairs there had been only two doors, but one of them had opened, just a fraction. He had hesitated—was it an innocent civilian, a child perhaps, coming from the bathroom? Or the suspect about to surrender?

The answer had come in the form of a 5.56-mm bullet fired from an Armalite that had sliced clean across his collarbone and through the throat of the corporal giving him cover from behind. They had both ended up at the bottom of the stairs, Darwin curled in a ball of pain, staring directly into the lifeless eyes of his fellow soldier. The corporal's widow had got a pension, Darwin had got sick leave and a commendation, and the IRA murderer a sentence of life imprisonment when eventually he had given himself up. That was eight years ago;

he could be paroled and out on the streets in less than another two. In Darwin's dreams the eyes of the dead soldier had stared back at him for months afterward. That wasn't going to happen again.

All the Bishop's men with the exception of the still writhing Dimitri had had their hands wired behind their backs; he grabbed the nearest and thrust him forward. Up the stairs. A shield. Insurance.

They climbed, and Darwin's senses were ringing; the nearer he came to the tin roof and the beating of the blades, the more insistent became the pounding inside his head. Even the wooden floor trembled. A sheet of metal roofing was working loose, beginning to bang methodically in the downdraft. Deafening. Like volleys of artillery fire.

Left at the top, the hallway dark and decorated like some Victorian boarding house. Prints, oil paintings, lamp shades with gently vibrating tassels, antique-stall bric-a-brac. And doors, too many bloody doors.

"You speak English?" Darwin had to shout directly into his prisoner's ear.

"I have a master's from Bristol University."

"You want to die?"

The prisoner shook his head.

"Then you open the doors. Very slowly. And start praying your friends recognize you."

He rebound the prisoner's hands in front of him, and they crept along the corridor, Darwin pushing his human shield, until they reached the first door. Gingerly the brass knob was turned, the door swung open—to reveal nothing more threatening than a linen cupboard. For a moment Darwin felt a fool, until he reminded himself that at least he was a fool who was still breathing.

Onward. Behind the second door was a bathroom, behind the third an unoccupied bedroom. A sense of urgency grew; he had to get on with it. Darwin wiped away the sweat that was dribbling freely into his eyes.

The next door unlatched in faltering fashion, the prisoner's damp and bound hand slipping around the polished brass. It opened a fraction, then a few more inches. And before them, back turned, looking out of the window in the pose of a statue dedicated to a Latin American warrior, stood the Bishop. Three respectful steps to his rear, attention also focused out of the window, was the missing guard.

They hadn't heard a thing.

With rising confidence Darwin pushed forward behind his shield, ducking down for protection, but as they crossed the threshold his prisoner stretched out with a boot and caught the leg of a chair, enough to send it toppling. The guard near the window swiveled, his mouth opened to shout, his gun leveled. He saw the human shield, recognized his companion, and fired. As Darwin fired back, the man in his hands flinched, grew heavy, and slowly toppled to the floor. Darwin could see two bubbling craters in his chest and could feel the spatter of warm blood on his own cheek.

The Bishop had turned now, attracted less by the noise than the fact that his guard who had been positioned some way behind him was now slumped against the wall at the foot of the window, his heart blown wide open by a single round.

Theophilos faced Darwin, examined the two bodies on the floor with great deliberation. He sought for options; there were none. Inescapably, it was over. An adventure too far. He shrugged, expelled a great lungful of disenchantment and slowly raised his hands, the sleeves of his cassock slipping high up his arms to reveal his favorite Rolex and a white silk shirt. His arms outstretched in silhouette against the glowing light of sun and fire from the window gave the impression of a crucifixion.

Darwin wiped the blood from his cheek, as he had done that day in Derry. As his eyes adjusted to the brightness he could see that Theophilos was smiling wryly. "I surrender," the Bishop mouthed—or might have been shouting; it was impossible to hear.

Darwin put a bullet straight through the top of the wooden cross that hung over his heart. The Bishop, lifted from his feet, fell heavily against and then backward through the window, which shattered into fragments like an exploding star leaving nothing but a gaping, lifeless hole. The last sight Darwin had of Theophilos was the tail of a flapping cassock, a pair of sandals, and two bright yellow socks.

Urquhart had been right. He'd apologized to Darwin, as soon as he'd finished briefing him over the satellite link about the layout of the Lodge.

"Apologize, Prime Minister?"

"Yes, Captain. The Bishop, if captured alive, will inevitably go before a Cypriot court. He has a lot of friends in Cyprus. I suspect he's more likely to get elected President than convicted. We don't deal with terrorists very effectively, do we?"

"No, sir."

"I remember in my own time, when I was a soldier doing your job in Cyprus, fighting EOKA terrorists. The Archbishop, Makarios, led the terrorists at that time, paid them from church funds, gave them their instructions. They killed not only our troops but many British civilians, women too. We knew it, even locked him up in exile. Then we let him become President of Cyprus. We're too soft, Captain."

"Yes, sir."

"Even if they lock him up for a while, it would achieve nothing. Like a serpent's egg. Put it away, and the menace only grows stronger until it breaks out in some more dangerous and reformed fashion. I've always believed there's only one thing to do with a serpent's egg."

"What's that, sir?"

"Crush it, Captain."

They had watched it all on the monitors. The shadows flitting between forest and kitchen window. The flash of confusion by the shutter at the front door. The fire drawing ever closer. The dark shape bursting forth from the first-floor window and falling like a sack of coal. Four grateful hostages rejoicing in sunlight for the first time in days.

And miraculously the fire had been doused, the aim and effectiveness of the rainmakers improving as rapidly as circumstances within the Lodge.

Much to Urquhart's private delight Youngblood had returned, commanded to do so by his superior who was insistent that, no matter how intolerably interfering and unreasonable the Prime Minister might be, a military representative had to be there to advise and, if necessary, to object. And even as Urquhart gloried in his victory, the argument was not yet done.

The military advice, from the commanding heights of the Cabinet Room all the way down to St. Aubyn on the spot, was to transfer the released hostages immediately to the safety of Akrotiri. But again Urquhart said no and insisted. This was no longer a military matter, it had become entirely political, and the politics demanded that the victory be paraded and lauded for the benefit of the legitimate government of President Nicolaou and for the disgrace of his foes. To skulk behind British barbed wire would wipe away all the President's newfound advantage.

So Urquhart decreed that the exhausted Nicolaou and the others were to rest overnight in a nearby hotel, and on the following morning, Sunday, St. Aubyn should prepare to drive them in convoy not to a British base but to the capital of Nicosia, to the seat of Government and authority. To the media networks that would spread the word of victory throughout the island. To the symbolic ruins of the Presidential Palace. To the humiliation of all foes. And to wherever Mortima's letter might be.

And, in order to maximize the magnitude of victory, Urquhart made a mental note to ensure that every television network and news cameraman his staff could get their hands on would be there to witness his triumph.

It was as dusk was falling and the last of the debris of captivity and assault was being cleared from around the Lodge that Urquhart knew, with a certainty that clung to his heart as ice, that something had gone wrong. The light was dimming, the sun setting, shadows stretching across the ground—as they had done all those years before on the side of that mountain. Urquhart was contemplating the scene of his triumph on the monitor when an ember, revived in the caress of a cool evening breeze, caught on the dried bark of a pine, settled, found renewed life. As he watched, and remembered, the tree burst into all-consuming flame.

Full circle. A cycle of life complete, finished. And from out of the screen, Urquhart saw the charred, accusing fingers of George and Eurypides pointing directly at him.

FORTY

Fear brings out the best in a man, strips away the complacency, and exposes the core. Those who are afraid to die have never properly lived.

Victory. It had been the lead item on the Saturday evening news, even though there were as yet no new pictures to illustrate the story.

"I asked not to be included in the formal War Cabinet. People would start speculating that I was being lined up for the succession—you know, the youngest Home Secretary since Churchill. We're in an election, not a leadership race. So I declined. But, of course, Francis consults me, all the way."

Across the table Booza-Pitt offered a smile that spoke of modesty, determination, achievement, I-know-you-want-to-touch-me-all-over-with-those-beautiful-lips-but-I'm-truly-very-important-and-business-comes-first. His dining companion purred in encouragement. After years of anguish she'd separated less than two months earlier from a parliamentary husband whose dedication to late-night lobbies, weekend surgeries, answering the telephone, and endless piles of constituents' letters was as utterly selfless as it was, to her, irredeemably boring. She knew getting laid by Booza-Pitt would be folly, but it had been such a long time and it might be fun, particularly if he was as practiced in the delivery as he was at finding the route. She hadn't climbed higher than a Minister of State before, let alone as far as a Home Secretary. She owed it to herself.

"Really?" she incited, wondering if his performance would be as inflated as his ego.

"It's pretty tricky right now—can't go into detail, you understand, but I advised that we should get in there as quickly as possible. Spring the hostages and teach those bloody Cypriots a lesson."

"A good spanking."

"Yes, something like that."

"You're magnificent, Geoffrey." She fluttered her eyelids outrageously, he smiled in self-congratulation—he was so lacking in subtlety that he belonged in a zoo. She hoped.

"It's a strain," he admitted, heavy eyebrows twitching. "Lonely at times."

Here it comes. He was about as difficult to read as a tax demand.

"You know what I would like?" he continued, staring at her across a glass of wine, which cast strange patterns across his forehead in the candlelight.

"To become Prime Minister?"

"I've no ambitions at present beyond..." he began the litany.

She reached out and touched a fingertip to his lips to put him out of his misery. Grief, he'd better be good in bed, he had no other redeeming features. At least it would avoid the complications of an extended affair.

"Tell me all your secrets, Geoffrey. I'm very good with confidences."

"Are you? Are you really?"

"Yes. Tell me—don't if it's truly a state secret, but—are you a Virgo?"

❖ ❖ ❖

"I wish you were here having breakfast with us, Mummy."

It was the one meal Claire insisted on trying to have with the children before politics dragged them apart for the remainder of the day. It didn't always work, even on a Sunday. "I know, darling, but you remember what election campaigns are like from the last time."

"Where are you?"

"Somewhere in the Midlands, to be quite honest I'm not sure where. I got picked up in a car yesterday afternoon from the train and the rest is all a blur. But I'll be back tonight. After you've gone to bed."

"I've run out of refills for my asthma inhaler."

"The blue one or the brown?"

"Blue."

"I'll find a pharmacy open somewhere." Claire scribbled a hurried reminder to herself in the margin of her *Sunday Express*, beside an exploding headline that shouted: FU's FALKLANDS. "Bring you one back tonight. And I hope you and Abby are wearing the clothes I laid out for you."

Diana ignored the question. Something else was on her mind. "Mummy?"

"Yes, darling?"

"What is war?"

"What do you mean?"

"We're fighting Cyprus, aren't we? Why?"

"Not the whole of Cyprus, darling. Just a few bad men."

"And all those ladies with the baby chairs."

"Not really."

"But Mr. Urquhart killed the Bishop, didn't he?"

"No, not Mr. Urquhart personally." Although something in her daughter's naivety rattled chains within Claire.

"But why?" Diana persisted, munching her way through a mouthful of wholemeal toast.

Claire hesitated. The morning's press had been crammed to capacity with plaudits for the previous day's success in the Troodos. Even those who were not supporters of the Government couldn't avoid copious reference to "Francis's Fusiliers." Some of the more serious newspapers carried reports of disagreement with military advisers and of the Prime Minister unusually and perhaps inappropriately having taken single-handed control of the operation, but in light of its success the military appeared to be playing down any sense of injured pride. Victory argues its own case.

So why did Claire feel so unenthused?

"I'll explain it all to you later, darling. And remember to brush your teeth."

"Gotcha!"

With a snap of exultation and a flick of his remote control, Urquhart wiped the Leader of the Opposition from his Sunday morning screen.

For almost twenty minutes on breakfast television Dick Clarence had been struggling hard to avoid his fate, but persistent questioning had worn down his linguistic ingenuity and overrun every defensive position his advisers had prepared until he was forced to capitulate. Finally he had no choice but to admit it. Yes, Francis Urquhart had done the right thing.

"Not long for this world, I suspect, young Dick," Urquhart reflected to Mortima. Fate was a harsh judge on an Opposition Leader who had lost the ability to oppose with only ten days of campaigning left.

From the other side of the breakfast table Mortima looked up from her newspapers. "The press seems already to have reached that conclusion." She passed across to him three editorials, carefully folded and highlighted, which effectively pronounced the election over.

He digested them alongside his Lapsang, then laid them to one side, shaking his head. "They rush to judgment. Clarence is dead, because he is congenitally useless. But there is still opposition."

"Makepeace?"

"Who else?"

"A man with no party."

"But an army."

"An army under attack, sir." It was Corder, who stood filling the doorway in the quiet way to which over the years they had grown accustomed. Mortima didn't even adjust her dressing gown.

"You have news from the front, Corder?"

"Yes, sir. Mr. Makepeace may have a battle on his hands. Since last night's news broadcasts, various of the extreme British nationalist groups have been organizing. Arranging a little reception for when he reaches Birmingham this evening. They want to do to him what you did to the Bishop."

"How unfortunate," Mortima mused with as much concern as if she were selecting tights.

"So what's to be done, Corder?"

"Depends on whether you want a riot on the streets of Birmingham."

"Violence is certain?"

"Could be. If you wanted it, Prime Minister."

"I think not, Corder. Too much uncertainty. Such things can get out of hand, make him a martyr. No, how much better if the threat of riots were sufficient to get Mr. Makepeace to abandon his march."

"You think he'd do that?" Mortima interjected skeptically.

"I doubt it. It would be the end for him. We could appeal, request, beseech, but I don't suppose he'd listen."

"So?"

"So we would have to get the Chief Constable to order

Makepeace to abandon the march as a threat to good public order, wouldn't we, Corder?"

"In my experience, sir, Chief Constables don't always listen..."

"He's coming up for a knighthood, he'll be all ears."

"...and aren't always listened to in such matters."

"But wouldn't that be wonderful?" Urquhart spread his hands in front of him as though confronting a heavenly host. "Makepeace. Already branded a friend of terrorists. Now challenging the forces of law and order in this country. The threat of riot would seem to be his fault as much as any other's. From martyr to public menace. We'd have to arrest him." He clapped, then subsided. "With great reluctance, and after copious warnings, of course."

"Public Order Act 1986, sir. Section Thirteen, I think. Three months and a fine."

"Precisely, Corder. Can do?"

Corder nodded.

"And then we would have all the loose ends tied up."

"Except for one, Mr. Urquhart."

Corder was clutching the red file. It appeared thicker than on the last occasion.

"Passolides."

"Yes, sir. We've been keeping an eye on him. Not simply a harmless old crank, after all. Appears he carries a gun, been waving it about. And a record as an EOKA activist."

He was standing right beside the burning tree, scorching his flesh as though an oven door had been opened in front of him.

"We should pick him up. But I wanted to check with you first."

The voices were at him again, warning, instructing, clashing and confusing. It was many moments before Urquhart was able to push aside the debris in his mind and speak.

"Where is he now?"

"Skulking in his tent. The one with no windows."

"Good. Then let us leave him there. Someone so close to Makepeace, armed, blood on his hands. British blood. Could prove very convenient."

"Even old men have their uses, sir."

"You might say that, Corder…"

Claire scurried through the swing doors of the local radio station, already a few minutes late for her interview and muttering darkly about faceless party officials who drew up election schedules. A woman needed a little more preparation time in the morning than some crusty Cabinet colleague who had no hair and wore the same soup-spilled pinstripe his wife had bought for him twenty years ago. Anyway, she'd had to try three pharmacies before finding one that was open and could fill Diana's prescription.

"I'm Claire Carlsen," she explained to the young and unkempt receptionist.

He didn't look up, loath to leave his examination of the sports pages. "Message for you," he muttered through a mouthful of gum, waving a scrap of paper at her. "You're to ring this number. He said it was urgent."

There was no name, she didn't recognize the number but it was a Whitehall exchange. "May I use the phone?"

He looked at her, less reluctantly now, his attention beginning to focus on the shape behind the name. He gave her a crooked smile before nodding slowly.

She dialed. It was Corder.

"Is this a secure line?" he inquired.

The receptionist had begun to examine her with ill-disguised lust, unwashed eyes massaging their way across her chest.

"If you mean can we be overheard," Claire replied, returning the stare, "not by any intelligent form of life."

Defiantly the receptionist blew a huge balloon of gum; both it and his confidence collapsed in a pink dribble across his chin. With a final sullen glance, he subsided back into his newspaper.

There was a brief silence on the telephone as Corder struggled to decode her cryptic remark. Irony was not his strong suit. "Your friendly driver," he continued cautiously, "is he on duty today?"

"No," she replied. During the last week the driver's time had been spent ferrying secretaries, correspondence, and dry cleaning between London and the route of the march, and he'd little to offer by way of fresh indiscretion. Claire had felt relieved.

Now she felt dirty. Corder knew. Her secret was spreading, as was her feeling of remorse. At the beginning she had regarded it as no more than a little idle mischief but she could no longer hide from the fact that it had been a mistake. The betrayal of a friend she still cared for. She had demeaned herself, got carried away. Acted like Urquhart.

The receptionist was staring once more, furtively; she turned her back on him, no longer able to meet his gaze.

"No, the driver's not on duty," she mumbled, feeling much like a prisoner in the dock being asked to plead. Not guilty, she wanted to insist. But who was she kidding?

"Good," Corder snapped.

"Why do you ask?" she was about to inquire, but already it was too late. Corder had rung off.

FORTY-ONE

Downing Street has a simple dress code. When you come in you should leave your principles at the door.

Makepeace stood on the age-worn steps of the parish church of St. Joseph's in Cannock, some fifteen miles north of the center of Birmingham, having attended early morning Communion and received the vicar's blessing. He was a committed if undogmatic Christian, not unaware of the benefits for a politician of displaying occasional touches of piousness, and many Christian groups had begun to join him on the march, gathering beneath a large "March for Peace" banner that had been draped across the bell tower of the church. Yet there were many others assembling that morning whose motivations were less spiritual, and two new elements in particular. For the first time, supporters and committed members of Dick Clarence's party paraded openly among the kaleidoscope of banners and protest groups in the crowd. They, like Urquhart, most editors, and many others, had perceived Clarence as a lost cause and already written him off. Stranded between the rock of despair that was Clarence and the hard, unforgiving place over which towered Urquhart, they had turned to the only banner of defiance they could find. Thomas Makepeace.

The second new element was still more noticeable, noisy in spite of relative lack of numbers.

Draped in Union flags and tattoos, their close-cropped heads appearing like battering rams above mean eyes and studded noses, surrounded by news photographers and penned in behind the hastily erected barriers of the local constabulary, the skinheads had begun to arrive, armed with their traditional weaponry of obscenity, spittle, and abuse. It was early morning, their enthusiasm for the task not yet fully warmed, but they formed the skirmishing patrols of elements that would gather later in the day in the guise of nationalist warriors.

"Scum's risen," Maria muttered to Makepeace.

"Not all of it. Too early for most of them."

"Urquhart's supporters come in strange and unwashed shapes. I suppose we should take it as a sign of success."

"I'd rather not. It worries me, these types, with all the families and children around."

"Don't worry," she reassured. "The police will take care of it all."

They were much slower to stir in the Troodos, even taking into account the two-hour time difference. In the early hours of the previous evening Lieutenant Colonel St. Aubyn had commandeered the top floor of the Pine Crest Hotel a few miles from the Lodge; it had caused the manager mild apoplexy and for a few minutes he was of a mind to refuse. But he was a German with an irregular work permit who had no care to tangle with the President of Cyprus, and was not paid enough to do so with several dozen well-armed troops. There had been an hour of shuffle and squeeze—and also indignation, guests responding with an eclectic mixture of insults when they discovered that they were not to be allowed to set foot outside the hotel until after the presidential party had left the following morning.

But Elpída had wandered around each of the dinner tables, thanking, explaining, asking for understanding. The harrowing details of her story plus the scar on her cheek had done much to repair frayed tempers, bolstered by the announcement that the Ministry of Finance would be picking up the bills for the entire week.

Of the President, however, there was no sign. Exhaustion had overcome him. As soon as he had talked by phone with a couple of his Ministers and ensured that his arrival the following day was to be expected, he had slept, until ten o'clock the following morning. Panayotis insisted on standing guard the whole night outside his door. No one had tried to wake him, there was little point. It would take only a couple of hours to drive to Nicosia.

By the time he rose the following morning the dew had disappeared and the crickets and martins on the wing had taken over from the morning chorus. It was a tender honey-colored spot, surrounded with cherry trees and with unspoiled views across the valley, so different from the tree-choked gorge in which the Lodge had been built. Nicolaou, like his daughter, made an attempt to circulate and thank everyone but the strain of his adventure was all too apparent in the awkward shuffle of his frame and the bruise-gray shadows about his eyes. He had aged, clinging to Elpída's arm as though afraid someone else would try to snatch her away.

St. Aubyn was growing impatient. It would be noon before they left, they would be traveling into the heat of the day and the President, already wan, was in no need of further ordeal.

"Do not worry on my behalf, Colonel," Nicolaou had tried to reassure. "I am a Cypriot. Used to a little heat."

The Lieutenant Colonel deferred to the politician, which seemed to be the order of the day. He'd been even less impressed with the instruction to head for Nicosia than his military superiors had been; the capital was a warren of intrigue where both streets and tongues forked in a confusion that offended the neat military mind. But as the Air Vice-Marshal had reminded him, soldiers don't get to choose.

The sun had passed its zenith but the thermometer was still rising when at last they set off, four-tonners in front and rear, Land Rovers in the middle, carrying forty-eight British servicemen and the four liberated hostages. They had debated long and hard whether to send more troops up from Episkopi, but had decided against. This was supposed to look like a victory parade, not another invasion.

Darwin and his team as well as the signals squad had been sent back to base, doused in gratitude from the President.

"You must come and visit us in Nicosia, Captain. Accept a little of our hospitality."

"And perhaps a medal or two?" Elpída added mischievously.

"It's been an honor, sir—miss."

The Captain saluted starchly, but the President was too overcome with emotion for military etiquette. He threw his arms around his savior in the manner of any Balkan bidding farewell to a much-loved brother, kissing both cheeks.

"Take care of yourself, sir," Darwin mumbled, coloring.

"Don't worry, my dear Captain Darwin. The worst is over. After what you have already achieved, the rest will be easy."

There was little Sunday spirit in evidence. With some three thousand people marching with him and more than ten thousand promised when he reached Birmingham city center, Makepeace should have been content, but all day long the skinheads had been driving up and down their route, blaring their horns and sounding trumpets, waving flags, leaning far out of car windows to raise clenched fists, spitting, goading, warning of trouble to come. Several supporters had tried to intervene and appeal for moderation, but by midmorning and Walsall, empty beer cans and other forms of garbage had joined the obscenities being thrown in their direction. A Morris dancer had already been knocked to the floor, and several marchers with young families had decided to quit.

Makepeace had appealed several times to the police to take some form of action to quell the disruption but the number of officers on duty was small and entirely inadequate to deal with the incitement. He was relieved therefore when, up ahead in the far distance, he saw a congregation of police cars, orange flashes on white, surrounded by a flurry of officers whose animation suggested they were intent on business. One was striding purposefully toward him.

"Chief Inspector Harding, sir." The officer introduced himself with a courteous salute. Makepeace gave no indication of stopping or even slowing, forcing the policeman to fall in alongside.

"Welcome, Chief Inspector, delighted to see you." He shook hands. "These yobs are proving a damned nuisance; they're deliberately trying to provoke trouble."

"I'm very much afraid you're correct, sir. Our information is that a countermarch is gathering with the objective of coming into direct confrontation with you in the city center. Many hundreds of skinheads, British National Union types, neo-Nazis, assorted maggots. Those you've seen so far are just the outriders. Has all the signs of a nasty bit of violence."

A car passed, horn blaring, heading away from the gathering of police cars. A pair of tattooed buttocks protruded from the window.

"Blast them," Makepeace snapped. "This is a protest for peace, a family event, not an excuse for mayhem. What are you going to do about it?"

"That's difficult, Mr. Makepeace."

"Don't just wring your hands; you've got to do something."

"My instructions are to stop it, sir."

"Excellent."

"I don't think you understand. My instructions are to stop all of it. The skinheads' march. And your march too, sir."

"You're bloody joking." Makepeace came to an abrupt halt. Flustered, angered, he motioned those behind him to continue. The marchers parted to either side of them.

The policeman persisted. "The two marches coming together will cause violence and disruption of the peace."

"Then stop their march. Mine is peaceful."

"For better or for worse—I sometimes wonder which, sir—we live in a democracy. They may be pavement scrapings but they also have a vote and equal rights to demonstrate."

"Sticking their unwashed arses out of car windows is demonstrating? Demonstrating what?"

"They are entitled to their political opinions, sir."

"This is a sick joke, Mr. Harding. Just sweep them off the streets, for heaven's sake."

"If I stop one march I have to stop both."

Makepeace was growing irritated by the other man's dogged sophistry. He began walking briskly once again, swept along by his supporters, but now he found himself accompanied by four uniformed constables who had fallen in behind their officer.

"This is crude blackmail, Chief Inspector."

"It's protecting the peace."

"I'm the one trying to protect the peace. That's why I'm standing for Parliament."

"And organizing a march of this size that in itself constitutes a strain on public order, that includes anarchists, militant animal liberationists, a group of extreme environmentalists calling itself 'One World Warriors,' the Anti-Nazi League, some..."

"The vast majority here are ordinary peace-loving families. I can't control everyone who wants to tag along behind."

"Precisely."

"Justice can't be this blind. It's a put-up job, isn't it, Chief Inspector?"

But Harding had no wish to debate further, not while swimming in a sea of Makepeace supporters. His brain locked into the appropriate criminal code and engaged gear.

"Sir, under Section 12 of the Public Order Act of 1986 I have reason to believe that this public procession may result in serious public disorder, serious damage to property, or serious disruption to the life of the community, and therefore, under the authority accorded to me by that Act, I am directing you to bring this procession to a halt and disperse your supporters."

"Not a chance."

The officer was bobbing up and down on the toes of his highly polished shoes in a state of some agitation. "Mr. Makepeace, I must warn you that failure to comply with the lawful directions of a police officer in this matter is an offense and renders you liable to prosecution."

"Bugger off, you bloody fool!"

The roadway down from the Troodos knotted and twisted like a child's ribbon, making the convoy's passage through the pines uneven and uncomfortable. Their four-tonners had not been designed for high-speed cornering. The air above the macadam boiled, throwing up little whirlpools of dust that irritated the eye and cloyed the tongue. From their right-hand side the ancient Amiandos asbestos mine glared gray at them as though it had been dropped from the far side of the moon, a dust-raped landscape destroyed by pickax and bulldozer. St. Aubyn licked his drying lips in distaste.

On the other side of the road they passed a small stone monument that remembered the Troodos of more gentle times, a drinking trough that trickled with the cool waters of a nearby spring. St. Aubyn read the inscription: ERECTED TO COMMEMORATE THE CONSTRUCTION OF THE NICOSIA-TROODOS ROAD–VRI 1900. Victoria Regina Imperatrix. A hundred years gone by and still the British were bailing out these people. Or still interfering, perhaps. He ignored the faded Greek graffiti.

Around the bend they encountered their first serious opposition, a BBC television crew, the advance troops for what St. Aubyn knew must be a formidable media invasion, waving their arms and pleading for assistance. They were standing beside the yawning hood of their car from which sibilant clouds of steam were emerging, the perils of an overhasty hire and an intolerably impatient editor. St. Aubyn looked the other way, passing by at the gallop.

The road continued to hug the side of the mountain, curling, dipping, disappearing around the bend into the pine trees ahead. That's when St. Aubyn saw the cutting, a man-made valley slashed through the rock, an angry scar whose steep sides and unhealed slopes seemed to cry with pain at the memory of the explosives and mechanical shovels that had blasted this great wound through the mountain's side, then inexpertly cauterized it with hot tar. Scree trickled like tears to either side.

It was inhospitable, claustrophobic, no trees or any form of vegetation seemed to want to grow here, this was no place to tarry. Then some fool up front stamped on his brakes.

There was a touch of Irish in Makepeace on his mother's side, buried a couple of generations deep, which seemed to rush to the surface at moments of indignation and perceived unfairness, blocking his judgment and making him desperate to find some physical outlet for his anger. As when he had crossed the Floor of the House. He was never entirely sure where principle stepped aside and old-fashioned Celtic passion took over, but that was his makeup, the way he was—anyway, there seemed little point in principle divorced from passion. Now there was some ridiculous policeman with pips on his collar standing in his way and telling him he was no better than some Nazi who stuck his bum out of a window. Nuts! As the Chief Inspector moved closer, Makepeace raised his hands to push him away. Or was he going to strike the man? Quickly Maria restrained him, reaching out before any of the constables had the chance.

"Don't give them any excuse other than a political one," she urged.

Makepeace had stopped walking and those following were beginning to falter, uncertain what was going on. They began to mill around Makepeace and the policemen, a march turning into a melee.

Harding attempted a placatory smile. "Please, Mr. Makepeace, no one regrets this more than I do. We want to make this as simple as possible for you, we've even arranged a venue about a mile down the road, a sports ground where we would be happy for you to wind up your march with your supporters. But with the threat of violence hanging over the whole community, there is no way we can allow you into the center of Birmingham."

Makepeace was blinking rapidly, trying to brush away the mists of rage and clear his thoughts. Maria was there first. "What of tomorrow, Chief Inspector? And the next day? And next weekend in London?"

Harding shrugged. "Not in my hands, miss. That would depend on the local police force. But if the threat of violence is still there…"

"So you would allow a bunch of thugs to run my election campaign completely off the road," Makepeace snapped.

"I'm sorry."

"And what will you do if I refuse?"

"Mr. Makepeace, I have given you a lawful direction to stop this march. If you don't, you would leave me with no choice but to arrest you. Neither of us wants that. Wouldn't do your election campaign much good either."

"You'll allow me to be the judge of that."

But others were also judging, pressing around more closely

as they began to understand that the police presence surrounding Makepeace was not for his protection. The mood was turning edgy.

"I don't pretend to understand politics, sir, but I have a job to do. So let's wind this march up peacefully."

"No, I think we'll take the other route. Arrest me or get out of my way." Makepeace began marching once more, trying to clear a path through the bodies in front of him.

"Please, sir…"

Harding was reaching out after him; Makepeace brushed aside the restraining hand. Harding hurried to bring himself alongside.

"Sir, you do not have to say anything. But if you do not mention now something that you later use in your defense, the court may decide…"

The rest was drowned in a growl of opposition from various members of the Akropolis weight-lifting team who had begun pushing forward through the crowd. Parents with children in arms were getting jostled, someone tumbled, cries of confusion sounded on all sides, the march had suddenly tugged on the edge of chaos. Is that what Harding intended? Makepeace arrested in the midst of violence without a neo-Nazi in sight? Forcefully Maria thrust herself between Makepeace and the advancing muscle, shouting reprimands in seaman's Greek and waving them to subside.

Makepeace had a constable latched on to either arm but he did not struggle or resist. Instead he, too, was calling out for order. "Relax. Get on with the march," he shouted to those around. "I'll be back with you as soon as I've got this nonsense sorted out."

But Harding's placatory smile had disappeared. "No, Mr. Makepeace, I don't think we can allow that. Not at all."

❖ ❖ ❖

The cutting had been blocked by a barricade of eight buses, ancient Bedford and modern Mercedes, parked sideways and four deep, fronted by a low rampart of boulders and pine trunks. There was no way through and, since the sides of the cutting rose steeply from the roadway, no way around. The buses were empty, doors ajar, curtains flapping at dust-streaked windows, yet the silence had an unmistakable menace that filled St. Aubyn's throat with bile.

"Back!" he yelled, waving his hand in a circular motion above his head as the driver made an agile three-point turn and started off for the far end of the cutting. The four-tonners snorted and complained like beached whales as they struggled in the narrow confines to follow suit.

It had been less than three minutes since they had passed into the rocky valley, but when they returned to it the entrance was not as it had been. Seated in the road as though engaged in a summer's picnic were two hundred chattering schoolgirls, in uniform, none more than fifteen. A barrier as unbreachable as rock. The Land Rover slid ungracefully to a halt in a cloud of dust.

Trapped. And he could see something else out of the corner of his eye. Shadows were falling across his path, cast down from on high. St. Aubyn looked to the top of the cutting, towering above him some forty feet, where the silhouettes of men were shooting up like a field of thistles. Every one of them was armed.

Then he saw two further dark shapes appear against the hard blue sky. Men holding to their shoulders not weapons, but television cameras.

With a certainty that sickened him, St. Aubyn suddenly knew he was going to be famous.

Makepeace was, of course, already famous, and about to move up to the category that would label him notorious. As soon as he had been arrested he had moved to the side of the road, out of the path of the march and against the wall of a church. There, framed against the statue of Mother and Child that dominated the churchyard, he refused any further cooperation. At least for the next couple of minutes. He had spotted a television van parking a short distance away, its crew tumbling forth. He needed to make a little time for them; there was little to be gained from being arrested if the drama couldn't be played out on prime-time television.

Maria was at his side, gesticulating to the marchers to continue, while Makepeace refused to budge, his arms folded and studiously ignoring the eye and the commands of the beleaguered Harding. But then all was ready, the mike boom was thrust forward, the red eye glaring on the front of the video camera.

Slowly, as though in prayer, he clenched his hands and held them well away from his body. Once more he was asked to cooperate; again he refused, shaking his head. He held the hands out still farther, his eyes shut tight. They took his arm; he shook them off. He was going nowhere. Reluctantly the Chief Inspector gave the order and a pair of handcuffs were snapped around his wrists.

When his eyes flicked open, they shone with vivid intensity. Makepeace held his cuffed hands aloft, like a warrior triumphant in battle, shaking them for all to see.

"The chains of an Englishman!" he exclaimed.

Maria held out her hands, too. Then another, and yet another. All around there were marchers asking, almost demanding to be arrested. The confused constables looked to the Chief Inspector for instruction. Hell, he couldn't turn it into a massacre of the innocents. Makepeace would have to be enough. He tugged nervously at the cuffs of his sleeve and shook his head.

Then, and only then, did Makepeace allow himself to be led away.

And the marchers continued marching. Every time a policeman approached they held their hands out in front of them, priests, mothers with babes in arms, children, even some in wheelchairs. And each time the policeman turned away.

Two issues confronted the editors of television news programs that night.

The first was how on earth to get political balance into their programs, to ensure that during the election period all sides got roughly equal coverage to avoid accusations of bias. In the end, most said to hell with the alternative of Clarence cuddling grannies on the seafront at Skegness. Delivered unto them had been the enviable combination of hard stones and gripping pictures, TV news at its best. They went with it.

The second was more difficult, to decide which of the two contending items should get top billing. Some chose Makepeace, most featured Colonel St. Aubyn. A "Double Whammy!" as the *Mirror* was to call it the following morning. Disruption, diversion, and editorial delight.

Mortima glanced across at Urquhart, creases of concern about her eyes. He recognized the look.

"I don't know, Mortima, how this will end. We don't control it anymore. Fools are afoot and our fate lies in the hands and upon the votes of the graceless mob."

"St. Aubyn. Makepeace. Are these stories of help or hindrance?"

"Who is to tell? All I am sure of is that these are contrary winds, and some boats will be quite swamped before the gale has blown itself out."

FORTY-TWO

Never show weakness, never. The only reason I bend the knee is in order to hit below the belt.

The custody sergeant was deeply unimpressed. A pack of tissues, a depleted tube of blister ointment, a couple of pens—one a cheap throwaway and the other a sparkling Parker Duofold—a comb, a watch, a paper clip, a mobile phone, and three envelopes containing letters of support thrust at Makepeace during the morning's march were all that he could produce by way of personal effects from his pockets. No cash, no credit cards, no visible means of support.

"I could 'ave you done for vagrancy," the Sergeant quipped.

"I was on a march, not an outing to John Lewis," Makepeace responded drily.

"Well, at least I can't book you for shoplifting, I suppose."

He finished completing the sheet of personal details, stumbling only over the occupation.

"Since Parliament is prorogued that means I'm technically no longer an MP," Makepeace explained. "Must make me unemployed."

The Sergeant sniffed, sucked the top of his pen, and wrote down "Election Candidate." Then he began reciting the words of the formal caution. "You are charged with the offenses shown below. You do not have to say anything unless you wish to do so..."

"Believe me, Sergeant, I wish to do so. I have no intention of staying silent."

"Which in your case makes for problems. As I understand it, Mr. Makepeace, it's your stated intention as soon as you've been released to go back out on the march—the very thing for which you've been arrested."

"Correct."

"Can't have that, can we, sir?"

"You going to arrest me again?"

"No. Not yet at least. Not necessary. Since you've made it clear you won't honor any conditions of bail, I'm proposing not to release you."

"You must."

"I can hold you for up to twenty-four hours, sir. That's the law. I suspect you voted in support of it, too. Give you a bit of time to consider, to cool down. Then we'll put you before the next sitting of the magistrates' court"—he glanced up at the wall clock, which showed nearly one on Monday morning—"which'll be Tuesday."

"I'm supposed to be in Banbury, almost halfway to London by then."

"Not this Tuesday, I'm afraid."

"Sweep out the tumbrel before you put me in it, will you?"

"Don't be like that, sir. You'll find your cell very cozy, I'm sure. Although we're fresh out of feather quilts."

"And justice."

"That's for the magistrates to decide."

"And, thankfully, the people."

The silver disk of the moon had risen to shed a pale, monochrome light across the cutting, supplemented at various points along the ridge by lamps that appeared to be powered from car batteries, and punctuated by the occasional brilliance of portable television lights. Across the road where the children sat, a line of candles had been lit, giving the cordon an almost festive appearance. Every twenty minutes or so some forty of the schoolgirls would rise and their places would be taken by a fresh contingent; they were running the human wall in shifts and by the coachload. But who "they" were was not yet apparent.

No shots had been fired, but the intention of those occupying the ridge was clear. Every time one of St. Aubyn's men approached within twenty yards of the barricade of buses, rifles were raised, chambers loaded, and triggers very audibly cocked. Even had the President and his daughter not been accompanying them, resistance would have been pointless. They had no cover, no way out apart from bulldozing through the children, so they sat and stared, sitting ducks.

Once the sun had melted from the sky and the inky umbrella of night emerged to cover them, they had discovered how insubstantial was the mountain air and how cold it could grow with nothing but starlight for warmth. Rations, too, were meager; no one had planned on this. And from beyond the cordon they could taste the smoky flavors of roasting lamb painted with garlic and rosemary. Torture on a hungry tongue.

Then three men emerged from behind the row of candles and made their way forward. One carried a battered oil lamp, another a large plastic bottle of water.

"Good evening, English," the man holding the lamp greeted St. Aubyn as he moved to meet them. The Cypriot, a wrinkled man in his sixties, sported a huge mustache that grew like ram's horns and entirely obscured his mouth. He held up his hand to indicate he was unarmed. "I hope you are uncomfortable."

"What is the point of this?" the Colonel demanded. "You know that a thousand British soldiers could be here within hours."

"And you and everyone in your convoy could be dead within minutes. But let us not deal in hypotheses, English."

"What do you want?"

"Your surrender."

"You cannot be serious."

"Deadly serious. We want to show you British that you are not welcome in this island, not as military occupiers who meddle in our affairs. And by holding you here until you surrender we want to show the world that your game is over."

"It cannot happen."

"I don't think you can prevent it."

"My Commander at Episkopi will already be organizing our relief."

"On the contrary, we have already spoken to your Air Vice-Marshal Rae and told him that if he lifts a single finger he will be responsible for an enormous loss of life, mostly British."

"You've already been in touch with him?"

"Indeed. We thought it only fair to let him know since we suspect your own communication facilities on the convoy are somewhat inadequate."

Damn right. Stuck in a cutting in the middle of the Troodos mountains with all the specialist communications equipment sent back to Episkopi, they might as well have been shouting down a drainpipe from the moon. St. Aubyn had been relying on a search party being sent out as soon as it was realized they were missing.

"And...?" St. Aubyn inquired uncertainly.

"It seems that he is seeking guidance from London. I am afraid you will have an uncomfortable night."

"We have no food. Precious little water," St. Aubyn explained, noticing the water bottle.

"Anyone who wishes either food or water will be welcome as our guests. But they will come unarmed and will not be allowed to return."

The man holding the water placed the bottle on the far side of the line of candles, tantalizing, just beyond reach.

"I fear that on this occasion we shall have to decline your Cypriot hospitality," St. Aubyn responded drily.

"For now, perhaps. But we shall see." He glanced up to the starscape that hung in the clear sky where soon would hang the fire of a Middle Eastern sun. "We shall see."

The Cypriots turned to make their way back beyond the line.

"By the way, who are you?" St. Aubyn demanded.

"Just ordinary Cypriots. I come from the village of Spilia."

"The Bishop's men?"

The old man turned and smiled wryly, a gold tooth glistening in the lamplight. "You don't understand, do you, English? Since yesterday, almost everyone on the island is one of the Bishop's men."

Then he disappeared into the shadows.

"Did you have any trouble locating the boys, Jim?"

"None at all, sir," the Squadron Commanding Officer replied. He'd been up at first light to fly the reconnaissance mission himself. "They're on the main Nicosia road, just below the village of Spilia."

He pointed out the location on the large wall map in the Air Vice-Marshal's office. "Bottled up in a cutting by a barricade of buses and"—he coughed apologetically—"what appeared to be a gathering of schoolgirls."

"You're kidding," Rae gasped.

"The schoolgirls appeared to be dancing, sir."

"What is this, carnival week?"

"It has some elements of that, sir. Long lines of cars and buses seem to be approaching the site from every direction. Looks as though it's becoming something of a tourist attraction. Whatever else it means, there's going to be no way to get a relief convoy up there without standing in line in a traffic jam."

"Helicopters?"

"We'd be hovering only feet above the top of the cutting with about as much protection as butterflies. They wouldn't even need to fire, just throw stones. Easier than a coconut shy at a fair."

The Air Vice-Marshal's voice dropped a tone. "So what's the answer, Jim?"

"Buggered if I know, sir."

Rae slumped in his chair over the telephone, which he knew would soon be ringing. "Tell you something, old friend. They ain't going to like this back in London. Ain't going to like it one little bit."

"Serves him bloody right."

The morning election press conference had approached a shambles. Urquhart had appeared on the rostrum at party headquarters beneath a neat Velcro slogan entitled "Growing Together." He had with him a carefully prepared press release and an equally carefully prepared Minister for Agriculture, intent on extolling the expanding fortunes of the great British farmer. The media would have none of it.

The position had been well rehearsed on matters Makepeace and military. No comment. The first was *sub judice* and up to the courts, the second a matter of national security. "You'll have to wait and see," the Party Chairman offered in his introduction, but of course they wouldn't. They attacked the position in waves.

"Is it true that our troops are being stopped by a bunch of schoolgirls?"

"It's really not that simple..."

"Can you confirm that the military advice was against this convoy heading for Nicosia?"

"Such private discussions must remain confidential..."

"But are there really lives at stake, or is this simply a tangle with St. Trinian's?"

"This is a serious matter..."

"Will you send in the SAS?"

"Better send in Michael Jackson," a colleague offered.

"Gentlemen, this has nothing to do with farming..."

"Dig for victory, eh, Prime Minister?"

The television lights seemed uncharacteristically warm this morning. He could feel the prickle of perspiration on his scalp and Prime Ministers aren't meant to sweat, to show pressure or exasperation. The cruel eye of television allows them nothing more than a cheerful glow, but he wasn't feeling cheerful.

"And what about Mr. Makepeace, Prime Minister? Has there been any contact between Downing Street and the Birmingham police about his arrest?"

Claire looked on from the wings, studying him closely while she twisted inside. Means, ends, truth, principle, pragmatism. Politics. Weeds choking the rose. She knew he'd have to lie, to deceive, perhaps she would too in his position—except she would never have got herself into that position, would she? She had been trusting, naive. She still had much to learn, even about herself. And much still to do.

The question hung in the air. Urquhart offered a reproachful glance at his wristwatch. "You'll forgive me, ladies and gentlemen, but this is proving to be an unexpectedly busy day."

She would attempt to make the walk that day even if she were on her own. Fifteen miles to Stratford-upon-Avon, from a sloping farmer's field outside Bentley Heath, south of Birmingham, where the M40 and M42 motorways intersect. To show Tom he was not alone.

She had arrived early after the confusion of the night before and had sat on the dewy grass, waiting. Time hung heavily upon the morning air, weighing down her spirits. There was, perhaps, little point in this gesture, but gestures have to be made. Sometimes that is all there is.

And others seemed to agree.

Like daffodils in spring, Makepeace's movement had grown, not yet in flower but already thrusting defiantly through the oppressive snow. They came, in families, with friends, on buses, by train and on foot, some solemn, some singing, carrying banners and babies, trickling into the field until they had grown to a river swollen on injustice. Then, with their unerring instinct for crowds, the first mobile kebab shops arrived. At last she ventured a smile.

She could imagine no more powerful symbol of success, of spring. The cuckoos of journalism would not be far behind.

By nine they numbered nearly five thousand. Not bad for a Monday morning.

Maria had grown with the movement, in confidence, in judgment and independence. She'd never stood before anything more formidable than a class of thirty infants, but armies march to the beat of a drum, and in Tom's absence someone had to do it. They looked to her.

She clambered onto the roof of the small Renault support van to face them. Slowly, the shuffle of noise subsided until all eyes clung to her. She had no words for what was in her heart, but somehow she felt that they all understood and shared.

The breeze caught her face, blowing back her dark hair and rubbing into her cheeks the flush of rebellion. Then, slowly and as though in great pain, she raised her clasped hands high above her head. As Makepeace had done the previous day, in chains. Five thousand pairs of hands rose toward the sky, clenched in defiance, and as many voices sang out in chorus.

From the control van parked in a lay-by beyond the entrance to the field, hurried conversations were flowing up the chain of police command, from the Inspector on the scene all the way to the Chief Constable's office. The marchers had started on their way before the decision came back down. There was little chance of the march being met by violent opposition, at least for the next few hours; skinheads wouldn't be out of bed yet. Anyway, the march was heading away from Birmingham, out of West Midlands' jurisdiction; so good riddance and the Warwickshire Constabulary could pick up the problem.

Anyway, what were they supposed to do, arrest the whole bloody lot?

"Kiss 'em good-bye, Inspector."

In the pink light of dawn the cutting glistened like the inside of a wolf's mouth, waiting to snap shut on its prey. It did not last. By midmorning the moisture had burned away and the rocks of pillow lava were batting the sun's rays back and forth in a cruel game of solar ping-pong. The temperature at the road surface was ninety and climbing.

Nicolaou had slept badly. The strain of the last few days was telling on a body that even in youth had been far from robust, and the reserves of character and resilience he had drained during his time at the Lodge had proved impossible to replenish. The sharp cold of the mountain night had cut through to his bones and he was in no mood to eat breakfast, even had there been any. His eyes had grown glassy, he was beginning to run a fever.

But there was still pride.

They had made him as comfortable as the circumstances would allow in the back of one of the four-tonners. He had uttered not a single word of complaint, offering only a brave smile for his daughter, but she was not fooled and refused to disguise her concern. And by midafternoon the temperature even in the shade was over a hundred.

St. Aubyn made hourly rounds of the besieged convoy, trying to maintain morale, emphasizing to all that had the Cypriots been intent on personal harm they would undoubtedly have inflicted it by now.

"Cypos are nice people, sir," a corporal confirmed, wiping his reddened face with a rag. "Funny thing is, though, when I was a kid we had lots of beetles on the farm. I never got into trouble for crushing them, it was only when I tried to burn the bleedin' things alive with a magnifying glass that me old man gave me a belt. Think I'm beginning to understand what he meant."

St. Aubyn passed on quickly, unwilling to tangle with such singular logic. The next truck was Nicolaou's.

"Fetch me a little water, Elpída," her father asked, as St. Aubyn appeared at his feet.

When she was gone he turned to the soldier. "Colonel, I am desperately sorry to tell you this, but I'm not sure if I shall be able to last very much longer."

St. Aubyn knelt beside him. "Mr. President," he whispered, "the water your daughter is fetching is all but our final cup. I'm not sure how much longer any of us will be able to last."

They were able to maintain intermittent radio contact with the outside world through the helicopters that flew surveillance at regular intervals high over the cutting. From this they were able to inform their base that their supplies were exhausted, and to learn that as yet no one had any idea how—or when—they might be released.

As dusk drew in a Wessex appeared on the horizon flying fast and low, no more than two hundred feet, the door to the rear cabin latched back. As it passed overhead two drums emerged, sprouted silken wings and began floating down, laminated red in the light of the melting sun. A straggling cheer rose from hoarse throats as the soldiers watched the water drums floating toward them and the Wessex begin its turn to start another supply run.

The drums were about a hundred feet from the ground when two shotgun blasts rang out on the ridge above. The parachutes exploded into a cloud of rag feathers and the supplies plummeted to the ground. On impact they burst, one drum almost taking a startled soldier with it into the afterlife.

With a dip of its nose, the Wessex abandoned its run and vanished into the evening sky.

Mortima woke to a clap of summer thunder. It was three a.m., the air dank and oppressive, outside the curtain of night was being torn by the white lightning of the storm. He was at the window; he hadn't slept.

She joined him, her arm snaking through his like links in a chain. "You are troubled, Francis."

"The gods are troubled tonight. I feel..." He shrugged, unable to finish.

"Francis, this is no time for secrets between us."

He breathed deep and tried again. "I feel as though they are waging war over me, the gods out there. Fighting over who will dispose of Francis Urquhart."

"Who will sit at his side in triumph," she corrected.

He did not argue, nor was he convinced. In the bursts of sharp light pouring through the window she could see nothing but shadow across his eyes, which made them appear as the empty sockets of a skull. Thunder rattled like the chains of the Underworld. The mood frightened her.

"What is it?" she demanded. "Don't lock me out."

His eyes flickered back into life, he bowed his head in apology. "We have always shared, Mortima. Everything. The triumphs and the wounds. But now I'm afraid to."

"Sharing a fear is to cut it in two."

"I haven't wanted to burden you."

"Am I so weak or loose-tongued you feel you have to protect me?"

"I wish to protect you," he chastised gently, "because I value you beyond all others. And my fears seem so infantile and superstitious. Yet so very real."

She squeezed his arm more tightly. The atmosphere was stifling, the storm was about to break.

"I told you about Cyprus. Of sacrifice, many years ago," he continued. "It took place not three miles from where the convoy is being held, near the village of Spilia. And it was marked by a symbol, a sign. A flaming pine. Like a torch that has flickered through my dreams in all the years since."

"Sometimes it's not healthy to dwell on dreams."

"I saw the tree again. The other day beside the Lodge. Burning once more."

"A symbol of future triumph," she offered.

"Perhaps a life come full circle."

"Then a completeness. A whole. Signifying strength."

"A life that has come full circle can never go around again, Mortima."

Mortality. With that she could find no argument. Yet the words had helped, he appeared more at ease now, the burden shared, his inner doubts confronted and out in the open. Better to see them. A mile away a trident's fork of lightning struck the BT Tower and a final, massive drum roll of thunder vibrated across the rooftops.

"What will you do, Francis?"

"Do what I have always done, the only thing I know how to do. Fight. And hope my gods win."

He turned to embrace her and the rains came. The gods' battle was done. They were ready to dispose of him.

❖ ❖ ❖

It was almost two a.m. when Maria heard the knock on her motel door. She hadn't been able to sleep, exhilarated by the success of the day's march and tormented by thoughts of what might happen to Tom in the morning. The knocking grew persistent. She threw the covers aside and was halfway across the room before she hesitated. Who was it? What could be so urgent and why the hell hadn't they telephoned? Anyway, she was wearing nothing but one of Tom's shirts.

"Who's there?" she inquired cautiously.

From out in the corridor a woman's voice replied; it earned no hint of threat. Maria opened the door but kept it on the chain.

"I've brought a message for Tom," the woman announced, addressing the eye and loose strand of hair that appeared around the door.

Tom. The password to Maria's new life. Resolved, she slipped the chain and slowly opened the door. It was Claire. Maria didn't fully recognize her, but Claire had already recognized the shirt—so it was true, they were lovers. The legs were great, long and finely toned. Tom always had appreciated good legs. "I think I'd better come in. Both you and I are a little too exposed here in the corridor."

The shirt, the legs, and the attractive face with its long and darkly rumpled hair made way.

"Hello, I'm Claire Carlsen," she said, extending her hand. "Francis Urquhart's PPS."

Instantly Maria took a step back and her look of sleepy half recognition turned to sharp disfavor. "Get out. I have nothing to say to you."

"But I have something to say to you." Claire held her ground. "Something for Tom."

"Francis Urquhart wouldn't lift a finger to help Tom."

"You're absolutely right. But I would."

"You?" She made no attempt to disguise her ill feeling. "Why?"

How could she explain, to Maria of all people? "Perhaps because in helping him I may be able to help myself."

Maria studied the other woman. The blond features were so different from her own. The salon-chic hair, the Italian shoulder bag, the considered, discreetly expensive style. Everything Maria was not. She had many reasons for distrusting this other woman, but there were also the raw eyes that said Claire hadn't slept, not since she'd heard of Tom's arrest and understood why Corder had been so keen to ensure that the driver was well out of trouble's reach. Trouble Corder knew to expect. Trouble he must have planned. And behind Corder stood only one master.

"I don't believe I want to help anyone associated with Francis Urquhart," Maria said firmly.

"We are all associated with Francis Urquhart, whether we like it or not. Tom above all."

Maria stood in the middle of the bedroom, her arms folded across the shirt, aggression squeezed aside by her concerns for Tom and, perhaps, feminine intuition about this woman.

"You would betray Urquhart?"

"I prefer to think of it as being true to myself. I don't think I have been at times in these past weeks. I want to make up for it."

"How?"

"By warning Tom. His arrest was no accident. There were politics behind it. Downing Street politics."

"Where's your proof?"

"I have none. It's no more than a suspicion."

"Not much to go on."

"Enough for me to take the very considerable risk of driving through the night to come here."

"Risk?"

"If Francis found out, there wouldn't be much point in going back."

"This could simply be a ruse, a distraction of some sort. Another trick."

"Please. Let Tom decide that. Tell him I think it was Urquhart."

Maria made no reply.

"One other thing," Claire continued. "Urquhart knows you are lovers. He'll certainly use it against you if he needs to."

"Don't try to threaten me." There was anger now.

"I'm trying to save you."

"He can't prove a thing!"

"My advice to you is to stay out of his bed until the election is over. And stay out of his shirts."

Maria started, looked down at her nightwear and then back at Claire, her intuition suddenly wide awake. "He said there had been someone who'd hurt him. Someone in politics, very different from me." She studied the tired eyes closely, trying to find the woman within. "Someone who would know his shirts."

"Someone who still cares for him very much."

"We have more in common than I thought," Maria acknowledged grimly. "He still thinks about you."

"And I still think about him, as you see."

"But more about yourself." Maria's tone carried accusation.

"Perhaps. And particularly about my family." She hadn't intended all this self-exposure and sharing of secrets, she wasn't sure it had helped. "What are you going to do?"

"What are you going to do?"

"I'm not sure."

"Funny thing is," Maria replied, showing her the door, "neither am I."

FORTY-THREE

Never trust a Greek man. The women of Greece don't, and they know them best.

A photograph of a grizzled old Cypriot dominated the front page of the *Independent*. He was seated on a splay-footed dining chair, old military beret pulled askew over his brow, a gap-tooth smile splitting his walnut face. A battered musket of pre-1914 vintage was propped against one knee and a lissom sixteen-year-old schoolgirl seated on the other. By such an army were the British being humbled, "held to ransom by a combination of hockey stick and blunderbuss," as the *Independent* claimed.

The *Sun* was less tactful—FU! SAY CYPOS ran its headline. Of the carnival atmosphere among the Greeks there was much coverage; of the growing fear and suffering among the British troops very little.

The message of the media was unanimous: FRANCIS URQUHART: FROM TRIUMPH TO TURKEY. Two days is a long time in Fleet Street.

"So what is the military solution, Air Marshal Rae?"

A smell of furniture polish lingered throughout the Cabinet Room; it takes more than war to disrupt a Whitehall cleaning schedule. Over the satellite link to COBRA came the sound of an apologetic cough. "That's difficult, Prime Minister."

"Difficult?" Urquhart snapped. "You're telling me you can't handle this?"

Across the Cabinet table, Youngblood began to color. Out of sight, the climate was changing in Cyprus, too. The Air Vice-Marshal was a man minted at Harrow and molded by his passion for the brutality of croquet; an unsuitable case for bullying. Rae blew his nose stubbornly, a noise that across the link sounded like a bull preparing to resist the matador's goad.

"Difficult, sir, because as you will remember this was an expedition that I recommended against."

"Schoolgirls!"

"Precisely. And I cannot envisage a military solution that would not risk endangering the lives of either those schoolgirls or my men, or both."

"Are you telling me you can find no solution?"

"Not a military one. A political solution, perhaps."

"You're suggesting I negotiate with a bunch of pirates?"

"They're not exactly that, Prime Minister. Which is part of the trouble. They have no clear leadership, no individual with whom to negotiate. These are simply ordinary Cypriots united around a common purpose. To get us out."

"What about President Nicolaou?"

"Seems they want him out, too. It's difficult to find much enthusiasm for politicians in this part of the world right now, sir."

Urquhart ignored what he was sure was the intentional irony. He needed Rae. "I have worked hard to bring peace to the island. If they throw out Nicolaou, they throw out the peace deal with him."

"They've never had peace, not in a thousand years. They're the sort who use sticks of dynamite even to go fishing. They'd manage to live without the treaty."

"Then if they want a fight, Air Marshal, I suggest we'd better give them one."

"How does the defendant plead? Guilty, or not guilty?"

Layers of dust and silence hung across the veneered courtroom, which was packed. Thousands more had congregated outside. The march had not happened today, they were needed here. Sunlight streamed in through the high windows, surrounding the dock in a surrealistic halo of fire as though Channel 4 were filming a contemporary adaptation of *Joan of Arc*. Did the defendant have anything to say before he was burned?

"Not guilty!"

Others apart from Francis Urquhart seemed prepared for a fight.

"If you can't get to the convoy, Air Marshal, then get the convoy to you. Drive it out. Smash the blockade. Call their bluff." Red-hot coals seemed to roll around Urquhart's tongue.

"You're willing to risk all those lives on a hunch they might be bluffing?"

"Strafe the ridge. Keep their heads low. Blow them off if necessary." He spat the coals out one by one.

"At last count there were also half a dozen television crews on that ridge, Prime Minister."

"You'd be surprised how fast a journalist can run."

"And what about the schoolgirls?"

"Tear gas. Scatter them." Out of Rae's sight, Urquhart was waving his hands around as if he were already getting on with the job.

"Schoolgirls can't run as fast as a speeding four-ton truck."

"Are you contradicting me, Air Marshal?"

"Stating fact."

"Enough objections. Take the simple route."

"The simpleminded route."

The exchange, which had thumped and pounded like hot blood through an artery, had suddenly faltered, its wrists cut.

"Did I hear you correctly, Rae?"

"This is not a game, Prime Minister. Lives are at stake."

"The future of an entire country is at stake."

"Forgive me, Prime Minister, if I find it more difficult than you to equate my own personal interest with that of the nation."

"Do I detect even at this great distance the stench of insubordination?"

"You might say that."

"Rae, I am giving you a direct order. Run that convoy out of there."

There was a slight pause, as though the digitalized satellite system was having trouble encoding the words. When they came, however, they sounded throughout the Cabinet Room with the utmost clarity.

"No, sir."

"How many others were arrested for participating in the Peace March on Sunday, Chief Inspector Harding?" Makepeace was conducting his own defense.

"None, sir."

"And why was I singled out for your attentions?"

"Because we believed you to be the organizer of the march, Mr. Makepeace."

"You were right, Chief Inspector. I was. The defendant admits it. I was, am, and shall be organizer of this march."

In the public gallery a portly matron with bright red cheeks and hair pulled back in a straw bun was about to start applauding, but Maria stayed her hand and advised silence. The Chairman of the Bench scribbled a note.

"So this other march, Chief Inspector, the skinheads. This avalanche of acne about which you had such concern for public order. How many were arrested from their number?"

Although the policeman knew the answer, he consulted his notebook nevertheless. It added an air of authority, and gave him time to think.

"Fifteen, sir."

The Chairman scribbled again. Clearly this had been a serious disturbance.

"For what offenses, Chief Inspector?"

"Offenses, sir?"

"Yes. Isn't it customary to arrest someone on the pretext of having committed an offense?"

Laughter rippled through the public gallery and the Chairman frowned until it had dissipated.

Harding consulted his notebook again. "Variously for being drunk and disorderly, behavior likely to cause a breach of the peace, four on narcotics charges, and one case of indecent exposure."

"Obviously a troublesome bunch. No wonder you were concerned."

The policeman didn't respond; Makepeace was being altogether too helpful for his liking.

"I understand the semifinal of the football cup was recently played in Birmingham. Can you remember how many people were arrested then?"

"Not off the top of my head, no, sir."

"I'll tell you." Makepeace consulted a press clipping. "Eighty-three. There were several hundred police on duty that day; you knew there was going to be trouble."

"Always is on a big match day."

"Then why didn't you cancel the match? Order it to be abandoned? Like my march?"

"Not the same thing, is it?"

"No, Chief Inspector. Not the Same Thing at All. Nor was the concert last weekend held at the National Exhibition Center. You arrested over a hundred then. So the disturbances that arose out of those trying to break up my march were really small beer. Barely even root beer, you might say."

Harding said nothing.

"Well, I might say that. I don't suppose you could possibly comment."

Even the Chairman let slip a fleeting smile.

"Then let me return to matters you can comment about, Chief Inspector. Indeed, matters you must comment about. These skinheads, neo-Nazis, troublemakers, call them what you will: arrested for drink, drugs, obscenity, you say?"

Harding nodded.

"Not for offenses under the Public Order Act?"

"I don't understand the point..."

"It's a very simple point, Chief Inspector. Can you confirm that I was the only person to be arrested for marching? All the others were arrested for offenses that would have required your intervention whether they were marching, knitting scarves, or performing handstands in Centennial Square?"

Harding seemed about to nod in agreement, but the head refused to fall.

"Come on, Chief Inspector. Do I have to squeeze it out of you like toothpaste? Is it or is it not true that of the several thousand people present on Sunday I was the only one you arrested for the offense of marching?"

"That is technically correct, sir."

"Excellent. So, we have confirmed that my march was entirely peaceful, that even the activities of the skinheads made it a relatively quiet day for the Birmingham constabulary, and I was the only one you chose to"—he paused for a little dramatic emphasis—"arrest as a menace to public order." He smiled at Harding to indicate there was no ill will. "Whose public order, Chief Inspector?"

"I beg your pardon?"

"Whose public order? Someone obviously decided that my activities would, if continued, represent a threat. But that was a judgment rather than a fact. Was that your judgment? Did you arrest me on your own initiative?"

"Why, no, sir. Only after the most careful consideration..."

"Whose consideration? Who was it? On whose authority were you acting?"

Harding had known this might be coming, they had to show the police action was not hasty but considered, right to the very top. Even so his knuckles were beginning to glow white on the edge of the witness box. "I was acting on the orders of the Chief Constable."

"And I wonder where he was getting his orders from?"

"How do you mean?"

Makepeace looked up to the gallery to catch the eye of Maria. He smiled. She nodded, understanding as always. He'd use Claire's information; what had he got to lose?

"Can you tell me if the Chief Constable's office was at any time before my arrest in contact with Downing Street?"

"I don't understand the question."

"It's easy enough, Chief Inspector. You seem to have had precious little grounds for arresting me as a matter of law. Therefore it was more likely to have been a matter of politics. Was anyone putting on the political pressure?"

"That's pure speculation."

"As was your opinion that my marching might cause trouble. Pure speculation."

"But an opinion that gave me the authority under law to issue directions and you the duty to obey those directions."

"Wouldn't have gone down too well at Nuremberg, would it, Chief Inspector?" Makepeace mocked. "Come on," he cajoled, "was there political pressure?"

"Of course not."

"You can confirm that there was no contact beforehand between the Chief Constable's office and any political office?"

"I...don't know." Harding was protesting truthfully, and beginning to fluster. The crossfire between a Prime Minister, his Chief Constable, and a former Foreign Secretary was way beyond his twenty-three years of experience. Early retirement beckoned.

"So you can't confirm that."

"No, of course I can't. I wasn't..."

"Let me be absolutely clear. Are you in a position to deny that there was any political pressure placed on the police to secure my arrest?"

Harding looked desperately at the Bench. The three magistrates stared back impassively, pens poised.

"How can I answer that?"

"A simple yes or no will do. Can you deny it?"

"No."

"Thank you, Chief Inspector Harding. I don't think I need to bother you any further."

COBRA was designed to resolve hostilities, not to generate them. It was not having a good day.

"Youngblood, I want Rae out and replaced within the hour."

"That will be difficult for me, Prime Minister."

"Confound you! Will argument take the place of backbone in the British Army? What on earth can be difficult about replacing one officer with another?"

"Nothing difficult in that, Prime Minister. It's simply that I won't do it for you."

"You are refusing me?"

"Exactly."

The Prime Minister used a short, foul word.

"I realize that for such a refusal you will require my head on the block," Youngblood continued, "but let me assure you that my speech from the scaffold will be truly magnificent. And forthcoming. I shall, for instance, relate how at every stage you have rejected and ignored military advice, brought this calamity upon yourself. I shall indicate how the nature and timing of our military efforts in Cyprus have been twisted to what I can only assume is an election timetable—I may be wrong about your motives, of course, it may have been folly rather than downright political fraud that caused you to act as you have done, but I shall be happy for others to make up their own minds." He cleared his throat, offered a perfunctory smile seeded with scorn. "I surprise myself; I'm rather enjoying this. I shall take considerably less enjoyment, however, from blaming you in public for each and every death, British or Cypriot, which might ensue from your folly."

"You wouldn't dare," Urquhart gasped; suddenly he was having difficulty breathing.

"Prime Minister, those are brave boys out there, *my* boys. And innocent children. If any of them comes to harm, I give you my word as an officer that I'll peg you out on an anthill in front of every polling station in the country."

The brown felt cloth across the Cabinet table had been rucked between Urquhart's clenched fists. A film of confusion had spread across his eyes, dimming their brightness. He stared ahead but could no longer see, blind. Or was it that there was nothing to see but darkness? He felt as though he were falling backward into nothing.

The General cleared his throat once again and gathered up the papers before him into a neat bundle.

"To contemplate what could turn into a massacre of children before the television cameras of the world is a form of madness. I shall have no part in it." He stood, straightened his uniform, adopted the pose of a Viking before the funeral pyre. "Now, sir. Do I have your permission to leave?"

❖ ❖ ❖

"I am brought to this court for no offense other than my politics. My views do not find favor with some. There were bullies on the streets who tried to stop my march; there are others, lingering in the shadows, who are their accomplices. Who will not accept an Englishman's right to disagree, to carve his own path, to decide for himself. We fought two world wars for those rights against enemies without. Now we must face an enemy within. I am called unpatriotic, yet there is no one who loves this country more than I do. I am accused of inciting violence, yet I march only for peace. I am brought before this court, accused of a crime, yet no man clings more closely to justice than do I. And of what am I accused? If it is not a defense for a man to argue that he acted improperly because he was only obeying orders, then surely there can be no offense if a man refuses to obey improper orders. Stubbornness is a quality much to be admired in English oak. I defied the police not because I lack respect for them, but because I have greater respect for the inherent right of an Englishman to say—stuff the lot of you! I want to do it my way. If it is a crime to be English, then I acknowledge that I am guilty. If it gives offense to love freedom and fair play, then, too, I am guilty. If it is a transgression to want peace, then yet again I am guilty. If it is a sin to believe that this country deserves a better form of politics, then condemn me and throw away the key. And do it now. For I shall not hide my views, nor compromise them for the sake of office, neither shall I do deals behind closed doors for things I cannot support in the open sunlight. I have no party, only my politics. And in those politics there is respect, for the law. Love, for my country. Sacrifice, for peace. And defiance for those who would trample over the rights of ordinary men and women. It is they, not I, who are trying to turn this court into a tool of political manipulation, and if they start and succeed here in Birmingham, in the heart of England, where will they stop? And do we have to ask who are 'they'?"

❖ ❖ ❖

"Sit down, sit down," Urquhart instructed, desperately attempting to reassess the situation. But Youngblood remained standing.

Urquhart felt drained; he reached for his glass of water. Everyone noted its tremble. He drained it in a savage gulp but it left trickles at the corners of his mouth and his upper lip damp. His eyes flickered nervously, staring up at Youngblood. "Sit down, man. There are lives at stake. Let us at least talk it through."

Stiffly and with evident reluctance, the General subsided.

No one spoke as Urquhart's teeth bit into a knuckle, trying to put himself back in touch with his own feelings, even if they were only feelings of pain. For a moment he seemed to be floating, freed from his own body, observing the group from a distance, gazing down at a man sitting immobile in the chair reserved for the Prime Minister, a man who seemed trapped like a fly in amber. One of history's victims.

"I apologize, General, if I appeared rash. That was not my intention." He could not feel the tongue that formulated the words, his voice unnaturally taut as though he had swallowed neat mustard.

Youngblood cast a look to turn milk, but said nothing.

"If it is your advice that there is no apparent military solution," Urquhart continued, still stilted, "what suggestions do you have to make?"

Youngblood gave a terse shake of his head.

"Anyone?" Urquhart offered, staring around the table. For the first time he realized he had scarcely once over the last few days asked other members of COBRA to contribute, but even rubber stamps can make a mark.

No one had anything to say. Then the General coughed. "Rae's the man on the spot. I trust anything he has to say."

Urquhart nodded.

"Rae," the General barked, "your thoughts, please."

"My thoughts, gentlemen," the voice carried across a thousand miles, "are that this is a political situation that can only have a political solution."

"Please feel free, Air Marshal," Urquhart croaked.

"Reluctantly I reach the conclusion that if the Cypriots want the bases back, there is little we can do to stop them. Now, next year, sometime soon. They would win. These things have an undeniable momentum."

"But the bases are our most vital listening post throughout the Middle East. Giving them up would be a military and intelligence disaster," Urquhart objected.

"Depends, sir. The Cypriots don't dislike our presence here, indeed they welcome it. Off the boil they're very hospitable. And the bases bring them vast amounts of income and jobs. What they object to is our being freeholders in their own country."

"What are you suggesting, Rae?" Youngblood pushed.

"If I were a politician, sir"—his tone conveyed his delight that he was not—"I'd be thinking about a deal. Keep us all as friends. Let them know we're happy to return the title to the base areas, then do a deal to lease them back. We keep the bases, the Cypriots keep the income. Everybody's happy."

"Intriguing," Youngblood muttered.

Urquhart's expression was of stone, his mind like an ice field that was slowly cracking. As he sat silently, independent thoughts began to swirl around him.

The Party Chairman shook his head. "It would be a political disaster."

"Not necessarily. Not if we made it our initiative," the Defense Secretary contradicted. "A solution that would keep our reputation as peacemakers in the island. After all, who could object? Dick Clarence has already publicly backed us in Cyprus, he couldn't bleat."

"And the only other likely source of sound is Tom Makepeace.

He's under arrest." The Attorney General sounded positively cheerful.

A mood of enthusiasm began to warm the room, gradually beginning to thaw Urquhart's frozen thoughts. Perhaps the fly was not entombed in amber; perhaps it had only brushed against a web and might yet struggle free.

A low knock at the door interrupted their deliberation. A tentative head appeared around the door, followed by the rest of a private secretary who made his way toward the Prime Minister's chair. He placed a piece of paper on the table, then retired.

Slowly Urquhart's eyes began to focus and read.

No matter how hard the fly struggled, there was no escape.

Thomas Makepeace had been acquitted.

FORTY-FOUR

The rules of politics are simple. Don't expect too much, don't attempt too little, and above all, never, never sleep soundly.

The dying sun had cast a hard shadow across the cutting. The temperature was still over a hundred but Nicolaou was shivering, as he had been all afternoon. His heartbeat was irregular, his voice a low tremble, but his mind had not lost its edge.

"I cannot leave, Elpída."

"If you stay, Father, you will die." She knelt beside him, mopping his brow.

"I'm not afraid. I've grown used to being threatened with death in the recent days." It was his attempt at being lighthearted to dispel oppression, but it failed. The atmosphere remained fetid, laden with failure. The pool of pale light cast by the lamp inside the truck had drained the color from his face, leaving only two small spots of protest that suffused the very tops of his cheeks. The rest of him looked like congealing wax.

"Come with me. Now." Her plea betrayed her desperation. She pulled at him, feeling every bone in his frail hand, but he refused to rise from his mattress of blankets. He was no longer sure he was able, even if he tried.

"You should think about it, sir," St. Aubyn intervened, his squatting form indistinct in the gloom that was slowly beginning to devour the far end of the truck. "There's nothing to be gained from senseless suffering."

"That is...noble of you, Colonel." Nicolaou's breathing was growing shallow; he was struggling for his words. "But you risked your lives to rescue us. I cannot desert our British friends."

"Father, grow up."

Her rebuke slapped across his face. His eyes, soft-glazed and distant, struggled to focus.

"They did not come to save our necks but those of their High Commissioner. And Mr. Urquhart," she continued. "Isn't that right, Colonel?"

St. Aubyn shrugged. "I am a military man. I do as I am instructed. A soldier isn't trained to ask why."

Nicolaou flapped his hand in feeble protest. "But Mr. Urquhart has been such a good friend to us, Elpída. The peace..."

"It is our peace, not his. And it's probably lost, anyway."

The old man flinched. His suffering had been borne on the hope that all he had fought for would yet come to pass; the contemplation of failure drained him like leeches. "Please tell me I haven't thrown it all away."

"You cannot fight on two fronts at once, Father, seeming to give so much away to the Turks while giving in to the British. As much as we want peace, we Cypriots also have our pride. Sometimes that's more important."

His hand shook in confusion, reaching for his daughter. "All I have done, Elpída, I have done for you and those like you. For the future."

"No, *Baba.* You haven't."

Nicolaou started choking in confusion. St. Aubyn leaned forward, whispering—"Steady on, miss"—but she ignored him.

"That's why I want you to leave here and join those people outside," she continued.

"Why? Why?" her father moaned.

"Because, *Baba*, they are right. And for the British to occupy Cypriot land as lords and masters is wrong."

"You never said such things before."

"You never asked me. Nor did you ask anyone else. But Cyprus is changing. Growing up." She turned to St. Aubyn. "Colonel, believe me, you will be welcomed in my house at any time. As a friend. But I don't want you in my house as of right."

He nodded, but said nothing. The concept of retreating from distant outposts was not a novel one to a British soldier.

"Why do you scourge me so, Elpída?" Flakes fell from the President's fading voice.

"Because I love you, *Baba*. Because I don't want your life to end in failure. Because if we cross the line, join them, you will not only be doing what I believe to be right for our island, but also what is best for you. Salvaging pride, yes, and a little justice from the wreckage that has been strewn about Cyprus by the British. Maybe even saving the peace, too."

St. Aubyn coughed apologetically. "The gentlemen outside, sir, have insisted that you and your daughter will only be allowed across the line if you submit your resignation."

"The presidency has become an uncomfortable bed on which to lie."

"You cannot make peace with the Turks, Father, until you have brought peace back to our own community."

"And, it would seem, to my own family." Nicolaou sank back onto his rough pillow of blankets, exhausted but alert. His bony fingers gripped his daughter's hand, flexing like the beat of his heart as he struggled to find a way through the maze of his emotions.

"What is to be done? Can I achieve more by remaining in office, or by resigning?"

"Father, you can achieve nothing by dying."

"To lose everything? The presidency? The peace? You, Elpída?"

"*Baba*, you will never lose my love," she whispered, and he seemed to gain strength from her words. He squeezed her hand with more certainty, propping himself awkwardly on an elbow, barely able now to see beyond the small pool of lamplight that lit his makeshift bed.

"Colonel, if I decided to leave, would you allow me to?"

"You are not my prisoner, sir."

"Then, if you don't mind, I think I shall."

The Colonel nodded and reached forward as though to help Nicolaou rise. Elpída waved him away.

"No, thank you, Colonel. If he can, I would like my father to walk back to his fellow Cypriots without leaning on a British arm."

"I do feel stronger somehow," her father acknowledged.

"Why do you think I have been kicking you so hard, *Baba*," she asked, kissing him gently. "You always become so stubborn when you get angry."

As she helped her father down from the truck she turned to St. Aubyn. "I did mean what I said, Colonel. That you will always be welcome in my house. As a friend."

It was twilight. The candles flickered, the gentle song of a Cypriot schoolgirl quavered on the evening air as the final colors of purple and fire stretched out along the horizon like fingers drawing on the curtain of night. Leaning heavily on the arm of his daughter, the President of Cyprus turned his back on the British and walked the fifty yards to rejoin his countrymen.

The new glass and front door had arrived that morning. A tax demand, too, along with an invitation to arrange a meeting with a sales tax inspector. Vangelis was ready to resume business and already the wolves were circling, drawing nearer.

He felt hounded in every direction he looked. On television

he had watched the scenes of Makepeace rejoicing outside the magistrates' court, raising his hands high above his head as though still manacled, receiving the same sign back from the spilling crowd and accepting their adulation and fervent endorsement. The victor. An Englishman who, so far as Passolides knew, had never set foot in Cyprus was now treated as his homeland's savior. Honor built on the sacrifices of others. Sacrifices, thought Passolides, like his own.

The screen showed scenes of rejoicing from the island itself, too, as old men, gnarled and bent double like ancient olive trees, danced with young girls and waved rifles and flasks like some scene out of *Zorba* in celebration of the defection and deliverance of Nicolaou.

Everywhere he saw the happiness of others, but Passolides had no part in the joy. These should have been his victories, his accomplishments, yet once again as throughout his life he had found himself excluded.

And the crown-encrusted envelopes of officialdom sat on the table before him. They were pursuing him, the agents of British imperialism, as they had done all those years ago, into his every hiding place, leaving him no sanctuary.

Inside he writhed like a worm cleft by a spade, a dew of despair settled upon his eyes, his mind blanked by bitterness. With a great cry of despair he lashed out, throwing the bottle from which he was drinking at the Satan's eye of a television screen. The bottle bounced off, hit the new window. Something cracked.

But Vangelis didn't care anymore.

Urquhart had watched those same newscasts as Passolides, his sense of despair equally profound. He had watched the clasped hands of Makepeace rise above his head, then fall, and rise, and fall again. To Urquhart it was as though Makepeace were clutching the haft of a dagger and he could feel the assassin's blade striking time and again into his own body. In Makepeace's triumph lay his own doom.

It was late; he had summoned Corder. "Still here?"

"Thought you might need some company."

"Kind. You're a good man, Corder. Good man." A pause. "I've got something for you."

Corder listened attentively, studying the Prime Minister all the while. Urquhart's stiff expression belonged in an abattoir, his voice strangely monotone, his reflexes mechanical. A man changed, or changing, struggling to hide the despair.

When Urquhart had finished, Corder could find only one word. "Why?"

He had never questioned an instruction before.

Urquhart's voice was no louder than a hoarse whisper; he seemed almost to choke on every word. "I have just given the order for the convoy in Cyprus to surrender; I have no option. To accept defeat is offensive to every bone in my body. It will kill me, Corder; they will flay me alive and demand my head on a pike. Somehow I must fight on, in any way I can."

"But why this way?"

"Please, don't ask me, Corder; I'm not even sure myself. Perhaps because it is all I have left."

The impact was catastrophic, utterly irresistible. Yet, like a dam that had held back the rising flood waters until it could no longer resist, the first visible cracks took some hours to appear. The news of the final humiliation, the announcement that St. Aubyn's men had set aside their weapons in order to engage in "unconditional discussions" with the Cypriots, came too late for the morning newspapers, and the TV images of the surrender shot through night lenses that appeared on breakfast news were too grainy and indistinct for full impact.

Nevertheless, the rumblings of internal collapse were everywhere to be heard.

The noise emanating from the Member of Parliament for Milton Keynes resembled not so much a rumble as a drum being repeatedly struck like a call to arms, unable as he was any longer to confine beneath the straining buttons of his waistcoat all the righteousness that had been building since his hopes of preferment at the last reshuffle had been dashed. "Tom has been a colleague and friend of mine for many years," he pronounced from the back seat of the radio car parked in his driveway. "Both Tom and I have served our party faithfully and I have enormous respect for Tom." He clung to the name like a life belt in stormy seas, as though by continued repetition he might convince others of what he had only just convinced himself. "The March is due to pass through my constituency later today and I very much hope to be marching with it."

The battle for the Blessing of Makepeace had begun.

"The party does not belong to Francis Urquhart nor to any one man. I believe Mr. Urquhart should announce his intention to step down immediately after this election. My choice for his replacement will be Tom Makepeace."

"And if the Prime Minister does not make such an announcement?" the interviewer asked from the London studio.

"Frankly, I don't think he's got any choice."

From party headquarters came reports of a flood tide of telephone calls from activists demanding resignation—whether of the Prime Minister or the Member for Milton Keynes, the reports did not make clear. In any event a press release was issued in immediate denial, but when journalists tried to check the story they couldn't get through. The switchboard was jammed.

And from Cyprus came news of Nicolaou's formal resignation and the first pronouncement of his successor, Christodoulou, the former Vice President who owned the BMW concession on the island. "We shall not rest," he told a tumultuous press conference, speaking into a bouquet of microphones, "until the blood shed by our fathers has been honored and all soil on this island has been returned to Cypriot control." Even many journalists started applauding. "And while I believe that we should pursue every avenue of peace with our Turkish Cypriot neighbors, I cannot sign the proposed peace treaty as it stands. A more fair division of the offshore oil resources is vital, and I shall be contacting President Nures immediately to seek further discussions." Standing beside him was Elpída, strained but seraphic, who nodded encouragement before reading out a statement of support issued by her father from his hospital bed.

Throughout the day the cracks in the dam grew wider, support draining away, the trickles of defiance becoming great bursting geysers of rebellion that were sweeping Francis Urquhart into oblivion.

By the following morning the mood approached hysteria. The van bringing the early editions of the newspapers into Downing Street had a loose hubcap; the noise echoed from the walls of the narrow street like the rattle of a cart over cobbles on its way to the Tyburn scaffold. Since elements of both main parties and any number of pressure groups now claimed Makepeace as their spiritual leader, the outcome of the election was utter confusion; party lines were crumbling into the chaos of a civil war battlefield, and among the tattered ranks roamed packs of reporters trying to find a yet more injurious example of defection from the colors of Francis Urquhart. A telephone poll indicated that less than ten percent of voters wanted Urquhart to remain as Prime Minister; as the accompanying editorial claimed, they must all have been supporters of the Opposition. Attempts were being made to contact sufficient Government election candidates to discover who in their opinion should be their next leader; the answer was overwhelming. Makepeace—if he would have it. But Makepeace was unmoved, saying nothing as his march wound its way toward the outskirts of Milton Keynes, growing by the thousand with every passing hour.

It seemed that with every passing minute the mob at the gate grew in size. Words that in the morning could be attributed only to anonymous but highly placed sources within the Government party by afternoon were having definitive names attached to them; backbenchers, under pressure from small majorities and small-minded wives, rushed to join the execution squad before they were placed against the wall themselves. Ministers were said to be in constant contact and cabal, to be in open rebellion. It was reported that at least two covens of Ministers would be gathering around the dining tables of London that evening to discuss the removal of the Prime Minister—not if, but when and how. The reports were so prolific that the venues had to be changed at the last minute.

And across the front page of Jasper Mackintosh's new journal, the *Tribune*, was the most extraordinary allegation of all. Against photographs of sick and weary British soldiers, some of whom were on stretchers recovering from dehydration and heat exhaustion, stood the headline:

FU PLANNED GERM WARFARE

It was feared last night that the Prime Minister planned to use chemical and biological weapons against the Cypriots before he was forced to surrender. The alarming condition of the British soldiers involved in the fiasco has led to allegations that they were contaminated by their own bioweapons which Francis Urquhart himself had ordered to be carried secretly on the convoy. "Such orders would make Urquhart a war criminal, guilty of the most serious breaches of the Human Rights Convention," a peace spokesman said...

Mackintosh was on his yacht in St. Katharine's Dock, the fashionable waterhole that nestles beside the looming columns of Tower Bridge, when the phone call came.

"Why do you print it when you know it's not true?" The voice was hoarse, with a slight Scottish Lowland taint, as happened when he was on the point of exhaustion.

"Truth, Francis? A strange new suit for you to be wearing."

"Why do you print it?" Urquhart demanded once more.

"Because it does you damage. Hurts you. That's why." From behind Mackintosh came the sound of an exploding cork and the tinkle of young female laughter.

"I thought we had an understanding."

"Sure. You would poke sticks in my eye for as long as you could. Then it would be my turn. You're through, Francis. There's nothing more you can threaten me with, no taxation changes, no monopoly references. Because one week from today they're going to hang you in front of every polling station in the country. And I'll host the celebrations."

"Is there nothing we can..."

But already the line was dead.

FORTY-FIVE

I would like to take my time about getting old, but there is a time and a place for everything. Even death.

Late that evening he called them in, one by one. His Cabinet. The Praetorian Guard whose bodies would litter the steps of the Capitol before they would allow any enemy to draw within striking distance of Caesar. In theory, at least.

Claire had counseled against calling them in separately, but he had been firm. They were agitated, like sheep, if one scattered the rest would surely follow. Herd them, isolate them, stare them down, allow them to find no strength in numbers; on their own he might cow them into support before they melted away into the mob. But at his core he knew they weren't up to it; they would fail him.

He sat in the Cabinet Room, in the chair reserved for the Prime Minister, the only one with arms. Three phones beside him. The rest of the table was bare, stripped of blotters and any other sign of Ministerial rank, covered only with a sad brown felt cloth. He wanted his Ministers to have no hiding place, no trappings of office, nothing behind which to hide. He needed to know. Outside it was drizzling.

He had intended to start with Bollingbroke, but the Foreign Secretary was returning from a Council of Ministers meeting in Brussels and there was a delay somewhere along the way. Instead he got Whittington—how he wished it had been Whittington's wife; then, at least, he would have found some solid response. There was a knock at the door and Claire brought him in. He seemed reluctant.

"Come in, Terry," Urquhart encouraged quietly. "It's my scaffold you're stepping on, not your own."

The Minister sat opposite and dabbed at his mouth nervously with a handkerchief that then slipped surreptitiously to his temple, wiping away the dew that was beginning to rise.

"Terry, let me get straight to the point. Do I have your continued support as Prime Minister?"

"You will always have my personal support, Prime Minister." A whimpering smile appeared on his damp lips, then as quickly evaporated. "But I can't see how we can win, you know, with..."

"With me?"

"With circumstances as they are."

He was bleating, even sounding like a sheep.

"Will you make a public statement of your support for me?"

The dew at Whittington's temples had turned into an unmistakable nervous damp. "It's so very difficult out there," he muttered, waving a rubber wrist. "I would hate to see you defeated, Francis. As an old friend, I must tell you. I don't think you can win. Perhaps, perhaps...you should consider announcing your resignation. You know, protect your unbeaten record?"

It sounded preprepared, secondhand. A ditty passed through Urquhart's mind, about something borrowed, something blue.

"And what does your wife think?"

"She feels exactly the same," Whittington added, too hurriedly. He'd given the game away.

Urquhart leaned forward. "A statement of clear support from

my Cabinet would help give a slightly less striking impression of a sinking ship."

Whittington's lips moved in agitation but he said nothing, merely flapping his arms about. He was already swimming.

"Then will you at least give me until this weekend to decide? Before you say anything publicly?"

Whittington's head nodded, falling forward, hiding his eyes. They were stinging; he wasn't sure whether from the sweat or because he was on the verge of crying.

With a flick of his wrist Urquhart dismissed him. Claire already had the door open. It was raining harder now.

Maxwell Stanbrook came in next.

"So, Max?"

"First, Francis, I want to tell you how grateful I am for everything you have done. For me. The party. For the country. I mean that, most sincerely."

"So you'll support me? Publicly?"

Stanbrook shook his head. "Game's up, old dear. Sorry. You cannot win."

"I made you, Max."

"I know. And so I'll go down with you, too. I'm honest enough to recognize that. Which is why you should recognize that I'm being honest about your situation."

"There is nothing to be done?"

"Get out on the best terms available, Francis. Which is to announce your resignation now, before the election. Give the rest of us half a chance. And keep your unbeaten record into the bargain. 'Undefeated at any election he fought,' that's what the history books will record. Not a bad epitaph."

Protecting his unbeaten record. The same formula used by Whittington. An interesting coincidence, if it were.

"Will you issue a statement of support on my behalf?"

"If that's what you want. But in my opinion it will do you no good."

It hurt. He'd had hopes of Stanbrook. Deep within he felt a shaking, of foundations crumbling, of new fissures beginning to appear below the waterline.

"Thank you at least for being so honest. Please, give me until this weekend. Say nothing until then?"

"You have my word on it. And my hand on it, Francis."

Melodramatically Stanbrook marched around to Urquhart's side of the table and offered his hand. At close quarters Urquhart could see the lack of sleep that bruised his eyes. At least it hadn't been easy for him.

Catchpole, the next, was in tears. He blubbed copiously, scarcely capable of coherent expression throughout the interview.

"What, in your view, should I do, Colin?"

"Protect"—*blub*—"protect"—*cough.*

"I think what you're trying to say is that I should resign now in order to protect my unbeaten record and place in the history books. Is that right?"

Catchpole nodded. Coincidence be damned. They'd been rehearsing, the whole wretched lot of them.

Except for Riddington. The Defense Secretary strode in, but declined to sit, instead standing stiffly at the end of the Cabinet table near the door. His double breast was buttoned, on parade.

"I have sat too long at your table, Prime Minister. In recent days at meetings of COBRA I have watched you abuse your position of trust for entirely political ends, putting the lives of British soldiers at risk for your own personal glorification and salvation."

"You never mentioned this before."

"You never asked me before. You never consulted anyone. You only bullied."

True enough. And Urquhart had expected no less from Riddington, who had refused to support him at the final gathering of COBRA, insisting with the others that St. Aubyn's men be allowed to bring an end to their misery.

Urquhart seemed to smile, parting his lips as though being offered a final cigarette. "So who will defend, if not Defense?"

"I beg your pardon?"

"I was merely musing. I suppose a public statement of support for me is out of the question?"

There was a whimsical tone in Urquhart's voice as though he found humor in his situation. Riddington offered an expression of bad oysters and did not reply.

"I have one last thing to ask," the Prime Minister continued. "You have sat at my Cabinet table for more than eight years. In return, I ask you for two days. By Saturday I shall announce my intentions. In the meantime, if you cannot support me, I'd be grateful if you could at least refrain from making public attacks. Leave me a little dignity. Leave the party a few pieces for someone else to pick up."

Riddington had on his most obstinate Dunkirk expression, but acquiesced. He gave a perfunctory nod, then turned on his heel and left.

For a long moment a complete stillness enveloped the Cabinet Room. Urquhart did not stir, did not appear to breathe. Claire, who had been sitting discreetly in a corner by the door, wondered if he had gone into a trance, so deeply did he seem to have retreated within himself. A tiny pulse on the side of his temple seemed the only sign of life, beating away the seconds until...Until. There was no avoiding it. Even he knew it. Then he returned from wherever he had been, and was with her once again.

"Like trying to stoke a furnace with dead rabbits, isn't it?" he muttered grimly.

She marveled at his composure, admired his resilient humor. "I wonder what *he* would have done," she asked softly, indicating the portrait of Robert Walpole, the first and longest-serving holder of the office of Prime Minister.

Urquhart rose to examine the oil above the fireplace, gripping the white marble mantel. "I've been thinking about that a great deal in these last days," he said softly. "They accused him of corruption, condemned him, even imprisoned him in the Tower. Called him a warmonger, even before Mr. Mackintosh got his hands on the media." His eyes seemed to dissolve like children's sweets. "They compelled him to resign. Yet he always found a way to bounce back from disaster. Always."

"A shining example."

"History has a devilish strange way with the facts. I wonder whether history will be as kind with me."

"Is it important to you?"

He turned sharply, his eyes burning with mortification. "It's the only thing I have."

The bitterness, hemmed around by dogged humor, was about to burst forth but at that moment there was a commotion from the door. It burst open, and in bounced Bollingbroke, breathless.

"Et tu, Brute?"

"Beg pardon?"

Urquhart closed his eyes, shook from them the venom and self-pity, and smiled. "My little joke, Arthur. What news of Brussels?"

"Full of bloody foreigners. Sorry not to have got here earlier, Francis."

"You are with me?"

"Till my last breath. I dictated a statement of support to the Press Association from the car telephone on my way in."

"Then you are doubly welcome."

"Bloody thing is, Francis, it won't do either of us the least bit of good."

"Why not?"

"'Cause you and me are for the high jump, there's no denying it. That bugger Makepeace has got this election by the balls."

And Makepeace marched on. To Luton. Every hour brought Makepeace more support, and closer to London. With every step the march grew in size, slowing him down and giving the Metropolitan Police Commissioner cause for concern. But after the fiasco in Birmingham, he dared not bar the march from the nation's capital.

So they marched, onward to Trafalgar Square. To Francis Urquhart's funeral pyre.

FORTY-SIX

Love colors life, but it is necessary to hate in order to make a man truly happy and give him a sense of direction.

He had stolen away by moonlight. Through the Downing Street press department, down into the labyrinth of corridors that connects Number Ten to the Cabinet Office on Whitehall, past the old brick walls where the Tudor King's tennis court used to be. Not even Corder was with him.

Even at midnight the center of the city was bustling with activity, mostly vehicular, Whitehall becoming something of a racetrack for delivery vans and late-night buses. The activity helped hide him, ensure he did not stand out. As he came down the steps from the Cabinet Office, past the startled security guard, he ducked away from the police presence that stood at the entrance to Downing Street. George Downing himself had been a rogue, a spy for both sides in the Civil War, a man steeped in duplicities and lacking in either principle or loyalties. Educated at Harvard. And they had given him a knighthood and named the most important street in the kingdom after him. Whereas he, Francis Urquhart, would be fortunate if they allowed his name to be placed even on a headstone.

There were monuments to the dead everywhere. The Cenotaph. The Banqueting Hall beneath whose windows they had with one blow severed the head of their liege lord and king, Charles I. Statues to fallen heroes, *in memoriam* and immortal. The entire avenue stood on what had once been the old funeral route from Charing Cross to St. Margaret's until the King, disgusted with the wailings of the common herd outside his window, built them a new cemetery at St. Martin-in-the-Fields so they could bury the dead without spoiling his dinner. At night in the shadows and with a scimitar moon overhead you could all but hear the creak of ancient bones in this place, a place of remembrance. And he so wanted to be remembered. What else was there for him?

He stood on the stone bridge at Westminster, gazing down into the silty-ink tidal water that lapped against the piers, its gentle murmurs haunting like the witching calls of Sirens. An emptiness yawned beneath him that seemed to offer peace, release, as easily as falling into the open mouth of a grave. What fragments he had left to lose could so readily be given up. Yet he would not do it, take the coward's way out. Not the way to be remembered.

He rattled the spiked and rosetted gates to New Palace Yard—the Members' entrance to the precincts of the House of Commons. Members of Parliament were forbidden access to the Palace of Westminster while an election was being fought, except for the sole purpose of collecting their letters. Even during elections constituents still complained, about drains, about neighbors, about missing social security checks, all the things that burdened a politician's life, and a carefully worded response might yet win a vote. The policeman who swung back the gate in answer to his call offered a respectful salute—Urquhart was well past, his heels clicking on the cobbles before the semislumbering officer had recovered sufficient wit to register what he had seen and wonder why on earth the Prime

Minister was calling in person and at midnight to collect his mail. But he was entitled.

Urquhart did not head for the Members' Post Office, which in any event was closed; instead he made his way up the stairs and through the stone archways to the rear of the Chamber; he met no one. But he knew he was not alone, the echo of his footsteps accompanied him like a cohort of distant memories. He had come to the long corridor that ran behind the Chamber, usually noisy with the bustle of errands and anticipation, now ghost still. Before him stood the great Gothic doors to the anteroom of the Chamber. They should have been locked, as should the second set of doors into the Chamber itself, but electricians had been busy rewiring the sound system and the constant unlocking and relocking of doors would have put them into double overtime. The doors swung open on their great brass hinges.

The darkness was intense, split only by pale splashes of moonlight from the high windows of the west wall, but he knew every inch by instinct. He had stepped onto this stage, the greatest stage of all, so many times yet it never failed to impose its majesty. The atmosphere, heavy with history, clung to him, lifted and elated him; he could feel the memories of centuries crowding around, the ghosts of the great whispering in the wings and waiting for him, Francis Urquhart, to join them.

He pushed his way past the waving Order Papers and jabbing elbows, stepping over the outstretched legs, making his way toward his seat. At one point he stumbled, forced to rest a hand on the lip of the Clerk's Table for support, sure he had been tripped by some extending ankle—Gladstone's, perhaps, the rakish Disraeli's or recumbent Churchill's? Did he hear the clip of a closing handbag, smell stale Havana? But then he had reached it, the space on the bench left for the Prime Minister, waiting, as it always had been, for him. He sat, embracing the formal subtlety of its leather, savoring the spice of great events that lingered in its fabric and brought forth the familiar rush of adrenaline. He was ready for them. But they were quiet tonight, everyone waiting to hear him, hanging on his every word, knowing that these were momentous times.

He stood to face them, his legs propelling him firmly upward until he was standing at the Dispatch Box, gripping its sides, rubbing his palms along its bronzed edging, afraid of no one. He would have his place in history, whatever it cost, show them all, those faint hearts and foes who surrounded him like men of Lilliput. He'd make them remember Francis Urquhart, and tremble at the name. Never let them forget.

Whatever it cost.

He pounded the Dispatch Box and from around the Chamber came answering echoes like the thunder of applause washing down across a thousand years. He could hear them all, great men, one woman, their voices a united chorus of approval, emerging from the dark places around this great hall where history and its memories were kept alive. They spoke of pain, of the sacrifice on which all legend is raised, of the glory that waited for those with character and audacity enough to seize the moment. And their thumping acclaim was for him. Francis Urquhart. A welcome from the gods themselves.

"Excuse me, Mr. Urquhart. You shouldn't be here."

He turned. In the shadows by the Speaker's Chair stood a Palace policeman.

"You shouldn't be here," the man repeated.

"You are of that opinion, too? It seems the whole mortal world is of the same view."

"No, I didn't mean that, sir," the policeman responded, abashed. "I merely meant that it's against the rules."

"My apologies, officer. I only came here for…one final look. Before the election. A chance to reflect. It has been a very long time."

"No worries, Mr. Urquhart. I'm sure no one will mind."

"Our little secret?" Urquhart requested.

"Course, sir."

And with a low bow of deference and a little light from the policeman's torch, Francis Urquhart bade farewell to the gods. For the moment.

It was Passolides's custom to rise before dawn, the habit of mountain warfare fingering in the mind of an old man. And while he embraced the cover of night and paid silent tribute to past times, he would gather the freshest of fish from the local market. A habit with purpose.

Unfriendly eyes watched him leave and it was while he was pondering over shells of crab and fillet of swordfish that hostile hands went about their work. Grateful, as Passolides had once been, for the cover of night.

When he tried to turn into the street, laden with paper-wrapped parcels of food, he found his way barred by a large plastic ribbon and a police officer.

"Sorry, sir. No one allowed in until they've finished damping down."

The parcels slid to the pavement.

"But that is my house."

A hundred yards away, hemmed in by fire engines, the windows of his home stared out sightless across the street, his newly restored restaurant now a gaping, toothless grin. He had been gone little more than an hour. It had taken considerably less than that to destroy almost every possession he had.

They set out that morning for Watford, on the very outskirts of London. It would be the final stop before their triumphal entry into the city itself, and already the route was lined with images of Makepeace and other trophies, strewn along their path like rose petals. A conqueror's welcome for a man of peace. And one day to go.

FORTY-SEVEN

Grasp the moment. Grasp the dagger! Destroy others before they can destroy you. And if that is not possible, it is better to destroy yourself.

Claire, in answer to his summons, found him writing letters in his study. He brightened as he saw her; he appeared pale with exhaustion but more at ease, as though he had ceased to battle against the impossible current and was finally reconciled to being carried downstream.

"Can I help?" she offered.

"You may help yourself, if you want. I'm writing out a list. Disposing of a few baubles and trinkets to those who have been kind." He looked at her intently. "My Resignation Honors."

"You have decided to go?"

"That has been decided for me, I no longer have any say in the matter. But in the manner of my passing..." He waved the piece of paper. "Can I find something for you?"

"There is nothing that I want," she replied quietly.

"For Joh, perhaps?"

She shook her head.

He fell to pondering. "My doctor. Corder, too. Mortima, especially Mortima. She must have something."

"You sound," Claire suggested slowly, "like a man disposing of his most personal possessions from his..."

"Deathbed?" He completed her thought. His cheeks filled with a little color, an expression of defiance began to erase the bruises around his eyes. "No!" he said with feeling. "I intend to live forever."

He returned to the papers on his desk. "Tell me, what do you think Geoffrey deserves?"

"You want to give him something?" The words stuck in her throat like dry biscuit.

"But he surely merits some recognition." An ironical smile played about his lips but reached no further. The eyes remained like old ice. "You may have noticed he was unable to attend our little session in the Cabinet Room yesterday, sent a message saying that he was away campaigning around the country. So I tracked him down by phone. He swore loyalty. To me. Which was why he was working so hard in the constituencies, he said. Tireless, the man is tireless. D'you know, it sounded as though he was almost in tears."

She shook her head in evident bewilderment.

"You misjudge him, my dear; our Geoffrey has never been idle or lacked passion."

"In his own cause most certainly, but in others'?"

"Why, I even asked if he would issue a public statement of support, which he readily agreed to do. I have obtained a copy."

He indicated a press release on the corner of his desk. She read it quickly. An appeal for party unity. Emphasis on achievements. A call to arms, of battles still to be fought and victories to be gained even through difficult times. Of faith in the future.

"But there's not a single mention of your name."

"Precisely. His trumpet sounds, but not in praise of me or even in epitaph. It's the first rallying cry in his own leadership campaign. He wants my job."

"You expected any less?"

"Absolutely not."

"So why do you want to give him something?"

"Language is important in this job, and I've learned to use my words with care." It sounded almost as if he were embarking on a lecture. "I asked you what he *deserved*."

"Disappointment. But are such things still within your power?"

"I may be mortally wounded but that makes me dangerous, not incapable. I am still Prime Minister. I can prick him, prick them all. If I want."

"Do you?"

"In his case?" He pondered, one last time. "Yes."

"Why are you so unrelenting?"

He picked up three envelopes, as yet unsealed. "Because some people are born to ruination. Geoffrey is one." He sealed the first envelope, addressed to the chairman of Booza-Pitt's local association, regretting that "in light of the new circumstances" the offer of an honor would have to be withdrawn.

"Because in that process of personal ruination," Urquhart continued, "Geoffrey would also ruin the party." He licked the gum of a second envelope, intended for the Chairman of the House of Commons Committee of Privileges, containing a copy of Geoffrey's letter of resignation with its tale of marital and financial malpractice. It bore the day's date.

"And because he has tried to betray me." The third envelope, also with a copy of Geoffrey's letter, was sealed. It was addressed to the editor of the *News of the World*.

"Power is there to be used, Claire. To command people and their destinies. We talk of economics, of ethics. But we mean people."

"Destroy others. Before they destroy us. Is that it?"

"No!" His eyes were sharp. "You must understand, yet you don't. We all talk about a vision for a better future but it is our vision and *their* future. People are our building blocks and you cannot build a temple without breaking a few bricks."

"As I said. Destroy others, before they destroy you."

He shook his head, but not in anger. "No. In politics, we destroy ourselves. We do such a good job of it we scarcely need the assistance of others. Although such assistance is so readily given."

He sealed a fourth envelope. It was for Annita Burke's husband. A photograph of her and Riddington engaged in the sort of detailed discussions that were impermissible even under the loosest interpretations of collective responsibility. A double blow to the ranks of those who might succeed him.

"It is given to few to cast their shadow across the land. If you desire success then you must stand tall, not constantly be bending down to commiserate with the masses huddled in the shade. That is for nuns."

"I am no nun."

"But I wonder what you truly are, Claire. Whether you know yourself."

"I am not you, Francis. Nor am I like you. That is why I want nothing from you. I already have what I want."

"Which is?"

"A view of power. From the inside."

"At the feet of a master."

"A man who has destroyed himself."

"Who may yet save himself."

"I can't see how."

"That's because, as you said, you are not like me. Because, after all, you are another who has turned away from me." She could detect no animosity in his tone. He sealed another letter. To the editor of the *Mail*. In it was a copy of Max Stanbrook's birth certificate, which showed him to be both illegitimate and a Jew. A doubly burdensome cargo that would surely sink his ship in the storm waters of a leadership contest. Pity. Urquhart liked Max Stanbrook and he was good. Perhaps too good, that was his problem.

"I haven't turned my back on you, Francis. I'm still here."

"And I ask myself why."

"Because I'm not a silly girl who flees in tears at the first sound of gunfire."

"No. Leave that to the grown men of my Cabinet."

"And because I can still learn from you. From all this mess. If you'll let me."

"You want to watch the autopsy."

"To find out how to do it better. When my turn comes."

"Oh, you have ambition?"

"I thought for a while you'd destroyed it, turned me off politics and their ways. But I want to find a better way."

"You won't have long in which to learn. But you may still have much to learn."

"Such as?"

"Who do you think will lead the party after me?"

"Tom."

"And if he doesn't want it? Or can't have it?"

"Stanbrook. Riddington, perhaps."

"But you see, they have all"—he straightened the pile of envelopes—"destroyed themselves. They cannot succeed."

"Then who?"

"I fear it leaves only Arthur."

"Bollingbroke? He would be a disaster!"

"He's popular. After the party is thrashed at the election they'd cling to anything that floats."

"He'd split the party."

"Probably." His eyes grew distant. "And then how they will sit around their campfires in the depths of fiercest winter and bemoan the folly of turning on Francis Urquhart. Not such a bad chap after all, they'll say. A great chap, even. One of the finest."

She hung her head in disbelief. "You are a remarkable man. Why, you're trying to write history even…"

"Even from beyond the grave." The clarity in his own thinking seemed to have brought about a remarkable transparency in her own. He rose and came around the desk to her. He took her arms. "Kiss me?"

He intended to have her, there in the study. Desire ran through his veins, a renewed sense of life. And lust. The final flicker of a guttering candle, perhaps, but a new energy, an electricity that stiffened his body and fueled his appetites. He would not back away this time.

She shook her head. "Once, perhaps, Francis, but not now."

"Have I misunderstood you?"

"No, you've misunderstood the time. And timing is everything."

It was well into the afternoon before they would allow Passolides to inspect the ruins of his home. He was allowed in with a fireman to see whether there was anything capable of salvage, before the place was boarded up.

It stank. He was surprised and disgusted at the overwhelming stench of rancid ashes and charred remnants of what a few hours before had been his life. It scraped his nostrils and stung his eyes, which began to pour.

"Upsetting, sir," the fireman commiserated, "but think of it this way. You were lucky to be out of the property. Particularly at that time of the morning. Have insurance, did you?"

Passolides detected the edge of suspicion.

"We'll have to put a report in. Some evidence that the fire was begun deliberately..."

The fireman prattled on as Passolides wandered desolate through the ruins, poking at the sodden ashes with his walking stick. Vangelis seemed so much smaller now that the upstairs floor had collapsed and all the partition walls had burned down. Everything was black, charcoal, rafters, and jagged wreckage scattered around like smashed bones at the bottom of a medieval burial pit. On a wall where the first floor had been, a washbasin hung at a drunken angle; the old enamel bath now lay overturned in his kitchen. In what *had* been his kitchen. He scratched, he prodded, hoping to find something of value that had survived the blaze when his stick struck metal. It was the British military helmet that had adorned the back of his door. Flattened like a plate. Vangelis had gone.

"Know of anyone who might want to burn you out, old man?"

Passolides was standing on the site of his food store. The walls had gone, the freezer had melted and all that remained amid the other odors was the reek of scorched flesh. He closed his eyes. Was this how it had been, with George and Eurypides? Burned by the same people, these British whose game of war and death never seemed to stop, even after all these years?

"They have taken everything from me."

"Got nothing?" the fireman inquired, compassion beginning to squeeze aside the suspicion.

"My clothes. My stick," Passolides responded. Then he remembered the gun. Tucked in his belt. He still had the gun. It hadn't all gone.

"Social services'll take care of you."

"I have a daughter!" he spat, fiery proud of his independence; he needed nothing from these British. Then, more sadly: "She'll be back tomorrow."

He sank onto the seat of the overturned bath, his forehead coming to rest on his stick, a bent and bleary-eyed old man, overflowing with miseries and exhaustion. In his dark clothing and beret he seemed to melt into the soot-smeared surroundings as though he would never leave this place. The fire officer, wanting to check the stability of the party wall at the rear of the premises, left him to his private sorrow.

As Passolides contemplated the end of his world, something

caught his eye, a figure standing in the screaming hole where yesterday had been the doorway. The stranger was clad in black leather and a motorcycle helmet with a courier's personal radio at his shoulder, and was calling his name. "Package for Passolides."

A clipboard was thrust at him and, in exchange for his signature, he was rewarded with a padded manila envelope. Without another word, the courier left.

The gnarled fingers fumbled as they sought to open the package. Tentatively he spilled the contents onto his lap. For a moment he did not understand. There was the photograph of Michael Karaolis, the young EOKA fighter with the defiant eyes and exposed neck around which in the morning they would put a noose. The photograph that, the night before, had hung on the restaurant wall. There was another photograph, a fading portrait of a young British army officer whom Passolides did not immediately recognize. And two scorched crucifixes that fell from his shaking fingers—God, how the memories pounded at him, made him gasp for breath, almost knocking him to the floor. The small engraved crosses were those he had given on their name days to George and Eurypides.

The dark world around Passolides seemed to stand still, only his tears had life, washing clean the ash-covered crucifixes as he retrieved them from the floor.

It was not finished. Two further pieces of paper slipped from the envelope. The first was a photocopy of a British Army service record, tracing the short career of a junior officer in a Scottish regiment from his induction in Edinburgh through service in Egypt. And onward to Cyprus. In 1956.

Passolides found the name at the top of the service sheet—now he recognized the officer in the photograph. Lieutenant, one day Prime Minister, Francis Ewan Urquhart.

And the second piece of paper. A primitive leaflet. Appealing to all to come tomorrow to the rally in Trafalgar Square.

At last Passolides knew the identity of the man he had been searching for. The man who had murdered his brothers. And, with a passion for Hellenic honor fermented over endless centuries, he knew what he had to do.

Mortima woke to find he had stolen from their bed again. She followed the noises to the narrow galley kitchen. He was busying himself at the refrigerator when she walked in.

"I am sorry if I disturbed you," he apologized.

"Why can't you sleep, Francis?"

"There seems so little to sleep for." There was a finality in his tone. "Anyhow," he offered in mitigation, "I was hungry." He had before him a large slice of Dundee cake and cheddar cheese, a favorite childhood delicacy the family gillie always produced during their beats across the Highland moors in search of grouse and deer. It had been years, he'd almost forgotten the sharp-sweet flavor. He began to consume the pieces slowly and with considered relish.

"You pay your midnight feast more attention than you do me in recent days, Francis. You've locked yourself away from me, looked straight through me, you've neither heard me when I've spoken nor offered answers to my questions. There's an anger, an impatience within you that drives you from my bed."

"Bad dreams. They distract."

"I've been your wife long enough to know it's not dreams that bother you," she rebuked.

"Go to bed, Mortima."

He took another mouthful, but she would not be moved.

"You're not running from your dreams, Francis, you're no child. And neither am I. You've never been like this with me before." Her distress was evident. "You are angry with me."

"No."

"Blame me for my folly with the letter."

"No!"

"Think that I have helped destroy you." She reproached him and reproached herself still more.

"We destroy ourselves. All that I have done would have been done whether the letter existed or not. And all that must be done, too."

"What will you do?"

He looked at her but would not answer. He began munching again, carefully breaking morsels from both cheese and fruit cake, gathering up the crumbs.

"You shut me out."

"There are some journeys we can only take on our own."

"After all these years, Francis, it's as though you no longer trust me."

He pushed aside his plate and came to her. "Nothing could be further from my mind. Or from my heart. Through all these troubled times you have been the only one I could rely on, could reach for in the darkness and know you would be there. And if I've hurt you through my silence then the fault is mine, not yours, and I beg for your forgiveness. Mortima, you must know that I love you. That you are the only woman I have ever loved." He said it with such force that there could be no doubting his sincerity.

"What will you do, Francis?" she repeated, demanding his trust.

"Fight. With all I have, for everything I have achieved."

"In what way?"

"So many men spend their lives in fear of doing something wrong, of making error, that they do nothing except live in fear and slip uselessly away." His eyes blazed contemptuous defiance. "I will not go meekly into the night. The world will hear of my going. And remember."

"It sounds so very final, Francis. You scare me."

"If my life were to end at this moment, Mortima, there would be only one regret, that I would be leaving you behind. Yet we both know that the time must come. What matters is what I leave behind, for you. A legacy. A pride. Dignity. A memory people will applaud." He smiled. "And that Library."

"I can't imagine life without you."

"As I cannot imagine life without all this." He waved his arms around the most private trappings of power. "But there comes a time when the body is worn, the spirit tires, the sword is blunted by battle—and even love must have its rest. What survives, for those chosen few, is the name, even after all else has faded away. Immortality. I want you to trust me, Mortima. To support me in whatever it is I have to do."

"I always have."

"And know that whatever it is I do, I do for us both."

"Then nothing has changed." She seemed to relax, understanding bringing a measure of reassurance. She had always known he was not like other men; he lived by his own rules, it could come as no surprise to her that he intended to depart by his own rules, too. Whenever the time came. A time perhaps of his own choosing. She managed a smile as she reached for him.

He kissed her with great tenderness. "I have so many reasons to be grateful to you, I scarcely know where to start. But let me start with your cake. It's delicious, Mortima. I think I shall have another slice."

"I'll join you. If I may."

FORTY-EIGHT

In the total darkness of fear and defeat, even a spark of misery can bring welcome light.

The morning broke wound-pink beyond the cupola of St. Paul's Cathedral, and already the preparations had been under way for many hours. Road diversions had been posted along the route to Trafalgar Square, lamp posts and shop windows festooned with posters and his portrait, banners were being painted, reporters were turning phrases such as "an Armada of faith" and "the irresistible gale of revolution." Makepeace was everywhere, the word upon all lips.

No one knew precisely how many would be joining Makepeace on the final stretch of his march from Watford or how many would be there to welcome him on his arrival, but after the derision that had been piled upon the West Midlands force following the fiasco in Birmingham, the capital's Police Commissioner had decided it was not a time for taking chances. Although there was no indication of trouble beyond the pressure of unknown numbers, the fountains in Trafalgar Square had been emptied, the great pump rooms beneath inspected for suspect packages, the metal crowd barriers collected like supermarket trolleys in neat rows across the square.

The population of pigeons, avian mongrels, complained at the unexpected clatter and noise, rising in feathery spirals of protest and darkening the sky before trying to settle once again, furious at the continued disruption. Their homeland was being invaded; for the day, at least, the square would be snatched from them.

Urquhart had bathed early, Mortima bringing him a great soup cup of tea in the bath while the steam and hot waters restored the color in his sleep-starved cheeks. She thought she heard him muttering, perhaps calling for her, but when she inquired he answered that he was simply practicing a few lines for his final election speech. She had noticed that the bulky draft provided by his team of speech writers remained untouched. "They believe I can't win," he explained, "and it shows." Neither had he touched his Ministerial boxes.

By the time he had completed his ablutions with a meticulous manicure, as though he had all the time in the world at his disposal, the crowd barriers were being put in place and interlocked around the square. A small number were left at sensitive points around Whitehall and particularly near the entrance to Downing Street, just in case. To keep the hounds from the bear. But little trouble was expected; in less than a week Makepeace's militia would be occupying the corridors of power as of right.

He selected from his wardrobe his favorite dark blue suit and a white cotton shirt, laying them out across his bed for inspection. He tried several silk ties against the suit; he wanted to wear the one Mortima had bought for him from the craft stalls beneath the castle in Edinburgh, a token from her last visit to the Festival, but it was hand-painted, a little florid perhaps. He put out his regimental tie instead. Then, attired in his silk dressing gown, he breakfasted. He was in good humor and of hearty appetite; the crossword was finished before his eggs had boiled.

There had been only two disputes concerning the organization of the rally that day. Superintendent Housego, the police officer responsible for security, would not allow into the square the two mobile kebab vans that had accompanied the march from its very first day. They were like mascots, Makepeace argued, veterans of some great battle who claimed their right to be present at the victory ceremony, but the Superintendent insisted that the congestion around them would be simply too great and potentially dangerous; in large crowds people could become so easily crushed, and in violent crowds such vehicles might become battering rams, barricades, or simply bonfires. No. Not worth the risk. Makepeace resolved the problem by inviting Marios and Michaelis, the two owner-drivers, to join him on the small podium that was being erected for his speech between the Landseer lions at the foot of Nelson's Column. "And next week you can drive all the way up Downing Street," he joked. It was the first time he had allowed himself even to hint that he would be there to greet them.

The second dispute concerned the numbers themselves; Housego wanted a limit of fifteen thousand but on this issue Makepeace was unable to offer any guarantee. He had no idea how many would be joining in. He did not control the marchers; on the contrary, as he explained to the Superintendent, they controlled him. But in any event the problem would be much reduced, he suggested with only a hint of perceptible irony, since it was customary for the police count at demonstrations to be so much lower than the reckoning of the organizers. Discretion being the better part of promotion, the Super decided to take his cue from Nelson and turn a blind eye. He would put on a couple of extra serials—self-contained police units, twenty-two strong—as a precaution. He saluted and departed content.

Others were also busy. St. John Ambulance set up a field station in the crypt of St. Martin-in-the-Fields, grateful at being able to borrow the facilities of the homeless shelter, while all morning television crews haggled to gain access to windows and rooftops around the square, determined to find the optimum vantage point and paying a handsome "disturbance fee" in hard cash to office maintenance staff. Even if they numbered only fifteen thousand it would still be the largest election gathering in living memory.

To it all Urquhart appeared oblivious. He nestled in his favorite leather chair, still wrapped in his dressing gown, and read. First from Margaret Thatcher's memoirs, *The Downing Street Years.* The final pages. Scenes from a great drama. Anger. Heartache. Betrayal. Then *Julius Caesar,* his favorite play. Another great assassination. Yet how much kinder they were to him than to her, Urquhart reflected, ending great Caesar's misery with a single blow, a final cut. Not lingering. In death to find the acclaim that those jealous and petty men around him would not confer in his lifetime. The way to finish great lives.

And Makepeace marched. All the way down Watling Street, the old Roman thoroughfare that led from Chester to the heart of London. Like the legions of old they tramped, five or six abreast, in a great phalanx that stretched for over two miles and which grew ever longer as the morning progressed and the great column drew nearer the heart of the capital. Two brass bands and a group of Scottish pipers appeared as if from nowhere to add to the carnival atmosphere, and garlands had been placed around the necks of Makepeace and Maria as they passed before a Hindu temple in Edgware. Even the mobile police control van that hovered in constant close attention had been decorated; policemen in shirtsleeves smiled and waved at the children as though competing to rub salt into the still-weeping wounds of their colleagues in Birmingham. The noise of celebration grew so enthusiastic that Makepeace had difficulty in making himself heard to the radio and news reporters who accompanied him all morning, but there were others keen to make up for any deficiency of sound bites. Waiting for Makepeace in Trafalgar Square was a patchwork quilt of pressure groups spread right across the political spectrum, all chewing media microphones and trying to identify themselves with Makepeace. Even Annita Burke was there, arguing that her "old colleague and friend" represented so many of the values that lay at the heart of what she and her party had traditionally stood for. When asked if tradition excluded the present, she smiled. "Perhaps the immediate past," she conceded.

As they proceeded down Piccadilly they passed by what had once been the town house of Lord Palmerston, a great Victorian Foreign Secretary who had become a still greater Prime Minister. Omens all the way; the flags that decorated the route seemed to stiffen in salute. The window of Hatchards was laden with copies of a book Makepeace had penned several years earlier and that until a few hours before had been heavily out of print; he signed several without breaking his pace. Drivers leaned on their horns, people waved from buses, tourists asked for autographs. The March for Peace had turned decisively into a celebration of victory. Yet even Makepeace was astonished as he came out of Pall Mall and into the amphitheater of great buildings that surrounded Nelson's victory column. He had lingered behind in Hyde Park, allowing the body of the march to move ahead of him. In that great river alone he knew there were some fifteen thousand souls, but what he had not known was that the river was flooding into the still greater sea of those gathered to greet him in the square. As they sighted him, led by a skirl of pipers, they broke into an emotional tide of waving hands and banners that washed back and forth across the basin of the square, growing stronger as it did so in shouts and accents that represented all parts of the country and some parts even beyond its shores. More than forty thousand people were gathered under the unseeing eye of Lord

Nelson until Trafalgar Square brimmed and overflowed with their enthusiasm. Makepeace walked through their midst like Moses carving his path through the Red Sea, his hands raised, clenched above his head, and they thundered their approval.

Even behind the thick shatterproof glass of Downing Street, Urquhart could not mistake the roar, like the cry heard by Christians as they waited in the pit of the Colosseum, armed only with their faith in God. Urquhart had never placed much store in Faith, not if it meant being devoured by lions and the bones being quarreled over by rats. How much better to believe in oneself, to die a Caesar rather than a humble sinner. There came another clamor as Makepeace mounted the podium. Only then did Urquhart set aside his books and begin to dress. He had forgotten to put out any cuff links; he chose the pair of nine carat gold engraved with the family monogram that had once belonged to his father. He stood in front of the dressing mirror, checking all aspects of his appearance in the manner of a suitor about to propose marriage. He asked Mortima for her opinion. She approved, apart from the tie.

"But what are you planning to do this afternoon, Francis, that you should be dressed up so?"

"Why, I intend to address Tom Makepeace's little rally."

Urquhart was adjusting his tie in the mirror, one ear tuned to the radio and the speech upon which Makepeace had just embarked, the other turned deafly in the direction of Corder. "Friends. Brothers. My apologies—and sisters!" he heard Makepeace exclaim, before Corder's voice pushed all else aside.

"You can't do this," the Special Branch officer was stating, emphatic to the point of shouting.

"You cannot stop me, my dear Corder," Urquhart responded with complete equanimity.

"There are no security arrangements in place."

"Our security is in the surprise. No one expects me."

"There are thousands of your opponents out there, Prime Minister. They've traveled from all over the country for the specific purpose of letting you know how much they dislike you. And you want to walk right into their midst?"

"Right into their midst. Exactly."

"No!" Corder's vehemence was genuine. "This is crazy."

"This is history, Corder."

"May I talk as an old friend, Prime Minister?"

Urquhart turned to face him. "So far as I am concerned, Corder, you always have."

"You've been under an immense strain recently. Might this have"—an awkward pause—"clouded your judgment?"

"Gently put. Thank you." Urquhart moved to place hands of reassurance on the shoulders of the other man. "But on the contrary, old friend, the immense strain about which you talk has brought great clarity. You know, the prospect of being hanged and all that? I know what I'm doing. I absolve you of any responsibility."

"They'll have me issuing parking tickets after this. You know that, don't you?"

"In which case you will be the first knight of the realm to be doing such work. I have already written out my resignation honors, Corder. I'm a Scot, not given to undue generosity, but you should know that you are on my list."

Corder blinked, shook his head to free himself of what was clearly a distraction from his purpose and returned to the attack. "I have to stop you."

"Corder, you cannot."

"Mrs. Urquhart," he appealed, changing tactic, "will you stop him?"

Mortima had, like Urquhart, been examining her appearance in the mirror, brushing away a few imaginary creases from her jacket. "I can scarcely do that, Corder."

"Why not?"

"Because I'm going with him."

"Are you, by God?" Urquhart exclaimed, challenging her.

She moved over to him, with care and great tenderness enfolded him in her arms and looked closely into his eyes. "Yes, Francis, I am. I have come with you this far, I'll walk with you a few steps further, if you don't mind. And even if you do."

His face began to move in agitation, trying to find some words of contradiction, but she placed a finger upon his lips to still them.

"It's only a little walk down the road," she whispered. "I won't hold you back."

FORTY-NINE

A man may die a thousand times in Westminster; on the field of battle, only once.

He stood on the front step of Number Ten, hand in hand with Mortima. Above him white clouds hung like gun smoke in the summer sky, while behind him Corder was ranting into his personal radio. Urquhart turned in rebuke.

"No, Corder! No great posse of police. I want no human wall to hide behind, no excuse for confrontation with the crowd. I'll not have it."

The tone was severe, brooking no argument. Corder muttered something into the radio and put it aside.

"Then may I accompany you, Prime Minister? As a family friend?"

Urquhart smiled. "In that capacity you have always been welcome."

They began walking down the street. As they approached the tall stressed-steel barriers at its end, a uniformed policeman outside the guard booth saluted while another jabbered excitedly down the telephone. But it was too late. The great gate swung open, and they were in Whitehall.

Large numbers of people were still trying to squeeze into the square, crowding pavements, beginning to clog the approach roads. The Superintendent had need of his extra serials, and more. And as the Urquharts made their way up Whitehall, recognition of them had an immediate effect.

"FU too! FU too!" barked one youth with the appearance of having been lifted from the front half of a dry-cleaning commercial, but Mortima turned to launch a look of sharpest feminine rebuke directly at him and he subsided, his voice faltering like a slipping fan belt. His chant was not taken up; instead, a ripple of attention ran through the crowd at the sight of the great opponent, normally only seen through television screens and surrounded by the trappings of power, who to all appearances was enjoying a weekend stroll in the sun with his wife. Cries of recognition the Urquharts received with a civil nod of acknowledgment, chiding rewarded with one of Mortima's most devastating stares. As they made their way the five hundred yards up Whitehall, past the mounted sentries at Horseguards, a tremor of interest rather than intolerance ran before them like a bow wave, heralding their arrival. By the time they had reached the crowded edges of the square, the tremor had become a shock wave that began to force its passage through the mass of bodies ahead. Urquhart was coming! Urquhart was coming! And many, particularly those who did not have a good view of Makepeace speaking on the far side of Nelson's Column, turned to face their adversary.

Urquhart's timing was providential—or pestilential, depending on the viewpoint. As Makepeace was about to begin his peroration, he sensed a distinct loss of interest among a substantial part of his audience. He looked out across the sea of upturned faces in front of him, through which a turbulent crosscurrent seemed to be sweeping past and dragging their eyes from him. Caught by their interest, Maria walked to the edge of the raised speaking platform to inspect the source of the disturbance; the look of alarm and confusion that took hold of her was enough to make Makepeace himself falter, serving only to fuel the distraction.

Superintendent Housego was there to meet them. At the first hint of the Urquharts' imminent arrival, relayed through the Information Room at Scotland Yard, he had uttered curses both profuse and profane. Then he had summoned the Tactical Support Group, his reserve of specially trained officers who were on standby in coaches parked in nearby Spring Gardens. But he hadn't enough; he wished he had a hundred more.

"I cannot allow this, Prime Minister."

"You cannot stop me, Superintendent."

"But I don't have enough men to force a way for you through the crowd."

"I want no force," Urquhart responded sharply. Then, more softly: "Please. Ask your men to stand aside."

Housego, bewildered, subsided.

Urquhart was still grasping the hand of Mortima when he crossed the roadway and came face-to-face with the crowd. From this point on he knew he would lose all control, becoming little more than another pawn in the great game upon which he had embarked. The faces confronting him were impassive, frozen by surprise. He nodded, smiled, and took two steps toward them.

The British are cynics, always willing to believe in human weakness and bathe in the oils of collective skepticism that seep from their daily press. Yet on a personal level they are civil to the point of deception, hiding their real feelings behind a cloak of wooden etiquette in much the same way as they ask for the *News of the World* to be delivered wrapped between the sheets of the *Sunday Telegraph*. Had Hitler flown to London rather than requiring Chamberlain to come to Berchtesgaden, the entire country might have queued to shake his hand. The British are bad at personal confrontation.

So the crowd in front of Francis and Mortima Urquhart began to shuffle back, to make way and allow them through. Many even smiled in automatic reflex. And thus the Urquharts, slowly and arm in arm like a couple stepping out onto a ball-room floor, made their way toward the rostrum.

The impact of these matters on Makepeace was devastating. He knew he had lost the attention of the crowd, now he could see it parting like concubines before the Khan. With a half joke about the arrival of unexpected reinforcements, Makepeace himself turned to the edge of the platform to inspect the cause of the disruption. He found Urquhart and his wife, with Corder a pace to the rear, at the bottom of the steps to the podium and already beginning to climb.

"Tom, good afternoon," Urquhart greeted.

"This I did not expect."

"Forgive me, I did not mean to disrupt you. But the deed is already done, you have won. I am tired of the fight, Tom."

"That is gracious of you." Then, suspiciously: "Why are you here?"

"To salvage a little pride and respect in defeat, perhaps. On the radio at the start of your speech I heard you say that you did all that you have done more in sorrow than in anger. In that same spirit I have come to express my hopes for conciliation, if not between the two of us then at least for our country."

"But why?"

"Because I love my country. Because I have led it for too long to wish to see the end of my career languish in bitterness and anger. I have made mistakes, been unfair to you. I would like the opportunity to apologize publicly."

"What—here? Now?"

"With your permission."

"Never!" Maria interjected. "You can't let him hijack your rally like this."

"I wish only to apologize."

"Then take an advert in *The Times.*"

"Maria, Maria," Makepeace chided gently, "this is our meeting, these are our supporters. Not his. I've just been complaining about the lack of free speech and compassion in the Britain of Francis Urquhart; is the Britain of Tom Makepeace to begin in the same ugly fashion? What have I got to lose, apart from his public apology? Anyway," he jested, trying to deflect her protest, "if I turn him back he's likely to get lynched."

"Then I may speak?"

Makepeace turned to the microphones. "It would seem that Mr. Urquhart is so impressed with our gathering that he has come to offer his personal apologies to us."

Released from the confines of face-to-face formality, the crowd indulged their true feelings. A chorus of wolf whistles and jeers erupted.

"No." Makepeace held up his hand. "Unlike some, we are forgiving and tolerant. Let us hear him. Before we condemn him."

The cries scarcely subsided as Makepeace made way at the microphones for Urquhart.

"I still don't care for it," Maria was complaining. "I'd rather watch the lynching."

How much more suitable she would have been as a leader than Makepeace, Urquhart reflected silently, if only she made a better choice of sleeping partner. He moved forward, Mortima at his side. The jeers grew in a crescendo. They volleyed back and forth across the square, gathering in pace and ferocity, the sea of arms and upturned faces turning turbulent and breaking like angry waves against the base of the great column, threatening to overwhelm him.

Suddenly Urquhart threw his hands in the air. "Marchers! Marchers for peace! I salute you."

It was as though he had thrown a massive blanket over a fire. Calm.

"We carve the mistakes of men upon their headstones, and

bury their accomplishments with their bones. If that is my fate, then let it be."

Even those few in the crowd who had continued to protest were now hushed to silence. This was not what they had expected.

"This is a rally to celebrate peace and I am indebted to your leader Thomas Makepeace for his permission to address you. I, too, have come in a spirit of peace. And reconciliation. For at the end of an election campaign it is time to accept the verdict of the people, no matter how personally hurtful. To bind the wounds. To move forward. Together. That is what I hope for our country today no less than when I first took office as your Prime Minister. I cannot deny that it was my wish to continue in Downing Street, and if that has seemed selfish on my part, then I accept the charge. If ambition is a crime, then I plead guilty.

"I have held ambition for my office, for there can be no greater privilege or higher accolade in a politician's life than to lead this country and you, its people. You have been kind enough to confer that accolade on me repeatedly for more than a decade, and if you choose to deny me that honor now then again I have no complaint. And certainly not against Tom Makepeace, for he is a decent man.

"I have also held ambition for the people, for it is only through the people that a country may grow great. And if their comfort and prosperity stand at levels that could only be seen as a dream some years ago, then I do not care one jot who is accorded the credit. It is enough for a leader to see those dreams fulfilled, and if others wish to ascribe such prosperity to the influence of Europe, to statistical euphemism, or even to economic accident, then, once more, I have no complaint."

There was a shout from the crowd.

"No! Not even against Tom Makepeace. For he was a member of my Government for so many of those years. And he is a decent man.

"Yet above all I have been ambitious for our country, to restore it to the ranks of those nations considered great. Great Britain. Not simply another anonymous land indistinguishable from the others, but one for which we can raise our heads with pride and say 'I am a Briton,' and for that bold claim to be respected anywhere in the world. And particularly in Europe. I am not anti-European. It is not that I would be the last European, but that I would be the first Briton. That has been my ambition, and if it is an ambition you do not share, as Tom Makepeace does not, then I have no complaint.

"Earlier today Tom Makepeace said that I owe you an apology and I listened to his words, the words of a decent man, with care. And if it is the view of you and other decent men and women that an apology is due, then it is freely given. As freely as I have given my heart and my life for you over these many years."

His voice seemed to be on the verge of breaking, and there was silence across the square. Maria was staring in hard reproach at Makepeace; he in turn stared stonily at his shoes. Urquhart appeared to be searching the crowd as though trying to reach for each and every one of them. Or searching for someone. On perches and pavements around the square, commentators were rapidly attempting to rewrite their scripts.

"But let me say that I have been brought to this place not so much for Britain as for Cyprus. An island I know well, and that I love. Many of you here will disagree not only with what I have done, but with what I tried to do in Cyprus. Say that I am guilty of confrontation and bloodshed. But that is not what I tried to do. My aspiration, as you all know, was to bring peace to the island. To stop the bloodshed. To bring together the communities. I have failed, but it is an attempt that has failed for over a thousand years in that unhappy place. Yet that prospect of probable failure did not stop me from trying. Yes, if you like, peace was my ambition, and why not? And if I should lose my office because of that failure, how much greater is the loss suffered by ordinary peace-loving Cypriots?"

And then Urquhart saw him, shuffling forward in the crowd, limping and with bent back, his features all but hidden beneath the beret. Drawing closer.

"There are those who do not want to see peace in Cyprus. Wicked men, men of violence. Who have never known peace and who cannot live with peace. Who linger over old death and lost graves rather than looking forward to new life. Who have tried to find division between Cyprus and this country, when some of us sought only reconciliation."

The attack on Makepeace was all too blunt yet it aroused surprisingly few cries from the crowd. "The bones. The bases," one protester yelled from the foot of the platform, waving a banner.

"No, do not misunderstand me. I do not come to dispute Tom Makepeace's views, decent though they may be; I come only to show that there is another, genuine way. And if there is a division between the interests of Cyprus and Britain then I for one make no apology for saying that I am British, the head of the British Government, and proud to accept the obligations that go with it. Perhaps I have loved my country too much. If so, it has been a fault—a calamitous fault. And calamitously am I asked to pay for it."

Maria was muttering vehemently into Makepeace's ear, nodding in the direction of the microphones, but Makepeace placed on her a restraining hand and shook his head. It was too late. The moment was indisputably Urquhart's. As if to emphasize the point, Mortima stationed herself close behind her husband's shoulder; if anyone were to make an attempt to seize the microphone, they would have to force her bodily out of the way first.

And Passolides had hobbled to the front of the crowd. He was leaning on his stick directly in front of the podium, less than twelve feet from where Urquhart was standing. He was looking up, the features beneath the beret contorted like an animal in pain, caught in a trap, who had chewed off its own leg in order to escape only to discover the hunter at hand. Urquhart lifted his club and began raining blows down upon his unprotected skull.

"There are some who will not forget, who cannot forget. Evil men who wallow in memories, in selfishness beyond belief, who will sacrifice an entire community in order to indulge their own personal vendettas." He was staring straight at Passolides. "That is the evil of ambition. Not the ambition to fight for peace, but simply to fight. Old battles, any battles. Sick minds that refuse to forget."

Passolides's mouth was working in the greatest agitation. His eyes had filled with blood. Urquhart studied him with analytical care as might an actor on a stage involved in the greatest performance of his life, feeling for his audience, reaching for their emotions, flaying them alive. He believed in this role without reservation, nothing else in the world mattered.

"I have no family, apart from Mortima." He turned to look at her, a look of absolute trust and gratitude. "I have no children. No brothers or sisters. Tom Makepeace has claimed you all as brothers and sisters today..." A fog had entered his voice; he allowed the words to hang across the square. There was no applause, no one any longer rushing to be identified with Makepeace. Urquhart had them, had turned them. The play was nearly at its end.

He smiled at Passolides. The same cold smile with the touch of British arrogance he had held when photographed as a young Lieutenant in Cyprus. Sneering. Contemptuous. Spitting the words at him. The old man was fumbling at his belt; Urquhart's eyes never left him.

"Perhaps he had the right to do so. But if he claims the living, then let me claim the dead."

Passolides seemed to be crying, his jaw adrift. Urquhart claiming the dead. George. Eurypides. This man was the Devil himself…

"The children and brothers and sisters who have dreamed fine dreams, as I have, who have laid down their lives in Cyprus over the years, sacrificed for the peace that I too have sought…"

And then he stopped. Caught his breath. Felt something on his chest. He looked down to see a dark patch beginning to grow on his crisp white shirt. Then a second patch appeared and he felt his knees begin to give way. But not yet. His body seemed reluctant to answer his calls but he turned toward Mortima, saw the look in her eyes, reached toward her, to embrace her, to protect her as another blow hit his back and pushed him into her arms. He slid to the wooden floor as he heard two sharp explosions very close at hand. His eyes were misting but he could see Corder standing with a gun in his hand, pointing it into the crowd. He could see Mortima bending over him, fighting to be brave. And he could see something very bright in his eyes. Was it the sun? Or a burning tree? It was growing brighter.

"Mortima? Mortima! Where are you?"

She was very close, but he could not focus; she was gripping his hand, but he could no longer feel. There was no pain. A sense of exhaustion, perhaps. And exhilaration. Triumph. At having cheated them all, even at the end. And cheated them by his end. Cheated them all, except Mortima.

His lips moved; she kissed them, cradled him as close as she dared, ignoring the blood and the screams about her.

He smiled, his eyes finding her once more, and whispered.

"Great ruins."

She kissed him again, long, until Corder bent over to separate her from the body.

EPILOGUE

A nation held its collective breath as it watched and rewatched the televised scenes of Francis Urquhart, his body already mortally wounded, throwing himself protectively in front of Mortima. A noble death. A great death, even, it was said.

Not so for Evanghelos Passolides. He died even before Urquhart, felled by Corder's bullets. It was never discovered why he had chosen to assassinate the Prime Minister, "Britain's JFK" as the tabloids put it, but the public knew who to blame. Thomas Makepeace. Close associate and, as was almost immediately revealed, adulterous lover of the old man's daughter. Criminal-conspiracy charges were considered but nothing could be proved in court, although the circumstantial proof against Makepeace had been established in the minds of the voters long before election day.

From Monday until polling day Urquhart's body lay in state in the Great Hall at Westminster where the public filed past to pay homage without pause. And on polling day itself they queued to return his now-united party in numbers unprecedented in modern electoral history.

He had won. The final victory.

Not everything was as Urquhart would have wished. The

chairman of Booza-Pitt's constituency party, on opening the letter withdrawing his knighthood, had a heart attack and died on his kitchen floor. He was never able to denounce Geoffrey, who claimed that the photocopied letter sent to the Privileges Committee and the *News of the World* was a forgery. Indeed, his hand had shaken so much in the writing that his claim was persuasive, and in any event the editor decided there was little profit in attempting to disgrace such a new and obviously grieving widow. So Geoffrey survived, for the moment, in the new Administration.

That Administration was led by Maxwell Stanbrook, whose Jewishness and dubious parentage proved to be distractions rather than direct hits during his campaign to become Prime Minister. The party decided there was nothing wrong with ability. And he made Claire a Minister.

It took a couple of years before Mortima, the Countess Urquhart, had founded the Library on a site beside the Thames donated by the Government, and it was many more years before peace talks began again in earnest in Cyprus. It was still longer before revisionist historians tried to dislodge the memory of Francis Urquhart from the hearts of a grateful nation.

They did not succeed.

THE END

ABOUT THE AUTHOR

Michael Dobbs is also Lord Dobbs of Wylye, a member of the British House of Lords. He is Britain's leading political novelist and has been a senior adviser to Prime Ministers Margaret Thatcher, John Major, and David Cameron. His bestselling books include *House of Cards*, which currently airs on Netflix, as well as *To Play the King*, *The Final Cut*, *Churchill's Triumph*, *Churchill's Hour*, *Never Surrender*, and *Winston's War*. Read more on his website, www.michaeldobbs.com.